BY ALLISON PATAKI

The Traitor's Wife
The Accidental Empress
Sisi
Where the Light Falls (with Owen Pataki)
Beauty in the Broken Places
Nelly Takes New York (with Marya Myers)
The Queen's Fortune
Poppy Takes Paris (with Marya Myers)
The Magnificent Lives of Marjorie Post
Finding Margaret Fuller
It Girl

IT GIRL

IT GIRL

A NOVEL

Allison Pataki

BALLANTINE BOOKS
NEW YORK

Ballantine Books
An imprint of Random House
A division of Penguin Random House LLC
1745 Broadway, New York, NY 10019
randomhousebooks.com
penguinrandomhouse.com

Copyright © 2026 by Allison Pataki Levy

Penguin Random House values and supports copyright. Copyright fuels creativity, encourages diverse voices, promotes free speech, and creates a vibrant culture. Thank you for buying an authorized edition of this book and for complying with copyright laws by not reproducing, scanning, or distributing any part of it in any form without permission. You are supporting writers and allowing Penguin Random House to continue to publish books for every reader. Please note that no part of this book may be used or reproduced in any manner for the purpose of training artificial intelligence technologies or systems.

BALLANTINE BOOKS & colophon are registered trademarks of Penguin Random House LLC.

Hardcover ISBN 978-0-593-87341-0
Ebook ISBN 978-0-593-87342-7

Printed in the United States of America on acid-free paper

2 4 6 8 9 7 5 3 1

1st Printing

First Edition

BOOK TEAM: Production editor: Loren Noveck • Managing editor: Pam Alders • Production manager: Sandra Sjursen • Copy editor: Katie Herman • Proofreaders: Liz Carbonell, Pam Feinstein, and Olivia Trzaski

Theater curtain art: serafima32/Adobe Stock; pearl art: Nataliia/Adobe Stock

The authorized representative in the EU for product safety and compliance is Penguin Random House Ireland, Morrison Chambers, 32 Nassau Street, Dublin D02 YH68, Ireland. https://eu-contact.penguin.ie

FOR CHARLOTTE,
MY FRIEND THROUGH SO MANY ACTS

IT GIRL

THE NEW YORK TELEGRAPH

July 4, 1906—It's a long way from Millionaire's Row to Murderer's Row, but the Playboy Killer has booked himself passage, surrendering his freedom on the same day that the rest of the country celebrates independence. Will Hal Thorne's final "suite" be the barred cell he now occupies in the Tombs prison? Or even more chilling a thought to ponder: Is the dreaded Tombs just a stop on the millionaire's way to the electric chair?

What—or Who—is the Cause of It All?

Love. That's right, there's a beautiful face at the center of this deadly dance, belonging to none other than America's Cinderella, the doll who now bears the name "The Girl Houdini" after last night's fatal shooting that rocked Manhattan high society.

In addition to the Playboy Killer and the It Girl, the *Telegraph* has now learned the identity of the third character in this dark drama, and it's the Boss of Fifth Avenue himself, the famous—and sometimes infamous—Stanley Pierce, who also loved the Girl Beauty.

Everyone loved Evelyn Talbot, the so-called Mistress of Millions, who soared to stardom with an allure that made her Broadway's most fêted Beauty, the nation's Prettiest Peach, our modern-day Helen of Troy, the enchanting Eve of our very own Big Apple.

But what would Miss T. of the famous face think of this fatal face-off between the two men who loved her?

Given how events have turned out, it's unlikely that anybody will ever know. . . .

That's what they wrote. That's what they read. That's what they talked about—talked so much that President Teddy Roosevelt himself had to step in, asking his pals at the papers to give it a break and let my poor beautiful body rest in peace.

Oh, I got my peace all right. I even got a laugh as I read the ink they spilled recounting the shocking details of my death, the tragedy of my too-short life, the dangerous perfection of each one of my curves and curls.

But it's not a new story, is it? They call me Eve, but I'm not the first of that name. Wasn't it Eve's fault that Adam ate the apple way back in that first garden? Or Helen's for having the face that launched all those ships? Salome's sins that cost men their heads and Cleopatra's cunning that brought down the Roman rulers?

I didn't make it as far in school as I'd have liked, but even I know that it's a story as old as storytelling itself: men blaming women for the wars they wage on one another, for the wars they wage on themselves. "The Crime of the Century," they're calling it—just put in a new beautiful face, a new batch of hapless men, oftentimes a snake or a sword for flair. This time it's a pistol and a fatal performance.

She drove him mad.

She drove him to do it.

He loved her, wanted to honor her, protect her, save her.

She's the cause of it all.

Stories written by the men, all of them.

And the problem here is that it's not the truth. At least, it's not the truth as I lived it. And it's my story, so what about my ending?

They always talked about my eyes. How they were too big and too deep and too dark and too haunting—they'd drive a man mad. Well, how about I tell you what it felt like, to see it all with these eyes? Because the truth? I remember it rather as something more like this. . . .

PART 1

Five Years Earlier...

Chapter One

New York City
1901

I FEEL HOW THE AIR CHANGES WHEN I STEP INTO THE ROOM. Crowded as Mrs. Vanderbilt's ballroom is, it all goes charged, crackling like this new electricity that Mr. Edison has begun to brighten our world with. I sense it in their eyes, their voices, the tilts and leans of their silk-clad bodies. I glide in, and the Four Hundred go silent.

My hostess stands in the middle of her guests and offers me the slightest of nods, the quick upward pull of an approving smile. That's my cue. I sweep farther into the massive space, taking center stage against a backdrop of gleaming marble and framed portraits of the dead Vanderbilts that line the walls. New money, these Vanderbilts. Arrivistes, but that makes them cleverer—and bolder. If they aren't necessarily *welcomed* by the likes of these Four Hundred, they'll settle for acceptance or at the very least tolerance. And they'll do things the others wouldn't dream of in order to gain that, like invite me—a fatherless girl from coal country—to their costume party. Give the blue bloods a salacious dance before supper. They won't pretend to be the arbiters of taste, these Vanderbilts. They are just richer than God, and they'll throw the best parties if it buys entrée into the clique.

Oh, but the keeper of the gates herself is here tonight, too. And surely that's part of why Mrs. Vanderbilt smiles so triumphantly as I take my place before her guests in this grand room of hers. It's because Mrs. Astor has deigned to accept her invitation to this flashy costume party. She's even donned a tiara for the occasion—dressed as a royal? Or simply herself? Mrs. Astor stands sipping champagne a few paces from her hostess, flanked by two mustached men. One I recognize instantly. He's always in the society pages. Mrs. Astor's partner and confidant, her closest ally in keeping people in their places, Mr. Ward McAllister, studies me with an appraising eye. And I can read his lips as he tilts toward his high priestess and whispers, not disapprovingly, "Look at her. Positively sinful." In reply, Mrs. Astor's pristine skin reveals the faintest and most tasteful of blushes against her collar of priceless diamonds.

I'm not sure who the mustache on Mrs. Astor's other side is, but he's gazing at me like a puzzle he'd like to sort. He's much taller than Mr. McAllister, and broad, with hair the color of dark copper laced with silver that calls to my mind the pelt of a fox. Under his full copper mustache are widely smiling lips.

Mrs. Vanderbilt's orchestra strikes up the first notes of the languid melody; they have the sheet music my stage manager provided. Tonight I'll be giving these fancy ladies and gents one of my most risqué performances, just as Mrs. Vanderbilt requested when she telephoned the theater to hire me. I shall be Salome, dancing beneath my seven veils, the biblical beauty who turned the king mad. The girl who drove Herod so deeply into his lust that he saw no choice but to grant her wish: the head of John the Baptist on a platter.

I close my eyes, draw in a slow, long breath. And as the music picks up volume, I allow it to pull me in, and I begin to move. I tug the first veil from my hair and raise it aloft. As my dark waves tumble loose and long, I flicker my fingers, and the rich scarlet covering flutters slowly to Mrs. Vanderbilt's floor. Small gasps of shock—and delight. I lock eyes with my hostess, who is done up elaborately as Lady Liberty this evening. Her lips part in a satisfied smirk as she watches my movements. And then my eyes slide to the tall man at her side, who is staring at the skin of my neck, which I've just laid bare. He's enchanted.

I drop the second veil. Deep purple. More scandalized gasps as my arms and wrists flash, uncovered. They are wondering how far I will go with this. Oh, so much farther, ladies and gentlemen. I flit my hands up and down, then over my head. My fingers flicker as the jewels of my rings catch the light of Mrs. Vanderbilt's thousands of candles. *The world is a dirty place. Keep her hands clean.* My mind wanders back to the advertisement for which I modeled earlier this week, a soap campaign. I was dolled up like a sweet little shepherdess in a pastoral scene, surrounded by fake flowers as I pretended to wash before a porcelain bowl. Each day a new costume, a new scenario.

I drop the third veil now. Emerald green. I see how they lean forward, and I can tell: I've got them. These plump and powdered matrons who hide behind their own veils of propriety, with their thick calling cards and butler-guarded foyers, but who delight in the diversions that women like me can provide. I'm holding them all. One lady nearby is ornamented as a swan, dripping in white feathers and ropes of pearls, and just over her head I spot a framed portrait hanging on the wall: a nude in repose. Some Vanderbilt ancestor? Surely not. More likely some French courtesan whose painted flesh they've acquired because the artist is in fashion and they can afford to own her. And yet, *I'm* positively sinful.

I drop the fourth veil now, ocher, and reveal my ankles, my calves. They titter to one another. They can't know that the further I unveil, the thicker my armor becomes. It's not Evelyn they are seeing, the showgirl who will return home to the cramped room in the boardinghouse, where Mamma will be asleep in our shared bed. Or worse, awake and weeping in her rocking chair, quietly lamenting our turn in fortunes.

I drop the fifth veil, sapphire, and the jewels of my necklace glisten alone against the bare skin of my shoulders, my collarbone, my décolletage. I gleam like the sensational new statue, Manhattan's infamous lady of burnished gold who spins forever and ever at the top of Madison Square Garden. And as the music winds on, I, like her, spin and spin. I don't grow dizzy, practiced as I am, but I can tell that they do. Fox Mustache at the side of

Mrs. Astor is smirking, and Mrs. Astor is hiding half her face behind her rapidly fluttering fan. But she's not hiding her eyes—no, she's still looking.

I drop the sixth veil. Fuchsia. Someone cries out now—"*Well, I never!*"—from farther back in the room. I bite down on my lower lip to stanch my smile, and I keep dancing. The music is fast now, and so are my steps. *Bold! Bright! Fresh!* That's what the papers declared as this new century came roaring in. Faster than the subway train that will soon make thunder under Manhattan's busy streets. Livelier than the jaunty notes of ragtime that bumped the waltz back into the last century. All of it new, the papers hailed, as they'd declared mine to be the face of this fresh century. The face enchanting enough to gain entry into this party of the Four Hundred. To dance before Mrs. Astor herself—something that, last century, would have never been possible.

I pluck the seventh veil. Gold. Hundreds of eyes go wide, taking in the warm sweep of my navel, my hips. My glorious figure that has made me the most in-demand artists' model on this island, the most sought-after doll to dance in the footlights of Broadway. I can feel it, the power I wield. I stand before them, my entire body thrumming, holding them in my thrall. And then the last notes play, and I raise my scarf before my body once more, ripping the view from their ravenous eyes. And they groan, as if in physical pain, when I take the sight of my figure from them, and I fly from the room. But as I go, I hear the place erupt. Applause, cheers, scandalized chatter. They loved it. They were shocked and horrified—and yet entirely seduced.

Like Salome, I could have whatever I want from them in this moment. But I want a very different ending than the one she got.

Chapter Two

Pittsburgh
December 1897

I'VE LEARNED HOW TO HIDE MY DISGUST. THE SIGHT OF THE men, their sounds, especially the way they smell—the reek of their skin, their breath, their desire. "You win more bees with sweet honey," Mamma always chides. So sweet honey I try to be, even when the task tastes like sour vinegar.

Rent collection day means I've got to knock on each of these boardinghouse doors and deal with whatever I find staring back at me. Mr. Jonas stands before me now, and he might just be the worst of them. His whiskey breath hits my face in a warm wave, but I keep my gaze steady. I resist the urge to recoil as he says: "I got it somewhere in here. Why don't you step in, and we'll have a look?" The short, thick man creaks his door open wider, offering just enough room for me to pass between him and the doorframe. There's no way I'm stepping into his room.

"That's quite all right, Mr. Jonas. I can wait." My voice is courteous but firm as I remain where I am, feet planted in the hallway, where any number of our fellow boarders might be able to overhear our exchange. Or my cry for help, should I need to holler.

"Suit yourself," the man responds, his stubbled face making plain his disappointment. "Give me a minute."

I nod, flashing a bland smile as he slumps his shoulders and lumbers deeper into his room to scrounge up the two dollars he owes for December rent.

Just get it over with, I think to myself, fidgeting where I stand outside the doorway. Each month it's the same: Mamma and our landlord, a crusty old man by the name of Mr. Leonard, have worked out this deal by which I traipse up and down the hallways of this dingy boardinghouse, collecting the two dollars due from each of its tenants. The place is filled with male boarders, save for Mamma, Kit, and me squeezed into our room on the second floor and one other couple—they claim to be brother and sister, but Mamma tells me she has her doubts.

"My girl can collect it all," Mamma suggested to Mr. Leonard. "Save you hours of haggling and irritation. Look how pretty she is. No man would ever tell her no."

When Mr. Leonard agreed to the idea, Mamma, ever the opportunist, slipped in: "In exchange, you just give us a break on ours, and we'll call it square."

So here I stand, every month, collecting rent in exchange for a quarter lopped off our bill. And each month I loathe it more than the last. These men have landed here in this dirty, dark boardinghouse for a reason. No wives, no children—at least, not any in sight. Not here in these single rooms that smell of coal dust and sweat and defeat.

Each month at collection time Mamma has me wash my face and tuck my nicest white blouse into my knee-length navy skirt. She ties back my hair with a ribbon and reminds me to smile. "You are to be sweetness itself, you hear?"

I get the money. Knowing that otherwise Mr. Leonard will be cross with Mamma—and Mamma with me—I make sure to get as close to the full amount as I possibly can. But it always feels as if I have to pay a steep price to do so. The way their eyes linger and rove as I appear alone outside their bedroom doors. They get to look, even as I stand far enough back that they can't touch.

Thankfully Mr. Jonas is now all that remains between me and the completion of this month's ordeal. He, like nearly all the others in this establishment, is one of the men who rakes coal, or sweeps the railroad tracks, or hammers and hoists out on the

Pittsburgh avenues where the mansions are being built. And then they come home to this boardinghouse, the misery wafting off them like the grimy sweat on their skin. He's loitering inside his room now, looking at me expectantly.

"Here you go." Finally, he puts a fistful of coins into my hand, his paw closing around my fingers. My heart lurches. Why is he grabbing me like this? My gaze flies up from the coins to meet his eyes. They are two small beads of smoldering coal as he speaks, his voice little more than a hoarse whisper: "You sure are pretty, ain't you?"

I swallow, saying nothing in reply.

"You know, a nice girl like you, you don't need to be in a place like this." My palm has gone clammy in his. He goes on, his hand closing tighter around mine. "I got a house. A big house, out in the country. So big you'd take a wrong turn finding your way from the pantry to the kitchen. But the maids would help you. I'm only here on business. But I'll be going back out there soon. I could bring you with me."

"Maybe," I say. "That sounds awful nice." When his eyes flash shock—and what is that, hope?—I seize my chance and dart backward before he can stop me. My fingers ache where he squeezed them, but they are yanked free. Holding tight to the coins, I turn on my heels and dart back down the hallway. I take the narrow dark stairs two at a time, and I don't stop until I'm out in the alleyway, the cold December air hitting me with a most welcome wave.

I take off at a trot, even though I know Mr. Jonas isn't following me. I want to put as much space between myself and the inside of that building as I possibly can. The coins jangle in my pocket, but I'd never dream of spending Mr. Leonard's money. No, I'll go scour the spot behind Haudenshield's Butcher, I decide. Scrounge up a little something special for Kit and me to eat. It is Christmas Day, after all—I remember this fact with a surge of emotion that comes at me too messy and muddled for me to even sort through it all, so I blink and try to stuff all those feelings back down, deep into that place between my heart and my belly.

The afternoon is frigid, and I'm wearing only my blouse and

skirt, so I begin an exaggerated skip in the hopes of warming myself. I shiver, but I force all the unpleasantness from my mind, banishing the memory of Mr. Jonas and his beady, expectant eyes. It was as odious a task as always, but it's done now. I won't need to make those rounds for another whole month. And my daily schedule of going to and from school is different enough from most of these boarders' work shifts that I likely won't have to lay eyes on the revolting Mr. Jonas before then.

I'm young and I've been gifted with an inherently sunny disposition—in spite of the trying circumstances in which Mamma, Kit, and I currently find ourselves—so I'm generally quite skilled at pushing away my unhappy thoughts. Skilled at it and well practiced, too. I've learned it the hard way: best to fight back at the first glimpse of gloom to keep an even bigger gloom away.

Like I did when Daddy left us. *Daddy.* Now I can't ignore the tugging feeling, the ache that pulls on that place deep behind my belly. *Daddy left us,* Mamma always says, her words tinged with the barbs of bitterness and resentment. As if he meant to do it. No, Daddy *died.* There was no choice in the matter. He'd never have left me had there been a choice.

Winn Talbot, my father—how I'd loved him. He was both the steady ground beneath my feet and the open sky above my head. Everyone loved him, friendly neighbor and small-town lawyer to all in our hometown of Tarentum. Daydreamer, he always teased me that we should slip away together with the circus troupe that passed through our town each hot July. And then in the cold winter, he'd take me skating across the frozen ponds; how I used to hoot and holler with joy, relishing both the risky thrill of the slick ice and the rock-solid comfort of knowing I was sure and safe in Daddy's grip.

'Course, Daddy's dreams for me were bigger than the circus—he always told anyone who would listen that I'd go to school, even high school and then college. Not only his boy, Kit, but his daughter, Florence Evelyn, as well. He taught me my letters, and I never saw him smile quite so big as when we'd settle in together and I'd read aloud to him and Kit. I'd take one of Daddy's arms around myself, and Kit would take the other. Daddy loved Horatio Alger the best. "Rags to riches, my sweet Eve. Not that you'll ever see rags. But you'll see the riches." When it wasn't the stories of Mr. Alger, it was the fairy tales of the Grimm brothers or the legends of King Arthur. "You're my Guinevere, darling. My little queen." Or the tales from *The Arabian Nights*. "Someday I'll take you as far away as these places. We'll ride on camels and search the caverns for lost treasure."

Yes, he was the sun and moon for me, and I was his star. Now, with Daddy gone, it seems as though there is no more light.

He died suddenly. Something burst in his brain, was all I was able to make out from the doctor's whispers with Mamma. She didn't ever explain more. She just burned all the photographs that showed Daddy's kind, smiling face and threw daggers with her eyes when I cried or asked for him.

We lost the house shortly after we lost Daddy. Sure, it wasn't anything fancy, but with Daddy alive it had felt bright and safe. Happy, with its tidy shutters and the sunny bedrooms that Mama had filled with color. But the gentleman from the bank had arrived at our door and told Mamma she couldn't keep it. Or the carriage, either, the big rig that Daddy had been so proud to order from Sears Roebuck so he could take all four of us out for rides on Sundays after church. We had to put it all up for auction—the kitchen table where he'd taught me to give thanks for our blessings, the upholstered sofa where he'd taught me to read, the books he'd been so eager to share with me and my brother, even the small piano he'd bought secondhand from the church and loved to play in the evenings, his jolly voice sounding to me like the most beautiful thing in the world.

We went to live with Mamma's cousins just outside of Tarentum—Mamma, me, and my little brother. "Just until we get back on our feet," Mamma kept saying. To whom she was speaking, I wasn't entirely certain. And she did try; she didn't sit idle. Mamma took in sewing and other people's wash—she worked with the needle and the lye until her hands were chapped and blistered. But it wasn't enough, and the hospitality of our relations soon reached its limit.

So that's when Mamma, Kit, and I got this room in the boardinghouse. "My talents with the needle are wasted in Tarentum," she declared. Mamma had gotten it in her head that this bigger city could give her more sewing work, that she'd even get to style some fashionable dresses for some of the wealthy ladies here. From Pittsburgh it's just a quick hop to Philadelphia, a still grander city with even fancier seamstress work. "Once we've saved enough, we'll set up a shop, make elegant dresses for the finest ladies." That's what she told me. And I smiled obligingly, aching for it to be the truth.

But she's talking about that plan less and less now. This boardinghouse does have a way of sucking the spirit from a human. Even I at my young age can sense that. "*What is to become of us?*" That's her more common refrain these days. Some nights she cries so hard that I worry she might die, too.

That's why I learned to sleep with my one pillow over my head—so I don't have to hear Mamma's wails. I throw my arm over Kit, and I pull him close, as much for warmth as for comfort, and I try my best not to think of all the things I miss about our old life back in Tarentum. Daddy. Our home. Our small school. I miss Mamma, too, even though her body's right next to mine in the narrow bed.

But I've learned not to talk about Daddy, or any of it. I've taught myself not to cry. Not to ask questions. Instead I've learned how to make myself disappear. Like in the fairy tales Daddy and I would read, only now there's no good fairy appearing to help us, and on some days, it feels like there's no keeping the wolf away. I've realized that my best hope is to just disappear so that the wolf won't see me. Because as bad as Mr. Jonas may be, with his grabbing paws and his whiskey breath, I have the suspicion that there are wolves far worse out there in the world.

Speaking of wolves, I could eat like one. We are hungry most of the time these days, Kit and I. With Daddy, the food was never fancy, but it was always enough. On a day like today, Christmas, Mamma would have made a roast or maybe a ham. Some potatoes with cream, fixed how Daddy and I liked them best. And I know there would have been a gift or two for me and Kit.

But on this Christmas Day, Mamma was still slumped in bed when I left for the rent collection, while Kit made mountains out of some empty tin cans before a dying fire. I don't know what we will eat.

Which is why I've made my way to stand in the alley behind Haudenshield's. Sure enough, just as I suspected, the butcher has tossed out several bags of stripped bones. I lean toward the quarry, relieved. I'll throw them in a pot and make us a Christmas soup.

"Oh!" I say, startling when I see the small figure moving at my feet. Looks like I'm not the only one who had the idea to come look for scraps. There's a little tawny cat, fur all rumpled and patchy. No collar or tag. A stray tabby, from the looks of it, and a survivor. She looks up at me and lets out a petulant mewl, telling me to back off her findings. I feel a pinch in my heart. Yes, she's a survivor all right; it's easy for me to recognize what I know so well.

I summon my softest voice. "We can share, can't we?" I lean down to her. To my delight, after a beat, she steps closer and curls herself right up against my leg. The warmth of her little body reminds me of how cold I am. I pull her, trembling, into my chest. "You must be near frozen, too, little one. This ain't no place for a fine little lady like you to be out." In reality she's not fine at all; she's got the look of a weary scrapper down on her luck, but I figure if I speak pretty to her, she might like it. She doesn't look like the type who garners many compliments.

I glance around the alleyway. It's getting dark, and it'll only get chillier. "How about we make some soup, huh? Don't tell me you got other plans for Christmas—lots of other invitations to go calling? Nah, you can come with me. Kit will love you."

Her little heartbeat next to mine thumps as thin as a bird's. I notice how she shivers. She's cold, like me. In fact I've been outside here without a coat for long enough now that I can feel the chill from my toes to my top. "And how long have you been out here?" She responds with another mewl. I decide this means she's accepting my invitation.

I tuck her under my arm and pick up the bag of scrap bones to make my way toward home. "I think you need a bath." She stinks to high hell, but I don't really mind. As we walk up the alleyway back to the boardinghouse, I nuzzle her ear and I whisper, "You can be my present." Because not only is it Christmas Day. It's also my thirteenth birthday.

Chapter Three

"Don't remove your shoes. We're going out." Mamma says it as soon as I open the door. I am surprised to find her up and dressed, my little brother bundled beside her in a scarf, mittens, a cap, and an overcoat. I walk straight to Kit, sliding my arms open to reveal the flash of orange, which appears even brighter in here against the drab colors of our cramped room.

Kit's eyes go wide, and then he exclaims, "Gee, that's bully!" He has the same big brown eyes as me, and I see them all full of tenderness now, so I nudge the trembling little cat toward my brother's open hands. Five years younger than me, Kit had even less time with Daddy, and that reality always hits me with a pang that I try to combat by showing him any extra kindness I can. If this stinky stray tabby can give him some joy on this Christmas Day and the days going forward, it'll make me happy. I figure it's the only gift either of us will get today.

"What is the meaning of this, Florence?" Mamma, in contrast, does not appear overjoyed, and she addresses me with the formal name I loathe—the name that no one in the world uses except for her. I turn to her now with a mask of innocence as I ask: "Isn't she sweet, Mamma? I figured she could be our Christmas present, plus my birthday."

This catches Mamma by surprise; I see it in the way her features hitch upward. Mamma has forgotten my birthday. Maybe even Christmas, too. And this opens a small window of hope inside me. "Can't we keep the poor thing?" I plead. Kit joins in.

Mamma lets out a slow, beleaguered exhale, and with that, I see the fight seep out of her. I press on, asking my brother: "Kit, what should we name this little lady? Something a bit grander than Muddy Paws. Do you remember Muddy Paws?"

I can see from my brother's crinkled expression that he doesn't, so I continue: "Muddy Paws was our cat back in Tarentum. All white except for the four brown paws that looked like he'd just stepped in the mud. Daddy let me name him. And do you remember, Mamma, how that kitten used to rile up our chickens?" I'm trying my best to keep my tone bright, in the hopes that some cheer might become contagious in this room, but my mother lowers her eyes without a reply. I lean toward my brother and say, "Muddy was always pestering the chickens, and they'd fight back with their feet so fierce that Mamma took pity on the poor kitten and sewed small leather shoes for each of her hens. To make the fights less scrappy while everyone learned how to get along."

"Never mind all that, Florence." Mamma's tone is as brittle as the cold air outside, and she waves a hand toward the shivering little body in my brother's arms. "I'll deal with this later. The creature can stay for a bit while we go out. Now fetch your coat."

"Where are we going?" I ask, as I give the cat one final stroke across its matted fur.

"Stonehurst," Mamma answers. Then, seeing my confusion, she adds: "The Thorne mansion, on Beechwood Boulevard."

Beechwood? That's a part of town into which we never venture. "Are we picking up their washing?" I ask.

Mamma flicks her eyes toward the doorway, irritated by my questions. "More like wishing them a Merry Christmas. All three of us, together. Now let's *go*. Kit, put that thing down before the night gets dark as pitch."

Outside it's the dusk of Christmas evening, the last thin tendrils of weak winter sunlight slipping through the gaps between the buildings. Mamma sets off at a brisk pace, her features pinched tight against the cold. I'm brimming with questions about the nature of our unusual outing, but I keep quiet and stay close to Mamma while she clutches Kit's hand on her other side. At the corner of the street, we pause and await a break in the horse and carriage traffic. The sleigh bells of a passing hansom lend a cheerful ring to the air as they mingle with the laughter of the passengers riding within. *I wish I could climb in and go wherever it is they're going,* I think as the hansom is swallowed into the night. But I'd never dare to say it.

Instead I see Mamma's breath when she speaks: "I hear that Mrs. Thorne is a churchgoing woman. I imagine that if we show up on her step at Christmas, she might be moved to some Christian kindness. Perhaps a warm plate of supper. Maybe even a few . . ."

A break in the traffic, and Mamma pulls us forward. I don't press her for more information, and I don't dawdle, knowing that to do either would mean catching a scolding. I keep with Mamma's pace as she crosses the street and leads us up the broad avenue, the buildings growing grander and farther apart as we make our way through their shadows. It's a long walk, and with the winter sun setting, it's only getting colder. I ignore the ache in my toes and silently hope this quest will be worth it.

Finally, the sign for Beechwood Boulevard appears before us in the flickering light of the elegant streetlamps; it's clear we've arrived in the wealthiest part of town. Even without reading the street name I would have been able to tell, for these are no longer houses tucked back above the wide boulevard, these are castles. And Stonehurst is exactly what you might expect from its name, and from the Thorne family that built it—the richest family in Pittsburgh, with the biggest residence on Millionaire's Row. It's more than a house, more than a castle even, it's a fortress, set back from Beechwood Boulevard behind a wrought iron fence and an imposing row of tall, winter-stripped trees.

Our cold little trio huddles before the pea-gravel lane, looking up at the hulking shape of the house, the quiet property draped in thick winter shadows. "Looks haunted," Kit remarks. He's got that right. Nestled in the gloom of the December dusk, the massive house is wrapped in a thick casing of climbing ivy. And yet, inside, the rooms are aglow. Probably even warm. I can tell because I squint my eyes and stare through the gracious floor-to-ceiling windows that pierce the ground floor, where I spy rich cranberry-colored drapes and, beyond them, the twinkling candles of countless sconces and what appears to be a very ornate chandelier.

Not that we have a prayer of being invited into the Thornes' warm drawing room, with its dark wood paneling and blazing fire. Mamma, however, appears undeterred. Wearing the grim expression of a general poised to ride into battle, she stares at the wide stone steps that lead upward toward the Stonehurst front door, and I see how she pulls back her shoulders.

Then, gripping my hand on one side and Kit's on the other, she states aloud to the cold night: "We are not urchins, nor are we beggars. We are honest, hardworking people. We've just had a spell of bad luck since, well . . . If she can't find it in her heart to show us some kindness on Christmas Day, then she's not the fine lady I've heard her to be." With that, we march up the lane, a determined little phalanx, the gravel crunching beneath our steps. When we reach the front, Mamma pauses, fixing me with a stern gaze. "Now, Florence, when the butler answers, you stay right beside me, and you be sure to offer him your most polite smile, you hear?"

I nod. Mamma studies me for a moment, her eyes sweeping from my heels to my head. She adjusts my wool hat, pulling a tendril of my dark hair over my left shoulder, and then she turns and raps the Thornes' cold brass knocker.

A moment later a silver-haired man in a formal tuxedo pulls the door back and appears in a sliver of light at the threshold. Surely this must be the man of the house? Would a servant be sporting a tuxedo? Perhaps in a home as fine as this, even the servants dress like this. Remembering my orders, I smile and throw in a small curtsy—just in case this fellow is someone as important as he appears to be. But I can tell I'm not the only one who's perplexed: the gentleman looks at me, then Kit, then his eyes land on Mamma. "How may I help you?" he asks.

Mamma takes a step forward. "Good evening. I'm Mrs. Goodwin Talbot." Hearing her mention Daddy's name, my throat tightens. I ignore that feeling, keeping the smile plastered on my face because *men are more inclined to do a favor for a sweet face than a sour one,* Mamma has told me more times than I can count. I want to look to Kit, but I resist that urge. Mamma goes on, saying, "I'm here to call on Mrs. Thorne."

A faint sound, the gentleman quickly clearing his throat, and then, arching an eyebrow, he responds with a question: "And Mrs. Thorne is expecting you?"

"I don't believe she is." If Mamma feels nervous, she's doing some job of hiding it.

"Very well, Mrs. Talbot," he says. "Have you a card which I may present to Mrs. Thorne?" So then he *is* the butler.

"I'm afraid . . ." Mamma shifts from one foot to the other. "I've left my calling cards at home."

"I see." The man's eyes slide once more from Mamma to me, then to Kit, then back to Mamma, and in his expression I detect two fleeting feelings—just a flash of each, before he's remembered his implacable mask of propriety, but I've seen them both: the willed patience of a well-trained servant, and the thin but undeniable undergirding of derision, or perhaps it's even pity.

A thought flies into my mind, and I can't help but wonder: *What number are we today?* How many other supplicants have appeared on this grand doorstep?

But the man quickly remembers his courtesy, holds fast to the unruffled civility required of a bannerman of the Thorne clan, and with another quick clearing of his bow-tied throat, he offers a bland smile. "If you'd be so kind as to wait for just a moment, I shall see if Mrs. Thorne is at home."

The door shuts, leaving us in the flickering puddle of light thrown down by the entryway sconces. Mamma lets out an audible exhale. "'Course she's at home," she says, her voice low. "Christmas Day, suppertime, where else would she be, the greengrocer's?"

"Church?" I venture.

Mamma shoots me a dart of a look, answering: "She needn't go to church when she can do some good right here. Doesn't the Good Book tell us to feed the hungry? And love our neighbors?"

But we aren't her neighbors, I think. We are from a very different part of town. I don't dare voice that aloud. A moment later the door opens again, and we all shift on our feet as Mamma rearranges her face into a look of graciousness itself. A woman stands before us. Older than Mamma and shorter, too, but with a ramrod posture that makes it look as though she's got an iron pole for a spine. Her thin hair is pulled back, tidy and high on her head, the same ashy color as her eyes. Her velvet gown is dark, the blue of a cold midnight, with a froth of white lace at the neck and wrists. Her gray eyes sweep our trio gathered on her doorstep, and when she locks gazes with me, I can't help but think of lemons, for it looks like she's just sucked one dry. "What is the meaning of this?" she asks, her voice so quiet that I take a step forward to hear better.

"Merry Christmas, Mrs. Thorne," Mamma says, managing a bright tone in spite of this woman's unsmiling, bone-white face. Mrs. Thorne, the richest woman in Pittsburgh, the widow of the legendary railroad tycoon and the lady of this sprawling castle, looks to be about the furthest thing from merry.

She throws a quick glance back toward the interior of her house, then meets Mamma's eyes as she answers: "And the same to you. And as it is indeed Christmas, I am occupied at present with my family. But I do not know you."

Nor does she wish to, from the look of it. I nod, hoping we can excuse ourselves and be on our way. But Mamma forges on, showing a determination entirely unlike her recent behavior. "The name is Mrs. Goodwin Talbot. Florence Talbot, if you like. And these here are my young ones. See . . . I'm a widow, like yourself, ma'am. And I work hard. I can show you my hands to prove it. But food isn't cheap. And with the two young ones to feed . . . and I figure, with it being Christmas and all . . ." Mamma's words drift off like the misting of her warm breath in the bitter night air.

Mrs. Thorne, somehow, pulls herself to stand even straighter. And then, her colorless eyes fixing squarely on Mamma, Mrs. Thorne declares: "You've come to beg for a handout."

Mamma lets out a puff of sound, then falls momentarily silent. I feel my heart hammering, and I see Kit fidget at her other side. I've had enough of this; I long to return home, even to that dingy boardinghouse, where at least the cat will be waiting for us. But with her gaze tilting downward, Mamma breaks the unbearable silence: "Well, ma'am, I heard talk that you're a churchgoing woman"—Mamma raises her eyes and glances around the place—"and blessed in ways that some of us aren't."

Mrs. Thorne folds her gloved hands before her slender waist, looking down at me and then at Kit. When she looks back to Mamma, Mrs. Thorne offers a tight nod of her chin, saying, "Of course I go to church. And I give generously there. Might I suggest you attend Sunday services, where you will find that not only your body but also your soul may be fed?"

Mamma shifts at my side. "I'll be there. Sunday morning. But until then?"

Mrs. Thorne throws another vexed look back toward the inside of her warm home, then she stuffs a hand into the fold of her fine velvet dress. A moment later she says only, "Oh, very well." And then she puts something into Mamma's hand. I steal a glance and see that it's a five-dollar bill. More than two months' rent! Sure, the rumor is that Mrs. Thorne's got hundreds of millions in the bank, left to her by her dead tycoon husband. But for us? This much money at one time feels like a fortune. Mamma was right—this outing was worth it.

Our benefactress offers one final scowl, two streams of warm breath slipping out of the nostrils of her narrow, patrician nose. And then, with a voice that sounds perhaps just slightly less irked, she says: "Walk around the side there. I'll have Cook send out plates for you."

"Thank you, Mrs. Thorne. We're so very grateful. Aren't we, children?" Mamma squeezes the bones of my hand so hard that I almost wince.

But I remember myself in time and flash the fine lady another big smile, another flourish of a curtsy. "Thank you, ma'am," I say, as Kit mumbles the same.

As we scurry down from the doorstep, Mrs. Thorne's shrill voice calls out into the frigid night: "But remember this!" We turn to listen, looking up at her figure, a thin wraith wrapped in the glow of her doorway's warm light. "I am not running an almshouse, and this is not a food canteen. You'd be better off putting your hands to good honest work and finding yourself in the church pew on Sunday. See to it that you don't come disturb our family peace again, Mrs. Talbot."

Mamma shifts on her feet. Mrs. Thorne slides away from the door; then she's gone, leaving her butler to shut the three of us out in the dark night. I can feel the fury seeping off Mamma like steam. Or perhaps it's shame. Probably both, I figure, as I feel her grip tighten around my hand and, with that, the hardness of resolution. Because a moment later, under her breath so that only Kit and I can hear, Mamma whispers through gritted teeth: "If that's the finest lady in town, who needs this place? Good riddance. I'll use her five dollars, and I'll get us out of here."

"To where?" I ask, as we resume our weary steps, back toward home, far away from this neighborhood with its stone castles and bare trees. It looks like Mamma doesn't plan to wait for the offered food after all, I realize, with a pang in my hungry belly.

When Mamma answers, her tone sounds as though it's the most obvious thing in the world: "Philadelphia, Florence. I'm going to make dresses for fine ladies, but I sure won't do it for Mrs. Thorne."

Chapter Four

Philadelphia
Spring 1898

"Flo? Florence? Ah, there you are." I can tell from the way Mamma bursts through the front door that she's brimming with news. I look up from where I'm sprawled on the hearthrug beside Kit, both of us taking turns dangling a piece of scrap linen over Titania.

"Yes?" I peel my attention from our beloved cat, whose hair is now less matted, even a bit glossy, thanks to the baths and the milk we sneak for her. Mamma strides into our small space, a rented room in a boardinghouse on Philadelphia's busy Arch Street. The place is bigger and slightly cleaner than the boardinghouse in Pittsburgh, and mercifully, I do not serve as the rent collector.

"I have news," Mamma says, slipping the pins out of her thick hair and pulling off her hat. "Good news."

About time. "What is it?" I sit up, attentive, as the cat paws my skirt.

"Tomorrow, you'll come with me to Wanamaker's."

"The department store?" My voice lifts with hope. Am I to have a new store-bought dress? Something other than the homemade patterns that Mamma styles me in? It's not that I'm complaining; she's an expert with the needle, and I enjoy sporting her creations. Even on the frequent days when we have too little to eat, I am always turned out well enough, thanks to Mamma's love of sewing and her eagerness to practice new styles.

"Yes," Mamma says, slumping down in the threadbare armchair beside our stove. Mamma works the day shift at Wanamaker's, selling fashionable dresses and other luxury finery to the ladies who live in the leafy estates out on the Main Line. Mamma leaves each morning right after breakfast, returning home after I've fixed supper. She doesn't love the work, but we need the wages. If she sells enough of Mr. Wanamaker's dresses, hopefully someday she'll get the chance to make some creations for the store herself.

"I've fixed it for you," Mamma says, ignoring the cat curling its tawny body against her legs. "You'll have a day shift on the floor. An errand girl at first, but if you put in good work, perhaps you can try your hand as a salesgirl soon enough."

"A day shift?" I repeat the words, my mind trying to catch up. "But . . . what about school?"

Mamma offers a beleaguered wave of her hand. "Oh, never mind that school."

Now I'm certain that Mamma can see my disappointment, and in spite of knowing better, I don't try to hide it. I've loved the past few months at the city school. We've been reading the writings of Benjamin Franklin and John Adams, and studying the spring plants. Walking to and from the school each day with Kit, our steps merging with the chattering crowds of other children, I've felt like I was where I was supposed to be for the first time since losing Daddy. I was even on my way toward making a real friend or two.

Besides, Daddy always told me how important it was that I study hard. I'm only a year shy of entering high school. *You've got the brains for it. You'll even go to college.* But how am I going to get there if I'm spending all day inside Wanamaker's?

Mamma keeps her eyes averted, suddenly preoccupied with watching the cat make waves with its spine against the legs of the armchair. It's in that moment that I notice how many new strands of silver lace her hair, which was once glossy and dark, just like mine. Daddy always waxed poetic about our gorgeous chestnut manes. But now hers is more salt than pepper.

When Mamma does go on, her voice is firm. "You'll learn more in one day just listening to and observing these ladies . . . and I mean the things that actually matter, Florence. Style, elocution, comportment. This will be the sort of schooling that'll help you get ahead in life. Now come here, I need to see your dress."

"Why?" I ask, stepping toward her. I throw Kit a questioning look; he answers me with a shrug that says he's every bit as puzzled as I am.

Mamma begins yanking on the bottom of my hem. Swiveling in the armchair, she riffles through her nearby sewing basket until she pulls out her small scissors.

"What are you doing?" I ask.

Mamma snips and tugs along the bottom of my dress as though I'm a block of ice and she wants to cut shavings. "I need to take down this hem," she says.

"But you always tell me it's good to keep my hem high. *The gentlemen like getting a glimpse of the gams.*"

Mamma stops snipping for a minute, letting out an exasperated puff of air. "At Wanamaker's you'll be working among the salesladies. A *lady,* you hear?"

But I'm a girl, I want to say, though I swallow back the words of my confusion, allowing them to drop into my stomach like stones.

"As such, you'll have to dress like one. And ladies wear long skirts. No more of these schoolgirl hems at the knees."

With that, she sets back to work, scowling as she focuses on the stitches. The room darkens around us. On Mamma's orders, Kit lights our one candle, and I stand there in the jumpy light, motionless, as I've been trained. I am Mamma's model, a statue, as she lowers my hem and works to turn me from a girl into a woman.

"Now, Florence, when we get inside, don't gawk. Mr. Wanamaker has constructed something called an elevator. It's a motorized trolley that floats up and down so the rich folks don't have to climb the stairs."

My wonder must show on my features because Mamma offers

me a curt nod, standing beside me outside the grand front entrance to the city's largest department store. She gives me a final once-over, smoothing down a stray tendril of my hair, which is swept up off my neck in a prim chignon just like hers, and then she speaks in a low voice: "Keep your wits about you, Florence. It won't do to gape like a fish."

I pat down my blue skirt, which now falls over my ankles, and stick close behind Mamma as we step off the street and into the cool, airy front atrium of Wanamaker's. All of Mamma's entreaties not to gawk and gape fly away as I get my first glimpse of the inside of the store. It is grander than anything Mamma could have prepared me for, or anything I could have imagined. I've never been inside any building this massive, all creamy white marble and shiny golden embellishments. And the ceiling! It soars skyward and I can't help but count the tiered balconies that striate the bright space, like an oversized confectionary cake: one, two, three, four . . . "Five stories, Mamma!"

"Yes, Mr. Wanamaker built his store to be as grand as the indoor markets in Paris and London." Now even Mamma lets slip a begrudging tone of admiration. And it's not just the sprawling space that I find so staggering—it's all the treasure stocked inside. The place is filled with riches! Glistening glass display cases and tidy lines of countertops boasting gloves, stockings, shoes and boots, pillow shams, chemises, hats. One could wear a new outfit every day, turned out from top to toes, and still never make it through all of these frilly, fancy items.

"What did I say?" Mamma chides, again in a low voice. "Don't gawk like you've never seen anything like it."

"But I've never seen anything like it," I reply. "Why, it reminds me of the caves filled with treasure that Daddy used to read about in *The Arabian Nights*."

Mamma grimaces, but I can see she doesn't understand the reference, so I ask, "Where did all this come from?"

"Mr. Wanamaker goes to Paris and London every year to pick out the finest items. Why, even the owners of Macy's in New York City look up to Mr. Wanamaker for his taste. And Mr. Macy could not claim to have an elevator in *his* store."

I'm wondering—and very much want to ask—if I might get the chance to ride that elevator, but Mamma chivvies me deeper into the cavernous front atrium. I draw in a slow breath, luxuriating in the aromas of the air, so clean and sweet, a swirling bouquet of many different perfumes and varieties of eau de toilette. We pass more elegant tables of gleaming dark wood and countertops piled with all manner of fine goods. I want to pause and study a particularly dainty pair of lady's gloves. I assume they must be fashioned of the softest kid leather and embroidered with silver silk thread, but I have no time to dawdle. It truly is like the caves of *The Arabian Nights*—look, but don't dare to touch.

We pass faceless mannequins and orderly rows of dresses. Garments of all styles and colors: chic polonaise gowns with bustles, day dresses for tea and calling, evening gowns with puff sleeves and frills, riding habits with clean lines of frogging and matching caps. In spite of all the variety, each piece of treasure seems to have what appears to be a sort of label dangling from it, and I pause to examine one.

"Ah, yes," Mamma says. "A price tag. Mr. Wanamaker's is the first store in the country to use them."

"But . . . what are they?"

"They tell the cost. No haggling, no vulgar negotiating in here like they do in more common establishments. Why, Mr. Macy liked the idea so much he brought it to Manhattan."

I stare at the tag between my fingers. "*Ten* dollars?" I gasp. "For one dress?" We could feast for weeks on that.

Mamma nudges me to keep walking. "I told you you'd learn in this place—what life *could* be."

We march toward the back of the grand atrium, where I spy a ring of circular counters sparsely populated by the other salesladies. Each woman gives off a tidy and prim sense of preoccupied purposefulness, clad like Mamma and me in cream-colored blouses with jabot collars and dark ankle-length skirts.

The place is brightly lit but not yet open to the public for the day, its employees seeing to their final chores before the massive clock in the atrium strikes eight. Just as we approach the rear of the store, Mamma takes hold of my arm and leans toward me, her voice low. "Be polite but keep quiet. Don't go out of your way to converse with the other salesladies unless they ask you a question. If you don't get in the way, then hopefully they'll leave you be. But remember, if anyone does ask, how old are you?"

"Sixteen."

"Good girl," Mamma answers, the skin between her two eyebrows hitching upward. I nod to assure her that I understand, that no one in this store will know that I'm a thirteen-year-old girl who hasn't yet made it to high school. And is wondering if I ever will.

When we step behind the counter, Mamma reaches into a drawer and then straightens back up, saying: "Put this on." She presses into my hand a white apron, pristine and starched stiff as a bone, which I dutifully slide over my blouse and skirt.

Fifteen minutes later, as the colossal clock in the middle of the store chimes eight times, the front doors of Wanamaker's open to the public, and the first shoppers begin to stream in, ladies entering mostly in pairs or trios. I can't help but stare all over again: they already look so fashionable, so elegant. What could they possibly need that brings them in here seeking even more?

"Here they come," Mamma says, turning her focus toward ensuring that the countertop before her is as spotless as can be. I feel my breath catch, and I immediately fix my eyes on the floor, hoping that these shoppers won't look too closely. Hoping that they'll allow me to stay and earn wages. That, I know, will depend on my making myself both indispensable and invisible.

My first shift, long as it is, passes in a blur of work. I measure the bolts of velvet and gingham like I'm told. I iron and fold the reams of chintz. I help Mamma drape swaths of lace over the mannequins while she pins the delicate fabric just so. I sweep before anyone has a chance to notice dust on the floor and polish a glass case as soon as I see the tiniest smudge. I am there to keep things running smoothly, to keep the salesladies happy and the display tables well stocked. At lunchtime, as Mamma and I sit in the back alleyway eating our cheese sandwiches, I miss Kit. And school. I wonder if my classmates are confused by my absence. I wonder, with a pang, how my little brother's day is going. Wonder if he'll miss me as he walks home this afternoon and has nobody but our cat to greet him at the door, passing the evening hours with only Titania for company. The store closes at six o'clock, and Mamma tells me our shift will end at seven once we are done cleaning.

But the work keeps me busy enough, and soon it's evening, and Mamma and I are folding one last pile of delicate undergarments before we may finally head home. I can't wait to get off my feet, plop down before the stove with Titania in my lap, and tell Kit all about the day. I hope he's been able to fix himself something to eat. And that's when it hits me—the realization of just how hungry I am for some supper of my own.

THE NEXT DAY I'm back at it. And the one after that. Each morning, once Kit has been bundled off to school, off I go with Mamma, in my long skirt, my stiff apron knotted tight at my waist. Every day but Sunday, from seven o'clock to seven o'clock, I am officially one of the breadwinning crowd, paid every two weeks. Tiring as the schedule is, that fact fills me with a sense of deep satisfaction. Someday soon, with Mamma's and my wages combined, we might be able to move out of our cramped room into lodgings with more space. Perhaps even a big window with a view of some grass or trees.

Since I miss school so much, I try to find other ways to expand my smarts. I practice sums in my head as I arrange fancy goatskin gloves from Paris, adding up their prices in case a customer ever asks me for a quick figure. I've learned to avoid the section on the second floor where the beautiful porcelain dolls are displayed, knowing that if I look too long, I might give away my girlish desire to pick one up, to stroke its honey-colored hair or admire the thin wisps of its blinking eyelashes. I've also learned to keep my eyes averted when ladies are shopping near me. Sometimes they look. Sometimes their eyes sweep my figure or linger on my face. But more often they just sail past me, focused on their quarry of fans or stockings or perfume.

And that's precisely why, on this one morning in late spring, I'm beginning to feel a bit uneasy as a lady shopper keeps looking in my direction.

I'm in the headwear section on the ground floor, assigned to dusting the shelves and stands where the hats are arranged in their colorful displays. It's a quiet morning in the store, and I'm pretending to be extremely preoccupied with cleaning a spray of Malmaison roses that are nestled on top of a broad-brimmed silk hat. The lady approaches, yet again, hovering in a way that calls to mind a pesky fly at a picnic. "Lovely," she says, to no one in particular.

I throw a sideways look in her direction. She's alone, unlike most of the ladies who shop in here accompanied by a friend or a daughter or even a maid. She's dressed more simply, too, in a day dress of pale linen and a simple straw hat. Her face is round and ruddy, her auburn hair pulled back as if it were an afterthought. She's staring at me, so I decide some sort of polite answer is necessary. I think she was remarking on the hat I was dusting, so I say, "Oh, yes, ma'am."

"I'm partial, however, to this one." She fingers a nearby hat of pale green. Of all the hats on the floor, this is the *last* one I'd be partial to. Perhaps it's the most interesting, for it has a jeweled serpent twisting around it. But I'm not certain what sort of an occasion might warrant such a piece. And it seems an odd choice for this lady, given her bland attire. I offer a noncommittal shrug. The lady moves on, picking up a cap of pink velvet with a profusion of silk flower petals. "When it comes to all these silk blooms," she muses aloud, "I'd much rather have the real thing."

"Don't keep as long, ma'am," I answer in defense of the fake flowers. But as soon as I've said it, I regret the words. Mamma would have told me to keep my eyes down and move along.

The lady, however, seems eager to engage. "No, I suppose they don't. But doesn't that add to their appeal? Prompts us to live with a certain sense of purpose, does it not? Urgency, even. To know our days are numbered. Our age is always advancing."

I swallow, saying nothing, turning to a cream-colored bonnet crusted with small pearls.

"Speaking of age..." she goes on, her voice unnervingly steady even as I feel the blood churning in my veins. "How old are you, girl?"

"Sixteen, ma'am," I answer, managing—I hope—a mild tone.

The woman lets out a small titter of a laugh. She's no longer even pretending to look at the hats—she's looking only at me. I don't meet her gaze, but she says: "You're not a day over thirteen."

"If you'll excuse me, ma'am, I'm needed elsewhere." I offer a quick curtsy and scamper off, feeling her gaze on me the entire time as I make my way back to the counter. There, Mamma takes one look at my flushed, harried appearance and her eyes go wide. I give a small shake of my head, and she does not probe me. She says only, "Florence, it's time for your break. Why don't you step away for a moment?"

I do as Mamma suggests, not looking back toward the hats, though I know that the lady shopper is still standing there, watching me as I go.

· ◆ ·

ONE OF THE best parts of the job is that we are allowed, through an unspoken agreement, to avail ourselves of the foodstuffs that have gone unenjoyed by our patrons. There is an elegant restaurant on the fourth floor of the store, where the ladies take their lunch and afternoon tea. There's even, I've heard, a soda fountain made of carved marble, splashing out drinks of cherry, vanilla bean, and sarsaparilla. While I've never set foot inside that space, I do know that Mr. Wanamaker, being a kindly man, gave the directive that his cooking staff is to put the extra food items out in the back alley at the end of each shift. There, I can grab cans of mustard or jars of nearly finished jam, ends of bread loaves, sometimes even leftovers of smoked salmon tea sandwiches. Discarded and undesired scraps that no one will miss but that, to me and Kit, taste like a feast.

And so that's where I go at the end of our shift that evening while Mamma waits out front. I find, to my delight, half a loaf of bread and I pounce on it, just like I used to do in the alleyway behind Haudenshield's butcher shop in Pittsburgh. I'm wearing my coat of pilled cloth, dark blue so it doesn't show stains, long sleeves rolled up. I tuck the bread into my oversized pocket and turn to skip back out of the alleyway to meet Mamma. It'll be enough for all three of us, even for some generous scraps for Titania. Because it's late and the sun is setting, because the alley is draped in shadow and my thoughts are already turned toward supper, I don't notice the other person back there until I've nearly bumped into her.

"Begging your pardon, ma'am," I offer, my tone contrite, but as I hurry to shuffle aside, the loaf slips out of my pocket. I look up at whomever this person is, concerned now; is she going to chide me for picking up Mr. Wanamaker's food? Sure, it's understood that we are permitted to do so, as long as we don't make a scene doing it. But will she complain to a store manager that some girl is filching like a stray at the back door? I stare at this stranger, begging her with my expression to show me a small scrap of kindness and let me pass. And that's when I see: it's the lady from before. The lone shopper, the one who looked at the green hat with the snake, before looking a bit too closely at me. And she's still looking too closely at me.

Please just let me be, I think.

Now, with her voice low, she says: "Goodness, my darling. Your eyes! You are breaking my heart right here on the spot."

Her words, her tone, her entire appearance catch me by surprise, and before I can manage to pull my features into a mien of composure, she says: "Goodness, and now look at you. So expressive."

She takes my chin in her hand, and I feel the immediate instinct to recoil. To turn and flee and keep on running. But then I realize: it's not like it is with the men in the boardinghouse, the way she's looking at me. It's not menacing. This woman is *studying* me. She's interested, as though she wants to know something. It's not desire in her gaze, in the gentle cradle of her fingers. And then she repeats her question from earlier: "How old are you?"

So I repeat my answer, just as I've been told to do. "I am sixteen, ma'am."

She frowns, allows her hand to drop and release my chin. Then she cocks her head to one side. "How old are you, really?"

"Sixteen," I answer again, my voice a bit more insistent.

"All right, you're sixteen. And a terrible liar." The woman glances up at the store sign. Then she sighs, gazing back down at me. "But they've accepted it. So I suppose I can."

I'm confused by this remark, and growing increasingly unsettled. Mamma is waiting for me at the front of the store, and if she were to find me speaking like this with a customer, she'd be furious. But the lady is not yet done with her questions. I am torn between two conflicting mandates: don't be impolite to a customer; don't engage with a customer.

The woman goes on: "Girl, have you ever posed?"

"Posed?"

"You know, for an artist."

I remember once back in Tarentum, Daddy arranged for a family portrait. Mamma groused about the expense, but she seemed happy enough to comb our hair and fashion new outfits for the occasion. A black and white image, all of us done up in our best. But I don't suppose that's what this lady means. "No, ma'am."

"Would you like to?"

I shake my head. I need to be going. I give her a quick curtsy and mumble, "Have a nice evening, ma'am."

But as I'm turning to walk out of the alleyway, her voice follows me. "I'd pay you," she calls out into the darkening evening. "A dollar for a sitting."

I halt my steps. I don't turn to look at her, but my whole body is coiled in attention. *Did she just say she would pay me a whole dollar?* Now I turn to face her, but something in me braces, tells me to wear a casual mask as I ask, "What would I do?"

"You'd sit for me. While I sketch. Inside, warm. Safe. And in the end, I'd give you the dollar." She looks at the scrap of bread I've taken back into my hand. Then she says: "I could offer lunch, too, if you wanted to come by around ten in the morning. How do you like roast chicken and apple pudding?"

My mouth waters just to hear of it. But I keep that mask fixed tight on my face. "I don't see what's so hard about sitting for a bit," I say, throwing in a shrug.

She steps toward me and hands me a small piece of paper. A calling card with an address scrawled on it. "Chestnut Street," I say, liking the way it sounds and wanting to show off to this woman that I can read.

"What is your name, child?"

"Evelyn."

"Do you have a last name?"

"Of course I do."

"Well, then, what is it?"

"Talbot. Evelyn Talbot."

"It's nice to meet you, Evelyn Talbot. My name is Mrs. Dawson," she says. "Leah Dawson. I'm a sketch artist, and that is the address to my studio."

"My mamma will want to come with me," I say.

The woman nods. "Of course. She is more than welcome. Quite frankly, my dear girl, with your doll looks, I wouldn't have you going anywhere without your mamma."

Chapter Five

"Heavens above, Florence, I don't know how you talked me into this. She's likely some swindler who'll take the shirts off our backs. Lord knows we don't have anything else to give her."

"Mrs. Dawson is a lady, Mamma. Fine enough to shop in Mr. Wanamaker's store, ain't she? And most respectable-looking." Plain, in fact, with nothing of the swindler to her appearance.

"Or she was there to prey on those less fortunate," Mamma retorts, her tone as sour as her mood. It's Sunday, our one day off from the store, ordinarily reserved for the washing, the mending, the cooking of whatever we've managed to put aside. And Mamma's day for hours of uninterrupted sketching and sewing. But today, instead, I've convinced my mother to come with me in search of this artist, Mrs. Dawson, leaving Kit and Titania at home. I told her what the lady said, a whole dollar just for sitting, but Mamma remains dubious.

We pause our steps before a modest brick building, four stories tall with black shutters. I reach into my coat pocket to retrieve the calling card, but before I've had a chance to verify the address, the door creaks open. Mrs. Dawson appears in the doorway with a smile, draped in a straw-colored apron and with that same untidy, upswept hair. She wipes her hands down the front of her apron and extends her grip to greet Mamma. "You must be Mrs. Talbot. I recognize you from the shop. I'm so happy you've come. Both of you, please come in."

We follow Mrs. Dawson into the quiet front hall of what looks to be apartment housing and up a set of stairs. At the second story landing, she leads us toward a door. She opens it without a key, and we follow her, stepping into a space that instantly strikes me as remarkable for two reasons. The first is that it is very long, much more spacious than Mamma's and my small room. The second is that it is so very bright. Floor-to-ceiling windows run the length of one entire wall, allowing sunshine to stream into a large, rectangular space. It's not tidy, but neither is it messy. The room, rather, appears full, a purposeful space where each well-loved item has its use.

In the front of the studio is a kitchen, with a deep soapstone sink and a wooden butcher block stacked with cups, plates, a bowl full of sand-colored eggs, a woven basket heaped with apples, and a few small posies of twine-wrapped herbs. The border of this kitchen area is a wooden table with six chairs, and just beyond that appears another space, crowded and colorful.

This must be where Mrs. Dawson does her art, for I see several easels and a tall wooden workbench covered in piles of paper, canisters stuffed with pencils and brushes of varying sizes, empty jugs and crockery bowls, sponges, and tubes of every shade. A haphazard scattering of canvases—some blank, some exploding with color—fills the space. Three stools are tucked back against the wall, and hooks overhead hold up a row of smocks dappled with varying degrees of stains.

Beyond that, behind a silk screen, I see the very end of a brass bed. Does Mrs. Dawson sleep in here, as well? She must. The space looks very lived in, after all.

"How very . . . bohemian," Mamma mutters, looking around the studio with a dour pinch to her features. I take in a breath, noting the smell of coffee and toasted bread and something else, something sharp, tangy.

"It's the turpentine," Mrs. Dawson says, offering half a smile.

"Begging pardon?" I ask.

"What you are smelling, it's turpentine. It comes from a tree and helps to bind the oil in the paint. It always strikes people their first time here. 'Course, I can barely smell it. I could open a window if it's too much?"

"Oh, no, I'm fine," I say.

Mrs. Dawson appears a bit formal today, much more reserved than when she sought me out behind Wanamaker's. She's dressed similarly to the other day, though, in a drab beige blouse and long skirt to match, her stained apron on top. I'm also wearing the same outfit I wore at Wanamaker's, my most proper attire: starched shirtwaist, full skirt, dark blue wool coat. Mrs. Dawson offers to take my coat and Mamma's, walking farther into the apartment and tossing them both onto the foot of the bed. Then, turning back to us, she says: "I hope you found your way here all right?"

"Oh, it was fine," Mamma says, her eyes still roving around the room. "Though of course we had to come on foot all the way, as a hansom would have been beyond our means."

"I appreciate you coming," Mrs. Dawson says. "And I'm happy to give you the fare for your return home."

"Much obliged," Mamma answers.

"Well, since time is precious." Mrs. Dawson claps her hands together and turns to me. "Evelyn, you said you hadn't done anything like this before, isn't that so? Sitting for a portrait?"

"I haven't."

"I could show you some of my other work, but I have half a mind, instead, to jump right in. Something about your eyes . . . your expressions. I've got this feeling you're going to be a natural, and I'd like to go with that, if that's all right with you?"

I offer a small nod; it's all the same to me. As long as we leave here today with the dollar she promised.

"I was thinking we could begin with you sitting on this stool, right here beside the window."

I look at the offered stool. "What . . . what am I to do?"

Mrs. Dawson narrows her eyes, considers her words for a moment, and then says, "You are to be as natural as you can be. I was thinking pencil sketches today, just to keep it simple. And we will have you stay precisely as you are, that blouse is fine. I'll work with your face. It was your expressiveness that caught me. The most important thing is that I want you to be comfortable."

"And me?" Mamma interjects.

"Mrs. Talbot, I'd also like you to be entirely comfortable. Can I offer you coffee?"

"I already had my cup."

"Then please, be at ease. Wherever you'll be happiest. This chair? At the table? I'm sorry it's not fancy. But I'm sure it makes this whole thing . . . well, less unnatural for Evelyn to have you here with her."

"Wouldn't have it any other way," Mamma mutters as she settles down at the wooden table and pulls a skein of maroon yarn from her sack.

Mrs. Dawson turns her gaze back to me. "Evelyn, you've never done *any* work with an artist?"

Mamma answers before I can: "Of course she has not! What do you take me for?"

"I only ask because . . . well, the command she has. But I suppose sometimes it can't be taught." Mrs. Dawson ignores the sharpness of Mamma's tone and keeps her gaze steady on me. "So then the first thing we need is for you to find your light." Mrs. Dawson leans over her kitchen counter and picks up a red apple. Then she turns back to me and curves her other hand over the piece of fruit, with just an inch between its red skin and her palm. "See this?"

"The apple?" I ask.

"Yes, but covered in shadow. A simple shape, barely any discernible colors. Not much to look at." Then she walks toward the window and holds out the apple before it, lifting her hand away, her eyes narrowing as she focuses on the small round piece of fruit. "Ah. Now I see a whole range of colors. Red, yes. But also yellow, gold, pink, a touch of green. I see here a small divot, a bruise. And the hint of the darkness under the skin right there. It makes my mind think, even without having to touch it, that the fruit is probably soft under that spot, a totally different texture. I imagine how it would feel to touch it. And there must be an entirely different taste, too, beneath that bruise." Mrs. Dawson is silent a moment, pensive, and then she lowers the fruit, looking back to me. "It's amazing what the presence or the absence of light will do for a thing. Visually, but even more than that. Looking at something in the right light allows us to see things, experience things, imagine things—all in a way we never previously thought possible." She's speaking now as if ruminating on something holy, sacred—not just any old apple. "Each face has its own unique set of shapes and contours, tones and textures, and the light will fall on it in any number of ways, depending on position and angle. And when something—or in this case, some*one*—is in the right light, why, she can look as if she's lit from within."

Mrs. Dawson takes two steps toward me, touches my chin with the rough tip of her finger, and gives it the gentlest nudge, so that my face angles toward the window. "Ah, see. Your cheek is a valley catching the sunrise, just beneath the beautiful mountaintop of your nose." She smiles at me with an earnest, searching look. "My girl, you glow like a pearl. Stay like that." With that, she hurries off, taking up her post behind the nearest easel, grabbing a pencil from the jar. I turn to watch her, and she tuts. "Please don't move, Evelyn. Keep just like we had you, staring toward the window."

I do as she says, rearranging myself. "Breathe," she says, so I do. "Can you soften your shoulders?" Again, I oblige. And then she falls quiet, and so do I, perched beside that sunny window. Mamma sits nearby, and my guess is that she's looked up from her yarn, but I don't hear anything from her, other than the rhythmic click-clack of her knitting needles. Soon the scratch of Mrs. Dawson's pencil on the paper makes it a wordless duet.

Mrs. Dawson moves through page after page, letting her papers slide to the floor before positioning a fresh one and carrying on. At one point she tosses her pencil to the floor and picks up a newly sharpened one. When she finally speaks, I have little idea of how much time has passed. Minutes? An hour? She says, "Pencil today, but it's really a shame not to have color in here. Your *hair*. It's got copper, russet, sunlit gold. I can't wait to explore it all."

Next Mrs. Dawson has me shift in and out of a series of poses. The sun has moved, which seems to thrill her. "These shadows! It's entirely new now."

As she works, scratching away, occasionally taking quick breaks to attack the tip of her pencil with a small sharpening knife, I slip into a sort of trance. At first I think of Kit, wondering how he's passing his day. I hope he gets himself out to play. There's a group of kids who play stickball in the alleyway just behind our boardinghouse any day it's not raining. Will he ask to join? I'm happy he has Titania at least. He's such a shy boy; he doesn't make friends easily, especially now that I'm not there with him.

Eventually, my mind goes blank. Like a sky without clouds. Staring off toward the window, I allow myself to take a break from any thinking or worrying, to just be. And when Mrs. Dawson looks up, declaring to the quiet room, "I think we are done," it feels as though I resurface from some deep and thoughtless place. I blink back to the present—the rectangular room with its mess of easels and brushes, the chemical tang of turpentine, the view of the kitchen table and Mamma with her knitting, which is now the full sleeve of a maroon sweater.

Glancing back out the window, I see that the sun truly has traveled across the sky. We arrived here in the morning; now it must be well into the afternoon. "How long has it been?" I ask.

"Five hours," Mrs. Dawson answers, making a slow circle with her wrist. There's a pile of papers scattered across the floor around her feet. "And I could have kept going. I'd gladly ignore the cramps in my wrist, but I fear for you. I don't want an unhappy artists' model."

I smile at this, a bit flattered to be referred to as an *artists' model*. It sounds so fashionable. But then a beat later, I notice my neck aches. My shoulders hum with a dull burn of fatigue. What's more, I'm famished. And I realize we haven't eaten—not lunch, not a bite since my early breakfast of bread and a small cup of coffee in our room before Mamma and I left for the day.

Mrs. Dawson steps slowly toward me, saying, "Evelyn, as I suspected, you are a natural. The expressiveness of your features. And the way you held your poses . . . why, I don't know that I've ever seen such total stillness from a model."

All those nights of forcing myself not to move, not to disturb a weeping Mamma beside me in bed. I suppose they were good for something.

"Excellent work today. I really mean that. As I said, a natural."

Funny that she calls it that, "natural." Feels to me more like being a statue. And then, as if skimming the thoughts directly from my mind, Mrs. Dawson says: "Surprising how much hard work goes into simply posing, isn't that so? It's more than merely being still. It's keeping your body and your face at rest, while also entirely engaged. Not many can manage it. As I mentioned when you first walked in, you have a command I've rarely seen. And without any study."

I don't look in Mamma's direction, nor do I feel the need to correct Mrs. Dawson, to tell her that I learned such total stillness from the schooling of our shattered life.

Mrs. Dawson goes on, "Bravo, dear girl." With that, she presses something cold into my hand. I look down to see four quarters. A dollar! For just a few hours of sitting there. I think no more of the cramps in my shoulder as I stare in amazement at my full hand, and then back up at Mrs. Dawson. She flashes me half a smile, then asks: "Would you like to see how they turned out?"

She takes my other hand in hers, and I walk with her toward the easel she was using. She leans over to pick up a few of the many pages. "See for yourself," she says, offering me the top one.

I glance down at it, stunned by the rendering of the face that appears before me in black, white, and every shade of gray. Mrs. Dawson has managed to create a glow that shines out of my dark eyes, with only a pencil on paper. I marvel at how she's shown the shadows of my face, the swell of my lips, the warmth of my skin. I so rarely see my own image—we have just one small handheld mirror, Mamma's. A relic of our previous life, the handle carved of rosy-pink enamel, small pearls forming the letters of Mamma's initials. Her wedding present from Daddy, something with which she refused to part. But she doesn't like me to touch it or look into it. Even so, the face that stares back at me when I *do* occasionally steal a peek has never looked as expressive or as interesting as the penciled faces I now see on the papers sprawled before me.

I look back toward Mrs. Dawson, and she's staring at my face on the paper with the same look of wonder—even disbelief—that I felt just a moment ago when she pressed four quarters into my palm. When she pulls her eyes away from the sketch and meets my gaze, a silent moment passes between us. Like before, it feels imbued with something akin to the sacred, silent and yet full of meaning.

The golden cord of that moment is ripped as a sudden commotion fills the front entry of the studio and a figure comes striding through the door. A woman. She looks at us, at the mess of papers across the floor, and declares: "Hope I'm not disturbing! Didn't realize you'd still be at it."

Mrs. Dawson, who appears entirely unfazed by the unannounced arrival of this woman into her studio, breaks from my gaze to turn toward the newcomer. And then, with her voice soft, she answers: "Yes, well, when you come across lightning, and you happen to have a jar, it's best to try to catch it."

Chapter Six

"We were on a bit of a roll, you might say." Mrs. Dawson looks to the newcomer, who strides boldly into the studio space, an overflowing parcel of groceries in each hand, as comfortable as if she owned the place.

"Well, then keep on rolling. I won't interrupt," the woman offers in easy reply. "The name's Rachel."

"My . . . roommate," Mrs. Dawson hastens to explain. "And it's no interruption. We had just finished for the day."

Rachel pauses before the kitchen butcher block and begins unloading her overstuffed bags—carrots, apples, bread rolls, a thick square of cheese, eggs. I realize, again, how hungry I am. Didn't Mrs. Dawson mention that lunch would be included? This new woman, Rachel, catches me staring and lifts an eyebrow, saying: "Leah, don't tell me you forgot to feed the poor thing?"

Mrs. Dawson looks from me to Rachel as embarrassment spreads across her face. "I, uh, well, I forgot about food entirely. It was . . . it was a productive session."

"Well, then I think an omelet is in order," says Rachel, pulling a red pepper out of her satchel. "Give me just a few minutes." She reaches into a drawer to retreive a series of bowls and utensils.

"Rachel works for a widow on Spruce Street, keeping house, laundry, cooking. She's an excellent cook," Mrs. Dawson says as she picks up her scattered papers from the floor.

Mamma, lowering her knitting and looking between the two

women, speaks up for the first time. "You are Leah and Rachel? What a biblical pair of names."

Rachel lets out a deep laugh, saying: "That's about where our resemblance to the Good Book ends."

Mrs. Dawson throws a scowl in Rachel's direction but quickly busies herself with tidying up her papers and pencils. In the kitchen, Rachel places a frying pan on the stove. I see how Mamma's eyes have widened as she looks once more at each of these two ladies, then toward the brass bed behind the partition. And then she turns toward me. I give a shrug; I don't understand what Rachel meant by the remark, but something about Mamma's expression tells me not to probe. And soon the scent of melting butter is so distracting that I walk toward the stove.

Mrs. Dawson, meanwhile, looks toward Mamma. "Mrs. Talbot, may I have a word with you?" When Mamma nods, Mrs. Dawson takes a seat, joining her at the table.

Rachel places a knife on the kitchen counter before me. "You like to cook, sweetie?"

I consider her question. Is it called cooking, what I do? Not really, as we don't ever have proper ingredients, but rather scraps we scrounge for and then toss together. Rachel, perhaps seeing my hesitation, goes on, "You know how to chop peppers?"

"Yes," I answer. That I can do. I've fixed dinner enough times for Kit and myself.

"Then get to work, darling, and make it fast because these eggs aren't going to wait on you." Rachel starts whistling a tune, bustling about the kitchen, pulling down four plates, plucking a finger's pinch of some green herb—parsley?—from a small basket on a shelf.

Soon the smells wafting around us are torturously enticing, and Rachel is telling me how she wants to travel to France someday. "The best cuisine in the world over there. If I could study there, why, I'd open my own café." She stares at a large print of a map that hangs on the wall nearby, labeled "FRANCE." Surveying it, she goes quiet, then exhales. "Leah and I will save up enough. Someday."

As I'm chopping, I can't help but eavesdrop on Mrs. Dawson's lowered voice nearby: "As you can see, Mrs. Talbot, your daughter has been greatly blessed. But I'm sure you are aware of that."

" 'Course I am," Mamma says, making less of an effort to keep her voice quiet. "Though I don't know whether I'd call it a blessing or a curse with this child. She's far too beautiful. Soon enough, she'll know it."

Mrs. Dawson sighs; I can hear it over the sputter of the eggs frying on the stovetop. I'm almost done chopping, but I pretend I'm entirely focused on the peppers as Mamma goes on: "Tarentum may be the ugliest town in America, but she was the prettiest baby in America. My, when she was born, people would come from places far away just to glimpse her face. They'd show up saying they'd heard about this beautiful baby born to the lawyer Winn Talbot. Sure, her daddy loved it. Completely agreed with all the praise."

This is news to me, this story of my earliest days. The knife has gone still in my hand, which I notice is now quivering as I think about Daddy, boasting with me in his arms as a baby. Mamma goes on: "Winn worshipped that child from the day she was born. I'd always tell him he had to keep it down, crowing on about what a beautiful little girl he had—such talk would go straight to her head and spoil it. Well, now he's gone, so we aren't hearing from him anymore...."

Mother's words taper off, but Mrs. Dawson's voice is low and warm when she speaks: "I can imagine it's been difficult."

"You *can't* imagine," Mamma answers, her tone bald, almost rude, and I wince where I stand. Rachel wordlessly slides the plate of peppers from me, finishing the last few slices and offering a wink as she scatters them over the nearly cooked eggs. I'm thankful that she allows me to remain where I am, silent, as Mamma goes on. "And it wasn't just him that we lost—it was everything. Maybe if he'd spent less time gabbing all over town about his pretty little girl and more time practicing law or seeing to his accounts, we wouldn't have been left in such a bind. But as it was, we lost the house, the horse and buggy, the furniture, all of it. And I got another little one at home, too. A son."

"Well, I'd be ever so willing to hire Evelyn again. And if the earnings help you just a little, then it's a favorable situation for all."

"I'll have to think on it." I hear Mamma's exhale. "I'm not sure, well . . . Is it decent?"

"I'd only do work that is entirely decent, Mrs. Talbot." Mrs. Dawson's voice remains even and calm. "There's so much to explore with her. The colors alone—her skin is the richest hue. She's not pale like many other girls. Her complexion has a warmth to it."

"That's her daddy in her."

"And her hair, it's like a waterfall, so thick. The most entrancing shades of chestnut and gold."

"That's thanks to me. I may not look like much now, but . . . well, I was young once, too."

"Yes, Mrs. Talbot, I don't doubt it. She's lucky to be your daughter. Oh, and her lips. We need to work with color to capture them, like two rose petals. Listen to me, I sound like a student of Shakespeare suddenly. But I assure you, my interest as an artist is what drives me. I'd love to pull out your daughter's gifts. Someday soon she may realize the treasure she has, and she won't have any use for my little studio. But until then, I'll paint her any day she'll give me."

Mamma declares once more that she has to think on it, and then Rachel announces that the omelet is ready, and all talk of posing is paused for the day. As Rachel slices into the eggs and serves up four steaming plates, my mouth begins to water. And as I sit down at the table, I realize yet again just how hungry I am, but not only for the food—also for the work that Mrs. Dawson has offered.

• ◆ •

AFTER THAT, I go to Mrs. Dawson's each Sunday morning. I sit before the windows in their ever-changing puddles of sunshine, "finding my light" as Mrs. Dawson has taught me to do. I always wear my starched white blouse, and sometimes, if she wants to draw a bit of my neck, I'll unbutton the top, but that's it. Sometimes Mrs. Dawson has me turn around and undo my braid or chignon so that she can devote her entire attention to my loose hair. Other times she focuses on just my eyes, moving me toward and away from a window for various amounts of light and shadow. "I don't think I've ever seen them looking this big," she says. Other times she studies my hands as though they hold some secret treasure that only she can find.

The view outside, originally one of spring trees newly in leaf, thickens and warms as summer approaches and then begins to ripen across the city. Eventually Mamma stops accompanying me to my Sunday appointments, assured of Mrs. Dawson's respectability and happy to have her one free day back to herself.

AFTER A FEW MONTHS, Mrs. Dawson declares that we are ready to begin incorporating props. "Art isn't meant to be passive; it's active," she explains to me. "And you are the most animated artists' model I've ever worked with. Let's begin storytelling."

So the following Sunday, on Rachel's direction, I tip my nose into a silk rose as though I'm entranced by its perfume. Next, holding the petals to my cheek, I stare off into the imagined distance. "As though you are pining for a long-lost love," Mrs. Dawson says, throwing me a playful wink. "Ever been in love?"

"Of course not," I answer, feeling my cheeks grow warm with bashfulness.

"Then you get to do a bit of theater, too, Evelyn. I know you've got several talents." Mrs. Dawson pauses, tipping her head sideways as she studies me for a moment. "Have you ever longed for anything?"

That I can answer in the affirmative. Yes, I've longed for a good many things. Daddy. Our old home. The life we lost. "There." Mrs. Dawson leans toward me. "That's it right there. Keep that." And so I try my best to oblige. To push the memories aside, wiping my mind blank, even as I hold on to the expression that the sad memories have summoned.

As I sit for Mrs. Dawson in silence, I hear the noises from the street outside—chatter, laughter, conversations as the girls and boys my age move about the city. It's always Sunday when I'm posing for Mrs. Dawson, a busy day when people take their leisure and make merry, as I sit here and work. Now that the weather is fine, the city teems with activity and, I notice, children.

Fond as I have grown of Mrs. Dawson, I do have moments when I long to get up and go. To walk the street on a Sunday afternoon like the other youngsters my age, an ice-cream cone perched in my hands, maybe a parent offering me a few coins to go catch one of the plays or musical revues showing in the theaters. But no, the dollar that Mrs. Dawson will press into my hand at the end of each sitting helps keep us fed. The Sundays of leisure will have to wait, I tell myself, certain that my face shows Mrs. Dawson plenty of longing.

Some Sundays Rachel is here for part of the time. Some days I don't see her at all. She always bursts into the apartment in a flurry of activity, acting as though we've surprised her by being there when she should know by now that I'm here every week. But then, one Sunday that autumn, she comes in with another woman in her company, and I'm the one who is caught by surprise.

It's a notable day for me: it's the first time Mrs. Dawson has asked me to change out of my ordinary shirt and skirt and put on a costume. Today I'm posing as the goddess Aphrodite. I arrived this morning with my hair in a tumble of dark curls, Mamma having braided two tight plaits for me last night, just as Mrs. Dawson requested.

And now here I am in her studio, my body swathed in a simple sheath of impossibly soft white satin, reclining on a pale sheet across the floor, a scattering of silk flower petals tossed around me. I felt bashful at first getting into this theatrical position, but I'm so comfortable working with Mrs. Dawson at this point that I quickly settled in. But when Rachel barges in with this new lady in her company, I feel entirely too exposed and bashful all over again.

"Oh, hello, Violet." Mrs. Dawson, for her part, barely looks up from her canvas. She's working in watercolors today, and she dips her paintbrush into her murky water, giving it a swirl as though she plans to carry on with her work.

I fidget in my place on the floor, the first time I've done that; I wonder if perhaps I ought to cover my arms, or pull back my unruly hair.

"Oh, Evelyn, don't move . . ." Mrs. Dawson begins, but then, seeming to sense my unease, she shifts in her seat, throwing Rachel and this newcomer a look.

Rachel raises a hand and hurries to say: "We aren't staying. Violet was just passing by and wanted to stop in and say hello."

I turn to look at this other woman, Violet, and my eyes lock with hers. She stares directly at me, as though she's been pinned in place. The intensity of her gaze startles me, causing my cheeks to grow warm. I cross my bare arms.

"Well, then, let's say hello," Mrs. Dawson replies. "Violet, this is Evelyn. Evelyn, this is Violet." Mrs. Dawson's voice has turned formal, even a bit cold. The woman, Violet, gives me a tight nod. And then, as promised, Rachel ushers her out of the apartment. Alone once more with Mrs. Dawson, I feel my body soften.

But Mrs. Dawson is scowling, holding her paintbrush across her knee as she looks at the doorway through which the two women have just left. "Now she'll be asking you to work with her; mark my words."

I swallow, saying nothing. Mrs. Dawson lets out a quiet sigh and turns her gaze from the doorway back to me. "Listen, Evelyn, I have a question. And it's just you and me in here, so I want *you* to answer. Do you like your work at Wanamaker's?"

"Yes," I answer, rearranging my limbs on the sheet.

"Do you really?" Mrs. Dawson presses.

I look toward the window, my head in a bit of a spin. I've never been asked that question before. I haven't even really bothered thinking it through. Sure, with autumn in the air, I've felt undeniable stirrings. As September began, I thought of the fact that I was so close to high school, and that had filled me with unpleasant pangs of yearning. I'd missed a few months in the spring, but now an entirely new school year was starting, and I was officially being left behind. But I hadn't allowed myself to dwell too long in that brooding.

Mrs. Dawson is no longer painting. She goes on: "The reason

I ask is because I'd be happy to give you more work. If you think your mother would allow it. I'd love to hire you for more than just Sundays."

This is something I'd never considered. I run my fingers along the silk of my costume, asking, "And you'd pay me . . . more?"

"Of course I'd pay you for your work. A dollar a day. But you see what that means, don't you? You'd have to quit your position at Wanamaker's."

A dollar a day! Why, that's more than double what I make at the store.

"It would be serious work, Evelyn. As a proper artists' model—no more of these sittings just for study. I do believe you are ready. I believe we are both ready."

"Ready . . . for what, precisely?" I ask.

Mrs. Dawson considers her words for a moment, then says, "I'd start selling the images. To the newspapers, the magazines, private companies for advertisements."

Selling images of me? To proper companies and advertisers? My words are quiet as I voice my question: "You really think someone would pay for an image of me?"

"I don't *think* it," Mrs. Dawson says, throwing a look toward her easel, where today's half-finished painting awaits: me as a goddess sprawled on white, surrounded by flowers. "I know it."

I DON'T RETURN to work at Wanamaker's. With Mamma's lukewarm assent, I quit my post as a department store errand girl, and thereafter I set out each morning for Chestnut Street and Mrs. Dawson's studio. It's a later start to the day, since Mrs. Dawson doesn't want me showing up at seven in the morning like I did at Wanamaker's. This means that Mamma sets off first and I'm able to help Kit finish his breakfast and bundle up. We leave the boardinghouse together, and I walk to work at the same time that the rest of the city's children are making their ways toward their schools. When Kit and I break apart at the corner of Arch Street, I keep my eyes lowered, pretending for all around us that I'm just heading toward a different school.

When I arrive at Mrs. Dawson's studio, often the bed is still rumpled; sometimes Rachel is still in it. *Do they share a bed?* I wonder, thinking that it probably helps for the warmth, especially now that we are marching toward winter.

"Morning," I say as I walk in, slipping out of my wool coat.

"Morning!" they both chime back. Rachel makes up the bed and dresses behind the screen, then brews us coffee. As Mrs. Dawson and I sit at the table drinking from our warm mugs, Rachel packs herself a lunch pail and sets out for her work on Spruce Street. Mrs. Dawson always walks Rachel to the door, and for some reason that I don't fully understand, I keep my eyes averted when they say their farewells in the doorway. Sometimes I see them embrace in what looks like a hug. One time I could have sworn I heard a sound like a quick kiss.

Once it's the pair of us alone in the studio, Mrs. Dawson sets out my costume for the day and tells me about the job. Each day our work is different. Some days I'm in lace and jewels, feeling fancy like a queen. Another time she drapes me in a boa of feathers and rouges my cheeks for a cigar advertisement. True to her word, she's begun selling our work to the newspapers and local businesses, and folks are interested in buying what we're making. We've got lots of offers. One day Mrs. Dawson tells me I'm to dress as a milkmaid for a local cheese maker off Rittenhouse Square. Another time she puts me in a floor-length gown of rich red silk and tells me my image will go on a chocolate box. Mrs. Dawson captures my likeness in oil, charcoal, watercolor, and pencils, slipping in and out of countless poses and expressions.

Mrs. Dawson and I make a good team; she tells me that, and I agree. And even when swaths of my skin show, or she looks at me with every drop of her concentration, I never feel uncomfortable in her presence. She's not looking at me as men have looked at me. She's an artist and I am her subject. Sure, I'm not always entirely clear on how my outfits tie into the products we are meant to be selling. "Why would a feather boa and rouged cheeks sell cigars to gentlemen?" I ask.

"Oh, it'll sell," she assures me. I trust Mrs. Dawson.

We have a good rhythm. Mrs. Dawson begins every session by

helping me to find my light. Then she tells me to settle my eyes. The eyes and the light, we can't begin until she's happy with both, and what she wants is always changing, depending on the work of the day. The key is to not hold *too much* in my eyes, Mrs. Dawson tells me. "They have to be expressive enough to capture someone's attention and tell a story, but still leave enough room so that people can put whatever meaning they want into the image."

We take breaks every few hours and drink coffee or tea. Together we sit before her broad windows, and Mrs. Dawson shows me what we've done so far. She speaks to me about our work like I'm her equal, perhaps even a partner.

Some evenings when we complete our work early, Rachel cooks for us, and each meal is more delicious than the last: tender pork filet, steaming fish stew, beef bourguignon so flavorful that the meat melts on my tongue. That map of France hangs near their kitchen table, and Rachel loves to point out from where in the country each meal comes. Both women speak regularly of their dreams of traveling to France—Rachel to study the cuisine and Mrs. Dawson to see the great artistic masterpieces.

Other evenings, I skip dinner at their place and stop at the library on my walk home. I love that time, picking up books for myself and Kit. I still cherish an ember in my heart, the dream from Daddy that someday I'll go back to school. Finish high school, maybe even apply to college.

Mrs. Dawson likes that I make these trips to the library, and she tells me to read as much as I can. "Reading is one of the only things in life that can take you out of yourself," she declares one afternoon when she sees my bundle of books that I tote to and from the library. "Art does, of course. And travel. And falling in love." She smiles, then carries on. "But reading will be good. It will stir your soul. It will enrich your imagination. Consider it your homework, Evelyn. Read for me and for your work—and most of all, for yourself."

So I do. When I read Victor Hugo's *Les Misérables* that winter, I imagine myself as the fatherless girl Cosette, who stays kind and good, even when faced with malice. Or bold, brave Éponine, who learns how to survive with nothing so that she need not compromise everything. And even Fantine, desperate to know every kind of love when instead she gets every kind of betrayal. Without school or friends my age, I use these books as my tools to learn and live beyond the boardinghouse and the artist's studio.

Another blessing to come out of my new work—I get long evenings with Kit. After I fix supper, we curl into bed beside Titania, and I read Arthurian legends for my brother just as Daddy once did for me. I tell Kit that someday soon we'll have enough money for a nicer room, maybe a little house with a yard. At night I go to sleep satisfied, knowing that I'm helping Mamma and providing for Kit. Knowing that Daddy would be proud.

And then one chilly afternoon that winter, the other woman comes back to the studio. Violet. She's with Rachel again, walking in as Mrs. Dawson and I are taking a break. We've just brewed some tea, and I'm savoring the warmth of the mug between my cold fingers. Mrs. Dawson gets up and greets them both at the doorway, giving both Rachel and this other woman quick hugs. Then all three of them turn toward me where I sit beside the window, done up in a yellow dress with a broad sailor's collar for a cookie tin advertisement.

"I'm Violet," the woman says, removing her coat as she takes a tenuous step closer.

I nod. I remember. "I'm Evelyn," I reply, unsure of what she wants. Or why she's staring at me like that. I throw a searching look toward Mrs. Dawson.

Mrs. Dawson folds her paint-stained hands before her waist, turning from me toward her company, and then back to me as she says, "Violet has been waiting patiently, and I was starting to feel like a greedy friend, keeping you all to myself."

And then Mrs. Dawson walks back toward me, sits down at my side. "Now Violet has come to us with such a golden opportunity, even greedy old I couldn't tell her no."

I still don't understand what this is about. Violet takes another step toward us. When she speaks, her voice is quiet. "Evelyn, I am also an artist. I work in stained glass, with a gentleman named Mr. Tiffany. Mr. Louis Comfort Tiffany. Does the name sound familiar?"

I nod again. Of course I know the name Tiffany. I worked in a department store—we all knew of Mr. Tiffany and his family's famous lamps, desired in New York City, London, Paris.

Violet braids her gloved hands before her midsection, and when she speaks next, it's with a tone like the one I use when I'm trying to coax a timid Titania out from under the bed. "Mr. Tiffany is working on a new church here in town, and he's hired me to cut the stained-glass windows. There are several scenes where I need an angel. I've been looking everywhere for the right artists' model. I've gone to New York, Boston, even Chicago. But I think I've finally found what I was seeking. And when I shared my idea with Mr. Tiffany, he agreed."

My heart has picked up its pace in my rib cage. Then Violet asks, "Evelyn, will you be Mr. Tiffany's angel?"

Chapter Seven

Late Summer 1899

I STAND BEFORE THE SMALL CROWD WITH MY BODY SHEATHED IN delicate white silk, the material soft as water as it clings to my curves and seeps to the floor. My loose curls, almost to my waist since Mamma and I have not cut my hair in so long, tumble over my bare shoulders, lending a touch of welcome modesty to the gauzy neckline. Mrs. Dawson looks on with unabashed approval, as do Violet and Rachel at her side. It's a sunny day with plenty of light coming through the tall windows, and Violet is explaining how she'll create the glow of a halo around my head with shards of gold-colored glass.

Kit, who lost interest in the art and my posing long ago, is playing at the kitchen table with some blocks Rachel conjured. He's building an Eiffel Tower, inspired by the large map of France, which Rachel was showing him.

The only person scowling is Mamma, but she's been unhappy for months. Even this prestigious job, posing as an angel for something as tops as one of Mr. Tiffany's stained-glass windows, hasn't been able to draw Mamma from her gloom—her frustration that after over a year at Wanamaker's, she still hasn't been permitted to try her hand at stitching some of the ladies' gowns. "I haven't been to *Paris*," she'll gripe at the end of her long shift, her face pinched with frustration and fatigue, and dislike for the floor manager who has told her of her inadequacies with the thread and needle. "I haven't studied at an *academy*. These folks don't recognize my talent when it's right before their eyes."

What's more, Mamma feels that Wanamaker's is draining her time and ability to pursue her dreams outside of the store. Twelve-hour shifts every day but Sunday. Serving women who either look right through her or harangue her with their complaints over merchandise she didn't make. She hasn't hidden her irritation that my work is wrapped up in about seven or eight hours each day and yet brings in much higher wages.

In spite of all that, she's made the effort to be here with me this evening, on the last day of this job, after which Violet plans to travel back to Manhattan to present to Mr. Tiffany the sketches she's completed of his "angel." Manhattan! Tiffany's! It all sounds so impossibly glamorous. I hope Mr. Tiffany loves what he sees. Violet assures me he will.

Rachel has insisted that we all stay late for a celebratory dinner. She's been cooking for most of the day, in and out as we've worked, and the studio is filled with mouthwateringly delicious aromas—a chicken roasting in lemon and rosemary, crispy potatoes drizzled in parsley and salt, and something else that smells like sweet stewed fruit. Suppertime can't get here soon enough.

At the end of my final pose, when Violet and Mrs. Dawson declare aloud to the studio, "That's it. We've got it," and Mrs. Dawson tosses her hands into the air, the three women erupt in applause. Rachel hoots as she twirls her wooden spoon overhead. Mrs. Dawson claps, then exchanges a hug with Violet, each of them looking over the sketches like a pair of proud parents.

Their celebration makes me feel even more bashful, so I retreat behind the screen to change back into my blouse and skirt. When I reemerge, Rachel is uncorking a bottle of red wine, and she pours a glass for Mamma, then one for Violet. She doesn't ask me, but when she extends a glass in my direction, I pull back, shaking my head. "Oh . . . I don't partake."

But Rachel is undeterred, still holding the glass out to me as she urges, "One glass, Evelyn. To season the food."

I throw an inquiring look to Mamma. Coffee, which I drink by the gallons some days, is one thing, but wine is quite another. With the eyes of our entire small party on her, Mamma lets out a beleaguered sigh. "Just one glass. But it won't do to make a repeat thing of it."

"I know, Mamma," I say, biting my lower lip to stanch a smile and eagerly accepting the offered glass. Rachel flashes me a quick wink and then says to Mamma: "Only for tonight's celebration, here with us. After all, she's worked like an adult on this."

Mamma grimaces at this but offers no reply. I turn to Mrs. Dawson to ask where she'd like me to put the angel robe costume, but she cuts me off: "Call me Leah, please."

This catches me by surprise. Rachel has only ever wanted me to address her by her first name, but Mrs. Dawson has never been anything but the formal Mrs. Dawson while we've worked together.

And yet, I can see that in this moment, with our labors complete, her expression is affable, more relaxed than I've ever seen, and she adds: "Tonight you are here as a guest in my home. You've done great work as a true artist, and we all wish to celebrate you."

"Hear, hear," Rachel agrees, clinking her glass to mine. "To Evelyn."

"To Evelyn," Mrs. Dawson and Violet repeat. I raise my glass to my lips to hide the tug of my shy smile. I swallow a small sip, feel the ripple of warmth that slides down my throat. The first taste of wine, the fragrant smell of the kitchen, the congenial company of supportive and artistic women who have worked with me as respectful partners—it all feels quite festive indeed, and now I no longer try to fight back against the urge to smile as I enjoy another delicious sip of wine.

"Dinner's ready," Rachel announces. We make our way to their wooden table, and we help her to pass around the steaming bowls of food—potatoes seasoned with fresh herbs, green beans drizzled with butter, roasted chicken crisped to perfection.

Violet takes the seat beside me and asks, loud enough for all to hear: "Have you ever been to New York City, Evelyn?"

"New York City? No," I answer, glancing to Mamma. Mrs.

Dawson—no, *Leah*—is fiddling with the gramophone as music starts to play.

"You ought to visit," Violet says.

"Your plate, dear," Rachel interjects, and she heaps a serving of chicken onto it. Next she serves Kit.

"I would love to visit," I go on. "Someday."

Violet slides a look toward Mamma when she speaks next. "She's good enough to work as an artists' model in New York City."

Mamma unfolds her napkin primly across her lap, looking down for a long moment. Leah returns to the table with a large pitcher of water, and lowering it, she says: "It's true, Mrs. Talbot."

Violet goes on, accepting a plate of food from Rachel. "Evelyn has the sort of face that you can't stop seeing, even long after you've walked away. Her beauty is haunting, like a ghost."

"Or an angel," Leah says.

"Well, that's right," agrees Violet with a grin. "That much we know."

I lift my fork, keeping my gaze fixed on my plate as they talk about me across the table. The night is darkening outside the window while we eat, and Violet goes on, explaining, "There's more work to be had in New York City for a girl with as much talent as Evelyn."

When Mamma does finally speak in response, her words catch me by surprise. And not only me, I suspect. "*I'm* good enough to be a seamstress in New York," she declares.

The table falls silent, everybody chewing on these words along with their food. I look up, glancing first at Mamma's pointed expression and then around the table. Rachel takes a slow sip of wine and eventually breaks the silence, answering: "I don't doubt that, Mrs. Talbot."

Violet swallows a mouthful of food. Then, her words slow and thoughtful, she says: "You know, it's something to consider. Both of you have dreams that might find their footing up there. Particularly in Manhattan, there's much to be done with the photographers." Violet raises her fork, and now she's looking directly at me. "When you work with a photographer, they have their image in a fraction of the time it takes a painter to get it onto the canvas. Five dollars for half a day, ten dollars for a full day. I don't think it's impossible to ask for that. Not with your talent."

I break my silence: "*Ten* dollars a day?" My head swirls; such a sum is hard to even fathom.

Leah leans forward and props her elbows on the table, looking from Mamma to me. I brace for what she's about to say—will she be irritated that Violet is suggesting I seek work elsewhere? But when Leah does speak, her tone is encouraging: "Think how much more work you could do in a day. Minutes to get your picture, rather than hours. And with that, so much more pay."

I'm no longer devouring my food; there's too much else to take in. I lower my fork and meet Mamma's gaze. "To think how much less my neck would ache."

Leah sips her wine, nodding as she does so. Violet turns back to her food, spearing herself a piece of chicken. Before she takes the bite, she points her fork at me. "Soon it'll be a new century, Evelyn." And then, turning to Mamma, she says, "She's ready for a new challenge."

I'm not entirely sure what prompts me to do what I do next. Perhaps it's the first taste of wine hitting me, or perhaps it's the camaraderie of women welcoming me to the table like an equal among the adults. Or maybe it's the glow of satisfaction I feel at completing such a big job for Mr. Tiffany. Or the tantalizing mention of such a large sum of money. I suppose it's the combination of all of it.

Whatever it may be, I feel emboldened in that moment to speak up, so I say: "I want to go to New York. I am ready."

• ♦ •

I AM. I'm ready for a new challenge: a larger canvas, more work, more money. It takes me only two days of persistent begging to convince Mamma. The major point that gives her pause—and me, too—is that we would not be able to bring Kit. If I'm going to be out all day for photography sessions and Mamma will be bearing the double load of chaperoning me by day and making a go of her sewing at night, she doesn't like the idea of Kit being left alone all that time in a strange new city, one as foreign and massive as New York. So with the funds we have managed to squirrel away, we enroll Kit in a small boarding school just outside of Philadelphia. He'll be safe there, he'll be getting a far better education, and he won't have to navigate and manage in the big city on his own.

As tearful as the rending is in the week before our planned departure, I know that it will be best for all of us in the end, if only we can make it through the pain of the short term. It's all part of a broader plan I've formulated in my mind: I will go to New York City, and I will get work as an artists' model. I'll make enough money to help set up Mamma with a small dress shop to sell her own wares.

Then, with the money that Mamma and I bring in together, we'll have enough for a safe and comfortable apartment in Manhattan, and we'll bring Kit up and enroll him in a good school in a respectable neighborhood.

The grand finale of this whole plan? Once Mamma and Kit are both happily settled and situated—I will go back to school. I'll complete high school and then even college. Just like Daddy wanted. "It's only for a short time," I tell my brother, hugging him close when he asks me why he has to go away. I have to look away from those big brown eyes of his, those eyes that look so much like mine, holding worlds of feeling inside them and mirroring back all the pain that I, too, am holding. "It's for the best," I repeat, my tone more resolute than I feel. This is the way that our dreams will finally come true.

WITH KIT SETTLED at his new school, Mamma and I turn our focus to our upcoming journey. We book two tickets for a northbound train. All our worldly belongings fit neatly into a trunk and two frayed carpetbags, and Titania will travel in my arms. It's our dreams that are too big for any bag to hold; those we carry in our hearts. Twin dreams, mother and daughter, headed for the island of Manhattan.

On the eve of our departure, with our small room packed up and our third-class train tickets tucked safely into Mamma's traveling satchel, I set out at dusk toward the butcher to fetch some sandwiches for our supper. No longer do I have to scavenge in the alleyway behind Haudenshield's.

I feel a fresh pang of longing for my little brother—it seems wrong to be getting supper for two, not three. Even though I know that this separation is what's best for him, for all of us, that does little to numb my pain.

My eyes begin to burn with the threat of tears as I recall our goodbye. "But *why* do I have to go, Ev?" he asked for the hundredth time as Mamma and I put him on his own train, bound for Chester. I'd sighed. How could I make him, a sweet ten-year-old boy, understand? That he was going away to school—a place where he would be able to learn, and always eat a full meal, and sleep in a warm bed, even make friends his own age. How could I help him to see how lucky he was?

I force back the tears now. I need to stay focused and hopeful for tomorrow's journey. New York City! But as I troop out into the street and the evening light, I nearly bump into a lady. "Begging your pardon, ma'am," I mutter before I look up into a familiar face. "Oh!" It's Mrs. Dawson. Leah. She looks happy to see me, but not at all surprised that I've barreled into her.

"Just how it all began," she says, her tone a bit wistful. "Do you remember how you nearly ran right into me in the alleyway outside of the store?"

"Of course I do," I say, rocking on my heels. Also how I was so frightened of her, how I thought she was going to get me into trouble. It makes my mind spin to think of it—how could I have known all that would come from our acquaintance?

"I guess the fates weren't subtle, in the matter of arranging our meeting," Leah says, looking into my eyes intently. Then she blinks, gives a quick toss of her head, and when she speaks next, her voice is less nostalgic. "I was just going to come knock on your door."

It's then that I notice her hands are full of papers. "I am on my way to pick up a light supper," I say. "But here, may I help you with your load?"

"Well, it's for you, in fact."

"For me? Should we go inside?"

"No, it's all right. Let's stay here, just for a moment." Leah throws a glance upward, toward the second-floor windows, then looks back toward me. "I'm glad for you, Evelyn."

"Thank you," I say. Does she hear all that lurks behind those two simple words? The thanks I feel—for everything. Not only for her wishing me well at the outset of my journey. But for giving me my start and then each nudge along the way. And for her not begrudging me for leaving.

It seems that she does hear it, because she goes on, "I knew you'd outgrow me, and Philadelphia. I'm just happy we did as much work together as we did. And speaking of work"—Leah looks back down at her hands—"you'll need your portfolio up north. Hope you saved some room in your trunk."

Leah leans toward me and transfers the folder of papers into my hands. I look down, then back up at her, confused. "What's all this?"

"Have a look. Go on," Leah urges me, gesturing toward my hands. I tear back the cover and take a peek. I see an image—it's me. I riffle through to the next drawing and the one after that. Page after page of me: my face, my silhouette, my entire frame in a multitude of scenes and costumes and mediums. All the days we worked together in her studio. I'm a milkmaid, a goddess, a schoolgirl smelling flowers. Scenes and clippings from advertisements and journals and magazines. But what catches me most off guard are the press clippings from the newspapers. I look at just the top one, which declares in large black font above my likeness:

MISS TALBOT, THE PEACH FROM PITTSBURGH!

But there's more.

RARE AND ENCHANTING BEAUTY
A FACE AS FRESH AS A MORNING ROSE
THE ALLURE OF THIS CREATURE WILL STUN

They go on and on, the words and the different renderings of my face, my hair, my body. I'm struck by the volume, by the variety. At how far and wide my image has flown when my own real world has felt so narrow. I swallow, my heartbeat in my throat. Breaking the silence, Leah says: "My dear girl, did you never know?"

I shake my head, letting out a quiet puff of breath. I've never seen these pages before—at least, not all together like this. Not this many of them.

"Evelyn, you're a sensation."

A sensation? Me?

"Do you know that I saw you, even before we bumped into each other in that alleyway?" she asks, her eyes holding mine.

"Oh, yes. Inside the department store. You were looking at a hat—or pretending to. But the whole time I was nervous you were really looking at me."

"You were right, Evelyn. I *was* looking at you. Couldn't pull my eyes away. I'd never seen your equal. I . . . doubt I ever will."

Her words are slow, heavy with meaning. I shift on my feet and say, "But the hat you were looking at was ugly as sin."

She laughs at this. How I will miss her laugh. "It was green silk, if I recall."

"With a big snake weaving around it," I add.

She nods. "I regret I didn't buy that hat. Would have been good fun to play around with images of your face beneath that serpent. Like the other Eve."

I smile, but my eyes slide downward, breaking from her gaze. We both know our time together is over. Leah puts her hand gently on top of mine; it feels warm and steadying. And when she speaks, her voice is also full of warmth. "It'll help you so much if you bring these clippings of your work to New York. So they see how much you've done. Don't be intimidated by the big city—this is excellent work. But here." She slips another package into my hands, this one much smaller, a thin envelope. "Hold tight to this. It will be every bit as important."

"What is it?" I ask, looking up into her kind eyes.

"It's a letter of introduction. For a Mr. Carroll Beckwith. Do you know the name?"

I shake my head, reminded once more of how provincial I am, how naïve. But Leah's words bolster me as she goes on: "He's one of the most in-demand artists in New York. Or anywhere, for that matter. His studio is on Fifty-fifth Street. Mr. Beckwith does work for the Roosevelts, the Morgans. He even did a portrait for Mark Twain. He's a living legend. If you get a commission with Beckwith, you'll have every artist on the island of Manhattan knocking on your door."

My heart hitches in my chest. "My word, Mrs. Dawson, er, Leah . . . this is, well, I don't even know what to say."

"Just . . . be careful, all right? Or I suppose I should say, be clever."

I nod, even though I don't fully understand what she means by this. But instead of asking about that, I ask the other question that pops into my mind: "Why?"

Leah arcs an eyebrow, confused. So I go on: "Why did you do all this for me?"

Leah flashes me a lopsided smile, and as I stare into her open, familiar face, it hits me again: How much I'm going to miss her. The way she made me feel safe—and worthy. As though she actually cared. Then, with a quick wink, Leah leans toward me and answers, "Someday I'll be able to say that I knew you first, and taught you how to find your light. Now go find more light."

"Thank you."

"I hope so," she says, her voice suddenly quiet.

I find it an odd response, so I let my face show that, and Leah adds: "I hope you'll thank me. And not curse me."

PART 2

The showgirl has a power that no one else does. Financiers trade in money, lawyers deal in documents, railroad men lay steel. But who else has the power to hold the heart and soul of hundreds at a time? Moving them across time and space in their own minds—why, it's a temporary madness she can conjure.

—Evelyn Talbot, in a letter written to Mr. Anthony Comstock, published after her death

• ◆ •

BUT THE PROBLEMS COME ONCE SHE DOES DRIVE THEM MAD.
Did I know I'd be a sensation? Did I know I'd drive them mad? Not yet, not right then.

Did I even want all of that? Not in any clear sort of way.

I just knew that I needed to climb. Up and out of that hole, higher and faster until the trouble that had been chasing us for years could no longer reach us.

So I did what I had to do. I did all that I could to ensure that we were leaving the past behind. Never thinking that to leave one trouble behind means to invite the next one in.

I played the part, and they played theirs, too.

Scene one, scene two.

I never imagined what was coming next.

Places, everybody, places!

Lift the curtain.

Chapter Eight

New York City
Autumn 1899

Mr. James Carroll Beckwith, venerated artist and established fixture of New York high society, gives me a pointed look. Seated on the sofa opposite me, he has a full mustache and unsmiling lips, but his eyes can't hide his interest. I let out a slight exhale when his eyes glide downward and he resumes his silent examination of my files, riffling through the images that we've placed before him.

On the other side of Mr. Beckwith's broad bay windows, I hear the midday bustle of the city, the horse and foot traffic filling Sixth Avenue. Here, inside this large sitting room of rich wood paneling and finely upholstered furniture, a charged silence hangs in the air. It's critical that this interview with Mr. Beckwith goes well, that this introduction leads to some offer of employment, for Mamma and I are nearly out of funds in our merciless new hometown, and he's our best chance at keeping a roof over our heads.

Mr. Beckwith pauses to study one sheet, concentration pulling his features. It's a charcoal study of my head, my hair falling loose over one bare shoulder. Mr. Beckwith's eyes flicker from the page to me, then back down to the page. "Extraordinary," he mutters, in a way that makes me suspect the word was not meant to be heard—but I've heard it. And I hear what he says next, too: "A nymph, in the flesh."

I fidget in my seat but say nothing, not looking to Mamma at my side, both of us allowing the artist to resume his inspection in unbothered silence. But I feel embers of hope as I nurture the possibility that I might in fact receive an offer to work with Mr. Beckwith, right here in his elegant studio in Midtown Manhattan, where he's created everything from rich oil landscapes to portraits of famed millionaires.

It would be such a relief. Mamma and I have used nearly every cent we have to set up Kit in his school outside Philadelphia and pay for our trip north. What little we had left over we've put into this month's rent on our small room in a boardinghouse on Twenty-second Street. It's nothing fancy, a back room atop a narrow flight of stairs with just one window that shows the brick exterior of the adjacent building. But it was all we could afford—and barely, at that. "Just until we get our feet under us," I said as we unpacked our garment bags and I tried my best to help Titania settle in on our shared single bed.

We have nothing in our cupboard but hard biscuits, and because the water in the building tastes like a foul mix of metal and eggs, we drink only coffee. *That's just fine,* I tell myself. It helps keep us warm in our frigid room. As it's autumn and a long cold winter is on the way, we are saving fuel until it's an absolute necessity.

"Pluck and luck," I've been reminding myself, ignoring Mamma's plaintive expressions as we look around our dim room that smells faintly of mold. I recall the stories of Mr. Alger, the heartening lessons that Daddy and I relished together. I know I can do this—I can secure work, and with the payment from a good job, we will turn things around.

So here we sit, with Leah's letter of introduction in hand, while Mr. Beckwith studies my portfolio of sketches, advertisements, and articles from Philadelphia. *Thank you, Leah.* I feel a pang of longing for her, for the safety and predictability of our routine together in a smaller city. The familiar tang of turpentine hangs in the air here at Mr. Beckwith's, but otherwise, it feels as though we are a world away from the sunny studio on Arch Street. Was it a mistake to leave Philadelphia for these unfriendly waters?

No, I tell myself—this is good. I was ready for a new challenge.

And here in New York, the coming of a new century means that anything is possible. I'm ready to work and make a name for myself in an even bigger world.

Eventually, after an endless wait, Mr. Beckwith looks up from the papers, fixing me with another pointed expression. I suspect he might be wondering what to do with the fact that I am not eighteen, and we all know it. He looks to be middle-aged, with dark hair laced by errant strands of silver, his well-groomed hands folded in his lap. He studies me for a long, silent moment, taking in the sweep of my white shirtwaist, my dark skirt, my chestnut hair pulled back in a loose chignon. I sit still; I can tell that he's almost won over. And then, something about his scrutinous gaze softens, and when he speaks, his tone is gentle. "Tell me about your work for Mr. Tiffany."

I resist the urge to fidget beneath his penetrating stare. "I was his angel," I say, flashing a winsome smile while trying not to sound boastful. Tipping my head to the side, I add: "For stained-glass windows."

"Yes, I see this praise from Violet Oakley. . . . It's telling. Violet is not easily impressed. Leah Dawson . . ."

Just hearing their names aloud, I feel another hitch of homesickness. A yearning for the warmth and familiarity of Leah's studio. The surety of their work and our brief period of financial stability as a family of three. Here in New York no one cares about me. No one cares whether I work or see my brother again— or eat. As is made plain by the hunger I feel in my stomach as I sit here in this fine room. I force another smile, looking toward my lap, adopting what I hope is a posture of unaffected and peaceful ease.

Mr. Beckwith is surveying the images again, pausing on a watercolor of me dressed up as a shepherdess. He doesn't look up as he continues on. "I'm not familiar with Leah Dawson's work, but I see here you've amassed quite an impressive portfolio in your . . . *eighteen* years."

I bite my lower lip as Mamma proffers a nod. "That's right," she hastens to respond. "Evelyn's was the most popular face in

Philadelphia, as you'll see written in the newspapers. That there was an advertisement for cheese."

"Quite a range, Miss Talbot, everything from churches to cheese." Mr. Beckwith clears his throat and looks up, meeting Mamma's gaze. "Has she had any formal study?"

"She went to school," Mamma says.

"As an artists' model, I mean."

"She's a natural talent," Mamma says, speaking about me as though I'm not in the room.

My cheeks grow warm as Mr. Beckwith turns his attentive eyes back to me and asks, "Miss Talbot, what cosmetics are you wearing at the present moment?"

I sit up a bit straighter, meeting his gaze. "Right now?"

He nods.

I throw a look at Mamma, then look back toward the artist. "Why, nothing, sir." I never wear makeup—Mamma doesn't allow it, and Leah never wanted it. Occasionally, when Mamma's not at home, I'll slash some pink or red across my lips and study myself in the mirror, but I always wipe it off before Mamma notices. She only has a few tubes remaining from her time at Wanamaker's, and she doesn't like me to waste them. We certainly can't afford to buy more.

"Nothing?" Mr. Beckwith arcs an eyebrow. "But what about around your eyes?"

"I have nothing on my eyes, sir."

"No kohl on your eyelids?" His voice sounds dubious. "No rouge on your cheeks?"

I shake my head.

"No tint on your lips?"

"No," I say, then add in a quick "sir."

Mr. Beckwith leans forward. "You mean to tell me, Miss Talbot, that if I were to ask you to step into the washroom just down that corridor and take a damp cloth to your face, nothing would come off?"

"Sir, I have nothing on my face," I tell him again, my voice thin but insistent against his clear suspicion.

Mr. Beckwith slumps against his sofa, exhaling as his back hits the silk cushion behind him. "High color. Extraordinary," he says, his voice faint as a whisper. Then, sliding his gaze toward Mamma, he says, "Mrs. Talbot, I would like to arrange a standing appointment with your daughter, twice weekly."

It feels as though my heart might dance out of my rib cage. But before I can react, he turns to me and declares: "I have been looking for an Aphrodite. You are familiar with the stories of the goddess?"

"Yes, sir," I say, as a fresh wave of giddy excitement ripples through me.

But Mr. Beckwith is all matter-of-fact as he goes on: "I'll pay you five dollars a week to start. We will explore a variety of mediums—sketch, watercolor—but I'd really like to paint you in oil. Does that sound agreeable?"

"Oh, yes, Mr. Beckwith"—my voice comes out sounding breathy—"yes, it does."

Mamma places her gloved hand on mine, bridling my obvious glee. Surely she must be feeling the same, knowing that this will mean steady income. But her voice is bland, even a touch cool, as she interjects: "When would you like to begin?"

"As soon as you can arrange to be here." Mr. Beckwith eyes us each in turn. "How might this Tuesday work?"

"I must check our diary," Mamma answers, her gaze holding the artist's. Of course we have no plans—we know no one in this city.

"And I shall plan for Tuesday," Mr. Beckwith says, offering a courteous nod to Mamma, and then to me. I lean forward to collect my papers, stuffing them back into our portfolio, and Mr. Beckwith rises, summoning a butler to see us out. As Mamma and I walk toward the doorway of the grand room, Mr. Beckwith's voice catches us at the threshold. "Oh, Miss Talbot, a word of advice, if I may?"

I pause, turn, and face the artist.

Mr. Beckwith's eyes are fixed on me, but it appears as though his words are meant for my mother, as well. When he speaks, his tone is not stern, but a hint of steel girds his words: "Do not go knocking on studio doors looking for work."

I frown, confused; isn't that what we've just done here today? Hasn't that led to my first commission of work, with the preferred painter of the Roosevelts? But our host continues: "Have you heard of the fad called French postcards?"

Mamma grabs my hand in hers, her body going rigid at my side. Before she can answer, Mr. Beckwith sighs. "I regret to say it, but there's quite a market these days for renderings of young girls dressed up, or often . . . dressed in too little. . . ."

My mouth falls open as Mamma gasps. Only Mr. Beckwith's face remains entirely composed, his voice steady as he adds: "You have gold here, Mrs. Talbot. And where gold is found, a rush often follows. Please don't allow yourselves to get taken away in it."

Chapter Nine

A RUSH IS PRECISELY WHAT FOLLOWS. A FEW WEEKS LATER, I'm in Mr. Beckwith's studio as we are finishing up an oil on canvas. I'm seated on his elevated platform, arranged in a prim posture with hands folded in my lap. Eventually, mercifully, he says, "I think we have it. Come take a look, dear." I soften with relief. It feels as though every bone in my body creaks as I ease my ramrod-straight posture and hop up from the stool, massaging my lower back.

"Yes, well, it was worth the effort, Evelyn." Mr. Beckwith eyes me with amused approval as I glide toward his easel. With a flourish of his hands, he invites me to see the canvas that has consumed so many of our hours together. "I was thinking of calling it *Girlhood*," he declares.

As I take in the image, I can't help but let out a small gasp of stunned delight. It's me, and yet, it's art. I'm in a formal dress of black velvet, its long sleeves ornamented in red trim. My hair is pulled back in a loose braid with a matching red bow nestled just above my neck. At Mr. Beckwith's direction, I'd coated my lips in lard and pursed them together in just the hint of a coy smile, then I'd tipped back my head and stared directly into the eye of the beholder.

"The *eyes*," he muses aloud. "What were you thinking about as you sat?"

The question catches me by surprise. I consider it for a moment, then ask, "Do you really wish to know, Mr. Beckwith?"

He hitches an eyebrow.

"Nothing," I say.

"Nothing?" Mr. Beckwith's expression is hard to read—I can't tell if he is smiling or frowning.

I nod. Then I say, "That's the key, sir. If I think, then I'll want to move. Either my face, or my body. I keep myself entirely blank."

"Brilliant," he says, his voice barely a whisper. "It works, that's for certain. You allow the beholder to see whatever he wants. . . . You give him his very own blank canvas. Opportunity. Power, even."

There's more I don't say, in part because I don't even know how to articulate it to myself, let alone to Mr. Beckwith. But the truth of the matter is that I *must* go blank, because otherwise my mind will rebel. I'll think of the hunger pang in my belly, the cramp in my neck after hours of holding one pose, the memories. . . . No, I've had to learn how to ignore it, and more than ignore—to silence it. Forbearance, that might be the word. Or perhaps more like mastery—over my mind, my body, my very will.

Mr. Beckwith interrupts these thoughts of mine as he rises to stand. "I have to be honest: the inquiries are getting more insistent."

"Inquiries about what?" Mamma asks, speaking for the first time from her place on the far sofa. I'd almost forgotten she was there, sitting silently with her stitching.

Mr. Beckwith throws a look in her direction, answering, "About Evelyn. A chance to work with her." Then he turns toward his workbench, where there are papers strewn about. *Are those all inquiries about me?*

Mamma perks up at this. "We do need the funds," she says, lowering her needle. "What with wintertime and the cost of fuel. Working only twice a week is not enough."

She doesn't mention that she has yet to gain a position as a seamstress, or even in any store. But Mr. Beckwith thinks for a moment, then says, "Evelyn is not the sort of girl who should take work simply because it is offered." He crosses the room to his workbench, where he riffles through the pile of papers. He selects one note. "I would suggest you consider this interview."

He brings the paper to Mamma, and she takes it in her hands, reading the name aloud. "Mr. Frederick S. Church." She throws an inquisitive glance at Mr. Beckwith.

"I know him well," Mr. Beckwith says. "Church is eminently respectable. It would make sense for Evelyn professionally . . . but also in regard to her personal well-being."

· ◆ ·

With Mr. Beckwith's letter of introduction in hand, we arrive at the studio of Mr. Frederick Church on Forty-fourth Street. The man who greets us reminds me of a good-natured grandfather, older than Mr. Beckwith, with white wispy hair and a broad, easy smile.

The artwork covering his walls delights me. I stare at the bright images in appreciation: storks carrying rosy babies in baskets, Santa Claus riding in his sleigh through a twinkling sky. And the animals! Bears dancing in top hats, turtles racing hares, tigers lolling about in sunny green meadows. Mr. Church has created miniature worlds that are lively and inviting. "Ah," he says at my side, his voice gentle. "*Aesop's Fables*. Are you familiar?"

"Yes," I say. Daddy and I loved *Aesop's Fables*. There's one image in particular I find impossible to stop studying: a girl lacing up ice skates beside a frozen pond as a friendly bear helps her in her task. How many times did Daddy and I ice-skate in a scene not too different from this one when I was precisely the same age as this happy little girl? Well, without the bear.

Mr. Church notices my attention to the scene. "Yes, that was a sketch I did for *Harper's Weekly*. Back in '75. Before you were born."

He hasn't asked about my age. And quite frankly, based on the purity and jollity of the scenes I see, I don't suspect it much matters. His work feels like art for children as much as for adults. But then Mr. Church surprises me by reaching up toward the framed image and plucking it down from the wall. "You may keep it."

I turn to him, throw him a look that must show my confusion. Mamma clears her throat.

Mr. Church repeats his kindly offer. "If you like it, you may keep it."

"Oh, but I wouldn't wish to take yours," I say.

"I have others." His pale features crease into an earnest smile, and in that moment, he doesn't look all too different from the Santa Clauses he has rendered. "I drew it, after all."

"Thank you, sir."

"My pleasure, dear girl." Next Mr. Church shows Mamma and me further around the studio, asking me, "Are you an animal lover? You seem to be."

"Oh, yes."

"As am I. I love painting animals. They teach us so much. They feel everything as deeply as we do. And yet, without the words to express themselves, they've found brilliant ways to convey it all. Studying an animal is an opportunity to study a broad range of emotions and moods."

"I have a cat," I say.

"Oh?"

"A tabby. I found her in an alleyway." I am not entirely sure why I am telling Mr. Church, world-famous painter, all of this.

"What is she called?" Mr. Church asks, genuinely interested.

"I named her Titania."

He grins. "A fine name. So then, you are a student of Shakespeare, as well as the great fables?"

"Yes, sir."

"Excellent."

My cheeks grow warm; I'm happy that Mr. Church knows this about me and seems pleased. Then he tilts his head to the side and asks, "Would you do me a favor?"

Mamma scowls, but I am expectant and attentive. He asks, "Would you bring your dear Titania back here tomorrow? Perhaps we can begin by painting the pair of you together."

The following day Mamma and I report for duty once more on Forty-fourth Street, this time with Titania in my arms. Mr. Church puts me in a white bonnet with blue ribbon and spreads a blanket across the floor. For four hours, he captures a variety of scenes as Titania and I sprawl across that blanket—Titania playing with a spool of yellow yarn, me offering her a porcelain saucer filled with milk, even the two of us lying flat in a pose of peaceful rest.

When Mamma and I return to his studio the next Wednesday, Mr. Church tells me that we will go outside for a walk. "To Central Park," he says. As Mamma declares her preference to remain indoors beside Mr. Church's fireplace, Mr. Church and I set off together, stepping out into a clear fall day that carries the scents of dry leaves and woodsmoke in the air.

We walk along the new Bridle Path that curves up the west side of the park. Mr. Church keeps a slow pace and pauses often—he is particularly interested in watching the birds. "Do you see how busy they are? They know that winter approaches."

And it's not just the birds. Mr. Church also takes a special delight in watching the squirrels. "Industrious creatures," he says, marveling in childlike delight as they scamper across the tree limbs. I can't help but study Mr. Church as he studies the animals—I can practically see his world-famous mind at work, watching and cataloging and enjoying. As though his pleasure in observation and creation wafts off of him like some sort of lively glow.

In no time at all, these walks through Central Park become a regular part of our sessions. One cold wintry afternoon finds us walking beside the edge of the pond, where a thin layer of ice has hardened the surface. We pause our steps, looking out over the scene, and Mr. Church says, "In the spring, we shall come back and watch the tadpoles as they learn to be frogs."

I nod, smiling, noticing how my breath is a silver mist in the chilly air between us. I am happy to think that I'll still be working with Mr. Church in the spring.

When we return to the studio, Mr. Church calls for warm tea, and we sit down before the fireplace, the pair of us, as Mamma has stopped joining me on my days working here. After we've warmed ourselves with the hot drinks and the hearth, Mr. Church leaves the room for a moment, returning with what appears to be some sort of heavy fur pelt in his hands. I glance up at him with interest.

"Tiger," he says, unfurling the massive sprawl of orange and black across his wooden floor. I gasp, looking it over as he smooths the pelt across the ground. "I've painted such creatures in real life," he explains.

"How did you get close to a real tiger?" I ask, approaching the fur, running a hand over its coarse surface.

"On my visits to the Barnum & Bailey circus. Have you been?"

I shake my head, forcing myself not to recall the small traveling circus that used to come through Tarentum. The fun that Daddy and I had watching the clowns as they juggled and danced. "You must go sometime," Mr. Church says cheerily, and I think I've succeeded in masking my melancholy. "Misters Barnum and Bailey know how to put on quite a show."

I nod, crossing my arms across my midsection but not yet daring to speak. Nor do I confess to Mr. Church how I used to laugh when Daddy would joke that we'd run away with the circus troupe together.

"But before you visit the circus," Mr. Church says, looking intently at me, "I'd like you to return here, next Wednesday, and I'll paint you with this tiger of the deceased variety. Does that sound suitable?"

"Yes, all right."

"Good," he says with a wink. "Only, don't tell Titania. She might not look too kindly on me for owning a pelt of one of her brethren."

I can't quite imagine what that sitting will involve. But I trust Mr. Church, and there's nothing that he would ask of me that I wouldn't do.

THE FOLLOWING WEDNESDAY, I report back to Mr. Church's studio, where he directs me to let my hair fall loose and he hands me a lightweight gown of diaphanous cream satin, into which I slip behind the dressing screen. As I emerge, with the soft material falling like mist over my neck and shoulders, Mr. Church directs me to settle onto the tiger pelt, which he's once more unfurled across his floor. He takes a bit of time arranging my dark hair around my face, and then he nestles a wreath of water lilies like a crown into my dark curls.

"Can you give me just the hint of a smile?" he asks, leaning over me. "Think of . . . Oh, how about you think of your mother telling you that you may run away with a rogue band of circus performers?"

The words slice through me, innocent as they are intended to be, and the smile I've been offering wobbles. *It was Daddy who offered to run away with me and the circus.* I'm sure my eyes betray the searing pain I now feel. I'm half expecting Mr. Church to chide me for losing my smiling expression. But, to my shock, he exclaims: "That!" He is staring down at me with a look of wonder. "Exquisite, Evelyn! Keep *that*!"

My mind is spinning, but I do as I'm told. I keep the thin smile on my face even as my eyes hold fast to the pain that just burned me from the inside. Mr. Church sprints back to his easel and gets straight to work.

And when Mr. Church's sketch of my face—wreathed in loose hair and water lilies, set off against the backdrop of a tiger pelt—runs in the Ladies' Home Journal, the editors dub me *"the most haunting and rarest of young beauties yet seen in the metropolis, with the face of an angel and the eyes of a sphinx."*

AFTER THIS, now that I've worked with artists as eminent as James Carroll Beckwith and Frederick S. Church, the Sunday American newspaper runs a two-page spread on me, calling me *"the captivating new creature of Manhattan's next century."* In a rare departure from her usually disinterested behavior, Mamma purchases a copy, and we open it together on the evening it comes out. My face flushes with heat as I take it all in: my images and illustrations are packed across the spread, images of Beckwith's work, Church's work, Violet's, Leah's. One would think I've been at it for a decade, rather than a year and a half. The paper gives me nicknames and labels that make my head feel dizzy, dubbing me *"the pristine and precious young Peach of Pittsburgh"* and *"the haunting young maiden of High Art."*

There are other words, too. The newspaper has printed an interview to accompany the images. I stare at it in surprise—and then confusion. These aren't my words. I glance up at Mamma. They are hers. "You gave an interview on my behalf?" I ask. "When?"

She closes the paper, suddenly flustered. "While you were working, Florence. Someone had to speak up. I wasn't going to let them harass you!"

My mind swirls. "Well . . . can I read it?"

"Oh, if you like." Mamma stands, as if she's lost all interest in the article. "But don't let it spoil your head. Remember, you're not even fifteen yet, even if the world thinks you're a woman."

I reopen the paper, my eyes sweeping the article, my mind racing to keep apace. *"She's our very own Venus, with a mouth as perfect as Cupid's rosy bow."* I feel my heartbeat hasten, and I read on. *"Raphael himself would have queued up for a chance to worship this creature, with her wildly abundant tresses and soft skin as luminous as a pearl."*

Mamma, at the bottom, reacts to their statements: " *'She's always been a beauty,' the proud Mrs. Talbot admits, beaming with heartfelt maternal adoration. But Mother Talbot is as doting as she is protective of her rare and precious pearl, whose eyes are dark and liquid, two pools into which one might happily jump, forgetting any desire to ever turn away. When asked of her daughter's allure, Mrs. Talbot assures us that it's young Evelyn's virtue with which she is more preoccupied. 'I'll never allow her to pose in the altogether,' Mrs. Talbot vows, with a prim shake of her head. And with that, perhaps not a few hopes have been dashed across America."*

"Mamma?" I look up at her, my mouth falling open as the words slide out. "Are you speaking here with this reporter . . . about my nude figure?"

"They kept asking!" Mamma raises her hands. "They kept making it seem like they were asking for the art. If you'd ever be allowed to model like a Greek or Roman goddess."

I sag back in my chair and close the newspaper, pushing it away.

"I knew what they were doing!" Mamma goes on. "The answer was no, of course. I'd never allow it."

Which is why what happens next comes as such a shock.

Chapter Ten

Winter 1900

"We have to think about this as artists and businesspeople." Mr. Beckwith is standing before us in his studio, having poured us each a cup of coffee.

"Go on," Mamma says, her tone wooden.

"Evelyn, Mrs. Talbot, it's a new century."

I know it is—and I'm more determined than ever to soar, to be the most in-demand artists' model in town. Mr. Beckwith seems to be thinking similarly: "Evelyn, you are the fresh face of our time. You've done everything from soap advertisements to stained glass."

My cheeks grow warm at his approval, but there's something new in Mr. Beckwith's expression. An intensity to his gaze. I know there's more coming, and he confirms this as he continues: "I am an artist. You know I've painted portraits for all of my career." Mr. Beckwith turns and fixes Mamma with his gaze. "You know I teach life classes to the artists in the Art Students League, yes?"

Mamma nods, but I'm having a hard time keeping up.

"As such," he goes on, "I work with nudes all the time. As does Church. As does every artist of any renown, not only here, but in Paris, London, Rome." Beckwith pauses, pulls in a long breath as if steeling himself, and then continues: "Evelyn, up until now, has done good work. Great work. But this would make her exceptional. Surely, since Evelyn is eighteen—or perhaps you're nineteen now, have I missed a birthday?"

He *has* missed a birthday, but I've turned fifteen, and my blood stills in my veins as I grasp for some response. But Mr. Beckwith does not linger on the point, carrying on as he says, "In any event, you are experienced enough. And I would make it perfectly tasteful, decent. Elegant, even."

Mamma turns her coffee cup in a slow circle in its saucer but offers no reaction, her eyes expressionless. I say nothing, entirely overwhelmed.

When Mr. Beckwith fills the strained silence, his voice is quiet, even soft, as he says, "My dear, you know I also do landscapes. There is no more beautiful landscape than the natural form of a woman. And you are an exceptional woman."

But I'm a girl! I wish to scream, my cheeks flaming. Up until now the most revealing poses I've done have been in dressing gowns or with bare shoulders. Mamma has always made it plain that she wouldn't stand for anything improper. But Mamma's behavior now is confusing. It's almost as if she's not offended. Perhaps she's not even opposed. And Beckwith appears expectant as he says, "Are you ready to be truly great, Evelyn?"

I slide my gaze toward my mother, my voice thin as I manage only, "Mamma?"

She lets a long exhale slip out. "If it were done in such a way . . . decent . . . elegant. And it truly would mean an advancement in her career . . ."

I shift in my seat, feeling as though I could be knocked flat with a feather. Are we truly talking about this? But Mr. Beckwith appears downright giddy, and he prattles on: "That's exactly right! If I were to paint Evelyn in the nude, it would be done with only the highest regard for decorum. It would be sold privately. With her looks and her fame and the demand there is for anything bearing Evelyn's image, why, such a piece could bring in hundreds of dollars."

Mamma threads her fingers together in her lap, staring straight ahead at the artist. "And we'd get a share."

This causes Beckwith to falter ever so slightly. He tips his head to the side, saying, "It's highly unusual for an artists' model . . . or her mother—"

"Manager," Mamma interjects.

"Manager, of course," Mr. Beckwith parries with a slight frown, but he carries on. "Well, to ask for a share beyond the sitting fee is not generally how these things are done."

Mamma unfolds her hands, takes her skirts in her grip as though preparing to rise from her seat. "As you said, Evelyn is not any ordinary artists' model."

"You are correct in that," Beckwith quickly agrees.

"And this is no small thing for which you ask, Mr. Beckwith."

"I understand."

"And a great number of artists would jump through hoops of fire to be having this conversation right now about my daughter."

"You are correct, Mrs. Talbot."

"So we shall not do this in the *usual* way."

Mr. Beckwith swallows, looks from Mamma to me, then back to Mamma, who repeats her demand, her voice like steel: "We would need a percentage of the high price which you have just mentioned."

Mr. Beckwith exhales, and I see the fight seeping out of him. "All right. You have yourself a deal, Mrs. Talbot. I will share a portion of the proceeds of the sale with you."

"Indeed," Mamma says, leaning back into her seat. I can see her triumph as I look at her and then at Mr. Beckwith. And it's in that moment that I realize: they've agreed to the terms of my nude posing, and I've not had the chance to speak a single word.

· ◆ ·

THE DAY OF the sitting dawns clear and sunny, and I step into Mr. Beckwith's warm studio feeling as though I've swallowed an entire bowl of butterflies. Mamma, at my side, appears less hesitant; in fact, she seems rather chipper. "It's a big day, dear. Are you ready for greatness?"

I pull in a long breath, wishing I could soften the coil of nerves in my stomach. I find it all so confusing, Mamma's reversal. I asked her why she'd agreed as we first stepped out of Mr. Beckwith's studio on the day he proposed the nude painting. She'd offered only a shrug, eyes fixed firmly ahead as she said, "He made a compelling argument. I see his point."

Was it the money? It had to be, at least in large part. "See here, if anyone can do it well, it'll be Mr. Beckwith. He does everything with taste and style. It's *art,*" Mamma added, her tone insistent. "And he sees greatness in you. It's an honor. Did you hear what he said?"

I've thought over what Mr. Beckwith said—that it's a fresh new century, and I am the face of this new era. But if I am the face of this new era, can't I be just the face? Why do I have to be the figure, too?

I haven't slept well for the past few days, knowing this sitting was approaching. I haven't had much appetite, either, with my stomach in a tangle. In truth, this morning came as a sort of relief. At least now I can get it over with. Ready or not, I'm here.

Mr. Beckwith has positioned the raised wooden platform in the center of his studio a few feet before his easel, just as he's done on countless other days. He tells me that the elevation will allow him to see my figure from a variety of angles, and though this is said in an entirely matter-of-fact and professional manner, his words make my cheeks burn.

Then he presents me with a silk kimono of soft rose-petal pink, a line of small tropical flowers dancing along the neckline. I take the garment into my hands, studying it. "Where's the belt?" I ask.

Mr. Beckwith throws a searching look toward Mamma, then looks back to me, before he answers, "No belt." A moment later his features soften, and so does his voice. "I will only paint you from the navel up, not to fear. But we shall allow the front to fall open."

He directs me to the dressing screen at the back of the room, and I walk slowly toward it, kimono in hand, wondering what the point is if the kimono will be slipping off in just a moment. "You may keep your bloomers on, Evelyn," he says. That's a relief. Such a relief, in fact, that I feel I could cry. He adds, "Hair down, please."

I wince as I slip away behind the screen; it's really happening.

Mamma takes a seat on the far sofa, and I can hear her yanking her needles and yarn from her bag.

A moment later I step out, barefoot, clutching the wrap tight, and I pad my way toward the raised platform. Once up there, I run my hands along the collar of the kimono. Mr. Beckwith is positioned at his easel, attentive, even expectant. My fingers trace the line of the seam down my chest, toward my waist. I pull in a slow breath, blink my eyes closed, and then open them. Before I can think too much, I allow the kimono to slip down my shoulders. I hear the click-clack of Mamma's knitting needles. I feel the whoosh of the fabric as it slides off my shoulders, and my eyes slant downward. The air is cool on the skin of my bare neck and shoulders.

"Very well. More, please," Mr. Beckwith says. And so I manage a gentle tug, and the silk whispers farther down my upper arms, until the small mound of my left breast is exposed. I look up for the first time and see Mamma facing the windows, her hands moving in their skilled stitching, eyes unavailable.

Closer by, Mr. Beckwith is all purposeful concentration as he approaches. He raises a tentative hand. "May I?"

I nod, feeling how shallow my breath has become. I don't wish to meet his eyes, this artist with whom I've worked so comfortably for countless sittings over innumerable hours. Now he may as well be a stranger, so foreign is the territory we are charting. Mr. Beckwith reaches toward me and with just two gentle fingers, he takes the silk in his grip, adjusting the kimono so that it slides off my arms and catches over my hips. I hadn't realized it was possible for my heart to hammer this rapidly. Still I look away as he stares at me in silence.

"Hold right here," he instructs, guiding my hands to my two hip bones. I've kept my bloomers on; that's a mercy. But they won't show on the canvas. He arranges my hair to fall down loosely over my right shoulder.

"Good. Now I want you to look directly at me."

God, that's hard to do. But when our eyes lock, I will myself to return his gaze. He narrows his own eyes, holding me in them.

"Evelyn, you look as though you've stopped breathing. Can you please take a deep breath for me?"

I blink now, as I force myself to pull in a long breath. And then another. The breath doesn't feel natural, but then, nothing about this moment does. *The sooner I do what he asks, the sooner it will be over.* I retreat inside to find that place of cool calm, that thoughtless void without movement or memory. But not without first repeating to myself: *I'll have a share of the hundreds of dollars.*

As Mr. Beckwith returns to his easel and his hands begin to work, I find my mind struggling to settle. I'm thinking of Kit. What would he make of me standing here like this? What if he ever finds out? *Dear God, what if Mr. Beckwith sells this image and it becomes widespread enough that Kit sees it?* And then my mind flies to the next terrible thought: *Daddy.* What would he make of this? Would he agree with Mr. Beckwith, who is a respectable leader at the Art Students League, that this is purely high taste? And then, hearing laughter on the street, I think of children, and school, and playing. What I might be doing today, on this very day, were Daddy still alive. Why, I'd be at school. In Tarentum with our rectangular house filled with sunlight from the big windows. I'd know all sorts of things from school, but I wouldn't know the first thing about who Mr. Church is or who Mr. Beckwith is or what the Art Students League is with its nude models.

My mind whirls until I realize that I've not been focused on my pose, and when Mr. Beckwith looks up from the canvas, I'm expecting him to chastise me for my unfocused expression. Instead, he merely stares into my face and says: "Good. That longing." He turns back to the canvas, and we don't say another word.

MR. BECKWITH CALLS it *Flower About to Bud.* And it does sell, as he said it would, for an unprecedentedly high sum of three hundred dollars. To a Mr. and Mrs. Barnes who wish to hang it in the boudoir of their mansion in Newport, which Mamma tells me is in Rhode Island. I'm glad it's far away in another state. I don't want to think about my bare breast on display all day and night in someone's home; likely I'll be the topic of many a scandalous dinner party and house tour. The idea fills my stomach with knotted nerves again. I'd rather not think on it at all, so I push the thoughts away.

After that, Mr. Beckwith's scenarios become bolder, but we do not revisit my posing nude. Instead I pose for him as a girl in a Turkish harem with jade bangles wrapped around my arms, beads hanging over my breasts. Another time I am Cleopatra, queen of the Nile, with a fake snake twined in my hands and dark kohl rimming my lids. In the next session he fashions me as Salome, the infamous princess in Jerusalem who danced with her veils for King Herod, demanding a man's head on a platter as payment for her performance.

And speaking of payment, the pay is so good. Given how in-demand I am, with artists writing to Mamma begging for a chance to work with me, I increase my fee that autumn to a staggering ten dollars a day. To think, we struggled back in Pennsylvania to pay two dollars a month in rent.

But I work to earn it, every dollar. I pour myself into each day's scenario, *becoming* the role. Cleopatra, Salome, the shepherdess smelling flowers for the perfume ad, or the girl drinking milk. It's tiring work, with long hours that make my muscles ache. But for the first time since Daddy died, Mamma and I aren't hungry, Kit is happy in his school, and we don't have to worry about losing the roof over our heads.

• ◆ •

WHEN I RECEIVE the note from Violet that she's in Manhattan and would like to meet up to sketch my portrait for a mural she's working on, I jump at the opportunity. Everything about the job appeals to me—it's a relief to think I'll be under a woman's gaze. She writes me that it'll be a pastoral scene, which means the scenario will be entirely chaste. Best of all is the thought of seeing my old friend, and hearing about the others in Philadelphia.

I meet Violet in Central Park on a crisp, overcast day in late autumn. As soon as I see her, something in my body softens, something that I hadn't even realized I was clenching.

"How are you, Evelyn?" she asks, pulling me in for a hug, placing a soft kiss on my cheek.

I ignore the question and offer, instead of an answer, "It's so nice to see you. I've missed you and Rachel and Leah."

As Violet unfurls a wide blanket and we settle onto the grass, she tells me that Rachel and Leah are doing well. "They send their love, of course. And Rachel wants to make sure you're getting enough to eat."

I chuckle. "I am, though I wouldn't turn down one of her roast chickens."

Violet nods knowingly. "She's still dreaming about running away to France to cook over there. Oh, and Leah complains often that she has not found anyone who can replace you." I smile and then tell Violet a bit about my work with Mr. Beckwith, Mr. Church, and the other artists. Then Violet explains the nature of our job. "It's a private commission. A family in Greenwich wants a mural in their salon. A pastoral scene, and you are to be their sweet country girl enjoying the roses."

I nod. It all seems straightforward enough. But something about the way Violet is staring, studying me, gives me a twinge of unease. And then, tipping her head sideways, still holding me in her searching gaze, Violet asks: "So, Evelyn . . . are you?"

I lean back, frowning. "Am I what?"

Violet's expression is intense, a bit too searching for my comfort. "Are you enjoying the roses?"

When I don't answer right away, she interjects: "Darling, you're the most popular model in Manhattan. I bet you have more offers for work than you have days in the week. But how are you?"

"Everything is bully," I say, conjuring a breezy tone as I offer her a quick shrug. "Mamma and I were able to move into a larger suite in our boardinghouse. We now have a bedroom and a sitting room. And Kit is happy in school."

Violet nods, but she keeps her gaze fixed on me. "That's all well and good. I'm happy to hear all of that. But you've yet to answer my question. How are *you*?"

I want her to stop prying. How am I? I want to scream: *Why bother asking such a silly question when the answer doesn't matter?* I want to tell her about the kimono, how I let it slip open so that Mr. Beckwith could paint my bare breast, how it felt when his fingers tugged on the fabric to show more of my skin and I could barely breathe. How it feels when I spread my body across the tiger pelt on Mr. Church's floor, staring up at the images of *Aesop's Fables* and wishing I could be sitting with my daddy, reading those books, instead of holding these poses for hours on end. About how my mind wanders when I hear the laughter of children outside the studio window and imagine what it would feel like to be in school, learning, laughing, like any other girl about to turn sixteen.

But I don't say any of that. Instead, I tell Violet about the good stuff, like how Mamma and I are no longer cold in our lodgings. About how we can take our leisure on most Sundays, with Mamma sewing and me occasionally walking to the art museum or the library. And how there's plenty of time to read Kit's newsy letters from school and plenty of food to fill a larder that was once near empty. About all of the other work I've done—the advertisements and magazines and newspaper images. "It's as though I get to play dress-up every day, acting out a new character." I keep my tone crisp, like the cool afternoon air.

Violet continues to hold me in her gaze, her eyes narrowed and searching. And then, finally, she offers what appears to be a mollified nod, and mercifully she sets to work. "I'll just get the lines down in charcoal, and then I'll put in the color later."

I slip into my working mode, my trancelike state, and the hours pass. Once she's got what she needs, Violet packs up her supplies and makes a suggestion. "How about some supper? There's a café right across the street. What do you say?"

Together we set off for the café, slipping indoors and enjoying the blast of warm, bright air. It's over our bowls of French onion soup that Violet says, "You know, Evelyn, I always thought you might someday dream of something bigger than simply posing."

I look up from my food, not sure of her meaning. Violet goes on, "Don't get me wrong; I'm not putting down your work. I'm an artist, after all, and I couldn't do what I do without talented models. I only mean that I always suspected I saw something of the performer in you."

"I do perform in my work," I say, a touch defensively.

"I mean the stage." Violet breaks off a piece of bread from the warm loaf on the table, dunks it into her soup, and then goes on. "Ever consider Broadway?"

"Er, no," I answer. Of course I haven't. I haven't even seen one of those shows, let alone thought about myself up there on one of those fancy stages.

"Well, you might want to think on it," Violet continues, as though it's the most logical thing in the world for me to mull over. "It wouldn't be all that different from what you are doing now. You act out a new character every day for your painters. Only, we'd get to hear your voice. Singing and dancing, that might be fun, right? Folks would get to know you for more than just your pretty face."

I take a slow spoonful of my soup, but I barely taste it. My mind is suddenly swirling with thoughts of what my friend has said, with the picture she's just painted in my imagination: me, on a bright stage, filling the space with song as my statue-still body breaks open and I begin to dance.

After the meal, as Violet and I stand outside the café to say our goodbyes, she reaches into her bag and retrieves a bulky parcel wrapped in tissue paper. I take it from her outstretched hands, confused. "From Leah," she says. "Open it."

I pull the paper aside to uncover a mound of green silk, and it takes me a moment before I realize what I am seeing. I let out a startled laugh.

"She said you'd understand," Violet adds.

Nodding, I look from the hat, with its green serpent coiled around it, back up to Violet. "This ugly hat. Leah was staring at it in Wanamaker's, the day we first met."

"Oh," Violet says, still eyeing the cap. "Well, that's an . . . interesting . . . gift."

"She said she'd want to sketch me wearing it. Like Eve with the serpent."

Violet snaps her fingers. "That reminds me! She wanted me to tell you: 'Don't believe that it was all Eve's fault.' Whatever she means by that."

I frown. I'm not sure about Leah's meaning, either. But I accept the hat, tucking it into my own bag because there's no way I'm wearing it as I walk home. I give Violet one final hug, thanking her for dinner and asking her to give my love right back to Leah and Rachel, and then she's gone.

I set off on foot toward Twenty-second Street, deciding to take the route that will bring me down Broadway. The Great White Way, the glittering avenue that only Manhattan can boast of having. A channel of bright faces and brighter façades, its lights that never go dark.

As I walk, I think back to Violet's words: *I always suspected that I saw something of the performer in you.* I allow my mind to drift, just a few paces, down the road she's conjured for me. I imagine myself once more on the stage, because what's the harm in a little bit of daydreaming? The bright warmth of the footlights, a full and adoring audience before me. Movement and noise instead of silence and stillness for hours on end.

As my steps carry me south and eventually bring me to the front door of our dimly lit boardinghouse, I chide myself, packing all that silliness away. I know I can't share even the ember of such daydreams with Mamma. *We are finally on a sure footing, Florence,* she'd surely say. It's a foolish fantasy I must cherish in secret, a golden kernel I'll have to hide deep in my heart. Perhaps this tiny little flame can give me a bit of sparkle and warmth through the cold winter months, but it would surely be blown out if I shared it with my mother.

Chapter Eleven

January 1901

Charles Dana Gibson. I know the name, of course. And I can see from Mamma's blazing eyes that she's just as tickled as I am that the famed sketch artist has written to her, explaining that he wants me to be his next Gibson girl. "Why, Mr. Gibson's work is everywhere," she says. "*Life* magazine, *Collier's*, *Harper's Weekly*."

"Oh, yes," I say, agreeing with Mamma. Every girl in America—and abroad—knows about the Gibson girl. In my solitary moments when I sneak a look in the mirror, I do my best to pile my hair high atop my head like the desirable Gibson girl, the symbol of sophistication and elegance.

Mamma and I promptly accept Mr. Gibson's invitation to a meeting at his gracious brownstone on Thirty-fifth Street. When we arrive on the appointed Monday that winter, we are shown by a gloved footman into a quiet, tastefully furnished drawing room. There we are greeted not only by our host, Mr. Gibson, but also his friend, a Mr. Condé Nast, who will oversee the pictorial for *Collier's* showcasing its newest Gibson girl: me.

Once Mr. Gibson has offered us all tea and cookies, the four of us take our seats on a pair of sofas arranged before the fireplace, and our host jumps right in. "Miss Talbot, Mrs. Talbot, I thank you both for coming."

"Our pleasure," Mamma says, polite yet reserved. Mr. Gibson looks from Mamma to me, and I meet his gaze. But I'm quickly distracted, because behind him on the wall are orderly rows of dozens—no, hundreds—of images. Each drawing is done in the ink and paper style that Mr. Gibson is so famous for, the unique black and white technique that has made him such an international sensation.

I force myself to look back toward my host, my eyes settling on him. He appears younger than most of the artists I've worked with—I'm guessing Mr. Gibson must be in his thirties. His face is pleasant and clean-shaven, without the shadow of a whisker, and he wears a tailored suit of dark charcoal with a black necktie. In fact, he looks a fair bit as though he's just stepped out of one of his dapper pen drawings, all crisp straight lines and shades of black and white.

At his side, Condé Nast appears even younger, perhaps in his twenties. He is also handsome and well turned out, sporting a three-piece suit of pale gray, but his face wears an impish smirk. And like Mr. Gibson's, his stare is fixed only on me.

It's Mr. Gibson who takes the lead in the conversation as he declares, "I need a fresh face for the new century."

I nod but remain silent, having heard this before. When Mr. Gibson continues, I am delighted to hear him add, "I'd like it to be yours, Miss Talbot."

Mamma nods her quick assent; there's little use in our acting as though we aren't already won over. But Mr. Gibson's next question catches me a bit by surprise. "Miss Talbot, may I ask you to step with me toward this window?"

I rise slowly and follow Mr. Gibson across the drawing room, with Mr. Nast trailing a step behind. Mamma remains on the sofa, but her eyes follow us. We pause a pace away from the broad window, and I look up at my host, who says, "Now turn to the side." I do as he says, as the gentle winter sunlight streams through the glass, grazing my cheek.

"May I?" Mr. Gibson asks. I offer a small nod, and he adjusts my chin, tilting my face with just his pointer finger until I'm peering slightly upward.

I remind myself to breathe, to keep my features steady, even as I can feel the famed artist's eyes boring into my profile, far more intense than the winter light that seeps in from the opposite direction. I've fashioned my hair like a Gibson girl, a high chignon, hoping Mr. Gibson would like it since it was he who first made the style a sensation. But to my surprise, he says, "It's the hair. Something's not right."

I feel my shoulders droop in disappointment. But Mr. Gibson's voice sounds animated, and he asks again, "May I?"

Once more I nod my willing assent, and now Charles Gibson is touching my hair. "No," he says, turning to Nast a beat later. "I am no use with these matters."

"Here, I have an idea." Mr. Nast steps forward. "Miss Talbot, may I touch your hair for a moment?"

"All right."

Condé Nast's hands are soft yet skillful as he pulls half a dozen pins from the bottom of my thick chignon. A moment later I feel the rope of my long hair fly loose, though the top remains fixed in place, so now it's like a pony's tail, with just ringlets of my chestnut curls winding down my back. Mr. Nast takes the loose tresses in his hands with a gentle grip, and then he settles them into place so that my hair tumbles over just my left shoulder. "That's it," Mr. Nast says, his voice soft as a whisper.

"Please, don't move," Mr. Gibson adds. He dashes across the room in just a few strides as I remain motionless before the window. And then, an instant later, I hear the scratch of pen on paper, and I know that Mr. Gibson is sketching. I hadn't realized we'd be starting right away, but from the feverish sound of his strokes and the quiet hum of concentration that pulses through the room, I can tell that Mr. Gibson has seen something he likes and we've gotten to work.

• ◆ •

"I MADE THIS for you, Evelyn. As a keepsake. To remember our work together." Mr. Gibson raises a hand toward me, and I see a flash of white in his grip. It's not one of his famous black and white ink sketches, but instead it's a paper silhouette. "I've always loved to cut silhouettes," he says. "Ever since I was a boy. Of course, they don't bring in what my sketches do. But I love making them."

"For me?" I smile, touched, as I look down at the delicate handiwork. It looks like a fish swimming through a series of waves. "Thank you," I say, meeting his eyes. It's our last day of work together—Mr. Gibson told me this morning that he's gotten everything he needs in order to get to work on the pictorial for Condé Nast and *Collier's*. And I'm happy to have this keepsake. I can't wait to see how our work turns out.

"Miss Talbot, may I ask you a question?" Mr. Gibson offers me his arm and begins to guide me slowly toward his front door.

"Of course."

"What is the most powerful force in the world?"

My first thought is hunger. It could drive a person to desperation. Or perhaps heartache? But I don't think Mr. Gibson means something as abstract as that. And then my mind turns back to the morning's news, the article I read on the front page over breakfast: a tragedy in the Five Points slum, a building turned to a hellscape inferno, the flames consuming the entire structure in mere minutes, killing seventeen of the poor people who lived inside, including two babies. A grisly reminder of how close to death Mamma and I could be at any time if my work were to stop and we were to move into a shabbier building. "Fire," I venture. "It can destroy anything."

Mr. Gibson chews his lower lip. "It's a clever answer," he says, surely having seen the headlines for himself. "Fire is powerful indeed. And yet"—Mr. Gibson raises his ink-smudged finger—"fire doesn't stand a chance before . . . ?"

"Water?" I offer.

"That's it!" He snaps his fingers excitedly. Mr. Gibson continues on, deep in his thoughts: "What's more, Miss Talbot, fire burns itself out, eventually, does it not? But water, why, it can never be overpowered. Water can and will change its shape to survive in any setting. It can carve rock, move mountains, change the entire face of the earth." A moment of silence stretches between us; the only sound I can hear is the clicking of the clock on the nearby mantel. And then Mr. Gibson goes on. "Think of the creatures that have learned not only to survive where fire can't, but to use it for their own good."

I look down at the cut-paper silhouette in my hands. "Like fish."

"Precisely, Miss Talbot." Mr. Gibson nods heartily. Then he leans close and presses his hand on top of mine, a gentle grip as he closes my fingers around the small paper fish in my palm. And when he speaks again, it's with a kind, almost paternal tone. "Learn to move, to adapt. Like water. In short, learn to swim. And then you'll survive."

Chapter Twelve

Spring 1901

"Come in, Miss Talbot. I have something to show you."

"Oh dear."

My face must drop as I step through Mr. Gibson's door, because he hastens to add: "Not to worry. Only good, my dear."

I slip out of my coat and take in the sweep of Mr. Gibson's drawing room. The space is usually immaculate and well appointed, but today it is cluttered, with easels displaying Mr. Gibson's black and white sketches all across the large, bright room. I focus on a few of the images and see that it is page after page of me—my face, my profile, my features in various expressions of black and white. Mr. Gibson has captured me from every angle in charcoal, colored pencil, graphite, ink and pen.

It is the series of me in silhouette that particularly catches my attention. I study one in which my dark hair winds its way down the whole length of the drawing. This was from the very first day, when I stood before the window and Mr. Nast draped my hair, like a pony's tail, across my shoulder. Under the black and white image, Mr. Gibson has written: "*Woman: The Eternal Question.*" He's drawn my dark hair to form a question mark around my profile.

A small sound like a stifled laugh escapes my throat. And when I turn to look into the eyes of Mr. Gibson, he says, "I can't wait to show you to the entire world, Miss Talbot. This image will run in *Collier's*. What do you think of it?"

What do I think of it? It's marvelous work. Thought-provoking, intriguing, playful, this *Woman: The Eternal Question*. But am I a woman?

The press seems confused, as well, because just as Mr. Gibson's rendering of me as *the* American woman catches the flames of widespread fame, my nickname in the papers becomes "The Gibson Girl." All the others are forgotten, and I am the only one.

The only what? Woman? Girl? I have to be both. I'm only sixteen, but the world thinks I'm older, and I've had experiences that most girls my age will never have. I certainly feel older than sixteen, especially on the days when I work twelve-hour shifts and return home drained and weary.

But there's not much time to stop and ponder it all. Now that my face has been stamped with Mr. Gibson's imprimatur, I'm more in demand than ever. Offers of work come pouring in every day, and Mamma fields them all. Managing my daily appointments has become her full-time job, and she's no longer even speaking about her dream of finding work as a seamstress.

That spring, Mamma books a job for me with the photographer Mr. Engels, with whom I've worked on several occasions. He's agreeable enough, and I welcome these photography jobs as a break in the monotony of portrait sittings.

"You will be my Helen of Troy in photographs for *Life* magazine," Mr. Engels announces as we arrive at his studio, a space that smells of flash powder and stale tobacco. "It had to be you, Evelyn. You're the woman for whom most men in this day and age would launch an epic war."

There it is again: *woman*. How old was Helen when she was snatched by Paris and spirited from her home? And how old before that, when she was snatched by Menelaus and taken to the marital bed—for who can imagine she would have chosen that hardened old man for herself?

As late spring ripens and the flowers along Fifth Avenue burst into riotous color, I find myself busier than ever. Mamma slots in as many photography sessions as possible, like a train conductor keeping the trains running on the crowded tracks. My face fills the covers of magazines and newspapers; I'm on postcards in the shops that line Manhattan's busy streets, advertisements for chocolates and toothpaste and soap. My work with Mr. Gibson has sparked a craze for the pony's tail hairstyle, and my images are snatched up for publication in *Harper's Bazaar, Ladies' Home Journal, Cosmopolitan.*

Broadway magazine, calling me "America's Eve," declares: *"Her desirability is due to the fact that both gentlemen and ladies want her. The ladies crave the soap or perfume she peddles. And gentlemen, well, they'd like to believe that they might offer her something she'd like to have."*

These so-called gentlemen write me letters postmarked from as far away as Chicago, Dallas, even the cities of California. We get so much mail that Mamma institutes a new rule: I'm not permitted to look through it on my own. Not until she's opened it all and made sure I'm not seeing "anything unfit."

Mamma usually tosses a good number of these letters into the fire after a quick perusal, but I surmise the general idea. According to Mamma, a lot of fellows are writing to ask for my hand in marriage. "Most of them can't even spell your name to save their lives," she grumbles.

Closer to home, right here in Manhattan, large companies now want me for their calendars. I love the work I do that summer being photographed for the Coca-Cola calendar because it means all the soda I can drink. Mamma doesn't love the calendar jobs, because she says that men will buy the spreads so they can keep the twelve images of me for a pittance of what real appreciators of art have to pay. She gripes, calling the calendar pages "pocket tokens." I don't know what that means, but I hear how she practically spits the words. "Your hard work is done in an elegant way with decent artists, but then those pigs turn it vulgar."

"What's vulgar about it?" I ask.

"It just *is,* Evelyn. And we won't speak about such things."

But you're the one who brought it up, I think, though I know better than to press her. Even though I do want answers—why would Mamma let me pose for work if it's being turned vulgar?

I decide to find out for myself. I wait until the next day, as Mr. Beckwith is finishing up with our afternoon session. Mamma often doesn't accompany me if it's a sitting for Beckwith or Church—she trusts them both so deeply at this point. I do, as well, and knowing how Mr. Beckwith has always acted in a cordial and respectful manner with me, I ask: "Mr. Beckwith, what's a pocket token?"

He winces, looking from his paper up toward me. "How did you hear such a term?"

I give what I hope looks like a casual shrug. "My mother told me that some of my nice, respectable work is being turned vulgar. She called them pocket tokens."

The artist rises from his stool, slipping his smock over his head before he answers. "Your mother is correct, Evelyn. And while it is unfortunate, it is also, sadly, unavoidable in this day and age."

"What is unfortunate, Mr. Beckwith?"

He chews his lower lip a moment, eyeing me. And then he sighs. "Men appreciate your beauty, even if perhaps it's in a different way than a lady would. Pocket tokens are, well . . . images that can be purchased at a lower price than your portrait work. They often sell such things to fellows in saloons, gentleman's clubs, casinos."

I consider all of this in brooding silence for a moment. Is it all that different from respectable companies using my face to sell milk or soap? Or that rich family in Newport that purchased my portrait to hang in their boudoir? Haven't artists like Beckwith and Church, even Leah, always told me that the beholder is going to see in my image exactly what he or she wants to see?

The next morning, while Mamma is still sleeping and the words of Mr. Beckwith are fresh in my mind, I do something I'm not supposed to do. Emboldened by my curiosity, as well as intrigued by the mountain of papers just sitting on the table, many of them addressed to me, I begin to riffle through it all.

I want to feel more worldly, less naïve, if I am to work like a woman, so first I take the newspaper into my hands.

AUTO SHOW COMING TO NEW YORK CITY!

The front page describes the new horseless carriages that can move entirely on their own. To think what it must be like to ride in one—I can only imagine! Excited, I read on, moving to an article about a new food coming out of the Midwest, something called "cereal," and there's an advertisement for it claiming it will cure all sorts of woes and ailments.

The next article I notice is an opinion piece by a Mr. Anthony Comstock. I throw a glance toward Mamma; she's still snoring in the rumpled bed, so I read on, careful not to rustle the pages. *"In an age in which proper and decent people know enough about human nature to put tablecloths over table legs, for fear of unwanted and most indecent stimulations, how is it that there are more than 25,000 women for sale in this city?"*

Mr. Comstock's words reek of offense and outrage. He goes on to applaud the recent arrest of a lady for her crime of smoking a cigarette on the street, reminding his readers of the many practices that the gentler sex should take heed to avoid. Crimes against decency, too often practiced in public in spite of their obscenity. Mr. Comstock reminds folks that ladies should not ride bicycles, read novels, listen to ragtime music, play tennis, or speak aloud any obscenities.

"It is God's work," according to Mr. Comstock, *"to combat the many vices which are winding their way into daily life, and it is only with a watchful and vigilant eye that we can see these crimes and root them out."*

I can barely pull my eyes away. Mr. Comstock concludes by lauding the work of the "Society for Prevention of Vice," over which he reigns. He thanks a gentleman, Mr. Hal Thorne, for his generous funding in support of this vigilante gang.

Thorne. I wonder if this Mr. Hal Thorne is any relation to the Pittsburgh millionaires. They certainly were known as a pious bunch. But then I read on, about how Mr. Comstock's primary aim is *"to protect the virtue and safety of the softer sex. These young girls who are being turned into bejeweled Bathshebas, right here in our modern-day Sodom. Once bedeviled, their only fate is to be brothel bound."*

I put the newspaper down, a current of unease running through my body. My heart is racing, and so are my thoughts. I can only imagine what Mr. Comstock and his Society must think of my work. Surely he wouldn't approve of my thin costumes as I dress as Cleopatra or Salome. Or my face on these so-called pocket tokens that Mamma deems so vulgar. *Or,* I think with a shudder, *a painting with my bare breast on display.*

Suddenly I feel unclean, as if Mr. Comstock has chastised me directly. My mind is troubled, recalling the stares of the men in the boardinghouse back in Pittsburgh on rent day. The smell of their breath. The hunger in their eyes.

Sickened by this, seeking a reprieve, I turn back toward the pile of mail. Next page. Anything to distract me. I see my name on an envelope, and I grab it. I'm most certainly not allowed to open this letter without Mamma's approval, but she's still snoring in the bed, so I tear it open.

It's not a proposal of marriage. It's something far better.

Chapter Thirteen

"I want to be more than a calendar girl," I declare to Mamma that evening as we sit down to supper. It's a simple meal, pork chops with potatoes, but it's more than we could have had even a few months ago, and with the window open to let in the gentle breeze of a mild evening, it feels almost pleasant in our room.

When Mamma offers no reply, I press on. "The long sittings, not being able to move . . ." Several years into this work as an artists' model, it's starting to take its toll, the fact that I'm not able to show any sign of life, when I feel as though I'm bursting with it. I want more. I crave some of the electric excitement of the city all around me. And I finally know the way to get it.

Lately, anytime I've been walking home from a sitting, I've taken the route that brings me down Broadway. There's some magnet pulling me in that direction, toward that bustling playground of song and dance, the Great White Way.

Why, that would be life, indeed. Those worlds of color and light. As I walk, I look at those theaters, and I think: *I want to go inside.* I want to do the work of the theater, where not only would I be allowed to move—I'd be dancing and singing!

Violet first put the idea in my head months ago, but the letter I opened in secret this morning took it from an idea to a most insistent desire. Revealing, quite possibly, a path.

The letter was from a Mr. Theo Martin, a stage agent who explained that he is currently working with the company of *Fair*

Flora and Fauna, a new show set to open later this year. He wrote in his letter about the chorus girls, the dance numbers, the tropical stage sets. As I read Mr. Martin's words, I was able to see it all in my mind—and now I want it.

"Mamma, think about it. I could still work during the days with the artists. My work in the theater would be in the evening. Imagine how much more I could bring in."

But Mamma doesn't appear willing to consider my idea. "Beckwith and Church already warned me this might happen. That the stage agents would come knocking. And they don't approve. It would be ill-advised," Mamma says, no doubt parroting the men who have made a lot of money off of my hard work. And then she adds, with a note of finality, "You are still a child, Florence."

I bristle at this, at her sudden concern for my innocence. "I'm earning like a man," I reply.

"Then why not keep earning? Mr. Beckwith and Mr. Church—"

"They want to keep me working with them, of course. And I will. But I think I can do more than simply sitting."

"We have a good thing going." Mamma's voice is unyielding.

But as I look around our small room, I respond, "We could have even more, Mamma. A double income. We could put even more distance between ourselves and the privations we've known in the past."

Mamma frowns at this, and I'm not certain whether it's because she is seriously considering my proposition or because she's recalling the privations of our past. Her face looks tired, so I press on, "Please, Mamma. One meeting with an agent? Just to hear his proposal. You'd come with me, of course."

IN THE END, it's only with the promise that I'll keep working as an artists' model, and we will only consider a job on the stage with a reputable agent in a good company, that Mamma agrees to one meeting.

"It's expected to be the biggest ticket on Broadway; it'll be a sensation, a packed house every night," I say, my voice a bit breathy from both the brisk pace of our walk up the crowded street and my excitement for the day's meeting. I've brought Mamma with me to the Casino Theatre, where Mr. Martin's new show will soon go on, set on a fabled island in the Pacific. Now that the building of the Panama Canal is all over the newspapers, such a setting and topic have captured everyone's imagination—written about with *almost* as much excitement and frequency as anything having to do with me.

Mr. Martin greets us at the theater door on Thirty-ninth and Broadway. He's dressed in a natty style, so unlike the artists I'm used to working with, turned out in a crisp checkered suit and crimson necktie. He ushers us inside with the air of a man who has got more things to accomplish than he has hours in the day.

Mamma and I follow Mr. Martin through the lobby, our heels clicking across the marble floor, and then down a hallway, where he guides us toward the third door. He closes us in together, and I take a look at the small rectangular space. Mr. Martin's office is a mess. His desk is strewn with papers—playbills, newspapers, letters both opened and unopened.

Mr. Martin takes his seat behind his desk and gestures for us to do the same in the two wooden chairs across from him. I hear the muffled sounds of a piano plunking somewhere above us. Without any ceremony, he jerks his chin toward his pile of correspondence and grins. "A few other gals want a place in the footlights."

Mamma and I exchange a glance, then he carries on. "They want to reel in a millionaire, mostly. To which I always say: you marry for the money; you end up working to earn every cent." He exhales a puff of self-important laughter, then offers a wave of his hand. "But when I saw your pictures, I thought, *Now, there's a girl who* should *be on the stage.* Only, now that I'm seeing you up close, Mrs. . . . er, Talbot, I'd say, well, it's not what I was expecting. From your pictures, that is. You're a bit . . . beyond . . . the typical age we look for."

I throw a look toward Mamma. From the tightening of her

features, I see she's as stunned as I am—by Mr. Martin's demeanor, his snappy style, his brash commentary—but most of all by his last comment. "Mr. Martin," she replies, "I believe there may be a misunderstanding."

The stageman hitches an eyebrow. "That so?"

Mamma leans forward in her seat and says: "It's my daughter here, Miss Florence Talbot." She gestures toward me. "My daughter has an interest in the stage. I am her manager."

Mr. Martin slides his gaze toward me. "*You?*" He quickly scans my appearance, my emerald-colored skirt suit that I selected for this meeting with such care because I thought it not only hugged my figure in a flattering cut but also made me look sophisticated. He takes in the matching emerald cap nestled atop my upswept hair, the hint of red on my lips, my cheeks. Then Mr. Martin flashes a grin, one I find hard to read.

"You're the girl in the Coca-Cola calendar?" His eyes dart back and forth from me to Mamma, a look of understanding breaking across his features. With a chuckle, he leans toward Mamma like he's about to share a secret. "I assumed she was your kid along for your meeting. How old is she?"

Mamma rearranges herself in her seat. "Florence is nineteen."

"Sure, and I'm the cow that jumped over the moon, lady." The flash of Mr. Martin's toothy grin hits me like a taunt, so I pull his letter from my pocket and slide it across his messy desk.

Mr. Martin peers down at his own handwriting, frowning, before looking back to me. "*You* are the Gibson Girl? You are Woman, the Eternal Question?"

I nod.

"But you can't be a day over . . ." He tugs on his red tie, a quick shake of his head as he says, "Sorry, but I'm not in the business of plucking babies from cradles."

And just like that, with a wave of his hands, this interview is over. Before I've even had a chance to open my mouth, let alone audition.

Before I know what I'm doing, I begin to cry. Hot tears. Tears of frustration. At the unfairness of it all, at how the world will use me as a woman in one instant and call me a baby the next.

"Now, now." Mr. Martin shifts in his seat, glancing from me to Mamma. "There's no need for all of that."

"But . . . you wrote to *me*," I say, picking up the letter that I'd placed between us, waving it like a flag before him. It's the first thing I've said to Mr. Martin since Mamma introduced us, and this behavior, coupled with my tears, can't be helping with his assumption that I'm a mere child.

Mr. Martin looks highly uncomfortable as he taps his pencil on his desk, eyebrows angling toward each other. "How old did you say you are again?"

"She's nineteen," Mamma declares, her tone flat.

"*Nineteen?* Why, do you take me for a—no, on second thought, you know what? Don't tell me. I don't want to know." Mr. Martin shakes his head, blinking rapidly. After what feels like an interminable silence, he ceases his pencil tapping and fixes me with a pointed look. "Listen here, kid. There's a rehearsal wrapping up right now. Let's just go up and have a look, shall we?"

Mamma and I follow Mr. Martin up the carpeted stairs in a brisk and wordless line, coming to the second story and a wide doorway that leads into a large studio. The tinny plunking of the piano has ceased, and rehearsal seems to be over: girls in leotards and dance shoes stream off the elevated stage to the left and right, scattering in two shoals of chitchat and chirpy laughter. I stand, motionless, and watch them in silent envy. Many of them appear fresh-faced and petite—are they really that much older than me?

There's a man rising from the piano in the front corner of the room, and Mr. Martin leads me and Mamma toward him. "Miss Talbot, I'd like you to meet Mr. Scharf. He's our musical director here at *Flora*."

I do a small curtsy for this Mr. Scharf, who is looking from me to Mr. Martin with a bemused expression.

"How was rehearsal?" Mr. Martin asks. "Is the second line coming together?"

"Every day we get a bit tighter," the man answers, gazing toward the doorway as though he'd like to leave.

Mr. Martin crosses his arms. "You got time to stick around for one more number? Miss Talbot here would like to show us her stuff."

Mr. Scharf looks as though he'd like to sigh, but he dutifully turns back toward the piano. "I don't see why not."

"All right, then." Mr. Martin hoists a hand in the direction of the stage. "Miss Talbot, let's see what you got."

"Now?" I thought he was bringing me up to see the rehearsal space. I didn't realize he wanted to see *me*. But I know how to do this; I know how to perform. And knowing, too, that this is my one shot, I draw in a deep and fortifying breath, pulling back my shoulders. I answer, sounding more confident than I feel: "Sure thing."

I march across the large hall, climbing the steps and striding out onto the stage. Mr. Martin and Mr. Scharf are watching, as is Mamma. The footlights are still on from the rehearsal, and I can feel their warmth like a row of small fires. It's strong, the bright heat, almost searing my legs, my chest, my cheeks, but rather than edge back as I might like to do, I step to the center of the stage and allow the lights to wash over me. I find my light.

I've thought so long and hard about getting this chance, all those days when I walked up and down Broadway, dreaming of getting not only a ticket into one of these theaters but a place on the stage. Here I am. I know what I'll sing for them. It's a song Daddy often sang to me as I sat perched on his knee at our piano. Or late at night while I was tucked into bed, when I had a hard time falling asleep. I can still hear his beautiful voice, feel his gentle embrace. And now the words strike me with a raw and ferocious poignancy as I pull in one more deep breath, filling my belly with air, and begin.

In the sweet by and by,
We shall meet on that beautiful shore;
In the sweet by and by,
we shall meet on that beautiful shore.

I'm singing a cappella, without any music, but I allow my body to sway. I close my eyes and raise my hands out at my sides, and I carry on, even louder now.

And our spirits shall sorrow no more,
Not a sigh for the blessing of rest.

In the sweet by and by,
We shall meet on that beautiful shore;
In the sweet by and by,
we shall meet on that beautiful shore.

The words pour through and then out of me. So does the melody as it rocks me with the force of a massive wave. How much I miss him, how much I long to meet Daddy again, as the words of this song say. How much I wish to be done with sorrow. To have a rest. Even to have someone who cares about me enough to know that I need one.

All of my pent-up feelings come surging out of me. This is the opposite of those hours where I have to sit like a statue, wiping myself clean of all thought and emotion. Here, not only am I allowed to feel, but it is encouraged and entirely necessary.

I finish, allowing the words to carry my voice to the very end of the wave, and then I open my eyes. Blinking, I come back to the theater, where I stand alone on the stage in a halo of hot light, and I see the men whispering in the corner. Then Mr. Scharf troops off, and Mr. Martin beckons me down from the stage, back to where Mamma stands at his side.

I can't read Mamma's expression, but Mr. Martin's is plain enough. The skeptical grin he's been wearing throughout our time together has been wiped off, replaced now by a far more earnest, even approving expression. When he speaks, his tone is no longer abrasive. "The light loves you." It's all he says, at first.

Thank you, Leah.

"And you've got pipes, kid, I'll give you that," he adds.

"Her father always had a nice voice," Mamma interjects. The remark nearly knocks me off my feet, but then she goes on, speaking as though I can't hear. "She got that from him. He played the piano with her before she was knee-high. She can sing like a songbird when she gets going."

My insides go warm, and I can feel that my face does, too.

Mamma's eyes meet mine at last, and there's something in there that looks almost soft when she holds my stare. And terribly sad. *So she remembers.* My own eyes begin to sting.

But Mr. Martin waves a hand and nods, his mind clearly at full thrum, and the tender cord between Mamma and me snaps. "We've got a doll, Lucia. She's leaving us in a bit of a bind. Heading over to the Knickerbocker to dance in another show, with our opening night only a month away." Mr. Martin glances toward the now-empty stage, then back to me. "We do need to fill the spot."

My heart clamors as Mr. Martin looks to Mamma, letting out an audible exhale. He leans toward her and says, his voice low, "I figure, with the costume on, the makeup, the company of the other gals . . . But let's keep it down a bit, shall we? On her age, I mean. Mr. Scharf didn't ask, and I don't want to talk about it. Better that way. We don't need Comstock and his vigilantes raiding our theater. All that balderdash about the stage being depraved." Mr. Martin makes a swatting motion with his hands. "You can come tomorrow for rehearsal, Miss Talbot. We can give it a try. Let's see if you crack up there when the pressure's on."

Chapter Fourteen

But pressure has never broken me. In fact, it fuels me. And the stage, though entirely new, feels like home.

Sure, it's not a quiet studio, and here I'm asked to jump and kick and dance for all to see, pushing my body to the point where my breath comes as stabbing rasps. But it's all just performing, really. It's what I've been doing for years. Only now I am allowed to act like I'm alive.

I fall in with the girls in the chorus line the next day at rehearsal as Mr. Scharf and Mr. Martin watch from seats in the fifth row. I allow my movements to be guided by the plunking of the piano, by the metered steps of the chorus girls all around me. It comes perfectly naturally to me, so much so that by the end of my hour-long trial rehearsal, Mr. Martin pulls me and Mamma aside and makes an announcement. "All right, part's yours, Miss T."

I can barely stanch my elation, so I bite down on my lower lip as he goes on, explaining in a matter-of-fact tone that I've got a spot dancing and singing with the chorus. He doesn't mince words: I have a month to learn it all before opening night—the songs, the steps, my cues, the costume changes. My role will be that of the "charming Spanish Maiden," part of the ensemble, but I do get one dance sequence of my own.

Showtime will be seven o'clock six nights a week, plus matinees on Wednesdays and Saturdays. At the end of each week, I'll be paid fifteen dollars. This in addition to what I'm making as an artists' model. Mamma and I will finally be able to breathe a sigh of relief, begin putting some money aside to eventually bring Kit up north to a bigger apartment.

To me, the Casino Theatre is a place of wonder and joy. Sure, it's a job. It's grueling—the rhythms of painting and then unpainting my face, quick changes into complicated and constricting costumes, hot lights on my skin, exhausting steps requiring all my stamina, punishing physical exertion that must always be done with a smile and a song, over and over. And that's just rehearsals. Once the show opens, there will be a mercurial crowd to be wooed and won each night.

But none of that feels *hard*. Being hungry for days on end is hard. Being cold in the winter when you can't afford fuel is hard. Losing the person you love most in the world, selling everything you have, and finding yourself without a home—that's hard. The Casino is in the heart of the Broadway theater district, and I've walked this city enough to know that there are girls my age working only a few blocks away, in the quarter known as the Tenderloin, filling the brothels and the betting houses—*that* is hard work, and I know what a short walk it is to get there. Or just west to Hell's Kitchen, or down to the Five Points, the slums where even a bed in a brothel would seem a luxury for the girls my age.

When it comes to performing in the theater, I know how to do this. I know how to become and embody a part. And at least here onstage, I'm not alone. For the first time in recent memory, I'm surrounded by girls. My guess is that I'm the youngest, though I don't breathe a word about my sixteen years to anyone. But still, it's a company of girls! After years of solitary work and the loneliness of speaking with only Mamma, maybe now—I allow myself to hope—I might even make a friend or two.

I put everything I have into studying the other girls, watching the ways they speak and sing and move, learning their names. They all sound so impossibly glamorous: Penny May, Annissa Sweet, Trixie Vaughn—who tells me with half a smirk that she's only recently joined this company after starring in *The High Fly*. "It's a burlesque," she says with a wink of her heavily kohled eye, and from the way Mamma blanches when I ask her what *bur-*

lesque means, I can tell that it's not something on which Mr. Comstock and his Society would look favorably.

I make my first friends with a pair that poses as sisters, Dinah and Dolly. "The Goodhue sisters," everyone calls them, inseparable as they are. They like to rouge their cheeks a fiery shade of red, not too far off from the matching red hairstyles that make them easy to spot instantly in any room. But as I study them up close, I begin to suspect that they are in fact a mother-and-daughter duo; perhaps they, like me, are here with Mr. Martin's admonition not to offer up any unnecessary truths.

Dolly looks young and is a chorus dancer. Dinah, who appears to be in her mid-thirties, has a bigger role, singing a solo at the end of the first act. And by golly, can she sing. She's got a pair of pipes that send vibrations through my own chest when she hits her high notes. As I watch her and the others, I feel inspired to be good like them. More than good. Perfect. I want to be perfect. And the only way to make that happen is to pour everything I have into practice.

I've got a few weeks to master the steps and nail my role before the curtain goes up on opening night. Mamma has mercifully been able to put off my modeling work for a few weeks, informing the artists that I have the flu and need to rest to regain my strength. They accept this for now.

So, with my days cleared for the first time in years, I give everything I've got to the stage. When I take my spot in between the other girls and that orchestra strikes up its first jaunty notes, it feels like a current begins to pulse through me. The music pulls like the strings of a marionette. I imagine that the sea of empty chairs is filled with our eager audience, and I dive deeper into my role.

Soon enough I can feel how my legs grow stronger, my breath comes easier, my lungs feel less squeezed. At first my calves and thighs would ache each morning when I'd rise from bed, but now I can hop right out, able and limber. *I can do this,* I think, and I find that I really do believe it.

With just a few weeks to go, the set and costumes begin to appear. It's all so wild: The bright panels of painted wood and silk, made to look like a lush tropical island. The costumes as colorful and rich as jungle flowers. One night, as I'm sitting before the long row of mirrors in our crowded dressing room backstage, about to dab my cheeks with some of the ever-present rouge that all the girls avail themselves of, I see Dinah appear over my shoulder in the mirror's reflection. "Here, you need this, kid."

I swivel in my seat to see what she's holding out. "What is it?"

"Poudre de riz," she replies with a playful flourish, then quickly clarifies: "Rice powder. Gives you that porcelain look that all the gents want. Then you put the rouge on over it. And don't skimp." One look at Dinah's flaming cheeks, and anyone could tell she certainly takes her own advice to heart. She goes on, saying, "It may look like too much in the mirror, but think about the fella in the back row who wants to see your cheeks with that rosy blush—it's got to be big and bold. Everything in the theater has to be over-the-top."

One week before opening night, I enter the final phase of my initiation into the backstage alchemy that will turn me from Evelyn Talbot of Tarentum into Broadway's Spanish Maiden. Powder, rouge, lip salve, half a dozen spritzes of perfume. The communal dressing room is a bouquet of lively scents, colors, and sounds. It's a place of art, not entirely unlike the studios of Mrs. Dawson or Mr. Gibson or any other artist, only here the tubes of oil paint are replaced with tubes of lipstick. The paintbrushes are replaced with cosmetic brushes. The canvases are the gorgeous faces and lithe bodies of the youthful girls who gad about the space, preening before an entire wall of mirrors framed in white circular bulbs.

I love it. I feel alive in the long rectangular dressing room, where the perfumed air thrums with the giddy energy and preshow jitters that spill out of each girl with laughter, boasting, encouragement. The grueling rehearsals that lead up to our opening night turn us girls into a team, maybe even a family.

"Here, need a hand with those buttons?" Dinah is at my back in the dressing room a few minutes before we are to take our places for the dress rehearsal.

"Actually, yeah, I do. Thanks." It's now one day before opening night, my first time running through the entire show—any show—in costume. I know the dance steps, my cues, the songs. I know how to work in costume. But do I know how to do all of it together, all at the same time? For a live audience? We'll see.

To become the Spanish Maiden, I slip into a wide peasant skirt that cinches tight at my waist, with scarves of emerald and purple, gold and scarlet, draped over it. My frothy white blouse shows off my shoulders and neck, a row of buttons running up the back. As Dinah finishes fastening the top one, she gives me a long look in the mirror and makes a clucking sound with her tongue. "What a find Mr. Martin's got on his hands," she says, winking at me in the mirror's reflection. "The fellas are going to fall to their knees when they see ya, kid."

AND THEN, SOMEHOW, opening night is here. A month has passed in a blur of work and memorization and practice and excitement. And though we are prepared, all of us feel nervous—I can see it in the pulled-tight faces backstage as we put the finishing touches on our thick makeup. But is anyone as nervous as me?

The house, empty during our rehearsals, starts to fill as the theater doors open. From where we stand backstage, the audience is just a low and distant buzz—the sounds of the expectant crowd filing in. And they keep coming: men in top hats and smartly tailored suits, women with gloves up to their elbows, all manner of jewels brightening their limbs and upswept hair. I can't help but peek at them from backstage, hidden in my spot in the wings. They all look so fine. All of them are theater regulars. How will we measure up—how will *I* measure up?

I wonder if they will spot me in the chorus line and recognize that I shouldn't be there, that I'm just filling the spot that another, more qualified girl vacated a month out from opening night. The thought makes my nerves twist, white-hot and electric. I stand motionless, in the shadowed wings of the theater, helpless to do anything but watch them.

Deep breaths, I remind myself. The air moves in and out but does not cool off the electric wires writhing in my belly. I shut my eyes, thinking maybe if I can sing quietly to myself, I'll be able to settle my nerves. For some reason the words that fly into my mind in that frantic moment are those of an old nursery rhyme Daddy used to sing to me and Kit.

"*Sing a song of sixpence, a pocket full of rye.*" I imagine the white coil writhing like a snake in my tummy, and then I visualize it unwinding, and then I send it slithering away. *Go pick on someone else,* I tell the monster in my belly. But then a real voice pulls me from my reverie.

"Hey, kid, look, first time you're in a playbill, right?" Dinah is gliding toward me, looking calm as can be, perfectly bedecked for the role of "Island Dancer." Dolly, at her side, is done up in a costume as colorful as a tropical flower. I see that Dinah's holding something in her hands, and I glance down at it: "PLAYBILL."

But my stomach clenches as I scan the list of names and roles. "I don't see my name."

"Here you are." Dinah points to the words: "*Spanish Maiden.*" And then, right beside it: "*Flossie the Fuss.*"

"Flossie the Fuss?" I say, my face creasing in confusion—and annoyance—as I look up at my friend. "What on earth?"

"Oh, Mr. Scharf does that all the time. Why, you think Trixie was born with that name? Heck, our last name ain't Goodhue; it's *Schwannstein.* But we're theater gals. We do what we gotta do to sell tickets."

This irks me, and I chew on my lower lip a moment before I say, "I'll sell tickets for Mr. Scharf and Mr. Martin and anyone else who wants to give me a chance." The nerves of just a moment earlier have evaporated. "But I won't do it pretending to be somebody else. I'm Evelyn Talbot, and I can tell you that after tonight, I'll be listed in the playbill with my name."

Dolly lets out a low whistle, looking to her mother—or her sister. And then, with half a grin, she turns back to me and says, "Look out, Mr. Martin! New kid's got some spark."

"More like sparkle," I say. And I make a decision in that moment, as the last few nerves flutter away and a feeling like resolve settles in their place. I decide that I'll dazzle them all. I'll sing and dance and hit every mark. I'll kick high, and then I'll kick even higher. And I'll do it all with the brightest smile. And then, tomorrow, I'll insist on a reprint of the playbill.

And now, as the stagehand calls out to us—"Time! Places, everybody, places!"—and as Mr. Scharf charges past us one final time, setting a flurry of heeled feet into motion before we each settle onto our marks, I feel the nerves no more. Deep within me, there burns only white-hot determination to shine even brighter than these blinding Broadway lights.

Chapter Fifteen

Summer 1901

After the show, the crowds that gather outside the Casino Theatre are even bigger than the crowds inside. Men, mostly. Silver-haired gentlemen in dapper three-piece suits with walking sticks and top hats, younger fellows milling about, both their attire and their demeanors of a less distinguished variety as they call out their offers to take us to dine, to drink, to dance.

One of the younger girls in our cast, Penny May, pulls me aside, winding her thin arm through mine as we step out into the warm Manhattan night following the Saturday show. It was a packed house. I'm looking forward to a few hours with the girls to cut loose and enjoy some carefree frolicking before it's time to collapse into bed. I've changed into a new dress of pale purple that hugs tightly at my curves, and though I've washed off a good amount of the stage makeup, I still feel dolled up and beautiful, young and buzzing with energy in spite of the hours I've just spent dancing.

"Don't fall for that type," Penny says with a jut of her chin, and I follow her gaze toward the nearby crowd of fellows who linger outside the theater's back doors.

"What would I fall for?" I ask, gliding alongside Penny past the mob. Some of the gents hold flowers; some of them cry out for our signatures. One even has the gumption to ask us for a kiss.

"Stage-Door Johnnies and Champagne Charlies. I don't have

to guess what they think of you, dollface." Penny gives a jaded roll of her eyes, then tilts her pretty blond head toward mine. "They promise the world, but most could barely afford to deliver a snow globe."

I take this in, recalling the man in our dingy boardinghouse in Pittsburgh, inviting me in, talking about his grand home out in the country. Little has changed, I suppose; only, here in New York, the men talk faster and, when they can afford to, dress with more flair.

Penny and I fall into step together, making our way up Broadway with a small gaggle of the other chorus girls, but she speaks only to me as she says, "All they want at the end of the day is the hootchy-kootchy."

I crumple my face at her odd expression. "The what now?"

Penny pauses her steps and, arm still linked with mine, throws me a teasing sort of look. "You are too sweet, aren't you?" Lifting an eyebrow, she fixes me with a look of mock sternness. "You better smarten up, kid. I'm just saying: don't get reeled in with lies or empty words. No, you want to hook yourself a real man. If he's going to make you promises, then make sure he puts his money on the line for you. Love, why, that'll come and then go, real fast. But the greenbacks? That's what keeps."

I nod as though I'm entirely up to speed, and Penny seems content to leave it at that. But in truth this is all so much to take in. This, right here, is what I want: a girlfriend with her arm in mine, our glamorous heeled shoes clicking against the pavement of Broadway as we make our way through the bright New York City night. Mamma at home, warm and fed, our days of privation feeling like a bad and receding memory. And someday soon, enough money put aside to bring Kit up north to us. Things, for the first time in quite a while, feel good. Men with cash, men peddling grand promises, why, their flattery might feel nice. But for now, this is all I want.

THE SHOWS ARE fun and fast-paced, but the nights afterward—those are even better. That's when we frolic and let loose, our playtime after the play. And because we are beautiful and young and starring in one of Broadway's hottest shows this summer, Manhattan is our playground.

We leave the theater as a small mob most nights, strutting out together to a supper club, a dance hall, or sometimes Annissa's apartment. One steamy night in late July, Dolly and Dinah talk me and Penny into joining them at a supper club on Broadway and Forty-fourth.

"Let's go to Rector's," they say brightly, and we agree, falling into step behind the Goodhue sisters, who seem to attract admiring stares everywhere they go. I can't help but giggle—it feels fun to be in a group of such vibrant girls. Even out of costume, the four of us make quite a scene, and the stunned crowds of Broadway cleave before us like the parting of the Red Sea.

When I spot our destination up ahead, it's my turn to be stunned. It looks more like a cathedral than a restaurant. "What is *that*?" I ask, pointing over the doorway, where a great big electric beast hulks as though he's just landed above the awning. It's like an eagle with wings, but it's got legs like a lion.

"Why, that's the famous Rector's griffin," Dinah explains. "It won't bite; it ain't real. Come on."

But I'm still dazzled by the scene unfurling before us, and my friend can tell. Dinah leans close, draping an arm over my shoulder as she says, "I remember how it felt, the first time I came to Rector's. I'd never seen anything like this where I came from, neither. They don't have places like this in Steubenville, Ohio."

I cut a sideways look toward Dinah. "Why, you're from Steubenville? I'm from Pittsburgh."

"I know you are, kid," Dinah says.

"Near your hometown."

Dinah tips her head to the side at a coquettish angle. "My dear little Spanish Maiden, you're not the only chorus girl who came east chasing dreams. Now, how about we enjoy this big city that is ours?" Dinah winks, and then she grabs Dolly by the hand and together they charge toward the door of Rector's. Before I enter, I pull Penny close, tugging on her arm. "Look!" I say, as I stare ahead at yet another new sight. "The door . . . it's turning in circles."

Penny's pretty features form an indulgent grin. "It's called a revolving door, Ev. First one in Manhattan. You'll feel like a hamster running around a wheel."

I watch the spinning glass door for a moment longer in appreciative silence before saying, "More like a mouse. A country mouse."

Penny takes my hand in hers, gives it a gentle squeeze. "Well, then, let's go, country mouse."

Following her lead, I run through, giggling. But once we've wound our way to the interior of the crowded place, I don't want to exit. I'm having too much fun. So I just keep on running, and Penny does the same, the pair of us wheeling round and round as the patrons in the restaurant watch our delight. Eventually, we allow ourselves to be disgorged by the glass revolving door and we sail into the place in a fit of near hysterics.

My laughter doesn't die down as Dinah places a flute of chilled champagne in my hands and declares she'd like to make a toast. "To the new kid. You sure are one quick study."

"Hear, hear," Dolly agrees.

"To Evelyn, the tiger's stripes," Penny adds.

I look at each of them in turn, my smile warming my cheeks as I take a sip of the bubbly drink. I relish the feeling as the cool ribbon of liquid slides down my throat and into my belly. For the first time in, well, perhaps ever, I have friends, people who see me, care for me. It's a thrill to think that on the stage where I found my light, where I'm told each night to take my place, I've maybe finally found it.

THAT EVENING I slip back into our room just after two o'clock, stepping quietly so as not to wake Mamma. But my efforts are useless, for she sits up in bed, and even in the dark, I can tell she's scowling. "Florence, what is the hour?"

Mamma doesn't love it when I return late, but because the

shows let out just before eleven, and then we have to change out of our costumes and make our way somewhere, it's often the early morning before I'm heading home. "It's late, Mamma. Sorry. I'm getting in bed now."

"Nothing good happens after midnight, and you know it. You're better off coming home and resting, rather than tipping the bottles."

I sigh at this, shimmying into my thin nightgown. "I didn't get into any trouble, Mamma. Promise. I was with Penny and Dinah and Dolly the whole time, and I only had one glass of champagne." That's what I always do—switching to soda water if I want something in my hand. Tonight it was mostly Penny and me blowing off steam on the dance floor. I may love to romp with the girls, but I'm not a fool. As much fun as it is to be a chorus girl both on and off the stage, I do remember that it's a job, and it's all that stands between us and destitution.

But Mamma doesn't seem to give me much credit. "You keep carrying on like this, your face will get puffy. Why, I bet you will be haggard tomorrow. And no one's going to have much desire to look at that."

I lower myself into bed with a thud, my happy feelings from just a few moments ago melting into the steamy summer night. Mamma isn't asking what I've been up to—where I've been, with whom. She doesn't care if I'm out getting debauched or corrupted. No, what she cares about is that I might lose my fresh-faced beauty—and with that, our paycheck.

But that ain't about to happen. I'm in good standing with the company. Within just a few short weeks after I first took my place onstage as the Spanish Maiden, the raves are coming in. I'm not deaf or blind; I hear how the audience calls out for me, how the Stage-Door Johnnies hooting and hollering out back are mostly calling my name as we all file past.

The lauds also come in print reviews. Since we have access to all the newspapers in the dressing room at the theater, Mamma no longer tries to stop my reading them. In addition to reporting in the society pages on what I wear, where I dine, and even how I style my hair, they also say that I'm a natural onstage. One well-regarded reporter, the *Evening Journal*'s Dorothy Dix, says my "*beauty is as vague and intangible as that of the lily, or any other frail and delicate thing. It lies over her face like a veil.*" Penny clips that article in particular and pins it over the mirror where I sit to fix myself up for the evening.

I am seated at that station when Dolly approaches me the following night. I'm surrounded by flowers, the bouquets gentlemen send after every performance, filling the space with their color and perfume. Dolly takes it all in—the bouquets, the cards and notes, the press clippings—then meets my eyes in the mirror's reflection. "Your ma and pa must be so proud."

I'm rouging my cheeks, so I keep looking into the mirror as I answer: "Daddy is dead. Mamma—well, it's complicated."

Penny, at my side, overhears this and sighs. "Isn't it always?"

Dolly nods, her fingers stroking a fragrant lily at my side. "If it weren't complicated, we probably wouldn't be back here . . . or up on the stage."

"We'd be in school," says Penny, and I hear the longing in her words. I *know* the longing because it's the same thing I've felt on so many occasions. Though I've never admitted my actual age to the girls, I suspect quite a few of us are teenagers, much younger than the "nineteen" we always answer.

I lower my makeup brush and square my shoulders, staring straight into the mirror. I know better than to succumb to melancholy, or even self-pity; and to be honest, this current life isn't so bad, what with the flowers and the champagne, the nights out with friends. "My school has been this," I say, trying to sound airy. And more savvy than I truly feel.

"That's right," Dolly says after a beat, nodding her ringleted head. "We've learned the ropes well enough, haven't we?"

"It was either that or hang." Penny rises from her seat and makes her way over to the massive wardrobe area across the room, where she starts riffling through flounces and feathers to find her costume.

But Dolly lingers beside my chair, still staring at me in the mirror's reflection. "Say, Ev, would you like to hear something kind of neat?"

"Sure."

Dolly turns back to the flowers, grazing her fingers over the petals. "I know someone in a position of . . . well, someone who'd like to meet you. And I think you might like to meet him, too."

I wheel around in my seat to face her directly. "What do you mean?"

"He's, well, a friend of mine."

"And why does he want to meet me?"

Instead of answering, Dolly waves her mamma, or sister, over. Dinah approaches, taking in my crowded space—the bower of plants, the cards—then her eyes rest on the newspaper article that's pinned up, filled with the praises of Dorothy Dix.

"Dolly says she'd like me to meet someone," I say.

Dinah puts a hand on my shoulder. When she speaks, her voice is like that of a doting mother. "Sweetie, we got someone who wants to meet *you*."

I sit up a bit straighter. Dinah goes on, patting a hand to her cherry-red coif as she studies her reflection in the mirror. "Let's just say he's a big supporter of the show. And he's been asking me to arrange an introduction with the little Spanish Maiden."

I glance around the colorful space, the room buzzing with nubile young bodies in various states of undress. Chatter, props, and costumes fill the scene, which thrums with all the usual preshow electricity. Then I turn back to my friends at my side. "You all are always telling me not to have anything to do with the Stage-Door Johnnies or other admirers who come calling."

Dinah laughs at this, putting a hand on her hip as she throws a look toward Dolly. Then, turning back to me with a smirk, she says, "Kid, this ain't no Stage-Door Johnny."

"No sirree, Bob," agrees Dolly, a touch of reverence in her tone.

Dinah leans toward me, looks me straight in the eyes. "They call him the Pharaoh of Fifth Avenue. He's a high society type. You know, a real fat cat."

I look at each of them in turn, but I say nothing. Dinah continues: "Not to mention, he's one of the biggest investors in our production. It'd be nice to make friends with him. Just a little group for lunch; that's all he's asking for."

I don't dine with men I've never met, so I answer: "Mamma would say no."

Dinah flashes me a wink, undaunted. Then, raising her hand, she gives my cheek one gentle stroke before taking my chin in the cradle of her fingers. Tipping my face up toward hers, she sighs. "Ev, your mamma might say no to you. But she won't say no to him."

Now it's my turn to chuckle. "What makes you so sure?" I ask.

"Because," answers Dinah, a mischievous smirk tugging on her flame-red lips, "no one says no to Stanley Pierce."

Chapter Sixteen

"What in hell's bells is *this* all about?" Mamma stands at our window the next morning, looking down on the street. For her to blaspheme, I know it must be something. I join her at the window and see Dinah stepping out of a gleaming cranberry-red horseless buggy, clutching her frothy skirts in her two gloved hands, and striding up to our front stoop.

A few moments later, we are welcoming my fellow starlet into our modest room, scrambling to clear our one armchair, with Mamma in a fluster about putting tea on.

"Oh, now, please do not put yourself out, Mrs. Talbot," Dinah says, her voice all prim and sugary, much like her daytime getup. She appears to be decorum itself as she adds, "This is a visit among friends. We are good friends now, aren't we, my dear Evelyn?"

I try to stifle my chuckle. Dinah is acting so proper, in a way entirely unlike her sashaying strut and playful banter backstage each evening. She's turned out in a day dress with a silk bolero bodice, and the thick scent of her gardenia perfume has filled the entirety of our small room.

"We are, Dinah," I answer, smiling, finding this act she's putting on highly amusing—as if she thinks Mamma is so proper. But why is she trying to impress Mamma?

"And I also come with a bit of social business," Dinah goes on, accepting a hastily poured cup of tea from Mamma but not taking a sip. "On behalf of another good friend. Mr. Stanley Pierce."

I tilt back where I'm perched on the edge of our bed, slanting a look toward Mamma. I've said nothing about Dinah's dressing room suggestion that I meet a friend of hers by the name of Mr. Pierce, but Mamma seems to know something about the gentleman. A slight flush pinks her cheeks as she rearranges the folds of her skirt. And then a moment later, with her voice sounding thin, she responds only: "Oh?"

Dinah folds her gloved hands in her lap. "You see, Mrs. Talbot, Evelyn here has been most fortunate in receiving a highly coveted invitation. To dine. At a luncheon given by Mr. Pierce."

Mamma makes a sound in the back of her throat. Perhaps sensing her opening, Dinah leans forward, pressing on. "Now, Mrs. Talbot, I can assure you that everything is perfectly aboveboard. Why, I would be there. And I'm even bringing my kid sister. Dolly's a good friend to Evelyn, as well. It's a luncheon at the Waldorf Astoria hotel. You know Mr. Pierce worked on the Waldorf for the Astors, right? The man is a genius."

Mamma offers a tight nod, though I'm not certain to which part she's replying. In the face of Mamma's silence, Dinah carries on: "Mr. Pierce is a great admirer of Evelyn's talent. He's a financial supporter of our show, so he knows her from the theater, but he became even more enthusiastic when he saw your daughter dancing at a private party for Mrs. Vanderbilt . . . ?"

My cheeks grow warm at the recollection of that recent evening in the lavish Vanderbilt mansion. "Oh, yes!" Mamma responds, beaming now. "Evelyn was hired as a *special* invitation. Mrs. Vanderbilt saw one of her pictures, Evelyn dressed up as Salome, and asked if she might offer entertainment at one of her private balls."

"Good for you, kid, getting invites to parties like that," Dinah says, staring at me searchingly. I clear my throat. What is it I glimpse passing behind her expression—surprise? Envy? It had been a good paycheck, to be sure, and a nifty scene to see, even if only for a few hours.

Mamma adds, her voice conspiratorial: "The fee Mrs. Vanderbilt offered, well, it was too high for us to refuse. And as it was Evelyn's night off from the show . . ."

"How nice," Dinah says, clasping her hands in her lap. Then, with a sigh, she continues, "I'd say this luncheon is another one of those invitations you'd be foolish to decline. And besides, Mr. Pierce has offered to get her there, door to door. You can see out that window."

I glance toward the street, spotting once more the cranberry-colored vehicle, and ask, "That's Mr. Pierce's horseless carriage?"

"He calls it an automobile," Dinah answers, as if she is sophistication itself.

I shift in my seat as Dinah eyes me intently, eventually asking: "Have you ever ridden in one?"

"No," I answer.

"Would you like to?"

I don't reply. The answer is *yes,* but I know better than to appear too eager. A ride in an automobile! A luncheon at the Waldorf! Why, of course I'd like to accept. It sounds bully! And I'd be in the company of two of my closest friends from the company. Why should I not?

But, bridling my hopes, I glance once more toward Mamma, whose eyes are slanted toward the floor. I cannot tell what she's thinking. Dinah, on the other hand, remains bright and undaunted, setting down her untouched tea. "Good then, that's settled," she declares. "Dolly and I will be here tomorrow shortly before noon to pick up Evelyn."

Though she claims she doesn't approve of the outing, Mamma is a flurry of activity that evening and the next morning, so much so that I suspect she might be changing her mind. Whistling as she scrambles to touch up my best white blouse, she fashions a broad sailor collar around the starched cotton neckline, then selects a pleated navy-blue skirt to pair with it. I look like a picture of a schoolgirl, skirt grazing my knees, very unlike the getups I wear as the Spanish Maiden. An hour before the scheduled outing, Mamma pulls my hair back, wrangling my thick curls into a taffeta ribbon. Then she grabs her own fanciest hat, a leghorn with a bow of creamy white silk, taking her time to angle the brim across my brow.

"You look simply precious, my darling," she says, making a turn around my figure and pausing once more in front of me. Staring into Mamma's eyes, I see something akin to warmth, perhaps even affection. Is it love? For me? Or pride in how well her handiwork has turned out, and I just happen to be the model?

As promised, the Goodhue sisters appear below our window just before noon in Mr. Pierce's gleaming horseless carriage—no, *automobile*—waving up toward me as the sleek vehicle rolls to a halt. I can feel the nervous excitement churning in my belly.

Once down on the street and staring through the windows of the shiny machine, I get a closer view of both of them. Dinah is in green taffeta and Dolly is sheathed in reams of snug-fitting lavender, its length covering more of her feet than her chest and shoulders. I see Dolly's flame-red waves are piled high atop her head in the Gibson-girl-style pompadour. The hairstyle I helped to make ubiquitous.

As the capped chauffeur helps me into the automobile, I take a seat on the rich leather bench and look around. "So this is an auto." I stare appreciatively.

Then I turn my focus to my companions. "Hello," I say, offering them a bashful smile. Dolly, up close, is a riot of textures and colors. I can see how tight the pale purple dress hugs her curves, gleaming pearl buttons running down the tailored bodice. A spray of fake pink flowers fills her soaring hairstyle, framing her heavily rouged and lipsticked face. "You look nice," I lie. In fact, she looks more done up than she would be for the stage, and reminds me of an overly frosted dessert.

"Thanks," Dolly answers, sweeping my figure with her light eyes. "You look . . . sweet."

I glance down at my own attire as the auto pulls away from my building and takes us east, turning onto Broadway. *Sweet*. I frown at my pleated skirt, my sailor collar. I feel even more like a schoolgirl now. Only it's the middle of the day in the middle of the week, and I'm most certainly *not* at school; I'm on my way to a fancy luncheon with two Broadway actresses at the Waldorf Astoria, hosted by some mystery man they've decided I ought to meet. It makes my head spin—that and the excessive perfume wafting off of Dolly and Dinah in this close space. All I manage in response is "Thank you."

But Dinah picks up the thread of conversation. "Mr. Pierce loves this lavender dress. He's got his eyes on my Dolly." Dinah's eyes hold Dolly with something similar to maternal affection. But the comment strikes me as odd. Is Mr. Pierce a suitor? A sweetheart? He can't be. Dolly doesn't look all that much older than me.

Eventually the auto rolls to a halt, and I look up at the building before us. I scowl in confusion. "This is the Waldorf Astoria?"

It doesn't look like the palace I've heard some of the girls rave about. Dinah shimmies across the leather seat as the chauffeur hops out to hand us each down in turn. I stare at the building as I step out of the auto. In truth, I've not yet been to the Waldorf Astoria and have little idea what it looks like, but I certainly didn't imagine it to look like this four-story brownstone on the corner of Twenty-fourth Street.

"Isn't the Waldorf Astoria farther uptown?" I ask.

"There's been a change of plans," Dinah says at my side, riffling through the silk purse at her waist. "Mr. Pierce wishes to host us at home. And, look, there's a toy store right next to the place. You should feel right at home, kid."

Dolly chuckles as Dinah puts a coin into the driver's gloved hand. "Say thank you, girls," Dinah chides, sounding the part of our school matron. "That ride was courtesy of Mr. Pierce."

I thank the driver and turn to peek into the ground-floor windows of the toy store facing the street before us. I smile at the playfulness of a small monkey holding drums, marching like a soldier. It's the sort of thing that Kit and I might have had and loved when Daddy was alive. I swallow, forcing that thought aside. I won't be sad today; why, I've just ridden in a horseless auto! And now I'm fixing to eat what will surely be a delicious luncheon, even if it's not in some fancy hotel. As my mood is rebounding, I'm startled by a door opening before us, the front entrance to the tall brownstone right beside the toy store giving way as if acting on its own accord.

I throw my friends a puzzled look, but they appear entirely unfazed by this door, which is now wide open. They enter through it, first Dinah and then Dolly. Following their lead, I step inside, into a quiet, cool entry hall. There's no footman or butler to receive us, which means that indeed the door has somehow opened on its own, seemingly magical. Through dim candlelight I see before me a flight of stairs, and without any chatter or explanation, we climb. At the top, on a second-story landing, another door opens on its own, revealing yet another stairway—but still no sign of a servant, or any human.

"Where are we going?" I ask, my voice sounding clamorously loud in this cool, dark stairway.

"To a place unlike any place you have ever been before."

I flinch, caught by surprise. It was a man's voice belting out those words in response to my question. My eyes dart up the stairs. I clutch the banister and tip forward on my tippy-toes. And then I see someone: a tall man, a broad-shouldered figure obscured by shadows, standing above.

Dinah and Dolly melt to the side, and Dinah indicates with a wordless wave of her hand that I ought to go first, so I do. I climb the remaining steps until I've reached the top stair, and just above me on the landing, the gentleman waits. He is so tall and on a step above me, so now he leans down like a curving tree limb, and he says, "Miss Talbot, welcome."

I'm struck by the deep baritone of his voice. Also, by a sudden wave of recognition, similar to what I experienced when I heard the name Stanley Pierce. Leaning close, he puts a quick chaste kiss on my cheek with his mustached lips, and I'm flooded with the scent of him, eau de cologne mixed with cigars, the hint of paper and coffee. It makes me a bit dizzy, so I grip the banister. Peering into his face up close, I can't help but frown; I've seen this gentleman before. The realization comes to me in a rush: the night of Mrs. Vanderbilt's ball. He's the fox-haired man who kept smirking at me.

As if landing on the same thought at precisely the same moment, the man gasps and says, "At last." He mutters, almost to himself, "I've been most eager to meet you, the Spanish Maiden and also Mrs. Vanderbilt's Salome."

I nod, letting out a small chuckle as my eyes tilt downward.

"And you, the famous Mr. Pierce, saw me perform in her home that night."

"Guilty." He grins, and I'm struck by how boyish and youthful his demeanor is. Suddenly I am entirely less nervous at the thought of today's luncheon. This man is no one to fear.

"Welcome, welcome, Miss Talbot. I would say it's a pleasure to meet you, but, well, we are already friends, aren't we?" Mr. Pierce's pale eyes are alight. "You have no idea how much pleasure it gives me to see you again."

Mr. Pierce takes my hand and without a word of welcome or even acknowledgment to Dinah or Dolly, our host ushers me up the last step and through a wide door, and suddenly the drab shadows of the corridor give way to an explosion of vivid color.

My eyes can scarcely take it all in, but I stare in appreciation and try my best, marveling at the rich oil paintings that line the walls, their textured scenes catching the flickering light thrown off by the countless burnished candelabras positioned around the large room. A thick Aubusson carpet enlivens the dark wood floors, with marble-topped tables boasting ornaments of porcelain figurines and cut-crystal vases overspilling with blooms. Divans and plush armchairs are arranged throughout the room, their red upholstery complementing the lush red drapes of velvet that hang across the floor-to-ceiling windows. For some reason, even though it is the middle of the day, these rich drapes are all unfurled so that the flickering of candles provides the only light in the massive space.

In the middle of this room hangs a grand crystal chandelier and under that an ornately carved mahogany table draped in a crisp white tablecloth. A crystal vase of fresh-cut flowers sits in the center of four place settings. I throw a confused glance at my companions, who have entered the room behind me—there are three of us. With Mr. Pierce, that makes a party of four. But I thought this was to be a grand luncheon?

Neither Dinah nor Dolly appears confused by this small gathering, so I decide it must be all right as Mr. Pierce strides toward the table and inspects the place settings. I study my host a bit more closely. He looks old, more than twice my age, with faded copper hair laced with silver and white. I remember well his full mustache, which is the same coppery shade, and his thick eyebrows that frame big gray eyes. Mr. Pierce looks up from the table just then and catches me staring, so I turn away, pretending to be entirely consumed with a small statue to my right.

"Ah, yes. The goddess of love and sensuality," he says, walking to my side. "I brought Venus home with me from Rome."

I face my host. "Rome?"

"Yes, the Eternal City. Have you ever been, Miss Talbot?"

"Oh," I answer. "Not yet."

"That's a shame. Well, nearly everything in here comes from over there. Europe, that is. Paris, Rome, London, Athens."

My head spins to think that this man has been to all the places he just listed. The farthest I've ever been from Manhattan is Tarentum. I turn my focus back toward Venus, studying the fresh and youthful beauty of her marble curves.

"Are you hungry?" he asks aloud to the room. Murmurs of assent sound from Dolly and Dinah. I am, as well. I imagine that with décor this lavish, his meals must be similarly sumptuous, and I can barely wait.

"Let's sit down, shall we?" Mr. Pierce guides us toward the table, where he pulls out a chair and gestures for me to take a seat. Then he helps Dinah and Dolly into their seats before he takes the place to my left.

So then it *is* to be only the four of us. I'm not sure what happened to everyone else, but I don't ask. As Dolly is arranging herself, primping the folds of her tight lavender dress, Mr. Pierce offers a benevolent smile and says, "I've ordered in from Delmonico's. Have you been?" His eyes fix on me.

"Not yet," I answer again.

"Ah, well, it's not quite as far as Rome," he says. "I'll have to take you there sometime."

"It's grand," Dinah says agreeably, leaning toward Mr. Pierce in her seat. As a small team of tuxedoed servants appears, bringing forth a staggering spread of food, I see what she means. I can't help but smile at the feast laid out on the table: deviled eggs, oysters on a platter of ice, fresh berries and cream, fragrant rolls with butter melting on them. Slices of steak, herbed potatoes. Lobster drizzled with liquid butter. Mamma will weep when she hears about what I'm eating with Mr. Pierce!

"Now, don't be shy." Our host looks from the platters of steaming food back toward me, gesturing for the nearby footman to begin serving at my place. "There's plenty more. We shall eat until we are fully satisfied." I accept a serving from every dish as it is offered.

Throughout lunch, Mr. Pierce behaves as if it were he and I alone. I have to temper my delight in the food to answer his questions, but he seems equally delighted to see how much I am enjoying the spread. He asks me about my experience in the company of *Fair Flora and Fauna*, how I like my role, how the stage compares to the artist's studio.

Mr. Pierce's attention, his interest, his warm hospitality—it all reminds me of the spotlight onstage. It's like a musical number where the light is fixed on one girl performing a solo, as others gather around to fill a bit of the faded light in the background, while knowing that it's really all hers. She's the brightest. That's what it feels like with Mr. Pierce fixing his interest only on me, Dolly and Dinah growing dimmer as the meal stretches on.

"Now, I hope you've saved some room for dessert," Mr. Pierce says, after I've had my last bite of lobster. He leans closer to me and presses a gentle hand on my forearm, giving it the softest squeeze. The warmth of his big hand sends a ripple across my skin. I nod, and then he rings the small silver bell beside his plate. A moment later the footman reappears, bearing a bottle of chilled champagne. Mr. Pierce doesn't ask, but the footman pours out four flutes of champagne. Next we are each served a dessert plate. "Cherry pie à la mode," Mr. Pierce says, eyeing me as if looking for my approval. I heartily offer it, along with my thanks.

After the meal, sated by the delicious spread and relaxed by my flute of champagne, I feel as if I could curl up on one of Mr. Pierce's plush sofas and slip into a lovely nap. But my host has another idea. "Now, Dinah and Dolly are my old friends; they've been here loads of times. But since this is your first visit, Miss

Talbot, would you like to see the rest of my home? I have something I think you'd get a kick out of."

I look to my friends, inquiring with my eyes: wouldn't they like to come along, too? Dinah offers a vague shrug in reply, Dolly just looks away, but neither of them makes a move. Mr. Pierce does, however, extending his arm toward me. "We won't be gone long. I'm sure they can find plenty of ways to entertain themselves. Right, girls?" Then he offers a wink and guides me toward the doorway.

I follow my host out of the room, and together we climb another flight of stairs. Mr. Pierce has me lead the way as he walks behind me. I hold tight to the carved banister and wonder where we are going. I don't see or hear another soul even though I know there's a team of servants tucked away somewhere. Once we've reached the fourth-story landing, my host guides me to yet another doorway and opens it, and we enter another large room.

I look around. There's a massive bed of rich wood draped with similar dark red velvet curtains occupying pride of place in the center of the space.

"Oh," I say, looking to my host with an expression that must show my confusion. I've never been inside a bedroom with a man, other than Daddy or Kit.

"This was what I wanted to show you," Mr. Pierce says, flashing a relaxed, good-natured smile as he guides me to the far side of the room.

"Is that a swing?" I ask, following his steps. "Indoors?" Now my delight overtakes my confusion. Like so much of Mr. Pierce's décor, the swing is covered in red velvet. I walk toward it and brush my fingers against it, caressing the fabric, its texture as soft as a kitten.

"How about a ride?" Mr. Pierce suggests, again with that boyish grin that makes me feel as though he behaves so much younger than his age.

"A ride?" I repeat.

"Why not?" he asks. "Don't tell me you've gotten so sophisticated as a star of the stage, Miss Talbot, that you can't still enjoy the simple pleasures in life, like a swing?"

The honest truth is I can't remember the last time I took a ride on a swing. I suspect it was before Daddy died. I swallow. Finding no reason to object, I shrug. "All right." I settle into the seat and clutch the velvet ropes on either side.

"May I?"

I nod, and Mr. Pierce begins to push me. As I glide through the air, I can't help but let out a small giggle. I forgot how much fun this was. I so rarely do girlish things nowadays. I look around the room again, and I notice a colorful parasol hanging from the ceiling overhead. Just another piece of Mr. Pierce's elegant and eclectic décor. Above that, I notice for the first time, the ceiling is all mirrors. What a space! It feels like something I could find in a theater, only this is the man's home.

"Evelyn . . . May I call you Evelyn?" Mr. Pierce continues to push me, and my reflection is smiling back from a dozen different angles thanks to the mirrored ceiling. "We're friends now, aren't we?"

"Yes, all right," I reply.

He gives me another strong push. "Do you think you can reach that parasol?" he asks, as though we are playing a schoolyard game together. I laugh at this. As he sends me flying once more through the air, my toes just miss tapping the parasol. We try again, and I miss again. "Almost," he says, cheering me on. The next time he pushes me even harder, and I stretch my legs a bit farther, and my feet do tap the parasol. We both let out a triumphant laugh. "Brava, my dear," Mr. Pierce says, and with that he slows the swing down, putting his hands around my waist to bring it to stillness. I'm slightly short of breath, and my heart is galloping as Mr. Pierce helps me down from the swing.

He's wearing that cheery smile again, and our eyes meet. We are silent for a moment, as I try to steady my breath. It is Mr. Pierce who breaks the silence, saying: "Thank you for coming."

"Thank you for having me," I answer.

"It's been lovely, but I must be off. Duty calls," he says, and he pulls his eyes from mine, glancing back toward the door. I nod, and then Mr. Pierce offers his arm to escort me out.

It *has* been an enjoyable visit. The food, the décor, the playfulness of our world-famous host. I'm sad that it's over, but I do not wish to be rude; of course Mr. Pierce has many things to do. So I follow him gamely as we walk back down the stairs.

Back in the grand drawing room where we ate, Dinah and Dolly are slumped on one of the dark red settees, and they barely look up as we enter. I don't know why, exactly, but I feel a pang of guilt. Surely their time wasn't as enjoyable as mine, for Mr. Pierce has scarcely spoken to either of them. Dolly looks like a wilted purple flower.

They seem to guess that the visit is over. Mr. Pierce walks straight toward Dinah and helps her to rise, then ushers her toward the door as Dolly and I follow. As we walk, Mr. Pierce says, "Take my auto. But before you drop her home, bring her here." Mr. Pierce slips Dinah a small piece of paper, and she looks down at it as he goes on. "The girl is perfection, but her teeth need a good cleaning. You just tell the fellow at the front that Mr. Pierce sent you and that she's a special friend of mine. You'll have no trouble."

Chapter Seventeen

The Goodhue sisters are cold as two blocks of ice that night at the theater. But it started before the evening; they barely spoke in the auto on the way to the dentist. Dinah was all business, doing as Mr. Pierce had directed her—whisking me in for a cleaning, the first I can remember having—and then she had the chauffeur deposit me at my front door without so much as a goodbye.

And now they pretend not to see me as I sit in the dressing room backstage before the show, rouging my cheeks and winding my hair into its chignon. I'm trying not to stare too long in the mirror at my newly white teeth, since I have the vague feeling that it would irk Dinah, and Dolly, too.

Later, after the show, feeling fatigued from the day's excitement and confused by my friends' uncharacteristically cool demeanor, I pull Dolly aside. "What's wrong?" I ask her. "Did I do something?"

Dolly fixes me with a thoughtful stare, her red lips pressed in a straight line. "I thought I'd ask you the very same."

I frown. "What does that mean?"

Dolly throws a look around the crowded dressing room, where the girls are buzzing about in the usual postshow air of euphoria. Penny is holding court in a small cluster, and she has the girls in fits of giggles as she regales them with her tale of nearly tripping onstage but then pretending she was woozy to go along with the song lyrics. I certainly won't be stepping out with them tonight;

I'm too tired. Then Dolly turns back to me, speaking in a low tone as she leans close. "You know, upstairs? With Mr. Pierce . . . What did you do?"

This sets me back on my heels, and I fall silent a moment before answering: "Nothing. I looked around some room of his."

"The Swing Room?" Dolly asks, her brows curving in a tight arc.

"Oh." I tilt my head to the side. "There was a swing made of red velvet, yes. One floor above the luncheon."

"What did you do in there?"

I shrug. "I rode on the swing."

"Did Mr. Pierce push you? Toward the parasol?"

"Yes," I answer, surprised that Dolly knows that part.

"And then what?"

"And then nothing," I reply, confused. "Mr. Pierce told me he had to work. We walked back downstairs, and you and Dinah brought me to the dentist."

Dolly's eyes could scorch with the intensity of her stare. After a long beat, she asks, "That's it?"

"That's it," I insist.

"Nothing more?"

"What more could I have done, Dol? I was only away from you for about five minutes."

"That's all it takes," Dolly says, throwing a look toward Dinah, and then, with a careworn shrug, she turns to walk away. But before she leaves me, Dolly pauses for just a moment, fixing me with one final pointed stare. Her tone brittle, she adds, "Just be careful, all right? Be smart."

But I feel the furthest thing from smart, because I can't puzzle out this riddle that Dolly's handing to me. Didn't Dolly and Dinah insist I meet Mr. Pierce? All I feel is confused.

THE NEXT DAY, an invitation arrives at our door. Another luncheon, once again hosted by Mr. Pierce, this one for both Mamma and me. But this gathering is to be held at his offices on Fifth Avenue, according to the card of thick cream-colored stock bearing

Mr. Pierce's monogram and the address of where we are to meet him. Mamma accepts this invitation more readily, having heard what a grand time I had at the first luncheon.

As a secretary whisks us into Mr. Pierce's imposing wood-paneled office, we see a fireplace nearly as big as our entire apartment and a table spread with a delectable-looking feast. Mamma gasps at my side. *Told you so,* I say with my expression. We lean over to admire the dishes: quail and partridge on silver platters, puréed potatoes still steaming, julienne carrots, a bowl of dark cherries. I can see that Mamma is just as giddy as I am for such a feast.

Mr. Pierce appears a few moments later and invites us to sit down with him, a party of three. He serves no champagne at this meal, only lemonade, but the mood in the room is festive and cordial. Unlike at the earlier lunch, where Mr. Pierce spoke only to me, this time our host is solicitous of Mamma, eager to hear about her passion for sewing, quick to compliment her on her adept job at mothering me through such an illustrious career. I see Mamma warming to him as the meal progresses, like a plant gradually tipping toward gentle sunshine.

When it's time for dessert, a tuxedoed footman steps out and, with gloved hands, presents each of us with our very own ribbon-wrapped box of Lowney's chocolates. I look down at the parcel in my hands and can't help but burst into a giggle. It's my image on the front of the box! I remember the day the photo was taken. Mr. Engels directed me to put a big red bow in my hair, while Mamma helped me into a white blouse with big puffed sleeves. I was made to hold a white pillow against my cheek for hours; Lowney's has turned that into an image of a fluffy white kitten. The language on the box, woven with red flowers, asks: "*Is there anything sweeter?*"

I look up into Mr. Pierce's eyes, and he flashes me a wink. "Even sweeter in person," he says. I happily tuck in to the chocolates.

After the chocolates, we end the meal with a delicious cup of coffee with cream and sugar—Mr. Pierce does not offer champagne at this point either, which is fine with me because I doubt Mamma would approve of my having a glass, and I left the detail of the champagne out in my retelling of our first luncheon together.

Full from the meal and happy to have eaten so much chocolate, I resist the urge to slump in my chair. Once the footmen have cleared our dishes, Mr. Pierce puts his elbows on the table and looks at Mamma, asking, "What does Mr. Talbot do?"

Mamma shifts in her seat, gives me a look, then returns Mr. Pierce's gaze as she answers only, "Mr. Talbot left us."

"He died," I hasten to add so that Mr. Pierce does not assume, as he very well might have done, that Daddy chose to abandon us.

Mamma shoots me daggers with her eyes, but Mr. Pierce's face goes soft as he says, "That must have been terrible for you both."

I nod, chewing on my lower lip. Mamma pulls her shoulders back, sitting even more upright as she says, "You can't even imagine, sir."

"So it's just you and Evelyn now?"

"I have a son, as well."

Thinking of Kit causes a pinching sensation in my heart, and my eyes tip downward. Mr. Pierce asks, "And where is he?"

"He's younger by five years. I couldn't afford to keep all three of us, not here in Manhattan. He's enrolled in school outside Philadelphia."

Mr. Pierce threads his hands together on the table. All three of us go silent for a moment, then he says, "That must be quite a burden for you to bear."

"Indeed, sir." Mamma frowns, then adds: "We send his tuition each month."

"How can you afford it?"

"With Evelyn's earnings," Mamma says. "I serve as her agent and manager."

"I see," he says, his features creasing in thought.

I shift in my seat, the sweetness of the dessert and my contented feelings from a moment earlier forgotten. It's Mr. Pierce who eventually breaks the silence. "This cannot go on." His tone is hard. He shakes his head, and I can see, beneath his mustache, that he is frowning. "Mrs. Talbot, you *must* allow me to pay for the boy's school. I won't hear otherwise."

"Mr. Pierce!" Mamma's face has gone white with shock—and something else. Incredulity? As she studies the man, this near stranger, is she trying, as I am, to gauge whether he is in earnest with such an outlandish offer?

But Mr. Pierce goes on before either of us can speak again. "The girl has no father, and, madam, you have no provider. I can never fill the hole left by Mr. Talbot's tragic departure. But I will do all that I can to make the privations less painful. I'm happy to be your protector."

Mr. Pierce's eyes glide from Mamma toward me, and he offers a kind smile. "I won't accept any answer but yes. You'll be my special ladies. We need Evelyn to be able to focus on her work, agreed? Her talent as a rising star. How can the poor girl do that if she's concerned with paying the bills?"

Mamma looks as though she might weep, but Mr. Pierce is animated now. "Speaking of Evelyn's talent, I know you've told the theater she's nineteen." *How does he know that?* But before I can ask, he adds: "I don't blame you for a moment. You had to say it, and now I understand even better why. But you can tell me the truth."

I swallow, slanting a look toward Mamma. Neither she nor I move. But Mr. Pierce leans closer, over the table, and with his voice like a whisper, he says, "I promise it'll be our little secret. But I'm not a fool, and I do want the truth. How can I be your champion if we aren't honest with one another? Mrs. Talbot, she's younger, is she not?"

Mamma blinks slowly, and when she opens her eyes, I see her make the decision to trust this man. I see it in her gaze before I hear her words. Her voice thin, she responds, "Yes. She's younger."

I'm surprised by her revelation. But then, most everything about this luncheon has caught me by surprise. Mr. Pierce is looking directly at me now, his pale eyes alight, and he speaks only to me as he asks: "How old are you, Evelyn? You can tell me the truth."

I glance to Mamma. She gives me a nod, and so I answer. "I'm sixteen, sir."

A moment of silence, in which I hear only the rhythmic clicking of Mr. Pierce's fancy clock on the marble mantel, and then our host nods once. When he speaks next, with his gaze still on me, he says, "Yes. Sixteen. Yes, that's more like it. Well, we'll keep that between us, won't we? And now that you've got me on your side, no one's going to give you any trouble."

Mamma's features break into a relieved—and weary—smile. I allow myself to absorb these words from Mr. Pierce and, with them, the warmth of a small but hopeful glow. This man is telling us that our troubles are behind us. Penny told me that many girls in the theater have benefactors; is that what Mr. Pierce is offering to be? Perhaps this generous and solicitous man really does wish to help us?

Our host appears entirely satisfied with the outcome of our meeting, not at all put off by the revelation of my true age as so many others before him have been. He says aloud to the room, his tone now cheerful: "I've known from the beginning that you are different, Evelyn. You're not to be treated like just any chorus girl. I've got big plans for you." My cheeks flush with warmth. "First order of business, we are going to get you out of the chorus line. You are star material, and everyone knows it. You just need to put in your time. You are winning hearts as the Spanish Maiden, so keep at that for a little bit longer. But you may rest assured that your friend Stanley Pierce is on the job."

With the luncheon over, Mr. Pierce sends us home in his chauffeured auto with enough food to fill us for a week. "My chauffeur will bring these baskets inside for you. I insist." Mamma and I watch with mouths watering as the servant loads parcels stuffed with pastries, croissants, more chocolates, cheeses, pears, and oranges. Food we would never be able to afford on our own.

"Only the best for you," Mr. Pierce says as he personally helps Mamma into his auto. And then he turns and extends his hand to me, helping me up.

As he shuts the door, he flashes me another wink, and I can't help but return his smile. There is something so undeniably vibrant, perhaps even a bit impish, about Mr. Pierce, the way his smile flickers. *Something magnetic,* I think, as I realize that I enjoy being near him. I like how he made me feel, during our first luncheon, as if he were shining a spotlight on me. Now, I find, I don't want to be out of that light.

Chapter Eighteen

The gifts keep coming from Mr. Pierce, growing only more lavish and generous. Lovely arrangements of flowers arrive daily at our door. Mr. Pierce sends cards with the bouquets, penning sweet notes:

> *Flowers to brighten the day for the little Spanish Maiden,*
> *who brightens our nights.*

And it's not only flowers. Mr. Pierce's generosity seems to know no limits. Footmen appear some mornings with baskets overflowing with grapes and peaches. Other days it's candied nuts and peppermints. One day it's a box of fresh-smelling soaps. The next morning he sends a bottle of honeysuckle and jasmine perfume for me, a scent of lemon and verbena for Mamma.

The best gift of all is the security that Mr. Pierce's regular gifts bring. Now that he's insisting on paying for Kit's schooling and he's taken over our account at the greengrocer's, Mamma and I agree that I can cut back my daytime work as an artists' model and focus almost exclusively on the stage. It was Mr. Pierce's idea, in fact. "This way, Evelyn stays fresh. Only take the posing jobs you really wish to take. But never again shall you work out of necessity to win your bread, dear. We all want to see you cheery and bright up there onstage."

Mr. Pierce comes quite often to my performances, and I love the nights when he is in the packed house, his broad smile shining like a second spotlight. I always feel as if I, too, smile a bit brighter, kick a little higher, when he's there. I want to earn his approval, to offer a flawless performance as thanks for his generosity and friendship.

Dinah is still cold to me, but Dolly is mostly back to her friendly self, if a bit reserved. I never did hear what my crime was. Had Dinah hoped that Mr. Pierce might become Dolly's benefactor? Or even a suitor? But I fear that to ask for clarification might only cause further offense, so instead I carry on being kind to both of them, hoping things will return to how they were with time.

Penny and I have become closer than ever after our months together onstage and frolicking across the city after the shows. Gentlemen and young lads continue to fawn over us when we step out, but I kindly demur their requests to dance, their offers to dine. I've been warned—and at this point, I'm most interested in working and enjoying my scant leisure time after the shows with the girls.

One night when Penny and I sidle up together to the gleaming bar at Rector's, the server tells us that he has a bottle of Pommery Sec champagne waiting for us on ice. I throw him a dubious look—we'd never order such an expensive bottle. But the man hoists his hands, brandishing the chilled bottle. "Mr. Pierce wishes for me to tell the Spanish Maiden that she should enjoy the finest French vintage."

"Cheers to that," Penny says, tilting a glass to accept the first pour.

"How did he know we'd be here?" I ask, clinking my own glass against Penny's before taking a sip. I close my eyes to appreciate the first taste, how the bubbles dance across my tongue.

"He must have eyes all over this city," Penny says, glancing around the packed supper club. She says it playfully, arcing an eyebrow as she leans close. "He's watching you."

I laugh at the quip. And then Penny, swallowing, says, "He's stuck on you, Ev."

"Hush," I reply. "He's twice my age."

"How old is he, do you think?"

I tilt my head sideways. "Forty?"

Penny leans on me, nuzzling into my shoulder and acting moony. "But you make him feel like a young lad, you lovely little Spanish Maiden."

"More like a protective friend," I am quick to retort. *But is that the full truth?* I wonder, even though I don't say it aloud.

"Do you mean to tell me, Ev, that you've never . . ." Penny eyes me with an appraising look. "That he's never, well . . . you know?"

"What?" I ask, my heartbeat quickening at the intensity of her stare.

"The two of you, you've never?"

"Never what?"

"Not even . . . a kiss?"

"A kiss?" I giggle the word. "With Mr. Pierce?"

She nods once.

"Never!" I gasp in reply when I see that she's being entirely serious.

Penny rests her elbow on the bar, eyeing me with a mixture of surprise and skepticism. "Honest?"

"Of course I'm being honest, Pen."

"He's never even tried? All those rides in the back of his motorcar?"

"No," I say, and she finally turns away, mumbling: "I guess, once in a blue moon, a girl may actually be as innocent as she seems."

Standing there, clutching my champagne flute, I certainly feel like the tender little naïf she apparently sees me as. But admitting that I'm confused would only make me look even more like a babe.

Later, as Penny and I slip out of Rector's with our arms linked, I spy Mr. Pierce's cranberry auto waiting across the street. We walk together to take a closer peek. Mr. Pierce is not in the car, but the driver appears to be expecting me, and he steps out now. "Miss Talbot?"

"Yes?"

"Mr. Pierce has asked for me to wait for you, to bring you and your friends safely home."

"Well, isn't that nice? We accept the offer." Penny gives my arm a squeeze, and then, so that only I can hear, she whispers, "See? What'd I say? Stuck on you. Smart fellow, too. Just make sure you stay smarter."

. ◆ .

THAT'S NOT THE *way of it,* I want to say. To Penny, to myself. I *am* smart. And Mr. Pierce is treating Mamma and me like true friends, with nothing untoward ever even hinted at. I remind myself of that as Mamma accepts and appreciates each one of his kindly gestures. And every time I think I've seen Mr. Pierce's generosity at its finest, he surprises me with yet another, even grander gesture—the grandest yet arriving the next morning.

Mamma and I are finishing a late breakfast. Our days are less harried now that we aren't shuttling back and forth to sittings before the theater. I've slept late, given the excitement of the previous night at Rector's. I have a slight headache from the champagne Mr. Pierce arranged, but I don't breathe a word of that to Mamma.

There's a knock on our door. Mamma flashes me a puzzled look, swallowing her bite of croissant. I reply with a shrug—I'm not expecting anyone. I can see what she's thinking: our room is so dingy, hardly a place in which we feel comfortable receiving guests. When she opens the door, several members of Mr. Pierce's household staff stand at the threshold. I rise from the table, joining Mamma by the door to greet his butler, two footmen, and a lady's maid.

Mamma has gone mute, so I step in. "Yes? Good morning. How can we help you?"

The butler stands straight as a sergeant. "It is *we* who have come to help *you,* Miss Talbot. Mrs. Talbot."

"Help us how?" Mamma asks.

The butler peers over our shoulders into our cramped little room. "We are here to pack up your belongings."

I look to the maid, to the footmen, then back to the butler, confusion evident in my tone as I ask, "And bring them where?"

"To the Audubon, mademoiselle," the butler says.

"The what?"

"The Audubon Hotel. Where your new suite awaits."

"I don't understand," Mamma says, crossing her arms as she looks to me and then back to Mr. Pierce's servants.

Neither do I, but the butler goes on. "Mr. Pierce insists you are not to worry about a thing; leave it with him, and he shall explain it all. Now, if you'd be so kind as to point us toward your personal effects, madam? Mademoiselle?" The man sweeps the room with his gaze and a wave of his gloved hand, glancing around as though beholding a meal for which he has little appetite. "Anything you do not wish to part with, that is." With a courteous smile hitching his tidy features, he adds: "Mr. Pierce told us not to bother with the furniture. He's had it all arranged."

In less than an hour, a cart is loaded with our trunk and bags, while Mr. Pierce's gleaming automobile awaits us. The chauffeur whisks open the door and helps Mamma and me into the plush leather interior. We roll away from the boardinghouse and Twenty-second Street in bemused but trusting silence, the motorcar not stopping until we arrive outside the Audubon Hotel in the much more affluent neighborhood of Madison Square.

A tuxedoed attendant stands sentry-like outside the hotel's wide glass doors. I still don't quite understand what is happening. As I step away from the auto and toward the hotel, I'm half expecting the man to turn us away; I've never set foot inside any place this grand, let alone spent a night.

But, to my shock, the man greets us with a most cordial smile, as though he's been expecting us for hours and is entirely delighted to finally see us. "Miss Talbot, Mrs. Talbot, it is our honor to have you here. My name is Mr. Carlton, and I am the concierge here at the Audubon Hotel. On behalf of our entire staff, I would like to say that we are most pleased to welcome you. We have worked with Mr. Pierce to ensure that everything is prepared, and you are to tell us if there is anything we might do to make your stay more comfortable. Though of course, it is our earnest hope that you shall never have to ask."

The sun is shining brightly, so I squint my eyes as I look from this man to the gracious building behind him, with its striped awning and façade of white limestone, tall windows and tiered balconies rising up toward the sky. Mamma, at my side, seems agitated now. "Our stay?" she asks, repeating the concierge's word.

"Yes, ma'am," the man answers, an unwavering smile painted on his features.

"And just how long is our stay arranged for?" she asks.

"Why"—Mr. Carlton clasps and then unclasps his gloved hands—"indefinitely, Mrs. Talbot."

"Indefinitely?" Mamma looks up once more at the building.

"As long as you'd like, ma'am. And we certainly hope that you shall have no reason to leave. If there is anything we can do for you, you need only to ask."

"You mean . . . this hotel room . . . is . . ."

"It's the penthouse apartment, Mrs. Talbot," the concierge interjects with a deferential nod.

"The *penthouse*?"

"It's been rented, ma'am." The man's placid cordiality does not falter. "By Mr. Pierce, for you both."

My eyes fly to the top of the grand building. How can this be true? It sounds like the stuff of some fairy tale that Daddy and I would have read together. No more boardinghouse but, instead, a hotel? And not just any hotel room, an entire suite of rooms on the top floor, surely with swell views of the whole of New York City?

I grab Mamma's hand, and together, without a word, we follow the concierge through the lobby of the hotel, where the cool air smells of fresh flowers and money, then straight into a private lift. I rock on my heels in giddy excitement—I can't help but think back to all those days at Wanamaker's when I dreamed of riding in the elevator. The lift chimes, illuminating a fancifully etched number six as the operator slides open the grated door. Mamma squeezes my hand, wordlessly reminding me to stop fidgeting, but I am finding it hard to tamp down my mystified delight.

At the concierge's polite insistence, we step out of the elevator and enter a bright foyer of impossible beauty. I gasp, ravenous to take it all in with my hungry eyes: gleaming marble floors and a soaring coffered ceiling, the large entry hall opening out into a gracious drawing room of rich wood paneling. I skip forward, entirely forgetting Mamma's entreaties not to act giddy—I'm so eager to explore. Adjacent to the elegant drawing room is an equally elegant dining room with a crystal chandelier hanging over an ornate table of carved wood and floor-to-ceiling windows with views all the way to the Hudson River.

I stare out those windows in wordless appreciation, finding it all too grand to even believe. *This is to be our* home? *Indefinitely?* Why, our entire room in the boardinghouse could fit in just the foyer. I'm desperate to keep exploring, but the sound of the concierge's voice pulls me from my dizzy reverie. I hear him tell Mamma: "Only a pantry, Mrs. Talbot, as all of your food shall be prepared and sent up from our kitchens. Anything you'd like, no matter the time of day, simply inform our staff, and we shall see to it."

Then the man asks if we'd like to see the bedrooms. "Bedrooms?" I gasp. Yes, he confirms, we are each to have our own bedroom. And our own private bathrooms, as well!

I haven't had a bedroom to myself since Daddy was alive. And a private bathroom with both a toilet and a bathtub to myself? Never. But first we walk through the spacious drawing room, where I spot a gleaming piano in the corner. "You'll see that we've decorated this room in Mr. Pierce's signature favorite—red velvet," the concierge explains. It's true: the drapes, the sofas, the settees, even the carpets are all in shades of red, claret, maroon, and cranberry.

But it's an entirely different décor in my bedroom, and I smile with unabashed delight as I walk in. The aesthetic is softer in here, shades of pink and peach and creamy white. The dresser and table are of a finely carved rosewood, and there's a three-part mirror trimmed in gold.

"My very own bedroom," I marvel aloud, to no one in particular. And so large! Why, this looks like the bedroom of a princess.

In the center of the room hulks a massive bed, so high there's a step stool to climb into it, with ostrich plumes spraying out the top of its four wooden posts. A soft lace cover is tucked in tight, and at the head of the bed is a mountain of overstuffed downy white pillows. "Satin, miss," the concierge says, and I nearly jump, having forgotten he was there. "For the bedding. Shall that be to your liking?"

It shall be indeed. "Oh, yes, that's grand. Thank you." I skip farther into the space and look around, hungrily, at every detail. Fresh-cut flowers sit in a small vase of crystal atop a dresser, and I lean close, breathing in their perfume. Beside the dresser is a large armoire with pink roses painted along its panels, and when I peek inside, I see it is stocked! Dresses of every shade, tailored skirts, blouses, coats, fine stockings, gloves, hats, ribbons. All in my size. Store-bought and impossibly chic. I can barely take it in. Never in my life could I have conjured a dream this sweet. I wheel around to face my new bedroom, feeling as though I'm now walking atop a cloud.

Speaking of walking atop a cloud, a plush white rug unfurls beside the bed. "Polar bear," the concierge explains. This strikes me as curious, the idea of a bear pelt beneath my feet every time I step out of bed. I'd change just that one detail, but otherwise I love the entire place.

"And Mr. Pierce would like me to remind you that you are not to make the bed," the concierge says.

I look askance at the gentleman, my confusion surely evident. "I'm not?"

"The chambermaids shall see to all of that."

A place for a princess, indeed, I think. *How can Mamma and I ever thank the man?*

MR. PIERCE CALLS on us that afternoon, just as I am preparing to leave for my evening show. He sweeps into our elegant new foyer, cane and top hat in one hand, his other arm extended toward me as an offering. "I thought I could give you a ride to the theater, Evelyn."

"Oh, Mr. Pierce!" Mamma exclaims, hurrying toward the door to receive him. "You've done so much!"

"I'm glad you like the place. And I can assure you," he says, flashing his coltish grin, "my joy at being able to do it is even greater than your joy at receiving it."

"That can't be true," I say, finishing the last buttons on my shoes.

"Mrs. Talbot, are you joining Evelyn at the theater this evening?" he asks.

"I'm not," she answers. "I thought I would remain to finish getting us settled." Mamma rarely comes to my evening shows.

"A fine plan," Mr. Pierce answers Mamma. "But do remember that you now have an entire fleet of maids at your beck and call, so be sure not to overexert yourself. Do you understand? And then order yourself something delicious from the dinner menu. If it's not on the menu, you simply tell them what you want, and they'll fetch it. Lobster, steak . . ."

Mamma's eyes go even wider, her cheeks darkening to the rosy tint of a young girl's, as she offers the broadest smile I've seen in years. Perhaps ever.

Moments later, beside Mr. Pierce in the back of the red automobile on the way to the theater, I feel as though I must try to thank him more heartily. For all of it: Mamma's beam, the food, Kit's tuition, the gifts, the impossibly lovely new home. "Truly, Mr. Pierce, it's too much."

"It's a joy to me, my dear," he says, grinning beneath his silvered mustache. "After all that you've endured. It gives me peace to know that you are out of that unsavory neighborhood."

I know he's a generous man, but still. Even if I were to work as an artists' model and a Broadway star every day for the rest of my life, there would be no repaying all that he has given us. Why, one night in that hotel must cost him more than what we were paying for an entire month in the boardinghouse. And somehow, he's happy to do this. "Mr. Pierce, I don't know how you can possibly be so generous."

He looks at me for a moment in silence, the automobile bearing us through the crowded streets of Midtown. Placing his hand softly on top of mine, he says, "I've worked hard my entire life, Evelyn. Everything I have, I earned for myself. Now I'm in a position to help others, and to enjoy the fruits of my labor. Please allow me to help you."

I look down at his gentle hand on mine, then back up into his light eyes, returning his smile as I reply, "If you say so."

After a beat, he asks: "Are you happy?"

I lean back in my seat, surprised by the question. Isn't it obvious? "I'm so very happy."

"Then that makes me happy." I can see from his face that he means it. "And you like the furnishings I selected? I do think the place came out top-notch. I oversaw every detail. And the piano in the drawing room—I've arranged for a teacher to come to you each week for lessons. Singing and playing. You don't do a matinee on Thursdays, right? So he'll come on Thursdays. I told you, we are going to get you to the center of the stage in no time."

"Mr. Pierce, you're spoiling me."

"Not spoiling. I expect you to work hard at your music lessons. I told that instructor he better have you singing better than Nellie Melba soon."

I laugh. "I'll practice hard."

"I know that you will. And what about your bedroom?"

"Oh, I love it."

"I know how you love fairy tales, so I planned it with that in mind, since you are so like a fairy princess."

I smile at this, but I turn away and look out the window. Only once I'm sure that he can't see my face do I allow my features to drop—just for a moment. If only this man knew how I used to scrounge in alleyways for discarded bones. Now he thinks I'm a princess, and he's put me up in my very own castle keep. It makes my head spin.

Mr. Pierce's deep voice pulls me from my gloomy brooding. "I didn't like thinking about you in that dingy boardinghouse. A beautiful creature like you should be in a beautiful place."

"Well, it sure is beautiful," I reply, managing a cheery tone. "Like a fairy tale indeed. Complete with the fierce beast," I say, chuckling. When his face crinkles in confusion, I clarify: "That polar bear pelt."

"Ah, yes, the bearskin rug," he says, his pale eyes narrowing, pinning me with a gaze that has suddenly turned harder to read. And then he asks: "Do you like it?"

I sense he wants me to tell him that I do. "Yes, it's all right. It's . . . different."

"Yes, well, that's good taste. It's a pristine pelt. Flawless. It's good for you to learn about all these things, Evelyn."

We've arrived at the theater. I look out the motorcar window, then back to him. It's showtime, and I feel the familiar backstage energy beginning to curl in my belly. But before I move to exit the auto, I lean toward Mr. Pierce and, with the sweetest smile I can summon, say, "All these things about good taste and proper furnishings . . . thank you for teaching me."

Chapter Nineteen

Autumn 1901

Mr. Pierce is always sending packages—flowers, candies of spun sugar, delicate lace—but this one catches me by surprise. Over breakfast one Wednesday I pull back tissue paper to find a cascade of plush red velvet. I gasp, running my fingers over a scarlet cape, hooded and trimmed with satin. Tucked into its soft folds is a note with Mr. Pierce's now-familiar handwriting:

> Dear Evelyn,
> Cooler weather is coming.
> Wear this on Friday evening after your show.
> I'll have my auto waiting for you at the theater.
>   Yours,
>   SP

Mamma is at my side in a flash, studying the material. "Oh, Florence, this is well done." She leans over my shoulder, admiring the fine stitching. "I'll make you something to wear under it. Red satin. Mr. Pierce will be so pleased." She seems to be, as well.

On Friday night, as usual, chauffeured cars and carriages line the street outside the theater. Plenty of the girls in the company have admirers and suitors ready to whisk them away for the evening, many of them offering their fine chauffeured vehicles to ensure that no other man interferes. Is that what Mr. Pierce is—my admirer? My suitor?

The question stops me in my tracks as I stare at the gleaming phalanx of autos. Is Stanley Pierce courting me, like all these other fellows lined up to pay suit?

Do I wish for him to be?

I enjoy spending time with him, to be sure. He is kind and thoughtful and he makes me laugh freely and often, in spite of the difference in our ages. He knows so much of the world and always has some spiffy new idea for a grand adventure. And I'm endlessly grateful to him for his generosity—a largesse that has saved my family. Whatever Mr. Pierce is doing, I certainly don't wish for it to stop. Though I can't say in this moment if our friendly relationship is one that I wish were more romantic. Nor could I venture to guess how he feels on that topic.

What I *do* know is that his waiting auto is the nicest of the bunch. And he's already in the car when the capped chauffeur clicks open the door and hands me in. I flash him a smile. Mr. Pierce takes in my appearance in the new red cloak, the hood draped around my dark hair, and he returns the smile. "You look delightful, Evelyn. Just like Little Red Riding Hood."

His approval fills me with a warm feeling, and I settle onto the leather bench beside him as the car pulls us away from the theater and its crowds, out into the cool Manhattan night.

"Did your new hooded cloak allow you to slip out and escape without too many of your lovestruck admirers nipping at your heels?" Mr. Pierce asks me with a teasing sideways glance.

Is he jealous? I parry his comment with a chuckle and then ask: "Where are we going?" Penny and Annissa were heading out to dance at Rector's, but I don't feel as though I'm missing out, as I'm sure that Mr. Pierce has something splendid planned.

"I figured it would be fun to take you up to my tower."

I lean my head to the side. "Your tower?"

"You know I built Madison Square Garden, right?"

"Everyone in this city knows that, Mr. Pierce."

"Would you like to see it up close?"

"Yes! Very much."

He nods, apparently content with this response. Then he narrows his eyes, holding me with his gaze. "Say, would you do me a favor?"

"Sure." After all he's done for me, I would do him any favor.

"Would you call me Stanley? Or better yet, Stanny? All this 'Mr. Pierce' business feels awfully formal. Like you work for one of my companies. But we're friends, aren't we?"

"Of course we're friends," I answer, finding it entertaining that Mr. Pierce, in his luxurious motorcar, is bearing me through Midtown toward Madison Square Garden, and yet *he's* the one asking me to be his friend, with a bashful manner not all that different from that of some shy boy in the schoolyard. How is it that this gentleman can be made to feel timid in front of me, a poor chorus girl less than half his age? It makes me a bit dizzy, this power that he seems to think I wield.

His eyes are smiling as they trace a line from my face down the trim of my cloak, not ceasing their study until the velvet fabric pools in my lap and then spills over my legs. When he speaks next, his voice is soft, even a touch conspiratorial: "I thought it was time I gave you a tour of the tower. It's a nifty place. Really, you could fancy yourself in Spain; I built it to look like you are."

I've never been to Spain, but this fills me with excitement. He goes on, explaining that the place has a theater, several restaurants, a concert hall, an exhibition hall, a ballroom. "But tonight I thought we could go up to the rooftop garden. How does that sound?"

"It sounds bully," I answer, without another thought for the girls dancing at Rector's.

We roll to a stop at the corner of Madison Square Park, where Mr. Pierce's behemoth of a building rises up in brick and stone, the highest building for miles around. As Mr. Pierce—no, *Stanny*—helps me out of the auto, I take in a closer view of the ground floor, which is hemmed by a forest of ornate columns. It does look like something one could see in Spain—not that I would know from experience.

The broad front entrance is dark and appears to be locked for the evening, given the late hour, but Stanny steers me toward a side entrance, where he knocks only once. After just a beat, the door swings open from within, and a young male attendant keeps his eyes tilted downward as he mumbles, "Evening, Mr. Pierce." Stanny ushers me inside. How many times have I walked past this building, admiring its soaring dimensions and grand façade? And now I'm walking in with the man who built it!

It is quiet and dark inside; other than the attendant at the door, we may be the only people here. Stanny and I walk through a foyer, my heels clicking clamorously loud against the marble floor, and he escorts me toward an elevator.

"My special elevator, just for me," Stanny whispers as the machine chimes before us and an operator slides open the grated door. Stanny tells the attendant: "To the top." With a quick nod and a "yes, sir," the young man slides the grated door closed and presses the designated button. Up we soar. It's dizzying, really, to think how far that little girl from Wanamaker's has come with her dreams to one day ride an elevator.

"Finest building in the city," Stanny interrupts my musing, his voice tinged with pride as the gears of the cab turn and grind, carrying us ever upward.

"Do we have the entire place to ourselves?" I ask, my words humming with the electric excitement I feel.

"Mostly offices up here. Nobody will be here this late," Stanny explains.

At last we come to the top, and the elevator chimes again. The grated door is heaved open by the attendant, and I step out onto the top of the world. With Stanny just behind me I look over the view, and I can't help but gasp. I'm in the sky! The streetlamps and illuminated windows of Manhattan appear miles beneath our feet. Closer at hand, all around me, I see that I'm standing in a lush and colorful garden. A garden in the sky.

"Welcome, my darling girl, to my very own paradise," Stanny says, hovering just a step behind me, so close that I can smell the hint of cloves in his cologne. I sense that while I'm looking out and all around, he's looking only at me.

I hear the elevator door creak closed, and a droning bumblebee sound tells me that the cab is now descending; just Stanny and I remain up here. I'm so dazzled by the view that I still can't speak, but he does. "What do you think?"

"I *can't* think . . . only of how swell this is!"

The city is lit up beneath us on the chilly autumn night. I pull my new plush cloak a bit closer around my shoulders, thankful for its soft warmth. "Lady Liberty," Stanny says, pointing out a distant pearl of light beyond the dark waters of the New York Harbor. Closer to us, around the perimeter of the rooftop space, glimmering sconces throw blue and green shards of candlelight across the floor and walls. "Courtesy of my friend, Mr. Tiffany," Stanny says, noticing my admiration for the nearest blue sconce. "I believe you've also worked with him?"

"Yes," I answer. The mention of that name causes my head to spin again, memories dancing to the forefront of my mind—modeling in Philadelphia, working with Violet and Leah. Before Mr. Gibson, and Mr. Beckwith, and the Broadway stage, and now Stanny. It feels like another lifetime.

The scene around me is unlike anything I've ever seen. Beside the garden terrace is a grand room with a soaring glass ceiling and walls made of alternating panes of floor-to-ceiling mirrors and windows, their trim etched with gold leaf, which has a most dazzling effect. I look around the space with a blend of mystification and delight. Bugs with big eyes made of ruby-red glass hang from the ceiling like whimsical chandeliers. In the middle of the room is a cluster of massive couches upholstered in Stanny's beloved red velvet, piled with overstuffed red pillows. The only other piece of furniture is a grand piano with a burnished bronze statue beside it. "Bacchus," Stanny says over my shoulder as I admire the piece. "The god of all things pleasurable."

But best of all, I decide, is the view of the goddess, the golden statue of Diana that presides over this tower. Up here, she is not some distant and miniscule figure soaring over all of us. Here, at the top of the tower, she's practically within arm's reach, and as I take in her strong, naked form, I see that she is fierce, noble, entirely unapologetic. Stanny's golden lady dancing for all of the city.

I stand for a few minutes in dazed silence and admire her as she spins in her naked glory, hundreds of feet above the rest of the world. I'm so absorbed in my admiration that Stanny's voice catches me by surprise when he speaks, though he is quiet, even a bit tender. "I wish I had known you, Evelyn. When I designed this Diana. I would have put you on top of my tower."

I wrest my eyes from the golden goddess, sliding them to meet his stare. His face is open and earnest, and his next words surprise me even more. "Never mind. Instead I'll just have to put you on top of the world."

I smile, unsure what to make of the remark. Of any of this, really. Including the fact that I do believe, in this moment, that Stanley Pierce is a man remarkable enough to make anything possible.

We are standing side by side now, before the balcony of the terrace, as he asks: "Do you like it?"

"*Like* it?" I gaze out over the view. "It's like I'm in Eden."

"Eden?" He tips his head toward me. "Eden was dreadfully boring. I was thinking something a bit more exciting. You know Bosch?"

"Bosch?" I grip the railing, looking down on the buildings far below. Buildings that, from the street, seem impossibly tall. How Stanny has a way of changing my view on things.

"Of course you don't know Bosch." Stanny shrugs and offers a smirk. "A great Renaissance painter. He did a thrilling work called *The Garden of Earthly Delights*. A scene of humans enjoying themselves in every way. That's how I envision *this* garden to be."

Before I can form some reply, Stanny goes on: "I'll take you to Spain one day to see the piece."

"Really?"

"It would be fun to see it together. You could learn a lot."

I thrill at these words. "Like what?"

Stanny narrows his eyes, holding me with half a grin, weighing his next words for a moment. "Things that you've probably never imagined possible. But speaking of delights—how about some food? You worked hard tonight up on that stage; I don't want you wasting away."

He's always so thoughtful. He guides me across the terrace and past the large hall, toward a smaller room just adjacent, one that looks almost like a greenhouse with its wrought-iron framing and wall-to-wall glass panes. "Oh!" I pause at the doorway, delighted, as I take in the next scene. There's a colorful Turkish carpet laid across the center of the room and on top of that a spread that makes my stomach groan. I clap as I walk toward it, seeing medallions of filet mignon and lollipop bites of roast lamb. Cheese, olives, strawberries coated with chocolate, and éclairs. "Are we going to eat like pagans on the floor?" I ask.

He flashes me a grin. "Could be fun, no?"

We settle onto the carpet, and Stanny serves me a heaping plate. Where are the servants who conjured this magical spread? I don't hear even a distant sound of footsteps.

Stanny, who has made himself a plate and settled in beside me, says: "Open that perfect little mouth of yours." I do as he says, and he places a chocolate-covered strawberry on my tongue. I close my eyes and bite into it, the sweet flavors exploding across my mouth. I smile appreciatively as I open my eyes and see the look on Stanny's face—he's staring at me with intent concentration.

He stares a moment longer and then asks: "If you could go anywhere in the world, where would it be?"

I barely have to think before the answer spills out. "Paris."

"Why is that?" He takes a bite of the lamb on his plate.

"Who doesn't want to see Paris?" I muse aloud, hoping I sound sophisticated. "Why, the buildings, the art, the food, the fashion."

Stanny chews, swallows, then offers a decisive nod. "Yes, you'd love it."

As I fill my belly with Stanny's delicious food, he fills my mind with images of the Seine, and the massive Notre-Dame Cathedral, the gardens, and the cafés where they serve pastries filled with liquid chocolate and sugared cherries.

Then he changes tack, pointing down to the fabric that pools all around my legs. "So, do you like your new cape?"

I shift, swallowing a salty bite of olive. "I do. It's warm, and it's soft, and I do feel as though I could be Little Red Riding Hood in it."

He leans toward me, tipping his head as he answers, "Well, then, I promise I will always protect you from the Big Bad Wolf."

"I know you will, Stanny."

"Stanny," he says, repeating the nickname, and for a moment I fear that I've been too familiar with him. That perhaps he regrets inviting me to be so presumptuous. But then he says, "I like that, when you call me Stanny," and a feeling of relief washes over me. With his voice quiet, he looks back down at the red material that drapes over my shoulders and says, "I would like to have you photographed in that cape."

I nod. This is not a surprising statement to me, given how much of my life is spent getting either painted or photographed. The only reason it catches me slightly by surprise is that it's the first time Stanny has suggested it. With his eyes still cast downward, he asks: "What do you have on underneath?"

"Oh." I shift in my seat on the carpet and show him, slipping the velvet aside to reveal the red satin dress that Mamma has fashioned especially for this evening. She had such high hopes that Stanny would like the way this new dress complements his gorgeous cape, but to my surprise, Stanny raises his hand and quickly slides the top garment back into place, covering my shoulders and my new dress entirely. "It's all right," he says, his voice sounding slightly scratchy. "Keep it on."

He gets up, walks to the far side of the room, and returns a moment later with a bottle of champagne, which he shows to me as if I'm a discerning society gal who might send it back. "Moët & Chandon," he says, his French pronunciation flawless as he fills two crystal flutes. "From Paris. Since we now have plans to go there together."

I can't tell how serious he's being, but even if it's just a joke, I like that it's our joke.

I accept a full glass, and he clinks his own against mine. I close my eyes to take a sip, savoring that first taste as the cool liquid bubbles across my tongue and down my throat. "Tell me more about Paris," I say, forcing myself to take slow sips.

Stanny stares off toward the skyline of the city. "Well, there's this spot where the girls dance, up on the hill of Montmartre. You think Broadway is something, I'll take you to the Moulin Rouge."

"Sounds grand," I say.

He tells me about the dancers who kick their legs in unison with a precision so tight that they look to be part of the same body. And the red—of their feathers, their lips, their headdresses. "You know how I love the color," he says, leaning toward me now with the posture of a relaxed picnic goer, and I smile, swallowing the last drop from my glass, my head swirling with the champagne and the images of stylish French girls clad in red, kicking their legs to the lively music.

I tip my now-empty flute toward him, indicating I'd like more. As I do so, the cape slides off my shoulder, revealing my bare arm. Stanny's eyes lock on the exposed skin of my arm, my hand angled toward him proffering my empty champagne glass. After a brief moment, he takes my outstretched flute into his hands with uncharacteristic brusqueness and throws me a pointed look that causes me to tip back in my seat. When he speaks, his tone is suddenly and uncharacteristically sharp. "I think one is quite enough for you."

Stanny is also leaning back now, and a chasm that feels inexplicably wide stretches between us. He does not look at me when he says, "I thought you were a nice little girl."

His words are chilled with an undeniable tone of disapproval, and I feel my body stiffen. I tip my head to the side, looking at him in my confusion, but when he meets my stare, I can't read his expression. "Do you ask other men to fill your glass with pour after pour?" he asks.

"No," I say, my head fuzzy.

"If you want to be the type of lady that I know you can be, you'd do well to heed this advice: don't let men pour spirits down your throat."

"But Stanny, you are the one who . . ." I'm so perplexed, but I stop myself before I might say something to further offend him. I don't mean my words as an accusation; I'm merely seeking clarification. For he's the one who poured me champagne. He's the one who brought me out here tonight, late as it is.

"I'm different!" His voice is gravel. "Haven't I proven that? I wish to protect you. Can't you see?"

My breathing has gone shallow. I can't understand this sudden turn. When I say nothing, he breaks the silence, his voice decisive: "I think you've had enough. Let's go."

"Where?"

"Home. I'm bringing you home. You need your sleep. And your mamma."

I pull the cloak snug around my shoulders, shivering beneath the plush red velvet as I rise from the carpet. I'm no longer interested in the view, the food, the distant lights of the beautiful city so far below. Now I really do feel like Little Red Riding Hood, wondering why Stanny—who mere moments ago was crooning that he was my protector, the friend who would take me to Paris and put me on top of the world—is growling at me like a wolf.

Chapter Twenty

I wake the next morning feeling wretched, as memories come back to me like a wave. The private elevator, the soaring tower, the champagne, the naked golden goddess dancing on top of the world. My mind lingers over the dinner spread and Stanny telling me about art and Paris—promising to take me there. I felt as though I already was on top of the world.

Then what did I do to offend Stanny? Stanny, who has always been so generous and gentle. I groan as I rise from bed, forcing myself to dress and move through my toilette before Mamma senses my worry.

She's ordered in a delicious spread for breakfast, and I join her at the table. I have little appetite, but Mamma would surely notice if I were to skip the meal, so I'm helping myself to a hot roll when she asks, "How was your evening? You went for dinner after your performance? With Mr. Pierce? I swear, that man was sent to us from heaven."

I take a sip of coffee, attempting to keep my face even, but Mamma arcs an eyebrow. "How was it?"

"Fine," I answer, holding the coffee cup in front of my mouth like a shield.

"Just fine?"

"It was nice, Mamma." I try to offer a smile, but I can feel my features wobble. *Don't cry,* I tell myself. But already I've revealed too much.

Mamma slowly dabs the corner of her mouth with her fine-pressed-linen napkin. When she speaks next her words are quiet but sharp as arrows. "Florence, has something happened?"

I sit back in my chair, slowly lowering my cup into its saucer. For some reason, I don't feel I can tell Mamma much of *anything* about the previous evening. Not the first part of it—the tower, the pair of us alone up there. Stanny asking me to open my lips as he placed the chocolate-covered fruit into my mouth. The champagne. Nor his sudden anger with me. She'll erupt into hysterics, chiding me that I must not offend our patron! I must not lose his friendship! She won't end up back in a boardinghouse!

I don't want that either. No, I am well aware of the fragility of our current comfort—even without Mamma's reminders. I am determined to set this right with Stanny, whatever it is that I have done wrong. So I reassure Mamma that our evening together was nice, and she settles down, picking up her coffee once more and taking a long, slow sip.

"Well, then, if everything between the two of you is hunky-dory, I think I'll ask him about next season's wardrobe. It is time to start shopping, and if we wish to send to London or Paris for new spring gowns, these things take time."

I've lost my appetite. I'm not certain that today is the day to press Stanny to make arrangements for us to visit the modiste and run up a bill on his account for a pricy order.

Nevertheless, I keep quiet, wandering over to my piano and attempting to practice, but feeling shiftless and agitated. And an hour later, when there's a knock at the front door to our suite, I feel as though my stomach holds a hard stone, because I know it will be him, and I don't know how this visit will go.

But it's not Stanny at our door. It's the hotel concierge, delivering a parcel. "A gift for Miss Talbot."

Mamma beams as a tuxedoed footman enters bearing the massive profusion of fresh flowers that Stanny sends each morning. "Lilies today. Oh, how lovely!" she exclaims, breathing in their perfume. But then there is another heavy parcel placed before me on the piano, and I thank the gentleman as I quickly untie the ribbon. It's a pile of weighty leather books. I glance at each spine: Milton, Chaucer, Shakespeare, Dickens. A note on Stanny's familiar stationery says only: *"For the cultivation of your mind."* Well, then. I don't suppose he's too terribly vexed with me. I allow my smile to spread as wide as Mamma's.

When Stanny does call on us an hour later, he sweeps into our salon as he always does, and I feel a great relief to see his friendly demeanor. All, it would seem, is forgiven between us. I'm still confused, but I no longer feel sick with dread.

It's over tea that Mamma brings up the topic of shopping. To my surprise—and delight—Stanny quickly agrees that we should order new dresses on his account, as though we were merely asking him to pass the plate of cookies. "You must order from Paris," he says, taking a bite of a petit four. "And someday soon, when Evelyn can take a break from her show, I should like to bring you both to Paris myself, to shop in person at the House of Worth."

Mamma's cheeks flush, and I stare down into my teacup, biting my lip to stanch a wide grin. It's a peace offering, and I know it; he still wishes to show me Paris.

"But before Paris, my dear Mrs. Talbot, I was thinking that another trip, one less far-flung, is in order for you in the more immediate future. And well past overdue."

Mamma's eyebrows lift in a questioning expression, and Stanny goes on, "Your young son, how does he do at Chester Academy?"

Mamma's smile slips. She looks down at the table and answers, "Kit does very well." And it's the truth. We know from his letters that Kit is in good health. The boy loves school, just as I'm sure I would have.

But Mamma misses him fiercely. As do I. "You look melancholy," Stanny says, eyeing Mamma with a probing, sympathetic expression.

"Oh, well . . ." she says.

"A very understandable maternal longing to see your dear boy?" Stanny ventures.

"Well, yes. Of course I miss him."

Stanny presses his hands on the table and leans toward Mamma. "Would you allow me to remedy that?"

"How . . . do you mean?"

"Later this month is Thanksgiving," Stanny says. "He'll have a break from his studies, I presume?"

"Yes," Mamma says, her tone tenuous. "The plan is for him to stay with a cousin of mine near Pittsburgh."

Stanny offers a decisive shake of his head. "I would love to arrange a splendid reunion for you and your boy. I'll make accommodations for you to travel first-class by Pullman to Philadelphia. I'll arrange for your Kit to join you there. I'll book you a suite at the Rittenhouse. The two of you can visit, dine, shop, tour the city together. By the end of the week, you will have enjoyed his company, and he'll be ready to return to school, refreshed by a visit from his dear mother."

"It sounds lovely. . . ." Mamma's tone is bright but unbelieving. "Only, how could I ever afford such a reunion?"

"You need not worry about a single detail, least of all the expense," Stanny says. "Leave it with me."

Mamma grips her teacup in her fingers, throwing a look toward me. "But Florence, er, Evelyn could never leave New York for a week, not during Thanksgiving. It's one of the busiest weeks of the year for the theaters."

"No, she can't," Stanny agrees. "You are correct in that. Evelyn will need to carry on with her work, as her company depends on her."

Mamma is looking at Stanny as the pair of them speak about me. "I could never leave her alone."

"*Alone?*" Stanny leans back in his chair, wearing an expression on his face as though he's been unfairly slighted. "My dear Mrs. Talbot, she will not be alone. Your darling girl will be in good hands. I would never let any harm come to her."

Mamma throws me a questioning glance, and I can see how badly she yearns to accept Stanny's offer—how much she aches for this reunion, albeit brief, with Kit. We haven't seen him since Mamma enrolled him at Chester, since the cost of a trip would have been forbiddingly high.

"Come now, Mrs. Talbot," Stanny coaxes. "I dare say you might relish the opportunity to return to Philadelphia . . . under your newly changed circumstances?" He arcs an eyebrow. "A victory tour of sorts, eh? Perhaps you might even pop into a few of the stores that you once dreamed of visiting?"

Stanny is smiling, and now Mamma is, too. And then she does something unusual; she asks me how I feel.

The honest truth is I could turn green with envy; I wish to see Kit every bit as badly as Mamma does. But I do realize that what they've both said is true: the company is expecting me to perform, and we've been warned that Thanksgiving is one of the busiest times of the year for Broadway. So I answer, "I will be fine." And it's true enough—I'm here in a hotel, not that ramshackle boardinghouse. I'll have food to eat and work to keep me busy. If I get lonely I can ask Penny to spend the night with me, and I have no doubt she'd be thrilled to do so. Besides, a reprieve of a few days from Mamma's presence wouldn't be so terrible.

Mamma appears almost ready to accept Stanny's outrageously generous offer, but he helps to seal her decision: "You deserve this, my dear Mrs. Talbot. I want you to worry about nothing. It's all in my hands."

Mamma looks as though she could weep as she says, "I swear, you are sent to us from heaven." With one quick, appreciative nod, her consent is given.

Stanny smiles at Mamma before throwing me a wink, answering: "Evelyn knows I think heaven is a bit boring."

As NOVEMBER TURNS dark and gray, and the week of Mamma's trip approaches, she sees to her packing and grows increasingly nervous about the idea of leaving me. "Perhaps I ought to stay," she says on the eve of her departure. But I know how much she longs for this, and Kit does, as well. As jealous as I feel at their imminent reunion, I don't wish for them to miss out on their visit. And in truth, I've been looking forward to a week to myself, free of Mamma's fretting.

"I'll be fine," I reassure her.

She sighs, folding a rose-colored scarf into her valise. Then, perhaps more to herself than to me, she says, "Mr. Pierce has promised he will be your chaperone around town in my absence."

You never even chaperone me around town when you are here, I think.

"You promise me you won't go out with anyone but Mr. Pierce?"

"For the one hundredth time, Mamma, I promise."

"And you'll obey him?"

"Yes."

"You do promise?"

"I promise, Mamma."

"Good. Then you listen to Mr. Pierce, and you do as he says." She turns back to her packing. "I swear that man is our guardian angel. I don't like to think where we'd be right now if not for him. It seems there's nothing he won't do for us. And I'd do just about anything to keep his friendship."

Chapter Twenty-One

Mamma leaves that Sunday evening—by private railcar, just as Stanny promised—which means I'm home alone on Monday, my one day off from the theater, when Stanny comes calling.

The hotel concierge sees him in while I'm sitting down to a late breakfast. I'm still in my wrapper, taking advantage of this break from Mamma to sleep later and move a bit slower, but Stanny says nothing about that, or my loose, unkempt hair, as he joins me at the table and pours himself a cup of coffee. We sit together in companionable silence for a while, him thumbing through a copy of the morning paper, before he says, "I have planned quite a day for us."

I perk up. "What is it?"

"Finish your breakfast, and you'll see."

As we are readying to leave the suite, Stanny asks me to bring along my new red cloak, and since it's a chilly November day, I happily oblige. His auto and chauffeur await us below, and we climb in. After the short drive toward Madison Square Park, I'm thrilled to see that he's bringing us back toward the tower.

As we sweep through the crowded lobby and step once more into Stanny's private elevator, I say nothing of our last visit here, and neither does Stanny. The floors click by as my ears pop, and I giggle as I chomp my jaw.

This time when the elevator chimes and we step out onto the expansive terrace, I see that we are not alone. There's a man already up here, and I know immediately that this is a photographer Stanny has arranged to join us. A new face, a fellow with whom I've not yet worked.

Stanny puts an arm lightly on my lower back, ushering me forward. "Evelyn, meet Mr. Barty Sidwell." I accept the man's quick handshake as Stanny says, "Barty, here she is. Ain't she something?"

The man makes a sweep of my figure with his keen photographer's eye, taking in the rich hue of my red cloak, the wild flyaways from my loose braid, the contours of my unadorned face, and then he looks at Stanny, and I see something pass between them. As if I'm not standing right there, the man mouths the words, "How old?"

My spine stiffens. This photographer thinks I'm too young to do good work? I may be just a few weeks shy of seventeen, but I could show him entire books filled with my clippings. In that loud and silent moment when the two men have their gazes locked, I click over into work mode, stepping forward with an air of willfully summoned confidence as I say, "Mr. Sidwell, lovely to meet you." I'll prove him wrong, like every other doubter before him.

Then I slant a look toward Stanny, hitching an eyebrow—he didn't tell me I'd be working today. Stanny reads the question in my gaze. "Evelyn, if you want to be a serious stage actress, you are going to need to spiff up your portraits. The advertisements are nice, sure. But you need serious prints and lots of versatility to move into a higher circle. We'll get you some shots today that will be top-notch."

Stanny points toward a massive cedar trunk a few paces behind Mr. Sidwell. "I've sorted it all out. Consider it a gift from your biggest admirer."

I don't quite know what to say, but feeling both his eyes and the dubious eyes of this Mr. Sidwell on me, I decide to walk toward the cedar trunk, and I heave it open. As the lid groans wide, I'm hit by a wave of scents: perfume, dust, leather, and fur. Then Mr. Sidwell is over in the corner prepping his camera, and soon I smell the flash powder.

We set to work, planning to run through a parade of poses,

costumes, and scenes as we shoot. We begin with my new cloak from Stanny. "What do you think, Barty?" he asks. "I had it made just for her. Doesn't she look just like Little Red Riding Hood?"

"Indeed," answers Mr. Sidwell, looking at me through the lens. "It's scary, all right."

Mr. Sidwell and mostly Stanny walk me through a series of poses as the camera clicks away. Stanny has me turn sideways and shut my eyes. "Tip your head back, so we can see that neck. Yes, there it is. Get that, Barty. Now open your mouth. Like you're frightened. You're acting here, remember? Show them how frightened you are."

Once Mr. Sidwell insists that he's got the shot, Stanny reaches into the trunk and hands me something simpler. "What is this?" I ask, holding the starched dress of white cotton with a high collar and simple stitching along the sleeves.

"A little Quaker maiden," Stanny explains, so I step behind a makeshift silk screen to assume my next role.

After that, I'm a shepherdess in white lace that slips off my shoulders. Stanny asks me to undo my braid so that my hair falls loose around my face. Then he strings flowers through my hair and hands me a tall empty vase. "Now hold it out for the camera." I find it a touch odd, this pose, holding an empty vase tilted toward the camera, but I do as he directs, as does Mr. Sidwell behind his lens.

Next I step into my favorite outfit yet, a floor-length sheath of bright purple satin, with golden embroidery and shimmering crystals adorning the trim. "A Turk, my dear. Remember, I said we need variety here." Stanny is in full director mode, looking with his world-famous artist's eye, and I imagine him leading subordinates on one of his remarkable building projects with this same scrutiny and clarity of artistic vision. "Haughtier with the eyes, Ev. You are not some concubine among many. You are the sultana. There, that's more like it. Ain't she a find?"

By now I'm having fun. It's all dress-up and playacting, and this is moving faster than most photography sessions do because Stanny has such a clear vision for each scenario and costume. And each piece that he extends to me is more beautiful than the last. I find myself embracing the roles, feeling powerful when the men fall silent in appreciation and attention.

But the final costume, though gorgeous, catches me by surprise. "What now?" I ask, staring at a garment of swirling blue and green silk.

"It's a kimono," Stanny answers. "I had it made just for you, kid."

I reach a tentative hand forward, gently grazing the pristine silk with just one finger. The last time I wore a robe this delicate was with Mr. Beckwith, and I prefer not to linger on the memories of that day.

But Stanny wears a proud grin. "This kimono cost more than most families make in a year. I've ordered it from Tokyo. You can keep it when we are finished."

I drop my hand and draw in a deep breath. There's no reason for me to fear—he's said nothing about any sort of nude photos. This is just another costume, and a beautiful one at that. I meet his gaze. "Thank you, Stanny."

I change into the kimono, and when I reemerge, I see Mr. Sidwell setting up the final shot, arranging what looks like a pelt of white fur on the wooden floor before the window. "It's your polar bear," Stanny says.

"From my bedroom?" I ask, stunned that he managed to get the pelt here without my noticing. He really did think of everything.

Throwing a look toward Mr. Sidwell, Stanny says, "The thing is pure white, unblemished. Like it's never been touched before."

Mr. Sidwell nods, checking his lens and focusing on the pelt on the floor. I kneel down and graze just the tips of my fingers across the fur.

"Soft, yes?" Stanny takes a step back, as if to survey the scene. "You make a splendid geisha, kid."

"Thanks, Stanny."

When I meet his approving stare, I note how his demeanor has changed; he looks a bit timid now, perhaps even bashful, entirely unlike his typical mien. When he speaks, his tone is uncharacteristically soft, and he jerks his chin toward the pelt. "Lie down."

I do as he says, folding onto my right side, tilting my face up toward the camera, my head cradled in the crook of my right arm. I'm awaiting artistic direction as to what sort of facial expression Stanny thinks best when he surprises me by saying, "Pretend you're asleep."

I glance toward him, confused. He gives a quick nod, saying, "Shut your eyes. That's right."

So I close my eyes. And I notice instantly that it's not hard to pretend at sleepiness. On the contrary—after the hours of work and the costume changes, I'm suddenly exhausted. The silk feels like the softest of caresses against my skin. The downy fur is the perfect pillow against my cheek, my entire body. I've done great work—and I know that I looked beautiful. Stanny is happy; even the photographer seems pleased. Now I'm set to have a book of work that will be better than anything I could have imagined. It's been an all-around smash of a day, and knowing that, I allow myself to surrender.

"Yes, so lovely," I hear Stanny say. This is the easiest shot yet. I lie still in contented repose, slipping almost into a trance, like I first learned to do back in Philadelphia working with Leah. The room is warm, the clicking of the camera so rhythmic, each shot an affirmation that I am doing good work. My breath is even, my heartbeat slowing. . . .

I do not stir from this trancelike state until I feel a soft hand gently nudging my shoulder. I blink my eyes open, taking in the shape of Stanny's outline hovering beside me. Has it been moments? Hours? A yawn slips out, and I smile, somewhat abashed at the realization that I may in fact have fallen asleep. I don't see the photographer anywhere.

Stanny is holding me in the tenderest of stares, his light eyes filled with a warm and affectionate glow. When he speaks, his voice sounds low and throaty, little more than a whisper as he extends a hand to help me sit up. "Well, my little geisha, that's all."

"Are we... Have we gotten enough shots?" I rise to stand, rearranging the loose silk around my legs.

"We have gotten perfect shots," Stanny says, his voice soft. "You've done wonderful work. And now let's get you safely home. Did I not promise your mamma I'd take care of you?"

Chapter Twenty-Two

I still feel giddy the next day. Stan called the session "a triumph" as he deposited me at the front door of my suite. To have won his approval at our first photography session together, when I know what a keen artistic eye he has, fills me with a warm glow.

My ebullient mood continues when, that evening outside the theater, I see him waiting for me once more. "Stanny!" I skip over to him, pulling my silver fur stole tighter around my shoulders against the chilly November damp.

"Hello, my bonbon." He looks just as happy to see me.

"I didn't see you in the theater," I say.

"I couldn't make it this evening, but I still wished to see you." Stan opens the motorcar door and hands me in.

As I'm settling in, I spy Penny stepping out of the theater door. She's chatting with Trixie and Annissa as they head out for the night, perhaps to Rector's. I feel a pang in my belly that only intensifies when Penny spots me, too, throwing me a cheerful smile and wave. And then she turns back to the girls, and the three of them are off, an undeniable part of me wishing I could join them. I stifle a sigh—there's no use longing for a night out with Penny and the girls. Mamma's orders. And besides, I've got the best companion in town sliding into the auto right beside me. "Where are we going?" I ask Stan.

"Why? Do you have other plans?" His demeanor is playful and a bit jealous.

"No," I say, chuckling as I settle into my seat. "You know I'm not allowed to go out while Mamma is away. At least, not with anyone but you."

"That's right," he clucks. "Mother's rules, you poor dear. Stuck with me. Is it a wretched fate?"

I toss him a sideways grin. "Not at all."

"Thank goodness," he says with exaggerated relief. "Thought I'd spare you from having to head straight home for a lackluster evening. I've set up a little supper in your honor at my place."

"In my honor?"

"To celebrate your work yesterday. With those prints, you'll soon have every stage company knocking on your door offering you a leading role."

I don't even try to quash my smile as I stare out the window of his auto, the glittering exteriors of Broadway's Great White Way streaming past like so many luminescent pearls on a necklace. To think—all of these theaters might soon be offering me roles. I have no reason to doubt Stan.

I feel as though I'm on top of the world. I also feel as though I could eat a feast, as usual after a show. "A dinner party sounds grand, Stanny," I say, offering him an appreciative grin.

We roll up to his townhouse on Twenty-fourth Street and I hop out, walking past the darkened windows of the next-door toy store. I throw a glance toward the displays but can barely make anything out. Stan opens his front door, and we step inside. The space hangs in silence and shadow, the line of sconces throwing off only a dim glow.

I grab the banister and begin to climb the stairs. Stan, behind me, says, "I recall how timid you were on these stairs the first day you visited. I called out to you."

I can't help but grin, remembering that day with Dinah and Dolly. How timid I'd felt, struck by confusion when I heard the sudden and faceless voice. "It sounded like you were the voice of God."

"Not too far off the mark, is it, my dear girl? Haven't I pulled you from hell and seated you at the finest banquet in paradise?"

I pause my climb for just a moment, turning to look at him over my shoulder.

Stan's mustache turns up with his half smile. "You know your mother calls me heaven-sent?"

"Of course I know that," I reply. I'm struck, yet again, by the fact that this man who sits atop the world seems to crave my adulation.

"Now you walk in like you own the place. Country mouse no more, my pet. You are my little city mouse." My cheeks go warm at this; I like appearing sophisticated and confident to a man like Stanley Pierce.

We arrive at the landing, and I lead the way as we enter his drawing room. Stanny helps me out of my fur stole, his hands hovering a moment on my shoulders, his lips brushing close to my neck as he says, in a soft voice, "In fact, I'd amend that. Maybe you aren't a mouse anymore at all. Maybe you're the cat."

I turn, leaving my fur wrap in his hands as I face him, and I see his appreciative stare as his eyes sweep my figure, draped in a flattering gown of sapphire blue, my collarbone and neck bare, save for a spritz of my favorite perfume and a thin strand of pearls. Both gifts from Stanny, of course. He is quiet for a long moment as he takes me in, and then, voice a bit hoarse, he says, "Why, the way you can play with my heart. Your sweet little smile just undoes me. Yes, you are the cat."

The last time we were alone together, truly alone, at that dinner on the floor on top of the tower, he got so cross with me—and so quickly—because he thought I wasn't acting like a good girl. But tonight, he seems different. He seems to want some playful banter, some impish flirtation. In fact he seems to be inviting me into it, so I oblige. "I'm the cat? And what are you?"

"The mouse." A smile tugs his lips upward. "Can I beg you not to be too terribly fierce? Perhaps don't be the cat. Can you be a kitten?"

I tip my head to the side. "That sounds better."

"My little kitten." He tilts forward and places a quick kiss on top of my head. As he does so, he breathes in the scent of my hair, a bouquet of jasmine and honeysuckle.

"You smell like perfection," he whispers into my ear, his breath pulling a shiver to my skin.

I bite my lower lip, my confidence wobbling for a moment. Something about the intensity of his stare, his voice, his entire demeanor—it feels unnervingly like fire now. A fire that could be dangerous or, at the very least, entirely new. But I force myself to meet his eyes. "It's the perfume you gave me."

He nods once, then looks away, around the room. "You know, Kitten, I said you walk in like you own the place. You *can* . . . own the place."

"What do you mean?"

"All of this. All of this could be yours. I've always sworn I would never bind myself to one woman. But . . . I never planned on you."

Is he proposing marriage? Is he telling me he loves me? He, who has always told me he's my protector, my benefactor, who has always looked after me with the care and solicitousness of a dear friend.

But of course I've known there was something more. Or at least, I've suspected it. The lingering, direct way he looks at me sometimes. I may be young and naïve, but I'm not a fool. I know the power I have over men, and have had almost since girlhood. And Penny made those quips, not to mention Dolly and Dinah. But Stanny has never crossed a line toward anything romantic. Is that what this is now?

Surely he can read my confusion because he waves his hands, as if swatting away a pesky fly, and his features rearrange themselves into an expression of jovial cheer, one I'm far more familiar with. "Let's just enjoy ourselves, shall we?" he says. "I want nothing more than to make you happy, at all times."

Relief washes over and through me, so much that I feel the space between my shoulders soften. I look around his grand salon, all too willing to drop the rope of tension that has unspooled between us. "Where is everyone else?" I ask.

"Everyone else? It's just us. Aren't I enough?"

"Of course. I only thought . . . since you said you'd arranged a supper . . ."

"Yes, Kitten, for us. To celebrate our work together yesterday and plan your bright future. You were a triumph, my darling. I can't wait to see the pictures. I've told the photographer he'd better make two copies because I want to keep some, too. Which costume did you prefer?"

As he talks, he offers me his arm and guides me to the dining table set for two, with gleaming candelabras throwing a soft amber light over the fresh-cut flowers and crystal stemware.

I consider his question for a moment as he helps me into my chair and takes the seat opposite. "The geisha," I answer. It was certainly the easiest pose, to lie there and slip into repose.

"I quite liked you on that white bearskin. You were the image of purity. Like you were dreaming."

"I *was* dreaming," I say. "I believe I fell asleep."

"Dreaming of what?"

I shrug as I fan the linen napkin across my lap. "Probably chocolate-covered strawberries."

He leans back in his seat, pressing his hand to his heart in a playful gesture, as though he's been wounded. "Not dreaming of me, then?"

"Why would I need to dream of you, Stanny? You make every day of my life a dream when I'm awake."

"I like that," he says, tilting toward me. "Yes, I like that. See, how can you deny it? You are indeed the cat, and you are toying with me. Or at the very least playing with me."

"I'm not, Stanny. I mean it. You make each day a dream."

"But you know, I dream of you." He leans over the table now, reaching his hand for mine, and I give it to him. When he goes on, I see that we've ventured into serious territory once more. "Awake and asleep. You are all I can think of. You have taken over my entire life."

My heart is knocking against my throat. Here it is again, this serious side of Stanny. I don't know what to make of it. Now I can feel my racing heartbeat in my fingers, as Stanny wraps his palm softly around my hand. I blink, and for a fleeting moment, my mind plays a trick on itself: I see another man gripping my hand. A dirty Pittsburgh boardinghouse, an invitation to step into his room. I blink again, and the scene rights itself as I see Stanny once more. This gracious room with this beautiful table. *I am safe,* I tell myself, trying to calm my frayed nerves.

As if sensing my agitation, Stanny looks down at our clasped hands and releases me. "Here I go, coming on too strong. You do have that effect on me. I'm sorry, my little pet. Where was I? Ah, yes, champagne. It is a party, after all."

He pours out two crystal flutes, handing me one. "To you, Evelyn Talbot."

"And to you, Stanley Pierce," I say, clinking my glass against his before taking a big sip, hoping that the cold bubbles will help to calm my rattled nerves and quell this uncharacteristic awkwardness that keeps rising up between us.

The first course, in addition to champagne, is oysters, and I eat almost a dozen. The delicious food does help to settle me, or at the very least, distract me. As we eat, we speak of the show; he asks after the girls and wants to know to whom I'm close. I tell him Penny is my dearest friend.

"Would you say she's your confidante?" he asks, forking himself an oyster and popping it into his mouth.

"A confidante? I suppose so, yes. Although, it's not as though I have much to confide."

I see the lurch of his throat as he swallows the raw oyster. Staring at me, he offers half a playful grin and says, "That so? You don't have any naughty little secrets?"

"I'm afraid not," I say, taking a sip of champagne. "The show, then home. Or out with you. Occasionally a night of dancing with Penny." Though my outings with the girls have become less frequent, now that Stan whisks me away so often. I take another sip of my champagne, then add: "Why, other than Penny, you probably know more about my life than anyone." Certainly more than Mamma.

"What about Dolly? Aren't you close with her and Dinah?"

I shake my head, frowning. "They've dropped me, it seems."

"Why?"

"I'm not entirely sure." I lower my glass to the table, then I make an admission. "Since the day I came here to meet you."

"I suspected that might happen." He dabs at the corner of his mouth with his napkin, offering a knowing nod. "They are jealous of you, Kitten. Or, at least, threatened by you."

"Threatened by me?"

Stanny takes a long sip of champagne before he says, "I think Dinah thought her daughter would be the next star."

"Well, can't she still be?"

He flashes a smirk. "Dolly can't hold a candle to you. No one can. You are incomparable, Kitten." Stanny reaches for the bottle of champagne, refills my flute nearly to the top.

I throw him a questioning look. "But I thought you told me . . . only one glass."

"We're having oysters," he says, flashing me a wink as he refills his own glass. "It goes too well with the oysters, does it not?"

I don't argue, happily accepting the second glass and taking a sip before helping myself to another oyster. I wonder when the rest of the food will arrive, since my stomach is still pretty empty and I don't think oysters alone will fill it. But until the next course is brought, I allow myself to enjoy the champagne.

We sit in silence for a moment, my mind turning back to Dolly and Dinah, but his voice pulls me from these thoughts. "Besides, you've shown me how much you have grown, my darling. I don't think you are such a little girl anymore. You steal the light from every other gal. And yesterday, why, you showed me you could be anything from a little shepherdess to a Turkish sultana. A queen. Yes, I think you're ready to be treated as such. As a lady. As a queen."

His eyes hold that fiery intensity again, and I'm tempted to fidget in my seat. But I'm spared as a footman appears in the doorway, declaring, "It is midnight, sir."

"Ah." Stan looks from the servant back to me, pressing himself away from the table. "If you'll excuse me for just a brief moment, my dear, I have to take a telephone call."

Stanny gets up to leave the room, but not without refilling my glass once more. *Odd, I think, that the footman appeared to tell him the time, not that there was a telephone call. And what busi-*

ness does he do at midnight? But my head feels fuzzy from the drink and the long wait for the food, from the fatigue of a full day, so I decide not to puzzle too much on the matter, instead raising my glass and draining my champagne as I sit alone in the large room.

It's a while before he's back, rejoining me at the table and pouring me more champagne from a freshly opened bottle.

"Who was it?" I ask, embarrassed when a hiccup escapes along with the words. I instantly put my hand over my lips.

"Pardon?" he asks, grinning at my hiccup.

"On the telephone."

"Oh. It was Mr. Edison. Thomas Edison."

"As in . . . the man with the glowing lamps?"

"The very one." He nods, leaning back in his chair. "Would you like to meet him someday? A real magician?"

"Oh, very much."

"Then I shall arrange it. I will do anything I can, Evelyn, to wave my wand so that you may live in a world of magic. But before that, how about some dessert?" He reaches into his pocket. I wish to ask: *What about the rest of the supper?* But he has retrieved a small nugget of what appears to be chocolate, and I simply love chocolate. That, and I don't wish to offend him when he's just served me oysters and champagne. He unwraps the tasty morsel and breaks off a piece.

I take the offered chocolate into my palm. "Aren't you having any?"

"I'm full." He pats his tummy. "But I know you can't resist your sweets."

I take a bite, closing my eyes in appreciation at the rich, nutty flavor. He refills my champagne again, but I don't wish for more. As I finish the nugget, the thought of my massive bed back at the hotel seems suddenly most appealing.

When a servant appears at the threshold, asking if Mr. Pierce would like him to clear the dishes, Stanny hastily orders the fellow out. "Leave us," he replies, his voice almost like a growl.

I look across the table and say: "I'm tired." The fatigue has hit me like a brick all of a sudden. I'm so exhausted that I feel as though I can barely keep my eyelids from closing. And my head feels heavy, unpleasantly so.

Stanny is looking directly at me, but makes no move from the table. "You should rest, my darling."

I want to fold over and drop my head right here on the table. "Can you bring me home?" I ask, hesitant to summon a hansom on my own. I doubt I would be able to stay awake for the short ride to the hotel.

"You can sleep here, Kitten. It's easier that way. My driver is gone for the evening."

This strikes me as unusual since Stanny always offers his auto to see me safely home after our postshow outings, no matter the hour. But my mind is beginning to fray at the edges, like a carpet coming unraveled. I find it hard to understand what he's saying. My bed is all I want. But then, he has no driver. And not having to travel does sound easier.

"I have plenty of room," he says. "You're not to worry." He helps me from the table since my feet feel suddenly leaden beneath me. I wobble silently up the stairs, his arm around my waist the only thing keeping me from tumbling down the entire flight.

Into the bedroom we go, the red room with the massive bed, the parasol dangling from the mirrored ceiling. The space we visited together on the day of my first luncheon in his home. It's past midnight, and the rich red drapes are drawn, and the room glows with a rosy candlelight that dances around me. The combination of the jittery flames and the deep, blood-red hue of the velvet furnishings strikes me as too much. I feel as though I might be sick.

The feeling only worsens when I look up, into the mirrors overhead. Stan, at my side, does the same, smiling at my reflection. "Surrounded by Evelyns," he says, his voice much more lucid than I feel, "just as I would always have it be."

But I don't like the way I can see a dozen of myself, as though I've been trapped in so many different shards of shattered glass. As though I myself have been shattered. I glance back downward, attempting to steady myself as the room sways.

That swing is in the corner, just as I remember it, and overhead that paper parasol. "This . . . Is this your bedroom?" I try to ask, but my mouth feels stuffed with marbles.

Stanny doesn't answer; instead he says only: "You can have my bed, darling. I'd like you to be comfortable."

The four-poster bed is the only thing in this room that appeals to me at present. I say, "Thank you," but again my words sound slurred.

"Would you like a quick swing before bed, Kitten?"

I shake my head, no. My face feels warm but not in a pleasant way, more like a fever. But Stanny is guiding me toward the swing, and I'm too tired to protest. He practically lifts me up onto the seat. I just want to shut my eyes. But then he's pushing me. I struggle in the seat; it's too much for me to hold on, though I try. I grip the ropes, grasping for—but not reaching—the words to ask him to stop.

He keeps pushing me. I'm dizzy, too dizzy, and now there's something like a drumbeat between my ears. With the mirrors above me, I see myself from every angle as the swing arcs me through the air. It's too much. But Stanny apparently feels quite the opposite: "Just what I want, Evelyn on all sides!" His voice sounds a thousand miles away. My hands have gone clammy, and I can't hold on to the ropes anymore. I can't even keep my eyes open. I slump, and the next thing I feel is the sensation of falling. Backward, off the swing, until I feel that his arms are there for me. And as I slip, finally, into a black slumber that won't release its grip, I think, *Oh, good, Stanny has caught me. I'll be all right.*

Chapter Twenty-Three

The drumbeat in my ears recedes, growing fainter and fainter, as I become aware of the feeling of silk against my bare skin. And under that, an ache, deep and unfamiliar. I blink open my heavy eyelids, pushing against a fog that doesn't wish to lift. Darkness. There are bed-curtains, and they are drawn, and that's the cause of the impenetrably inky black. I'm in a bed.

The sound next to me is slow, rhythmic—rasping breath. A snore. I am not alone! I squint to take a closer look. I know that large body. Stanny is beside me. Stanny, asleep and undressed.

I look down: the silk against my skin is the bedsheet and nothing more.

I, too, am undressed. I scramble to pull the sheets higher to cover my breasts.

I notice it again, that deep ache. I swipe the bed-curtain aside, allowing in a sliver of light, for it is daytime, early morning I guess, and I peer down under the sheet. Two smears of red run along the tops of my thighs, a brighter color than the rich velvet bedding all around us. And before I can think, I start to scream.

Stanny rouses from his slumber, his eyes opening into two wide coins. He seems far less dazed than I feel, for he immediately sits up and declares: "For God's sake, Evelyn, don't!"

"What happened?" I begin to cry, my throat raspy and dry, my tears coming hot and fast. Tears of confusion and fear and shame. *What have I done? Lord, help me. What will Mamma say?* I heave another sob, unable to stanch it even in spite of Stanny's censure.

"Put this on," he says with a sigh, reaching through the bed-curtains to grab something. Even just that view of his bare back, pale skin stippled with copper and gray hairs, his white arms—it all makes me want to curl up and sink through the bed. And then he's facing me, and he tosses me a scarlet kimono. Oh, I've had enough of this blasted red. My head aches. And so do other parts of me, parts that I've never before named.

Stanny's facial expression softens. His demeanor is suddenly tender as he reaches toward me and pulls me into an embrace, his fingers stroking up and down the bare flesh of my arms. "Please don't cry, my darling. It's all over. You've done very well. And now we belong to one another. We love each other, don't we?"

I don't understand what he means. *It's all over.* What is over? But I nod, because I need to be out of his arms. Out of this bed, this room, this very house. "Can I go home?" I ask, my voice sounding choked, more tears seeping out.

"Yes, my darling. I'll have them bring round the auto. Shall I ride with you?"

"No, I'll be fine," I say, hoping he'll believe my lie. I scramble out of the bed, feeling a fresh assault of stomach-curdling shame as I bend over to pick up the heap of my clothing from the floor, the beautiful sapphire dress of last night, which I have no recollection of shedding.

BACK IN MY room at the hotel, alone, with the door locked, I fall into my bed, but there is no sleep to be had. My head aches and my mind fails me: I cannot make sense of any of this. How did I end up in Stanley Pierce's bed, naked and in pain, with him asleep beside me?

The day brightens to midday, and New York teems outside my window like a menacing, unknowable place. I remain in bed, unable to move in any way other than this unstoppable trembling.

Mamma has me booked for work this afternoon. I am to pose for a Mr. Willard, who has hired me as his model for a marble piece called *Maidenhood*. I telephone the hotel concierge and ask him to send my regrets to Mr. Willard. "I'm unwell," I say, my voice shaky. I *am* unwell; it's the truth. Then I ask the concierge to also send a messenger to the theater to let them know I won't be able to make it for the evening's show. I picture Penny and the crowded preshow dressing room, but it feels nauseating to think of them all there together, colorful and carefree, so I blink and force the scene away. Tonight, for the first time since I've started working on Broadway, I will miss a performance. They will pull another chorine to dance as the Spanish Maiden. I'm not a maiden anymore! I collapse back into bed, clutching the bedsheets tight to my neck.

The sky darkens outside my window. I know I should bathe—I should wash the scarlet evidence of my stains off my thighs, but I can't bring myself to rise from bed. So there I lie, numb, as the hands of my clock make their slow and unrelenting rounds. Later, when I hear a knock on the door of the suite, I still don't stir.

I know who it is. Of course I know. I glance once more at the clock on the marble-topped bedside table—it's nine o'clock in the evening. The show is well underway.

Stanny lets himself in. He has a key, I realize. He's knocked all those other times, waited for a servant to announce him as a show of courtesy. But of course he has a key. He's the one paying the bills. It's his suite, after all. I'm here only at his pleasure.

"Kitten?" his voice calls out in the dark foyer. I don't answer. My whole body clenches as I hear his footsteps against the cold marble floor, hear him fumbling around in the dark, for I haven't clicked on a single lamp.

He does knock this time, at the threshold of my bedroom. "Evelyn?"

I make a sound like a groan, my voice hoarse, but he takes this as his invitation to enter. When he switches on the nearest lamp, it makes my head hurt even more. I wince as he asks, "Have you eaten anything?"

I force myself to look toward him, and I see that he's carrying a tray of food from the kitchens downstairs. My stomach flips at the thought of sharing another dinner with him. The shame alone could make me sick.

Stanny lowers the tray onto my bedside table and sits, perched at the edge of my bed. I roll over, hugging my knees into my chest.

Stanny puts a tenuous hand on my back, and my frame stiffens. I hear him heave a sigh, but otherwise the room pulses with silence. A silence that he eventually breaks: "My darling, we did what two adults do when they are in love."

Am I an adult? Are we in love? My head swirls, but this time I don't cry. In place of the hot tears and raw ache, this time my entire being goes numb. I say nothing, so Stan eventually goes on. "Did you . . . well, did you know what that was?"

I shake my head. I'm still not sure, only that we did *something*, and it can never be undone, and now my thighs are stained, and my insides ache, and I don't feel as if I'll ever be able to look another person in the eyes again.

Stan sighs again, and when he speaks, his tone is that of a gentle and patient elder. "We offered one another our bodies for pleasure." He must see my confused grimace, because he tries another tack: "Do you remember the painting I told you about, by Bosch? *The Garden of Earthly Delights?*"

I nod. That feels like another lifetime. Another girl saw that painting. Everything that happened before last night was in the life of another girl. *Do you remember . . .* The last thing I remember from last night is seeing my reflection in a million mirrors of shattered and splintered glass.

Stan goes on. "Why, it's really only meant to be that—pleasure. You weren't so unwilling last night. You never once told me no, or even asked that we stop."

Is that true? I can't remember; I don't know. The shame is a white-hot coil in my stomach. I have to say something. "But . . . I didn't know—"

"Isn't that what I'm here for, my beauty?" Stan interrupts. "To teach you all the things that you don't know? To show you all the wonderful things that make this life good and pleasurable? You told me yourself how thankful you are that I am teaching you about all of the finest pleasures in life."

The room is tilting sideways. I blink, trying to understand.

"Was it . . . 'good and pleasurable'?" I repeat his words, but I can't bear this, so I close my eyes in shame.

"It certainly was." He sits up a bit straighter on the edge of the bed. "You really don't remember?"

I shake my head. I'm trembling again.

"There, there, no need for all this."

But now I'm crying, and I can't stop. Stan is still the patient and enlightened instructor opposite my wayward pupil's demeanor. "Kitten, darling, you must pull yourself together." He exhales slowly. "I heard that you had the hotel staff telephone the theater and tell them you are unwell. One night is fine. Everyone takes sick once in a while. But we really must get you back on your feet. I want you at work tomorrow, all right? You don't want to give people any reason to doubt you. Or worse, gossip."

Stan's tone, his words, everything he's saying to me right now reminds me that Mamma insisted I do as Stan said while she was away. I promised her I would.

Mamma! Just thinking about her makes my stomach flip on itself again. What would she say? How will I hide this from her?

Stan interrupts these miserable thoughts. His words are quiet, barely a whisper even though we are alone in the suite, as he leans toward me. "You *do* know that every girl does it, right?"

I swallow, and it feels as if I have shards of glass in my throat. But my curiosity gets the better of me, and I meet his gaze. "They . . . they do?"

Stan's tone is one of unassailable certitude as he answers: "Yes, they do."

"Everybody does . . . what we did?" *Dinah? Dolly? Trixie? Even Penny? And yet I've never heard about it?*

Stan nods. "Everybody does what we did, my darling. It's just that nobody talks about it. At least, nobody who is smart."

I let out a long exhale, realizing as I do so that I've been holding my breath. I don't know if I believe this. Every night when we are getting dressed backstage, and singing, and rouging our cheeks—all those girls around me, they've also done whatever it is I did with Stanny last night? Is that why Penny asked me about kisses during my rides in the back of Stan's motorcar? Did she assume we'd done so, because that's what she does with fellows?

"Now, then." Stanny makes to rise from the edge of my bed. "I'm going to leave so that you can rest. And you ought to eat something. I'll leave this supper here. Take a bath, Kitten. Hopefully by tomorrow you'll feel back to yourself. Before I go, I'm going to give you a kiss. Nothing more, my darling. Just a kiss, because that's what adults do."

I shut my eyes, clenching everything tight as I feel his body lean toward me, and then he places a quick, chaste kiss on my lips.

When I open my eyes, he's looking at me appraisingly. "Was that so bad?"

"I suppose not," I say, but my heart is hammering, and my stomach feels tight as a knot. I'm glad that it was only a quick kiss. I don't want anything more from Stanny. I want him to go, to leave me alone, so that I can try to think about all he's just said.

At the threshold of my dim bedroom, Stan turns, hovering in the shadows. "Remember, don't be a chatterbox, Evelyn." His voice is cool now, with a hard edge. "That's most unbecoming. Doing this . . . there's nothing wrong in it. It's the talking about it that gets a girl into trouble."

Chapter Twenty-Four

I move like a wraith around my rooms. All solid substance feels vaguely foreign; even my own flesh feels as though it is no longer real, not part of me. Flesh, after all, has betrayed me. I bathe, hating the too-sweet scent of the soap that Stanny gave me. Scrubbing my thighs, washing away the stains, the taunting evidence of my brokenness. I close my eyes and remain underwater for as long as my aching lungs can bear it and then a bit longer. I am a carved-out casing, hollow and cored, the only thing inside me a dull and constant throbbing.

I'm glad my mother is not here. She'd know; she'd see my unraveling. *Mamma*. But she'll be back in a few days. It's as Stanny says: I must pull myself together before she returns. Before she, or anyone else, can sense that something deep within me has shattered.

I do as Stanny insists: I get myself to the theater for the next evening's show. I feel a bit wooden, a bit tense, but I make my way through the steps, even my solo number, and the audience applauds as if they don't notice anything too terribly amiss. They are all just happy that I'm back.

The girls are their usual bubbly selves backstage, and I do my best to smile and play the part of the Evelyn they all know. I'm grateful that the makeup and costumes do their bit to hide me. Only Dinah seems to guess something is amiss, holding me with a lingering look before she leaves for the night, but otherwise the evening goes off uneventfully.

Or at least, that's what I'm thinking. But when Penny lingers beside the backstage door and grabs me on my way out, my hopes of getting through the night without incident are dashed. "Kid, everything all right with you?" she asks.

"Yeah," I answer, not meeting her eyes as she hooks her arm through mine.

"You seem . . . not your usual self."

"I had a sore throat." We emerge into the chilly night, and Penny pauses our steps. She's staring at me, but I still won't return her gaze. I wish I could—but to let her look into me might break me open all the way.

She keeps her pointed gaze fixed on me as she whispers, "You'd tell me. Right, Ev?"

"Tell you what?" I blink, fighting against the needling in my eyes.

"You'd tell me if there was anything wrong? If you needed my help?"

"'Course I would." I shrug, sliding out of her arm, pretending to be distracted by the hoots and hollers of the men gathered all around. But I can't stop thinking about Stan's words: *You do know that every girl does it*. Does Penny do it? But to ask her would be to reveal that I did. Or, at the very least, to open myself up to further questions. No, I can't possibly broach all of that with her. Not now, not yet.

It's for that reason that I'm actually slightly relieved to see Stan's cranberry-red auto waiting for me outside the theater. I kiss Penny's cheek, tell her good night, and hop into the warm back seat. I'm less relieved, however, to see Stan seated inside. "Oh, hello," I say.

"Hello, Kitten. Surprised to see me?"

I fumble for words to form some reply.

"It *is* my motorcar, after all. And chauffeur." Stan offers me a playful wink. "Good show. I'm proud of you."

"I didn't see you in the theater."

"I couldn't make it tonight. But I heard from . . . I heard you did well."

"Oh," I say, turning away to look out the window. *What, does he have spies reporting to him from inside the theater?*

I don't have anything further to say, but he does. "I thought I'd see you safely home. Get you some dinner ordered up from the kitchens. I promised your mamma I would take care of you."

Now I pull my gaze from the window and look at him, incensed by the fact that he's brought her up. "I doubt Mamma would approve of . . . you know. . . ." I arc an eyebrow, but he doesn't take up the thread of my words. It's as though he wants *me* to say it. So I do. "Of what you did the other night."

"What *we* did," he corrects me, shifting in his seat. He throws a look toward the chauffeur in the front, and then turns back to me, his words barely a whisper. "Evelyn, darling, you're absolutely right."

I'm so surprised that he's agreeing with me that I remain silent. He goes on: "Kitten, your mother would be so terribly jealous."

"*Jealous?*" I nearly spit the word.

"Darling, it's always been the three of us. I've always taken care of you both. And I always will. But now, well, this is something special that only you and I share." He leans his body toward mine, and I feel the instinctual urge to recoil. Whether he sees that or not, I don't know, but he narrows his eyes and flashes half a grin as he says, "Yes, she'd be green with envy."

I rip my gaze away, looking back out the window and the stream of lights and buildings that whir by. But I don't see any of it. No, because my mind can't stop seeing the image of his pale back beside me in the red bed. *Mamma would be* jealous?

"We can never tell her," Stan goes on, his low voice filling the tense quiet. "We don't want to hurt her, do we?"

Before I find any words to answer, the auto rolls to a halt. Stan looks out the window. "Ah, we're here. The Audubon Hotel. It really is such a lovely establishment. You're happy here, right? I'll leave you to enter on your own, Kitten, now that I've brought you safely home. Is that all right?"

It's more than all right. I nod, sliding toward the door as the chauffeur opens it, stepping out into a blast of cold night air and feeling as though I could weep with relief as I leave Stan behind me.

· ◆ ·

As much as I loathe the idea of agreeing with anything Stan has said, I do have to figure out a way to get myself back on an even keel before Mamma returns from Pennsylvania.

That'll mean figuring out how to stop feeling this ache. Or, if I can't stop *feeling* it, then I must at least figure out a way to tolerate it. To block it out until maybe, eventually, I will be able to forget it.

It'll be the work, I tell myself, after a good night's sleep and a long bath. It'll be keeping busy. Rescheduling the missed sitting with Mr. Willard for his marble bust and then taking home my fee. Showing up at the theater each night and playing my part. Painting my face and stepping into my costume. Kicking and singing and smiling for the packed house.

Why should I weep? Weeping won't bring my innocence back. Tears will do as little in this moment as they did to lift my father's lifeless body from the dirt. Or put food into our empty larder.

To hear Stanny explain it, he's given me a gift: he's initiated me into adulthood. "It had to happen eventually, Kitten, somehow, someway. Shouldn't it have been with me, who cares so deeply for you?"

He joins me for breakfast at the end of the week, on the day before Mamma's return. Sipping his coffee across the table, he eyes me with an appraising look. Then he says, "Think of it this way: from the day we met, I've done nothing but give you gifts. You were always thanking me, asking how you could ever repay me. The champagne, the car rides, the piano lessons, the clothing, the home. All of it. And I won't stop. I'll keep showering you with gifts. This was the one gift you could give me in return. I appreciate it so much, my darling. I really do."

I absorb all of this in a sullen silence, rolling it around in my mind, finding that I no longer have much appetite for the warm croissant I've just buttered. But Stanny interrupts my brooding. "Now, I have good news. I've secured us a very special invitation."

I chew my bite of pastry but don't taste much. Taking a sip of coffee, I notice Stan's expectant expression, so I ask: "What's that?"

Stan lowers his own coffee cup as a smile tugs on his lips. It's the look I used to love because it always meant he was about to spoil me with something delightful. Now I don't feel much of anything. His voice is tinged with enthusiasm as he leans toward me. "I've secured for you an invitation to dance for Lina, er, Mrs. Astor. In her ballroom."

Mrs. Astor's ballroom? The place she guards with such unyielding snobbery?

"Lina's a good friend of mine," Stan hastens to add. "And it seems she enjoyed your work so much at the home of her rival that she's agreed to hire you for the evening. To dance for her and her society ladies. She'd like a reprisal of your dance of the seven veils."

"Salome," I gasp. Why, for Mrs. Astor to follow in anything that Mrs. Vanderbilt has already done—she must have been impressed by my dance, indeed.

I lean back in my chair, just as the clock on the nearby mantel chimes. So Mrs. Astor has invited me into her ballroom. But only if I arrive as Salome.

I'll do it, I decide. I'll dance for these coddled society ladies. And like Salome, I will get what I want. Served up on a platter.

Chapter Twenty-Five

New York City
Summer 1902

"Do you know what the latest write-up says?" Stanny looks at me with a rakish grin, the latest copy of the *Journal* spread open beside him.

"No," I answer, sitting across from him at his dining room table, the summer sunshine melting into a soft gold outside the window as evening settles over Manhattan.

He reads in a theatrical tone: "*This fresh rose bears no resemblance to any living woman you have ever seen. This starlet has sung and danced before Manhattan's millionaires; she's inspired living legends such as Misters Gibson, Beckwith, Church, and Pierce; why, she's even received a private invitation into the rarefied inner sanctum of the selective Mrs. Astor herself. And yet, even to mention such a roster of elite names alongside hers, one must say: the truth is that Evelyn Talbot exists on a plane unto herself.*"

Stanny's eyes dart back toward me as he quirks an eyebrow. "And they don't even know the half of it." With that he leans back in his chair, a pose of total contentment, and I allow myself to smile as I take a small sip from my sherry glass.

Stan reaches his arms in my direction, pawing at the air as a little child would do. "But, my beloved, you're too far away over there. Come here, please." I oblige, taking a perch atop his knee. Stanny burrows his face into my neck, breathing me in.

We are at his place on a warm Monday evening, the one night the theater goes dark. Stanny is covetous of any time I can spare; work has been busier than ever now that I have a bigger part, playing the dancing girl Lakshmi in the new show *Wildflowers,* running at the Knickerbocker. Just as Stanny promised, I've moved out of the chorus, and my star continues to rise.

Stanny carries on tickling my neck, nuzzling against my dark curls, which hang loose over my shoulders—just how he prefers it when we are alone at his home. I give his head a playful tap. "Are you some pagan?"

"I am," he answers, wrapping his arms around my waist. "I worship the goddesses. And you are my goddess. I am helpless before you."

I know it's true—that he worships me, that I have some undeniable power over him. That the youthful enthusiasm and mischievousness I detected in him from our first meeting have now translated into a full-blown boyish infatuation with me.

Life has changed so much in the past year, it makes my head spin. Stan and I have been sweethearts, as he calls us, since that eventful Thanksgiving week when Mamma went away and he first declared his love for me. True, we are still keeping the details of our association secret for the time being, because Stan values discretion and he also feels it would upset Mamma—a point on which I readily agree.

After my initial shock at what the bedroom act actually entailed, I allowed myself to believe Stanny. It's like he told me on that first night: all the girls do it. I've been backstage long enough now to see how many of the girls have arrangements with fellows of their own. Each arrangement seems to have circumstances and rules uniquely its own, but the general idea is the same: We call them our patrons, our benefactors, our friends. The gents are often older. The girls are always more beautiful. We have the talent on the stage; they have the greenbacks with which they will willingly part. No one knows what goes on between each actress and her benefactor when the two are alone, and no one asks.

Now that I'm the lead in a new show, my place in the dressing room and the company in general is different. The girls in the *Wildflowers* cast are kind and affable enough, but they treat me with a sort of reverential distance, just as I once treated the beautiful leads in *Fair Flora*. Besides, I'm almost eighteen, no longer the naïve new kid in the bunch. No, now I feel downright worldly. I see the bright eyes, the flushed cheeks—the fresh-faced girls who come nervously into our sorority at sixteen, even fifteen. I don't blame them for padding on a few years to land their spots—just as I did—but neither do I believe their fibs.

WITH STANNY AT the helm, New York City has become my playground. Together, we walk the beach at Coney Island, eating popcorn and hot dogs, taking rides on the Razzle Dazzle. On days when we wish to stay closer to home, Stanny takes me for carriage rides through Central Park, or he arranges yachting outings up the Hudson. Even after all of these months since we first "gave ourselves over to one another in pleasure," as Stan describes our intimate encounters, he remains infatuated and attentive.

And Mamma does not raise a single objection, nor does she press for details as we step out together. She doesn't even mind when I sleep over at Stan's brownstone. "I'd rather know you are safe under Stanny's roof than frolicking on your own throughout Midtown." She thinks of Stanny as a dear and trusted friend, and she's right—he *is* a true friend, to both of us.

All he needs to do is remind Mamma of how many other men are pursuing me, men with less money and far less to offer us. "You know that magazine man holds a candle for your daughter?" Stan will say to Mamma as the fragrant bowers of fresh-cut flowers arrive at our hotel suite from Mr. Condé Nast. "And Bobby Collier, that handsome heir living off the Collier entertainment empire, he'd pay court to her like a prince, but his intentions are more like those of a rogue."

Mamma practically shudders when she hears Stan's words, when she thinks of me throwing everything away for a dalliance with a dashing young bachelor like Condé Nast. But how can they compete? These fellows cannot, not with Stanley Pierce, a man who has traveled the world and now wishes for nothing more than to enrich mine.

My favorite nights are when he takes me up to the top floor of his tower. Diana, naked and golden, spins before us, unapologetic and untiring. Stan and I clasp hands and climb up his narrow, winding staircase, not pausing until we reach the very top, where the city sprawls before us. Church spires, apartment buildings, even glittering Broadway with its theaters, none of it can reach us. The elevated train that flies up Sixth Avenue sounds like music beneath us, a distant and gentle drumbeat. That granite bridge that crosses over to Brooklyn looks like lace unfurling in the evening lights. Farther down I can see the shimmering water of the harbor, where that other woman, Lady Liberty, welcomes the masses into this miraculous city.

Even Stan, who has seen the world, seems a bit cowed in those moments we share up there. He'll wrap his arms around me and whisper, his voice low and tender, "It was my city. Now it's *our* city."

It's true. He built this city, and then both he and his city fell in love with me. It's all ours. As the wind whips around the top of Stan's skyscraper, I fold into his massive chest for a hug, and I feel both safe and loved. And then he grips my shoulders, giving them a series of gentle squeezes. "What are you doing?" I ask, tilting my face up toward him at an angle that I know he loves.

"I'm checking for wings."

"Wings?"

"I think you fell into my arms from some magical land. You are my fairy, the object of my every wish."

And when he leans forward for a kiss, I feel how this man, so powerful, who presides literally on top of the world, trembles for me and surrenders to the power that only I seem to hold over him.

Chapter Twenty-Six

Christmas Eve 1902

THE CHRISTMAS EVE SHOW HAS A PACKED HOUSE, WITH HUNdreds of families turned out to see me in the new role of the Sleeping Beauty. The air is warm inside the theater, heated by the bright lights and the hundreds of bodies, as a fresh snow falls over Broadway outside. I dance my way through my lines and musical numbers, moving the crowd like one giant wave—pulling laughter from them as I frolic in disguise, fooling the besotted prince. Then I pull tears from them as I fall to what they believe is my tragic death. And, finally, I deliver joy, relief, even more laughter and tears as I rise and reclaim the love they feared I'd lost.

Brava, Evelyn!

I take my final bow, catching a few of the roses they toss my way. Cries and cheers and deafening applause—I am quite drunk on it all. That's when I spot Stanny, in his favorite seat, toward the back. I can feel the warmth of his beam from across the theater. One of hundreds of admirers. They adore me, all of them. And as I stand there, soaking it all in, it's almost enough for me to forget the Christmases I've spent that were empty of this joy. Almost.

After the show, Stanny and I leave together. As we step off his private elevator and into the large Madison Square Tower room, I look around with startled delight. "How did you make it snow inside?" I ask. Stanny has set up a winter wonderland: banks of fake snow, a team of stuffed reindeer harnessed to a red sleigh, peppermint trees taller than I am, a life-sized gingerbread house covered in bright candies. "Why, it's magic!" I drop his hand and run into the gingerbread house.

Peeking my head through one of the candy-trimmed windows, I smile up at my lover. "Here, Kitten, try this." Stan palms a handful of the fake snow and puts a drop on my tongue. "What does it taste like?"

"It's sweet," I answer.

"Spun sugar."

"More, please."

He obliges. "Come out of that house. I wish to spoil you on the day before your birthday."

"But Stanny," I say, doing as he says, "you spoil me every day."

"True. But today I'm going to be even worse."

Mamma is in Pennsylvania visiting Kit for his Christmas break from school; Stanny insisted he treat her to the trip, since I had to work the entire holiday. This means that I get to enjoy both Christmas and my birthday alone with Stanny after my shows. As we sit down to a delicious spread of lobster and tender lamb chops, I feel that there's no one I'd rather be with in my final hours before turning eighteen.

After the meal Stanny presents me with a small box wrapped in a red bow. I giggle nervously as I take the ribbon in trembling fingers. *Is it a ring?* My stomach tightens at the thought. Stanley tells me all the time how much he loves me, and I feel incredible affection for him. But do I wish to marry?

My stomach unclenches and my eyes go wide as I open the box to find not a ring but a long rope of pearls with a large diamond clasp. "Stanny!" I gasp. My face bursts into a wide smile. I love the necklace, and I realize in that instant, I'm undeniably relieved that he hasn't proposed marriage on the eve of my eighteenth birthday.

Stan looks satisfied by my happy reaction. He grasps the pearls as he says, "They reminded me of your skin, Kitten. The way they glow. And the diamonds because, well, you are a diamond. Do you like it?"

"Like it? Why, I adore it," I answer as I lift my hair for him to clasp the necklace around my throat.

"Ready for more?" he asks.

"There's more?"

"Of course there's more. Why, it's your eighteenth birthday. No one can say you aren't a woman now."

I unwrap the next package to find a pristine stole of snow-colored fur with a matching hat and impossibly soft hand muff. "The precious white fox," he says, a noticeable tinge of pride in his voice.

"Oh, darling," I marvel, stroking the plush fur. "You're better than Santa Claus."

"Then call me Stanny Claus."

We both laugh at this, and then Stanny's eyes turn serious. Glancing from the pelt in my hand back up to my face, he leans closer. "I want to see you in it. But first, one more thing."

With that, a man walks into the room, and I take a step closer to Stan, startled by the sudden appearance of a stranger in our private winter wonderland. A beat later I realize this man is dressed up as Santa Claus. I gasp in surprise and then delight. "What is the meaning of this?"

Stan wears a proud smile. "I wanted you to have the chance to ask for anything you wanted, my darling."

I glance from Stan back toward this Santa, clad in white and red, an expectant grin fixed on his ruddy, bearded face, and I'm overwhelmed by the realization that I have not had a visit from Santa Claus since Daddy died. I barely marked Christmas or my birthday after that, after all illusions and innocence, even joy, died with him.

Until Stanny appeared in my world, breaking it apart like an earthquake and then building something new, something better than I could have dared to imagine. And as the jolly man asks, "What do you want for Christmas, my dear girl?" I just shake my head and clutch Stanny's hand. For I have a fresh realization in that moment: I don't want for anything.

It's not until later, after I've modeled and then shed my pristine new furs, when I lie wrapped only in my pearls and Stanny's arms, that I tell him what I really want. What only he can give me. "I want more of the same," I say. What we have, in this moment, when I feel so very loved and cared for. And then I kiss him, breathing into his ear as I whisper, "I don't want this magic to end."

Chapter Twenty-Seven

Winter 1903

But of course, like all magic, the spell must eventually end. And it does. The bad news arrives in the form of a telegram. "From Chester," Mamma says, her face going ashen. "Kit."

I fly to her side and read over her shoulder, staring at the words in mute disbelief.

Diphtheria. My brother, my beautiful little boy, has fallen to the dreaded disease that is sweeping through the halls of his boarding school. This infection, which has been ravaging the nation in recent years, has made its way to Pennsylvania. And now we have to return there, as well.

Mamma and I travel like two phantoms back to Tarentum, but this is a nightmare from which there is no waking. Stan arranges for our first-class rail travel the entire way, and has Kit's body cleaned and placed into a walnut coffin, which he arranges to be transported directly to us in Tarentum.

Back in coal country, wrapped in black mourning weeds, we revisit the grave site where Daddy's body rests. We do battle with the frozen earth to lay Kit into the ground beside Daddy. A small crowd gathers to pray with us as the village priest stands over Kit's lowered coffin. A trickling stream of dour-faced distant relatives and former neighbors offer their condolences, many of them pausing to tell me just how proud they are of my fame. One matron even shows me a clipping she's saved from a local newspaper, proudly brandishing my crumpled image as though tempted to ask for my autograph. Mercifully, she does not, but I'm grateful for the black netting that drapes from my hat, concealing my face from their gawking, probing stares.

I don't say much for several days. Not to these neighbors or to the priest, not even to Mamma. I try not to think much, either. Every time I *do,* all I can think about is how I missed out on years with my brother. How Kit was tucked away at school while I occupied a different world. I always thought we'd get our time, eventually. Someday, he'd join me up in the city. Until then . . .

I always felt this grinding need to work, to provide for his future. But in doing so, I missed out on his life. Years I can now never reclaim. I got so wrapped up in myself, in my climb toward comfort and perhaps even security. Illusions, all of it. What does it matter on this bleak winter day? No luxury can bring back my baby brother. Kit, like Daddy, was snatched away in an instant.

Daddy. It's the first time I've been back to his grave since his awful burial, so many years ago. All these years later, I'm just as confused as I was then. Why did he leave so suddenly? And why did Kit have to follow? And how will I, without them, be able to carry on?

Well, I know the answer to that one. Because this frozen ground is the exact spot where I first learned it. This grave site is the very place where I first had to do it, all those years ago. I have to push my tears back down and force myself to walk on.

• ◆ •

BACK IN MANHATTAN, I pour myself into work. Penny is a constant and reliable comfort, offering walks and chats, dropping by for visits on the mornings when I find it hard to rise from bed. Stanny takes me to supper, or we order in and eat quiet meals at his brownstone. My body, in spite of the cruel fates that have befallen the two people I loved most in this world, carries on with youthful vibrancy and energy. And so, as winter unfurls, I carry on with life, playing for packed houses. What other choice do I have?

But that spring finds me staring glumly at the calendar, lamenting other news: Stan's work will take him to the Continent for the upcoming summer.

"I've put this trip off for far too long, and that's down to you," Stan says, kissing the tip of my nose as I sit on the edge of his massive four-poster bed. "I can't be away from you for a day, let alone months. But it's time. It's past time, in fact. Why, before you, I went abroad a few times a year. I cannot put it off any longer; my warehouses are almost entirely empty, and my clients are growing frustrated. Of course, I haven't told them my reasons—that there's a little kitten who holds me in her grip and makes it unbearable for me to leave."

I wanted another magical summer with Stanny. Another season of boat rides on the Hudson and beach outings at Coney Island. Most of all, I don't want to be apart from him. Stan's presence in my life is the only anchor these days that gives me any feeling of security.

So then, since I can't keep him with me in Manhattan, I beg, "Take me with you to Europe."

"Not this time, Kitten."

"But you promised," I press. Paris and London and Venice—as he outlines his itinerary, I yearn to go, not only to be with Stanny but also to see these fabled places he's spoken about so often.

"This trip is work, not play," he says. "Better that I go, see to what must be done, and return to you as quickly as I can manage." I can tell from his tone that he's decided.

I flop onto the bed, hoping to summon him to me, but he appears uncharacteristically impervious to my presence, so preoccupied is he with packing his trunks.

As he sorts through a pile of neckties, he goes on. "I'll bring you some nice things, I promise. And besides, you'll be so busy this summer, you'll hardly notice I'm missing. Though I'll confess: I do hope you miss me at least a bit. I don't want some cad swooping in to fly off with you. If your mother is a wise woman, she won't allow that to happen."

"It would serve you right if one did," I retort, my tone as sour as my mood. I'm being petulant and I know it. But he's the one who filled my imagination with tantalizing images of Paris and London. And after all his talk of loving me madly, telling me his world is mine, wouldn't this be the best time to show me? And to show others, as well?

I can't help but suspect that at least a part of his reluctance to bring me stems from the fact that he does not wish to reveal to the wider world that we are a romantic pair. And that irks me. I'll be nineteen this year. I'm a wildly successful artists' model and a celebrated Broadway performer. I'm not a child. I'm ready to tell the world that my lover is Stanley Pierce. But why won't he claim me as his?

When I finally meet his eyes, I see I've wounded him. No, it's something else. I've offended him. Stan's lips are a tight line, and when he speaks, his words are cool. "I am going to forget that you said that, Evelyn, because I do not believe you truly feel that way. I think you are being childish, and it's not a side of you that I enjoy. I'm going to excuse myself. When I return, I hope to find that you've regained your composure. That, or you may excuse yourself until you have."

Stan leaves the room without another word, and I sit there alone on his bed, chastised, feeling every bit the child he has just accused me of being.

Our first quarrel, I realize. I draw my knees up into my chest, refusing to cry. Nor will I follow him and beg for his forgiveness. I won't be made to look even more immature. I turn away from his open trunk, rolling onto my side on top of the bedcovers. And that's when I see something I hadn't previously noticed. On his side of the bed, right next to the bedside table, lies a small leather-bound book.

Thinking it must be some sort of diary—the sort that I'd never keep, for fear that Mamma would find it and read my secrets—I now can't resist the urge to peek at it. I throw my eyes toward the doorway. No sign nor sound from Stanny. He's so cross with me that he'll probably stay away for a while, hoping I'll cool off. I look back at the little book. Perhaps Stanny has written about me? I slide over to his side of the bed, and I take the book into my hands.

One more glance toward the door, and then I open the diary. But instead of a diary, it appears to be a list. Or a series of lists. *Packing arrangements?*

The first column is labeled "*New York,*" and there follows a long series of names, scrawled in Stanny's familiar handwriting.

Adeline
Alva
Annie

I swallow, noticing how my heart is hammering in my throat. But I force myself to read on.

Belle
Bernice (London for the winter season)
Beth
Blanche
Cara
Cate
Dee
Dinah
Dolly

The paper quivers in my hands, but I carry on, still on the New York list.

Edith
Elene
Elinor
Elizabeth C.
Elizabeth V.
Evelyn*

My stomach curdles, I feel as though I might be sick.

Fanny
Frances

Gillian
Greta
Hannah
Hattie
Hilda
Hillary
Ilsa (travels often to Berlin)
Ina
Ingrid

I'm still only on the New York column, but I can't go on. *Are these . . . lovers?*

The room has tipped sideways, and I drop the book, my body collapsing alongside it on the bed. Could Stan really have had that many lovers? All before me? Or—terrible thought—is he still carrying on with these other girls? And why is he packing this list, this book, for his summer travels? The pages go on and on, and that's only New York. I flip ahead and come to a list labeled "*London*." Pages later, "*Paris*." And then "*Rome*." "*Berlin*." "*Venice*." "*Vienna*."

I have to stop. I drop the book again, my mind reeling. I know that Stan travels the world for both work and leisure. Perhaps these are the names of friends he visits as he travels? But even as I hope for that, I know it's nonsense, and a mad laugh slips out of my mouth. There is my name. Not far below *Dinah* and *Dolly*. Now I really do think I might be sick, and I climb out of the bed and charge toward the door, clutching my stomach.

But before I reach the threshold, I nearly barrel right into Stanny, who has just reappeared in the doorway. "Oh, Evelyn," he says, startled, putting his hands on my arms. He takes one look at my wild demeanor, and then, peering over my shoulder, he must see the book spread open on his bed, right where he left me just moments earlier. And then his gaze careens back toward me, and he stares once more into my ashen face. He knows I've seen it. He knows that I know.

I force the words from my mouth, even as my whole body is trembling: "So then, I'm between Elizabeth V. and Fanny?"

He grimaces at this. But a moment later, when he speaks, his voice is unnaturally calm. "That's simply a question of alphabetization. I'd put you at the top. At least, for the moment."

I feel as though I might collapse, so I brace myself on the frame of the doorway. *Lists for Paris, London* . . . It's no wonder he won't bring me along this summer. I may be young, but I'm no fool. Again, that sound like a madwoman's laugh slips from me.

My voice is thick and low, but mercifully I am able to keep the tears back. "Lots of work to be done this summer, yes? I see how busy you'll be." I force myself to meet his icy gaze. "Will you be revisiting the names already in there, or adding new ones?"

Stan's face is wiped clean of all feeling. He looks more like a statue of carved marble than the man I know and love. "I suspect a bit of both, if all goes according to plan."

I hadn't realized it was possible to feel any worse, but a wave of fresh horror washes over me. And in its wake, a vile brew of shame and anger. Heartbreak. I'm so hurt, in fact, that the most overwhelming feeling I have in this moment is a desire to hurt him back. So I turn on my heels, and I march toward the bed, and there, before I can lose my nerve, I hurl his horrid little book into the fireplace.

Now, at last, I finally get a reaction out of this marble-man Stan. But it's not what I had hoped it might be. He rushes to the hearth, his cheeks flushing with their own scarlet flames as he growls: "How dare you?" And then he bends over to fetch his book. This makes me even more furious, how committed he is to keeping his list. Is it so that he may be proud of his many conquests or so that he can keep straight his plans for future trysts?

Watching him jabbing at the small book with a poker, frantic to rescue the names of his many mistresses from the flames, I feel myself reeling with both humiliation and hatred. When I speak next, my voice is shrill. "Do you know how many millionaires have asked for my time, Stan?"

He manages to retrieve the book, cursing as he burns his fingers, and he sits back on his haunches beside the hearth. The charred leather smokes at his side, but he says nothing.

"Do you know how many men have made me offers of support?" I press on, feral and furious. "I've not entertained a single suitor. Because of you!"

When he finally looks up at me, his lips curl in a grin, but not a happy one. With a shrug, he says, "I'd like to hear what you think after getting on top of some rusty railroad man. Let me know if he teaches you anything useful."

Fresh horror surges through my entire body. Who is this man before me? So indifferent, so callous and cruel! When was my sweet, tender Stanny replaced by some unfeeling monster? "How dare you treat me like this?" I ask, well and truly mystified.

This comment further displeases him; I can tell from the blaze in his gray eyes as he rises to stand. "I've treated you with nothing but kid-leather gloves," he responds, his voice hard as crushed gravel. "Why, I was patient; I was gallant. I let you take your time. I have put you on top of the world."

My mouth falls open. "But . . . you told me . . ." My mind whirls. "Was it all a lie? Everything you said to me? You told me you loved me."

"Oh, grow up, would you?" Stan bends over and picks up the charred book, holding it like a hot cake between his fingers. I hope it burns him. He stares directly into my eyes as he says. "You know how this world works. How these arrangements work. How dare you act aggrieved? You've had it as good as can be. Too good, in fact. You know what I did wrong, Evelyn? I spoiled you. Because, yes, the fact of the matter is, I *do* care for you. So I let myself act like a lovesick fool. And now here you are, acting like a spoiled little girl."

Did I mean so little to him? What we had between us, what I believed was love—what he *told* me was love—it was all merely transactional, temporary, until I no longer kept his interest? But he's not done. "I've been a very patient man, Evelyn. And surely you see I put the star next to your name. I did treat you like you were special, because I do think you are. But you're pushing me with this rudeness. And my patience will eventually run out."

The last drop of air leaves my defeated body, an audible exhale, and I turn to leave the room. I'm more shattered than I felt even on that other day when I fled this bedroom in shame, that time when he had broken my body. For this time, he's crushed my heart. Because I allowed myself to believe in him, in us. He'd told me he loved me, he asked me to love him in return, and I did as he asked. I gave myself to love, even after he betrayed my trust that first time. And now he's done it again. Fool that I am, I never saw it. This whole time, it was some great illusion, and I was simply playing a part. Less real than my work at the theater each night.

Back in the hotel suite I avoid Mamma as I storm straight into my bedroom. I find my jewelry box on the shelf beside my bed, and I yank the top open. I've kept all my letters from Stan in this precious jewelry box, tucked in against the lining of pearls and pink satin. A gift from him. My jewels are in here, too. Also from him, of course. Incomparable pieces from Cartier and Tiffany's, but the truth is that his letters always meant more to me than the diamonds. His promises of love and devotion, words that had kindled in my heart such hope and happiness.

How many other girls have boxes like this one, lined with Stan's jewels and his words?

Priceless jewelry beside empty, hollow words. And now here, in this room, my own insides are hollowest of all.

PART 3

To shift roles, a girl has to put everything she's got into total transformation. It's a change of costume, tempo, scenario. Each time I'd face that same pesky fear that the audience wouldn't fall for it. And yet, they always did.

—Evelyn Talbot, in a letter written to Mr. Anthony Comstock, published after her death

• ◆ •

AND PERHAPS I DID, TOO—FOR A TIME.
Did I choose to keep changing it all? The scenery, costume, role? In the same way a butterfly could not tell you why or when it chooses to spin its chrysalis, nor could the creature tell you with any certainty what, if anything, will emerge, I could not have told you in those days what divine wisdom was guiding my steps.

The music in the orchestra pit doesn't stop just because a showgirl falters. No, her job is to keep kicking, keep moving, keep putting on the show.

Each stumble of mine led to the next act that would reveal itself. The music kept playing; I had little choice but to keep dancing.

And like the butterfly breaking its way through wind and weather and past all dangers, my wings could not help but grow stronger.

Chapter Twenty-Eight

Hudson River Valley
Summer 1903

When Daddy told me the tale of Rapunzel, I'd often wonder: What's that girl got to complain about anyway? She's in a beautiful tower with enough to eat and a doting Mamma who loves her so much that she just wants to keep her safe. Isn't that what every girl would want?

But now I understand. Now that I'm Rapunzel. Locked up with Mamma, not *by* Mamma—but by a man who wants to keep me for himself, even though he's made it clear that he's not mine alone, nor will he ever be.

Stan left for Europe at the start of the summer. I'm not certain whether he took the charred remains of that leather book with him, but something tells me he won't have too much difficulty finding ladies to spend time with as he travels for the next few months.

And after our quarrel—our first ever, and big enough to end with me writing him a one-sentence note: *I never wish to look at you again*—Stan arranged a private meeting with Mamma. I didn't know he'd asked for it, nor do I know precisely all that they discussed, though I have a very good guess at a few of the topics Stanny did *not* raise. So much for his claims at their first introduction: *How can I be your champion if we aren't honest with one another?* All hogwash, everything that man told us from the start.

Who knows what yarn he spun for Mamma this time? All I

know is that Mamma came out of that closeted meeting insisting I needed a break for the summer. "We are going away," she declared. "Let's leave the close-packed heat of Manhattan and take our leisure with some good, healthful country air." Parroting Stan, from the sound of it.

He is paying, after all. He's rented us a sprawling castle on a leafy hilltop overlooking the Hudson River, forty miles north of Manhattan and yet far enough away to feel like a different world. Members of a prominent New York family Stan knows, the Harmonds, are abroad for the summer, touring England's Lake District, so they have allowed Stanny to rent their place along with their staff for July and August.

"She deserves a break," I overheard Stan telling Mamma as I eavesdropped on them huddled together in our hotel sitting room, the day before he set sail. "She looks tired to me. And pale. And her behavior has been a bit . . . concerning, of late."

"Oh?" I heard the alarm rise in Mamma's voice. "It has?"

"Nothing to worry about. Just an isolated episode here and there. But her line of work is grueling. It's crucial to give Evelyn rest, both her body and her spirit, so she doesn't become like all of those other used-up chorus girls who age ahead of their time, weary from exhaustion and overwork. You hear about it all the time, sadly. But we won't let that happen to our Evelyn."

How rich! How my stomach curdled to hear Stanny's exaggerated fears for my *body and spirit*. And since when has Mamma ever cared about my exhaustion or overwork?

True, I *have* been working nonstop for years. But all this time, Mamma has never once batted an eye over the punishing load I've been carrying.

Now though, hearing that I might compromise my looks or my energy—and thus my profitability—or that my behavior hasn't been entirely pleasing to Stanny? She took his bait like a fish before the hook. And so here we are, tucked away in the country while Stanny sweeps through London, Paris, and beyond.

I groan just thinking about it. Work, he told us. I know what sort of work.

We barely spoke before he left. After I sent him that letter, he dealt almost entirely with Mamma before bundling us off to the country in his chauffeured auto.

But Mamma sensed the tension between us. She asked me about it, this "episode" to which Stanny had fleetingly alluded, but the daggers I threw with my eyes hit their mark, and so miraculously, mercifully, she did not press me. Stan seemed concerned for my health and was all too willing to pay for a castle for the pair of us for the summer, so I suppose, for the moment, that was good enough for her.

Now, TUCKED AWAY in our stone aerie overlooking the Hudson Valley, with an attentive staff to see to all our needs and the most beautiful natural scenery one could hope for, I should be perfectly happy this summer. It's the first time in years that grueling physical work hasn't dictated my hours both sleeping and awake. I couldn't possibly conjure a world less like Broadway with its lights and its call times and its constant noise and chaos. There's a quiet and a peace to this landscape, picturesque panoramic views of a wide river and the granite hills that cradle it.

And yet—I'm miserable. As I sit by myself on the terrace on a warm July morning, taking nothing for breakfast but a cup of coffee, I know that all of the peace and pastoral beauty and, yes, boredom, are not helping. Jumping from a life of work to a life of leisure is making my melancholy all too apparent and ever present. I miss New York City. I miss being busy. I miss the girls. I miss . . . *No.* I won't allow myself to miss him.

I'm glad he's gone, I remind myself. I certainly don't want to carry on as number eighteen on his list.

The sun is getting stronger as it climbs up from its morning perch; the birds are quieting down. I look down at the coffee cup trembling in my grip and frown. My hands have boils on them because I keep scratching at my skin.

That's when I decide: I need to find some way to fill my time. Walks along the trails of this mountain yield swell views, sure. And there's a small pond filled with fish, where the staff have offered to set up a picnic luncheon, and the coachman has offered to take me on a carriage ride down the hill so I can stroll along the river. But I need to see some other people, some company other than just Mamma.

Mercifully, today promises a slight reprieve from the boredom, as we've received an invitation from the neighbor. I gather from Mamma that it's a cousin of the family who built this castle, a lady who lives just down the hill, where she's invited us for a luncheon in her home.

Mamma and I arrive shortly before noon, the Harmonds' coach bearing us past two stone pillars that boast the name of the neighbor's estate: Water's Edge. Up ahead I see a gracious white Victorian house, three stories high, with two wings that open like arms around a spacious forecourt.

"Not too shabby for the cousin who lives down the hill," Mamma remarks under her breath as our coach rolls to a halt. Our hostess, Mrs. Hollis, stands ready to greet us. In her written invitation, Mrs. Hollis explained that she is a widow who lives alone in the sprawling mansion, though she referred to it as her *"tidy little cottage at the base of the mountain."*

We step out of the carriage, and Mrs. Hollis rushes toward us, embracing us like we ourselves are long-lost kin. "Mrs. Talbot, welcome! Miss Talbot. It's so good of you to come." The words come gushing out. "In just a few moments I shall introduce you to my dear nephew, Arthur. Though I suppose he likes to go by Art nowadays. Oh, he is a very polite fellow, and he does his best to entertain me, but I can see he longs for some young blood! We've been craving company, you see. So when I heard there was a mother and daughter pair staying up at Stonetop, I simply had to meet you. Oh, but where are my manners? I'm Alice Hollis. The neighbor—guilty, that's me. And family, too. My grandfather built that castle, you know, as a gift to my grandmother. Romantic gesture, isn't it?"

I offer a curtsy to my hostess, and then I turn to Mamma, slightly flustered by this rush of information, and not quite sure which point to respond to first. But a response proves entirely unnecessary, for our hostess chatters on: "But my dear Mrs. and Miss Talbot, you have caused quite a stir in our sleepy little river town, don't you know? Why, a Broadway star! The Gibson Girl, right here in the neighborhood! Miss Talbot, we've all washed our hands with soap bearing your image. To see you now, in the flesh, it's as though one of Botticelli's goddesses has appeared before me."

My face burns at such an onslaught of praise, and I manage a modest dip of my eyes. Mrs. Hollis strikes me as someone who has so many words bubbling up inside her, and such a need to speak them to someone, that they cannot help but come spilling out. "Oh, but you are even lovelier than your pictures," Mrs. Hollis prattles on. I breathe out a puff of laughter at this. I'm turned out very simply today, in a cream-colored silk day dress with pale blue frogging down the front, a large-brimmed hat tipped across my brow. Mamma is similarly attired, both of us doing our best imitation of what we presumed to be the wardrobe of country ladies of leisure. It's nothing like how I might dress to frolic at night on Broadway, and certainly not in the style of a Botticelli goddess.

Of course Mamma saw to an entire new summer wardrobe for both herself and me before we quit the city, and of course Stanny paid for the entire thing. But I've had so little verve or vigor lately; what is the point of a huge effort to just sit tucked away in my country exile? Though, to hear our hostess now, today might in fact turn out to be the first bit of fun I've had all summer. "I sent out many invitations, Mrs. Talbot, assuming that most of our friends would be gone, but they've all accepted. I think they all wanted to catch a glimpse of you, Miss Talbot!"

I perk up at this—at last, perhaps some lively company. "Oh, and here they come now," our hostess says. She and I both turn and see the first horse-drawn carriage rolling in, and after that, a steady procession of carriages drops off pairs and individuals in the forecourt as Mamma and I sit nearby on the lawn, sipping lemonade. I watch the arrivals and see, with a sinking feeling, that all the people descending from these coaches are much older than I am, even older than Mamma. Our hostess pilots each one of her guests in turn as I'm introduced to a stream of inquisitive smiles.

I meet the Fish family, the Benjamin family, the Gordons, the Sloanes.

And then, just as I'm about to give up all hope for some lively companionship, at last, someone my age appears—not from an arriving carriage but rather from the home, a young gentleman, and I find myself sitting up straighter in my chair. He walks out into the bright sunshine and crosses the lawn toward us, his slender body swathed in a suit of pale linen, a straw hat hiding his face in shadow.

Mrs. Hollis raises her arms toward the young man. "Ah, here he is at last. Mrs. Talbot, Miss Talbot, please meet my nephew, Mr. Arthur Darrow."

The young man pauses before us, and I look into a pair of green eyes draped in the shadow of his straw boater. But even through shadow, it's easy to see that it's a fine-looking face. Perhaps he's a few years older than me. "Miss Talbot, so lovely to meet you," he says, extending a hand in greeting along with an easy, open smile.

"And you, Mr. Darrow," I say, accepting his handshake. I feel a fluttering in my stomach as his gentle grip closes around mine, even though I have gloves on.

"Now that my dear Art has joined us, our party is complete." Mrs. Hollis gestures toward a nearby stand of gracious oaks, which throw out a pleasing canopy of shade under which a wicker table is set for the midday meal. "Shall we dine?"

We follow our hostess to the table, and Mr. Darrow helps me into a wicker chair. To my delight, he takes the seat at my side. I keep my gaze straight ahead and unfold the linen napkin across my lap as a team of attendants appears around us, bearing a procession of delicious-looking platters.

Mamma, on my other side, nods appreciatively as the attendants serve us a feast of summertime delights: a salad of diced eggs and dill tuna, sliced peaches with cream, oysters on ice, cheeses, caviar. I accept a serving of everything, including a glass of chilled champagne.

Mamma is immediately pulled into conversation with Mrs.

Fish on her right, who keeps a summer estate just up the lane and has many questions for Mamma about our accommodations at the castle.

As I'm taking a sip of champagne, Mr. Darrow leans closer to me and, with a hint of sheepishness, whispers: "I beg pardon if this is terribly rude of me to ask, but you see, my aunt told me nothing of what today was to be. I've been visiting friends up in Rhinebeck, and I only just arrived back here by train this morning to find my aunt all aflutter about a party. All I was told was a 'luncheon with some friends and a few special out-of-town visitors.' I presume you are the latter, since we have never met?"

I smile, lowering my flute of champagne. "You are correct. I'm up from Manhattan. Visiting with my mother for the summer. And no need to apologize—I was similarly ill prepared as to the specifics of this gathering."

"Then I'm not alone," he says with a playful sigh, and I allow myself to meet his gaze. He's removed his boater hat to reveal a head of honey-colored hair, tidily combed back off his handsome, suntanned face. But he's looking at me with a quizzical expression, and I resist the urge to fidget in my seat. Then he says, "This might sound like a most preposterous question, but when my Aunt Alice said your name just now . . . I can't help but wonder: Are you Lakshmi?"

I tip back in my chair, unable to suppress my grin. These days, for me, it's so rare to meet someone like this, with no prior associations or assumptions on their part. "So you've seen *Wildflowers*?" I ask.

Mr. Darrow's eyebrows shoot up, perhaps because I have not denied what he presumed would be a preposterous question. "Yes, I've seen it," he answers, his voice breathy. "But you're not . . . Are you really . . . ?"

I give a small nod, biting down on my lower lip.

"You're *the* Evelyn Talbot?"

"Last I checked, Mr. Darrow." I am trying not to giggle at how wide his green eyes have gone.

"But she might have given me some warning," he mutters,

more to himself than to me. "Why, you're really Evelyn Talbot? Miss Talbot, you're nothing short of a sensation."

"That's kind of you."

His tone is still slightly incredulous as he says, "*Of course* I've seen you in *Wildflowers*. And everywhere else, it seems. The papers, the advertisements, Mr. Gibson's sketches. I follow a lesser-known artist based out of Philadelphia, a woman, in fact. Violet Oakley? She's also worked with you as a model, I believe?"

"Yes." I feel my cheeks flush with warmth, and I'm sure it has little to do with the midday sunshine. Summoning a demeanor of unruffled interest in the lunch spread, I scoop myself a spoonful of the peaches and ask, "Do you enjoy much theater, Mr. Darrow?"

"A fair amount, yes. Especially the shows featuring Miss Talbot."

I dab my lips with my napkin, concealing the grin that pulls on them. "You are generous to say so, Mr. Darrow."

"Please, would you call me Arthur? Or Art?"

I throw him a sidelong glance, and he tips his head toward mine, speaking in a hushed voice as he flashes me a lopsided smile. "Come now, considering we are the only two at this table, quite possibly in this town, who are eating this meal with all our teeth still intact, we might as well become friends."

Now I laugh, taken with his unexpected irreverence. My voice is quiet, but my tone is wry as I lean toward him and say, "I believe my mother's teeth are all intact."

"Oh, that's a relief," he answers with an exaggerated sigh.

"But I do hear your point," I add. "I was despairing of seeing anyone even close to my age all summer, before you arrived." I'm surprised at my own candor, at my casual chatter with this young man whom I've only just met. But something about his affable and guileless demeanor has put me quickly at ease.

"I'm on a mission of mercy, you see," Art says, taking a bite of his salad. I look to him with a questioning glance, and he goes on. "Aunt Alice is the dearest of souls. And it's her cousin who lives up at Stonetop, and with them gone for the entire summer, she's quite alone here. She refuses to travel with them. Her one child, my cousin, is something of a musical genius, but he lives in Berlin. She wouldn't dream of sailing to see him. Won't even go see her friends in Newport. She's a fixture of this neighborhood. *'The next time you'll see me leaving this place will be when I'm carried out in a wooden box, and you better get me a nice one.'"*

I can't help but laugh at his good-natured impersonation of his aunt, at how spot-on the fidgety mannerisms are. Art goes on, "But I feel guilty, you know? With my uncle and cousin gone, she's a widow without much company. She gets lonely. She never complains, but I know she must feel it. Both my parents have passed, so she's the only family I've got, and she's always been good to me. So I make these visits up whenever I can. It's not a bad spot to spend a few weeks in the summer."

"Indeed, it's gorgeous," I reply, looking around, my eyes resting for a moment on the languid sway of the broad Hudson below where we sit. "And a few weeks sounds like just the ticket. I only wonder at how I'll make it two months." The words are out before I realize I've spoken them aloud, and then, fearing that I have insulted this place that clearly means a lot to him, I pivot: "And what do you do when you're not bringing cheer to a solitary aunt out in the country?"

"I'm a cartoonist," Art answers, his tone brightening. "I live in Manhattan. I draw for the *Journal,* Mr. Hearst's publication."

"Oh?" This I had not expected. I'd expected the well-heeled nephew of Mrs. Hollis to say that he was studying the law or perhaps dabbling as a financier on Wall Street. But a cartoonist for Mr. Hearst? No wonder he is so familiar with my modeling work. I tilt back in my seat, staring at him appraisingly: "Art the Artist."

"Has a nice ring to it when you put it that way."

We share a smile before I remember myself, and pull my gaze away from his pleasing face. As I spear myself a sliver of chilled cucumber, he asks, "And how about you, Miss Talbot?"

I'm not sure precisely what he's asking, considering he's just let me know that he's well versed in my career. He goes on, "Did you always envision for yourself a life on Broadway?"

"I didn't, actually," I answer. "In fact, for the longest time, I thought I'd attend university." I swallow, then add: "I still hope to attend university."

"Well, then," Art says, raising his flute of champagne and tipping it in my direction, "I have no doubt you shall make it happen, Miss Talbot."

"You may call me Evelyn."

His eyes go wide. "Are you quite certain?"

I reach for my own glass and take a sip. His questions about the stage have stirred up thoughts of Stanny, and I don't like the feeling. Nor do I like thinking of Daddy and his dreams for my schooling. So I push all that aside, and I turn back to Art, allowing myself to stare into the cool, kind green of his eyes for perhaps a moment longer than is entirely appropriate. Enjoying the appreciative way he's staring back at me, enjoying the champagne and the lovely view, the grass-sweetened summer air, and my relief at having finally found someone close to my own age—a handsome gentleman, at that, and one who clearly finds me pretty—I lean just an inch closer to him and say, "It's as you said. . . . We are quite outnumbered here. Might as well be friends, right?"

His eyes hold mine, direct and earnest. "I'll be your friend, Evelyn." And then he looks away, down at his plate, and takes another bite. I do the same, but I can feel how my heartbeat has sped up. *I'm flirting*, I realize. *With a man other than Stanny*. And what's more, I'm enjoying it.

After a moment, Art breaks through my giddy thoughts: "So how about you, then? What did you do to get exiled to the country for the summer?"

I swallow my bite of food, take a quick sip of water as I try to arrange my thoughts into some suitable answer. "My mamma and my . . . er, friend . . . thought I needed a break. Felt the Broadway lifestyle was getting too grueling, that I should take a few months away from the stage. To revive my spirits."

Art is staring at me intently as he asks, "Is it working?"

I shrug. "I'm well rested, if that's anything. Then again, I don't have much else to do *but* sleep."

Art nods. Then he asks, "Are you bored?"

"Terribly," I admit. Because the truth is, up here, where the Broadway showtimes mean nothing and the hours stretch long and empty, I'm just an eighteen-year-old girl, restless and lonely.

"I can fix that," Art says, offering me a playful wink. I feel something hitch in my belly.

"I have one week remaining in my stay at my aunt's," he explains. "I shall make it my personal duty to show you a good time. And—how did you put it?—*revive your spirits.*"

Chapter Twenty-Nine

I see Art every day. True to his word, he finds ways to fill these idle country hours with entertaining outings—and nonstop laughter. Each morning when my new friend comes calling, winding his way up the dirt lane to my mountain hideaway, the sound of his aunt's coach crunching the gravel brings the most welcome break to the otherwise endless quiet. I force myself to stand still and composed behind the doorway as Art halts the horses and hops down, even though my entire body hums with the thrill of anticipation, giddy at having a friend and eager to hear what new amusement he will propose for the day.

It feels like an eternity to wait, but when the footman finally announces, "Mr. Arthur Darrow here to see Miss Talbot," and I see the first glimpse of his fresh morning smile, his body so lean and energetic in his crisp pale suit, his boater hat coming off to reveal his thick mane of golden hair, I think: *How happy I am that Mrs. Hollis has a nephew in the neighborhood!* Suddenly I am entirely grateful for my new summer wardrobe, and my morning toilette no longer feels like a pointless exercise as I sit before the mirror and comb my hair or pick a flattering new day dress.

On the first day that week, Art brings me into the nearby village, and we visit a local artist's studio, admiring the small but lovely exhibit of watercolors. We stroll slowly past the canvases featuring plein air scenes of the beautiful landscape all around us. "It really is such a picturesque setting," I say. "It can't help but inspire."

"It's true," Art says, walking a few paces behind me. "I remember drawing my first sketches out here as a young lad on my summer visits with Aunt Alice. It was she who always set me up with paper and pencil beside the river."

"Have you come here your whole life?" I ask, studying this man as he studies the art before him.

"Mm-hmm, yes," he answers, leaning close to examine the technique of the brushstrokes. But I'm still staring at him; there's a question on my mind, and it might be terribly rude to pose it, but it's been niggling at me since we met at the luncheon. "Art, how old are you?"

He looks up at me now, a smile brightening his light eyes. "I'm twenty-two," he answers, his expression unguarded. "And you?"

"I'm eighteen," I answer quickly. I want the truth out before I can lose my nerve. That question that I've been asked more times than I can count, that question I've been drilled and trained on for years, always ready and willing to lie. Something in this moment, in this place, with Art beside me, fills me with a longing to be honest. Perhaps I don't want Stanley Pierce to be the only man who knows the truth about me. Or perhaps with Art, I don't feel as though I have so much to hide. That realization comes with an undeniable feeling of relief—and even something akin to delight.

The next day we eat lunch in a quaint inn beside the Hudson, chattering about whatever pops to mind—the pleasing weather, his work as a cartoonist, my work on Broadway. Art is eager to hear what my life in Manhattan is like. His curiosity feels genuine and straightforward.

After lunch, we stroll the riverbank with a pair of ice-cream cones Art orders from a vendor near the water. As I'm enjoying my scoop of chocolate, Art pauses at my side, throwing me a quizzical stare. "What?" I ask. "Why do you look at me like that?"

"Evelyn, you are grinning wider than the Cheshire Cat. While I'd like to think it's the pleasure of my company and my witty conversation prompting such a look, I must ask . . . why do you smile as though you could break out in laughter?"

"Ah," I say, licking my lower lip as I glance down at my ice-cream cone. So then he's noticed. Art seems to do a lot of that—noticing. Especially noticing things about me. I look back up, meet his eyes, and answer, "I was just thinking to myself that . . . well, I'm eating ice cream and taking a walk."

Art's face creases in a thoughtful expression. "Yes," he says after a moment. "I'd say that's an accurate description of what we are doing. And that is so highly amusing because . . . ?"

"Because it's something I've always wanted to do," I say, no longer about to laugh. Now my tone is full of feeling. This moment feels so much larger than simply a walk with an ice-cream cone. And even though the simple pleasure was deferred for years, now that it has arrived, I'm so very glad that I waited, so that the first time could be with this kind young man who treats me like such a dear friend.

ON THE THIRD day of our time together, Art borrows his aunt's small rowboat and brings me down to a pebbly patch of the river landing. He helps me into the narrow seat at the bow of the wobbly rowboat, and he pushes us off, guiding us out for a slow cruise up the Hudson. We come to a break in the rocky riverbank where a small sandy beach offers us a soft landing. The day is a warm one, and a thin sheen of perspiration slicks Art's suntanned brow from the exertion of his rowing. He asks me if I'd like to alight from the boat or carry on. Though I'm enjoying myself immensely, I feel as though he could use a reprieve.

"Let's take a break," I answer, and without warning, I bend over and kick off my boots and roll down my silk stockings. Grabbing my pale blue skirt in my fists, I hop into the shallow water and relish the cold as it wraps around my ankles and bare feet.

"It feels so nice!" I call to Art, who remains seated, bobbing in the rowboat. His expression is a bit stunned, and I suspect it's not due to the bright sunshine but rather my abrupt disembarkation from the boat, and even more so my sudden decision to show the flesh of my ankles. I suppose he temporarily forgot that I'm a showgirl—I show much more than my ankles on a daily basis. But his chivalrous innocence strikes me as adorable.

"Won't you join me?" I try to coax him into the water with a small splash in his direction.

"Oh? Oh, all right," he says, his usually relaxed demeanor noticeably ruffled as he lowers the oars into the boat and kicks off his own shoes. After removing his socks, he hops into the water with one agile leap and drags the boat safely ashore. "Chilly, but refreshing," he says, smiling in my direction. I'm twirling in the water, the bottom of my skirt getting soaked, but I don't mind.

Art stands in silence, watching me. After a minute, with my breathing a bit heavier, I pause, staring at him. Taking a step closer, I say: "Art the Artist."

"Yes?" His cheeks are flushed, ruddy from his rowing and the heat, and perhaps something else.

I cock my head to the side. "I find it unfair that you've seen me at work, but I've yet to see you do yours."

He lifts a hand to his brow, as though seeking a break from the bright sunshine. "What do you mean?"

Still twirling my skirt in my hands, swaying like the waves of the river, I say: "Only, I'd like to see some of your sketches."

Art considers this for a moment. "I could draw a sketch just for you."

"Even better," I answer, my head tilting sideways. "And what would your subject be?"

He doesn't miss a beat before he answers, "You."

"Me?"

He nods.

"You can turn me into a cartoon?"

"I'm not certain there's any turning that face into a cartoon, but I can try."

THE NEXT DAY we set up at a small park just a short walk from Aunt Alice's home, where there's a charming little gazebo and a flat meadow of thick summer grass stippled with wildflowers. Art spreads a white sheet for me to sit on, and I settle in, fanning out the skirt of my cream-colored day dress. I feel uncharacteristically nervous, though I've posed more times than I can count. But now, trying to quell my jumpy nerves, I pull in a slow breath and hope that I've chosen an outfit that suits Art for his drawing.

I'm not the only one who appears anxious. "I'm trying not to think about Mr. Gibson. Or Mr. Beckwith," Art admits, flashing a lopsided grin as he sharpens a thin pencil. "A fair bit of pressure."

This puts me at ease, to hear that he's also feeling shy about this collaboration. "And here I thought I was supposed to be off duty for the summer," I say.

"Consider me your charity case, then. A young new artist in need of practice."

"Charity indeed; I doubt you could afford me." I regret the words as soon as they've slipped out. Thoughtless words—I meant them as a joke, but I see the way Art's smile drops.

Quietly, he says, "I certainly could not, Miss Talbot."

"No, no," I hasten to add. "I'm only joking. Please, I remember all too well that it was *I* who asked *you* to show me your sketching. I've never been done in cartoon before, Art. This is a special treat."

He nods, and I see—I very much hope—that all is right between us once more. Picking up a blank sheet, Art sets it in place on his small wooden easel, and his expression shifts to a mien of purposeful attention. He's looking at me with a studying, observant gaze. So this is Art the Artist, at work. I like seeing this side of him.

We sit in quiet for a while as Art's hand moves in quick strokes behind the easel. My body settles into position, and so, too, does his. I see, gratefully, that he appears to have recovered his equilibrium, even his happy and congenial manner, when he jokes that my hair alone would require him to take a master class. "Especially with this breeze."

I feel the breeze; I notice how it flutters my hair, my skirts, but after a while my muscle memory kicks in, and I slip into the peaceful trancelike state that has always carried me through my hours of motionless posing. Cartoon in pencil is done much more quickly than oils or watercolors, and when Art asks me if I'd like to take a peek, I hop up happily, thinking how pleasant a sitting it was.

And then Art shows me the paper.

A gasp slips out of me as I see his work. I feel my lips curl into a surprised smile, and it takes me a few moments to find words. "Why, Art." I look to him, his gaze eager and expectant, then I turn back to his drawing, which is unlike any rendering I've ever seen—though I've been captured in countless poses, costumes, and scenarios. "You've painted me with wings."

"I did," he answers.

"And why is that?" I ask.

"I thought you could be a bird. Or . . . an angel." *Don't say fairy. Please don't say fairy.* He doesn't. He goes on: "Because I wanted to give you the gift of flight."

I swallow, then I ask, "So that I might fly to . . . where?"

"Anywhere," he answers, his voice soft. "Freedom."

I tip my head to the side, looking out over the river just as a bird flaps its own wings over the smooth surface of the water. I watch it rise until it eventually disappears across the distant bank. But I'm not yet ready to meet Art's gaze, though I know he's still holding me in his.

Stanny told me on so many occasions that he thought I might have wings, that I was a fairy. A fairy *he* conjured. That I'd fallen into his world as though through a rip in heaven's seam, some fateful error that had led me to him, as the embodiment of all his desires. Art wishes to give me wings so that I can fly to my freedom.

I study the drawing a moment more in silence. I take in the lines and curves of Art's strokes, the shading of my features, the dynamism and depth of my expression. Finally raising my gaze to lock with his, I say, "You've drawn my face to look a bit sad."

A small nod as he agrees. "Just a bit."

"Do you think I'm a bit sad?"

"Sometimes," he says. And then, his green eyes crinkling into a playful smile, he tilts toward me and says, "But not when I'm around."

I laugh at this, then look once more at my drawing. "Will you sign it for me, please?" And as he does so, I realize that, of the dozens of men who have drawn me and studied me, of the hundreds who have looked on my face and figure in flesh and print, Art Darrow is the first man who has looked with the purpose of truly seeing me.

Chapter Thirty

"You walk first, in front of me," Art says, gesturing straight ahead up the narrow forest path. "It's better that way, in case of rattlesnakes."

"*What?*" I throw him a horrified look. "I'm not certain I wish to be joined by rattlesnakes."

"It's possible. They do nest up here. But that's why I'm having you walk first."

I'm confused, and he sees this. "They are sleeping, in the heat of the day. Our walking could wake them, but if you go first, you'll just get the drowsy warning rattle. It's the second fellow who gets the strike. So you'll be fine. Just promise me, if I perish, you'll hold me in your arms? I couldn't imagine a sweeter ending."

"Art!" He's joking, but still, I'm not all that comfortable with that image.

"We'll be fine. Don't you trust me, Evelyn?"

I fall silent for a moment as I realize that, yes, I do. I trust Art. So I resume my walking. He chatters on, entirely unfazed, just one step behind me: "If we move at a brisk pace, we can slip by without tipping off the devils," he reassures me, and he sounds so unconcerned that I decide to take his word for it. We carry on up the narrow, wooded path through the forest.

It's our sixth day together. I've been counting all week with a thickening knot of dread, because I cannot help but suspect that he will be leaving soon. Any day now, I would imagine, given the fact that he told me he had one week left at his aunt's home. I haven't asked for the exact day of his departure, because I don't wish to think of him leaving. Especially when I still have a month to go up here in the country. What will I do without his company?

As we walk along together, I have to admit to myself: it's more than his company that I enjoy, in truth. It's *him*. It's everything about him.

As we come to the end of our path, stepping out onto a hilltop clearing with a sweeping view of what appears to be the entire Hudson Highlands beneath us, I gasp. "Why, Art, it's stunning!" I look down on the water far below as it curves between the two banks.

"Isn't it?" I can hear his breath at my side. I can smell his fresh scent, peppermint and something else, like sun-warmed grass. My heart is racing from the hike, but also because of his proximity. We stand together and admire the scene in companionable silence. I don't want to spoil the moment by asking the dreaded question: When does he leave?

"The river that flows both ways," he says eventually.

"Pardon?" I turn toward him.

"It's what the Lenape call it—Muhheakantuck, the river that flows both ways. Because the Hudson moves with the tides. Most extraordinary."

Learn to move, to adapt. Like water. In short, learn to swim. And then you'll survive. Mr. Gibson's advice from what feels like another lifetime. Have I learned to move like water? I've survived, so far.

Looking at Art, I think: *With him, I wouldn't have to simply survive. With him, I could live.* A beat later, another thought fills me—no, it's more than a thought, it's a longing—I wish for Art to kiss me.

"Most extraordinary, really," he says, as his eyes meet mine. His voice sounds thick with . . . something. Is it also longing? The same longing I feel?

But Art turns away, looks back over the view one more time,

and begins to walk toward the wooded path. He simply leaves me there, alone on that precipice, ready to leap. But with no one to take the leap along with me.

I RETURN TO the castle an hour later, having descended from our hike to bid farewell to Art, my legs tired, my mind unsettled.

Art Darrow offered to be my friend, and that seems to be all that we shall be. For now, I suppose, he will depart his aunt's home any day. *Not tomorrow?* I wonder in a sudden panic. No, for when he took his leave today, he did not mention a departure. Surely, he'd tell me. He'd give me a proper farewell. Perhaps even suggest that we meet up again in the autumn, once we are both back in Manhattan. Oh, but I don't wish for him to leave me alone here in the country.

I slip away to my bedroom and flop down in bed, clutching my sketch that Art made for me. Of all the renderings that any man has done of me, this one is the most treasured. It occurs to me just then that I've never seen the photographs that Stan had Mr. Sidwell shoot. Stan told me they would be for me, for my portfolio.

He's kept them for himself. I am sure of it. I can hear his voice in my head; I know precisely what he would say if I were to press him for the photographs, the images that he told me would be mine and would help me in my career. *Haven't I gotten you enough work, Kitten? It's not like you're suffering from a shortage of offers.*

The thought of Stan makes me seethe. Repulsion, resentment, a noxious brew that boils too uncomfortably close to shame. No, I don't want to think of him. Not when I am here with Arthur, who makes me feel entirely the opposite in every way. I blink, pushing all thoughts of Stanley Pierce aside, and I look once more at my sketch, at my wings, at my face. Art, who drew me with such attention and care. Art, who somehow saw beneath so many layers to find the sadness I've learned to conceal. Art, who had observed that I'm sad but then said, "*Not when I'm around.*" It's true. Art, who makes me happy, who makes me laugh.

I wallow through the remainder of the afternoon as though in some sort of agitated fever dream. I'm still feeling melancholy when I find Mamma in the dimly lit corridor before dinner. Her pinched features halt my footsteps. I quickly tuck Art's sketch away, out of sight into my skirt pocket, as she turns to me. She doesn't notice or inquire about the paper I was holding, and in fact she's holding two pieces of paper in her own hands.

One item she does not mention or offer to show to me, but I can guess: it's a telegram. The second paper, she extends toward me. It's a clipping from a newspaper. The *Herald*. There's no image, but there is text, and I feel my heart squeeze as I quickly scan the headline.

CARTOONIST WOOING MISS TALBOT!

I glance at Mamma, whose face is hard as stone, and then I read on.

> Arthur Darrow, a sketch artist in the employment of Mr. Hearst, is seizing his moment with the Broadway Beauty who has most recently delighted audience members as the lovely Lakshmi. The young pair were seen strolling outside of Manhattan on a day filled with summer sunshine and even sunnier smiles.
>
> Miss Talbot, a bright light of the Great White Way, has been on hiatus from the stage this month, leaving theatergoers bereft, but she looked to have nary a thought for her legions of disappointed devotees as the handsome Mr. Darrow offered his arm. Nor did Miss T. seem to be pining for her oft-seen companion, celebrated architect Stanley Pierce, as he travels abroad this month.
>
> Readers may be wondering: While the Cat is away, will this pair of Country Mice play?

I lower the paper with trembling hands, but force myself to look directly into Mamma's eyes. I see how pale she's gone. I take in a fortifying breath, and then I say: "Well, someone's spied on us, it would seem."

Mamma's words are toneless as she asks: "But they saw correctly?"

"I've been out with Mr. Darrow, yes. You know that, Mamma. We've certainly taken a few walks this week, and yes, he has offered his arm at times. But I'm not entirely sure why that would warrant a headline."

"You know that the papers always want news of you, Florence," Mamma retorts.

"There must be a shortage of other news," I say, affecting a look of disinterest and giving a casual shrug as I offer the paper back to her.

"The implication is that the pair of you are . . . well, that it's become romantic. Florence, you cannot really think to take up with that pup?"

Mamma's words are so like something Stanny would say, I can't help but laugh. It's a joyless laugh. And now I know who sent the telegram. The collusion between them—the secret communications, their efforts to control my every move—it makes me want to anger her, not assuage her. "Why shouldn't I take up with him, Mamma?"

It works—my words hit their mark. I can see the heat rise in my mother. Rage—or something else. Fear? "Stanley will be back from Europe any day. You know he hears everything. Why, what if . . ." She shudders, gives a quick shake of her head. "No, it doesn't bear thinking. You will not receive that Darrow scoundrel again."

"Scoundrel? *He's* the scoundrel? Why, if only you knew, Mamma."

Another defiant toss of her head, as though she won't even allow my words to take purchase in her mind. "Enough! Leave me. I don't want to see you. Not until you've seen reason."

"Very well," I say, wheeling around and charging away from the dining room.

"You will listen to me. I'm your mother!"

I'll listen to her; she told me to leave. So I slip right out the back door of the castle, and in the pale light of the settling dusk, I walk down the hill.

I don't stop or even slow my pace as the lane curves away from the castle, past the brook, and down toward the fields that nestle into the bottom of the hillside. It's nearly sunset by the time I reach the border of Water's Edge. I glance toward the river, its gentle curves awash in the fading light. It'll be suppertime for Art and his aunt. I don't bother to suppress my frown.

I turn and look out over the purpled meadows, and I wonder if Mamma has noticed I'm gone. I very much doubt it. I suspect she railed and told the servants to make her a tray, which she's taken to her bedroom without an inquiry after me.

The long walk gave me plenty of silence and time alone with my thoughts, but still I feel that I've arrived at no answers. What is happening here, between me and Art? Is it, as the article implied, a romantic liaison, or does he merely see me as a friend? Even a lonely charity case?

I know that he was taken with me when we first met, and certainly there have been moments when he's looked at me in such a way that I suspected he did harbor some feelings that were more than simply friendship. And yet, he's been such a gentleman; he's never tried anything untoward. He's the exact opposite of Stanley Pierce.

What will I do about Stan? What do I envision for my life when I return this fall to the city? How could Mamma and I possibly carry on with our New York life without him as our benefactor? But far worse to consider is the alternative—taking back up with him as we were before.

I could not. The thought makes me shudder.

And why have I walked to Water's Edge? Did I truly intend to come here and knock, then waltz in for supper with Art and Aunt Alice? No, no. I need to sit and think, before I do anything rash and foolish. But before I've done so, a voice calls out across the warm evening air. "Evelyn? Is that you?"

My cheeks heat with instant embarrassment as I spot Art, standing in the candlelit doorway, and I know that he's seen me. Lurking here, alone and uninvited, in his aunt's garden.

I try to offer a laugh, but it comes out like a puff of air. "Oh, Art! Hello!"

"Hello," he answers back, his confused features rising in a smile as he steps out into the evening.

"You must think me terribly rude to appear like this."

"On the contrary, I couldn't be more delighted." He looks relaxed, the jacket of his ever-present suit unbuttoned, cravat off, and the top of his collar undone. His hair is uncombed, even a bit messy. He really is impossibly handsome, and my heart tips sideways with longing for his young and unspoiled beauty.

Art pauses a few steps before me, crossing his arms in a casual stance. "You may appear in this garden anytime you like. Only, when I glimpsed your shape from my window, I believed I must be seeing things. Hoping so badly to see you that I'd imagined your likeness as some illusion."

So then, he did want to see me. The sound of the evening all around drones in my ears, the crickets, the peepers, plus the thrashing of my suddenly quickened heartbeat. I pull back my shoulders and decide that I will meet him in a place of candor, too. "Art, I'm afraid that you and I have caused a bit of a stir."

He narrows his eyes. "Oh?"

I tell him about the *Herald* article and Mamma's admonition that I am to stay away from him. He uncrosses his arms, a thoughtful look creasing his features. "But I'm confused. Why can't we be seen together?" he asks. "What's the harm in that?"

A fluttering of hope dances through my belly like the wings of a butterfly. Art does wish to be seen with me! But just as quickly, that joy flies away. In its place, a terrible worry settles like a leaden weight: Am I ready to discuss everything with Art?

I sigh. The only way to remove this stone I've been forced to carry is by taking it up. So in that moment I decide: I must tell Art the truth. Or at least enough of it for him to understand—me and my highly unusual, complicated life.

I draw in a long, steadying breath, and then I begin. "I had a . . . friend . . . back in New York City. He's taken a particular interest in my career. He's an investor in several shows. You could say he's been very generous toward me, and my mother, and . . . my brother." My voice falters, and I feel myself careening toward the loss of all my resolve and composure. But then I swallow and will myself to go on. "But this fellow might get, er, that is to say, he might not be happy to see reports of me spending time with another man. He might become, well, jealous."

I hear the sound of Art's exhale. *What must he think?* The silence stretches between us, filled with the pulsing of my unease and the sounds of the crickets and other nocturnal creatures until, after what feels like an eternity, Art says only, "I see."

Does he? Can he truly know what it means to be starving, as I was? To find a temporary salvation on the stage, only to learn the hard realities of that place? Can Art, or any man who has never been kicked out of a home for which he could not pay the rent, understand how it feels to be a fatherless showgirl? Forced to accept a rich man's largesse in a most terrible deal, in order to save herself and her family?

But Art doesn't press for more details, and I'm so unbelievably grateful for that courtesy that it gives my heart another pinch. Then follows another thought: *Mamma.* Am I being selfish here, risking everything? Not for myself. I could survive on my salary. But there's Mamma's life, too. I can't carry all of it on my own earnings. And God forbid, if I were to break with Stan, would that put my work in jeopardy? He's an investor in so many of these theater companies; it's smoothed the way for some of my work. If I offend him, might that have the opposite effect?

It's getting darker now as evening settles more fully around us. I see Art's face only through the graying shadows, but when he speaks at last, his voice is steady, and I can hear deep feeling in it. "Listen, Evelyn. I don't know much about the world of Broadway. Or the life you live in New York. The life you've had to live. All I know is that I want to. To know more. To know you."

I'm so relieved that I could weep. That Art is not horrified by me, by any of what I've revealed to him or even my abrupt and inelegant appearance outside his door. But then he takes one step closer, eliminating the gap between us, and to my further surprise, he reaches forward to take my hand in his, saying, "You've caught me entirely unaware, Evelyn."

My heart twinges. "I know. I'm sorry. I shouldn't have just come without—"

"No, I don't mean finding you out here tonight."

I swallow, and my throat feels thick. "Oh?"

"No, I mean all of it. I mean you." Art lets out a low laugh. "I came up here, supposing I'd have a quiet visit with Aunt Alice. And instead, you appeared before me. And well, I am no longer even aware of what's night and what's day. I'm not sure of anything. Only that I now spend my time counting down the minutes until I can see you next."

My entire body could melt with relief—to hear Art speak these words that echo my own frantic thoughts and entirely unexpected longing. Without thinking, without giving myself time to summon restraint or reason, I lean toward Art, and I press my lips to his. I hear his small gasp of surprise, feel the slight tensing of his startled body. But he's not the one in pursuit; it's me, so I lean even closer to him, hoping to give him permission to receive my kiss. And to return it.

But he doesn't. Instead, Art pulls back, cleaving his lips from mine. And he whispers one cruel and heartbreaking word: "No."

I'm confused. And crushed. Did I misunderstand all of what he just said, what I took to be a confession of his feelings for me?

"No," he says again, another stab to my heart. But then he goes on, "Not here. There's something . . . There's a place I'd like to show you. Would you walk with me?"

He's still holding my hand, and I can feel his gentle tug. "What place?" I ask. "In the dark?"

"Yes, I know it well enough, I could lead you there with my eyes closed."

"All right," I agree, returning the gentle squeeze of his hand and falling into step beside him. We walk in silence for several minutes. Art guides me through the dark and up a slight incline until we come to a halt, and I can't help but gasp in surprised delight. It's not dark here, even though night has fallen over us. "Where are we?"

"We are in Aunt Alice's orchard," he replies.

"What . . . what are they?" I ask, looking around at the flickering lights, too many to count.

"Fireflies," he answers, and I can hear the smile in his voice.

"When I was a child, Aunt Alice would bring me up here on summer nights. They love the fruit trees. They really are something, aren't they?"

"Fireflies, yes," I repeat. Though I haven't seen a firefly in years, living in cities as we have, I remember them from when Daddy was alive, from my summer nights as a child. There must be thousands of them here now. They light up the dark all around us. *Forget your tower lights, Stan,* I think. The air glimmers as the glowing creatures dance around the fragrant fruit trees, casting their spell of pure and pastoral magic.

"What do you think?" he asks.

"I think we could be in *Midsummer Night's Dream,*" I reply, laughing, dropping his hand, and running up the nearest row of trees. "How long will they be here?"

"A few weeks," he answers. "For the summer, but not after."

"That makes me sad," I say, pausing my steps. "I wish it could last forever."

"Evelyn." When Art says my name, I can tell he's right next to me. I can feel him, the heat from his body, the energy that seeps off of him. It's desire, and it's the first time I've ever sensed him overcome by it; it's the same need that overpowers me as I turn toward him. Finally, as he leans toward me, and he kisses me, I kiss him back with all of the longing that has been building inside me. And when I raise my arms to twine them around his neck and pull him closer, his courteous timidity melts away at last. He kisses me with a hunger that feels as though it could swallow us both.

"Art," I whisper his name. There's something happening inside of me, something I've never experienced before, and I'm begging him to help me because he's the only person who can.

He removes his jacket, laying it down on the ground. As I lower myself onto it, I reach for him and pull him to me. His body curls over mine, and I can feel the desire that pulses in him, in both of us.

I need to be closer to him, to peel away layers until there's nothing separating us. He's guiding me out of the folds of my dress as I'm pulling at his buttons. When I feel the warmth of his skin, my own flesh ripples in delightful response. I've never known anything like this—his fresh scent, his taut limbs, his body that fits so perfectly against mine that it feels as though we were formed for each other.

Still I crave even more of him. I know what comes next; of course I do. But I've never longed for it. Not like I do now. "Art, please." I'm beneath him, awaiting him, in need of him to deliver me.

Just as I think I can't bear it a moment longer, he pulls back. "Evelyn, my angel." His voice is raspy. "We shouldn't."

"Don't you wish . . . ?" My hand slides over his body, my touch whisper soft as I trace a line down his back. I sense his own body crying out for more. But he stills my hands, pressing his own palms gently on top.

"Of course I do, my beauty. Every ounce of my being longs for you. But not like this. Not unless . . . Oh, Evelyn, I know this sounds rash, but I'm certain of it. I've never been more certain of anything. Will you marry me? Be mine not only right now but forever?"

I answer first with my lips, pulling him back to me. "Yes, Art, I will," I murmur into his ear. And with that, I feel the very last drop of resistance leave him, and he gives himself over to me as our bodies meet in the deepest of places. We ride the swell of our shared desire together. I need him just as madly as he needs me, and we can only make it to the other side of this perfect torture if we cross over as one. I tremble as his body loves mine; it's unlike anything I've ever experienced, the pressure and the pleasure building until there's nothing left to do but to break apart. And when, at last, we cry out together in our shared joy, I feel as though our promise of eternity has already been consecrated.

Chapter Thirty-One

"Where do you live, Art?" My body is folded into his, both of us lying beneath the canopy of fireflies and, beyond that, the stars. It's in this moment of sweet repose that I've realized how little I know of the details of his life. An inevitability, I suppose, given the fact that our entire acquaintance has extended little more than the length of a week. But now I have questions. "I know you live in Manhattan, but where?"

His finger traces a slow circle around my bare shoulder. "I have rooms in the Algonquin."

I laugh at this, propping myself up on my elbow.

"What's funny?" he asks.

"I also live in a hotel."

"Yes, you do. Now you live at the Algonquin. With me."

I place a soft kiss on his earnest face as a tendril of my dark hair slides over my shoulder. Art takes it in his fingers. His touch is so tender, so gentle, and that, combined with the immense relief I feel as I realize that I can leave my suite at the Audubon—with the daily visits from Stan—is enough to make me break out in a full peal of laughter. But I don't. Because just then another pressing question pops into my mind. "What will we do? When we are back in the city?"

"We will do whatever it is you want, Evie. I'll continue to work for Mr. Hearst. You'll continue to sing and dance. But that's only work. What will we do—in life? We'll do everything and anything. We will walk the streets of Chinatown. Or eat bowls of red pasta on Mulberry Street. Drink flagons of red wine."

"I prefer champagne."

"Champagne? All right. Then you shall have it. We can fill our entire bathtub with it."

But the thought of the hotel suite has planted an unsettling thought in my mind: *Mamma.* She may not have noticed I slipped out this evening, if she retreated to her own bedroom for the night in a sulk. But surely she will notice by the morning. And how would Aunt Alice feel if she knew I was spending the night here? But I push those worries from my mind, sliding closer to Art and nuzzling my head into the crook of his neck. The scent of him is intoxicating. For now, the night is dark, and we are protected. For just a few more hours.

I find my lover's face, and I give him a long kiss, which leads to his hands seeking out the soft curves of my back and pulling me closer to his own body. I sigh in willing and delicious delight, happily yielding to his roving touch.

As the night hours stretch on, we do not spare a thought for sleep. The noises of the darkness continue all around us, so many living creatures calling out in high summer for mates and companionship, and we, too, offer up our own cries to the chorus. And when the sun begins to send its first hints of pale purple through the dark, I am still in Art's arms. Sated and yet still eager for more of his touch, I smile with giddy joy, knowing that it's to be a new day for me.

BUT WE CAN'T REMAIN. Not at Aunt Alice's and certainly not with Mamma in the castle. The papers have already scented our trail, but if and when it comes out that we are engaged, it will be a full-blown frenzy.

While I'm used to being photographed and written about in my life in Manhattan, I do feel the prick of guilt for bringing my chaotic life to Aunt Alice's private, peaceful idyll. Nevertheless, I know we must face her. We owe her that courtesy at least.

Art and I find her at the breakfast table. We walk in, arms

linked, and I see from her wide eyes that Aunt Alice is stunned, wondering what I am doing in her home. Art explains, as matter-of-factly as if he were describing the balmy summer weather, that I arrived last night, and that we have decided to marry.

"You . . . you spent the night here?" Aunt Alice asks me, her toast slipping from her fingers onto the table.

"I did," I answer.

"And . . . your mother, dear girl?"

"She's up at Stonetop," I answer.

A heavy sigh, and then the old woman's quiet, almost mournful words: "I see." But Aunt Alice still has many questions, as is evident from her strained expression. And she appears now to be wrestling with her own propriety in determining whether or not to ask them. Arthur preempts her, declaring for a second time that we wish to marry.

"Well, then, that's that." Aunt Alice clears her throat. For as lovely and welcoming as she's been to me, I doubt a stage girl and artists' model is the bride she envisioned for her beloved nephew, but she does not say that. Instead she asks, "Have you secured your mother's blessing?" She looks to me and then her nephew.

I answer, "Not yet." I shift on my feet, but Art's hand holding mine gives me a jolt of much-needed confidence. "She may need some convincing. But . . . the decision is mine."

Aunt Alice takes the handle of her teacup in her fingers, turning it slowly in the saucer, but doesn't take a sip. "Well, if your mother still needs some convincing, I suggest you get to work. And quickly. The quicker the better. One likes to have these things buttoned up before they become a scandal."

I throw Art a sideways look and see that he feels the same relief I do—Aunt Alice, though clearly caught by surprise, is not withholding her blessing. She is not going to dress us down for our indecent or backward way of going about our courtship. Nor will she disown her nephew. That's one less obstacle in our way.

But neither Art nor I has any illusions—the next steps shall be far more complicated. We make a decision that morning: the best plan, at this point, is to climb like scolded children into Alice's coach and ride back to New York City. I'll collect everything I can from the Audubon and move into Art's suite at the Algonquin. Before going, I'll write to Mamma, a long and thorough letter explaining everything that's happened. Requesting her blessing for our marriage, asking for her attendance at our wedding, the details of which we have not yet settled. First, I must bring her around to this reality. I don't know precisely how the next few days or months will look, but I know that, as long as I'm with Art, all will be well.

And so that night, as we roll back into Manhattan, keeping our heads down as we alight from the coach and skitter quickly into Art's hotel, we hold hands and can't help but laugh like giddy youngsters evading a censorious chaperone. We feel excited and optimistic; we are at the outset of a grand adventure, a life together. Art leads me up the stairs and hoists me into his arms as we trundle across the threshold of his suite. Our suite. Our new home. There, alone, we decide to christen our shared space the best way we know how, by collapsing into each other's arms and landing on the bed, falling together into the all-consuming pleasures that push all worries away.

Chapter Thirty-Two

I ALWAYS THOUGHT IT WAS AN ODD TERM, *LOVEMAKING*. I DIDN'T understand what it was getting at. With Stanley, the physical act was a one-way transaction in which nothing new was *made*; something was only taken: he longed to consume me, to take from me to slake his own rapacious desire. After the first few times it was no longer outright unpleasant, but it was never pleasurable, either. It was something for him to enjoy and for me to bear.

But now I understand why it's called lovemaking. Each time Art pulls me into his arms, we fall further in love, and we make more of the love that exists between us. We leap together and find that we can fly.

Our first days together back in New York City, it really does feel as though we are flying high. Tucked away in a place all our own, with the world still unaware of our secret, we have interest in little other than exploring each other's bodies. Savoring our private vows. Giving and receiving pleasure with generosity and tenderness. We are young, and we are strong, and we are enraptured—and every time we come together, it is a further proof of the fact that our bodies were made for each other.

When our physical frames occasionally exhaust themselves, there are plenty of other entertainments just for us in our private little bliss. Art sketches me, or I sing for him. He reads aloud from magazines as I luxuriate in the bathtub. We laze in bed and order in food. We doze and we talk. We talk about life, and the plans for our future. We play with the question of whether we ought to move to Newport or perhaps even California.

After a week passes in this isolated and deliciously indulgent way, even we begin to realize that we must soon face reality. I posted a letter to Mamma my first day back in Manhattan, and I know she must have received it by now, but she's sent me no response.

I am still on hiatus with the *Wildflowers* company and not expected back at work just yet, but Art will soon have to return to Mr. Hearst's offices. Our sweet summer idyll must inevitably come to an end. But I'm excited for our life together. I can't remember ever feeling this excited for all that is to come, except for maybe the times when I was a little girl and Daddy promised me we could run away to see the world. But that was never reality; I see that now. This, what Art and I have, is real.

· ◆ ·

My fiancé and I are returning from an afternoon stroll in Central Park, discussing where we ought to get married. My first choice is Aunt Alice's—an exchange of vows at the small stone church just up the lane and then an intimate luncheon at Water's Edge. It's where we started our courtship. It's where I'd like us to start our married life together. Art promises he will write to Aunt Alice and ask her if that would be all right. He suspects that, as long as I have Mamma's blessing and Mamma is in attendance, Aunt Alice would be happy to oblige.

But as we turn the corner onto Forty-fourth Street and I see the familiar limestone façade of the Algonquin, I notice before it another familiar—and in this case most unwelcome—sight. The cranberry-red auto. And Mamma, standing beneath the hotel awning, with Stan at her side.

In the same instant I see the pair of them, they see us, and Stanny's eyes take in the sight of my arm woven through Art's. I stop walking, but I do not lower my arm. In fact, I edge even closer to my lover, so our bodies meld together.

Mamma turns away, staring off toward the busy street with a look of disgust. But Stan says: "You're not taking much care to be discreet, are you?" Nothing else. He does not say hello to me or to Art. He merely looks at us as if we ought to be ashamed of ourselves.

But why should we feel any shame, any need to hide? No, *he's* the one who has long had to be discreet, because what he does is illicit and sinful. Art and I are in love and engaged to be married. Why must we hide?

We do not take another step toward them, nor do I answer Stan. Instead, I say only: "Hello, Mamma." I haven't seen her since the night I left the castle, the night Art and I spent together under the stars. "Did you receive my letter?"

Mamma looks to Stan but doesn't meet my eyes. Infuriatingly, it's Stan who speaks again. "What are your intentions, lad?" He's looking at Art like a piece of debris he's just peeled off the sole of his shoe.

But Art is defiant as he stands a bit taller at my side, his tone unapologetic. "I've asked Evie to marry me."

Stanny and Mamma exchange a glance, as Mamma's face goes a shade paler. But Stanny looks back to Art and offers a derisive smirk. "And what did she say?"

"I said yes, of course," I interject. I've had enough of this, of Stan speaking *about* me but not *to* me. "Mamma, I wrote you. We are engaged to be married." Still she won't meet my eyes.

Stan appears relaxed, even a bit amused as his lips curl into a smile beneath his mustache. "How do you plan to pay for the wedding?"

This is a preposterous question, and I let Stan know that I think so. "It's not a concern. We don't want anything lavish."

"Oh, but after that?" Stan arcs an eyebrow, briefly glances toward me before fixing his cool stare back on Art. "How are you going to afford all this, boy? You know this girl expects oysters and pearls. What will the two of you live on?"

"We will live on love," Art answers, taking my hand in his and giving it a squeeze. I feel how his skin has gone clammy, but I pull back my shoulders, meeting Stanny's eyes dead-on. He is silent for a moment before his gaze slides back toward Art. "Have you been prudent?"

This catches me a bit back on my heels as I'm not entirely sure what he's asking. Is he asking whether we have been intimate? It's none of his business.

Neither Art nor I says a thing, and then Stan, for the first time in this exchange, appears to lose his equanimity, and he practically growls, "You're both idiots, is what you are! Damned fools, the pair of you!"

His ire only serves to chill the blood in my veins, and I summon that same iciness to my voice as I say, "Stan, I really don't feel it's your place to—"

But he ignores me entirely, taking a step closer to us and practically spitting into Art's face as he carries on. "You very well may have just ruined her entire career, her life, and you know it." Then Stan cuts his angry eyes toward me and holds me in his gaze, but I resist the urge to withdraw, or wince. Ours is a wordless but deafening face-off, and I hope he sees the steel of my will. No one says a thing. After a long moment, it is Stan who looks away, to Mamma, and he says: "She needs to be seen by a doctor."

Mamma winces. "A doctor?" I ask, confused by this abrupt turn. A moment ago we were speaking about the wedding. I'm standing here before them full of health and vim. In love. Feeling better than I can ever remember feeling.

"I can assure you, I feel just fine," I answer, taking care to keep my voice low as I say it, for by now a small crowd has begun to gather around us. We are in a busy part of town, and I'd venture a guess that Stan, Art, and I are three of the most recognizable faces in the city, as the papers have been swirling lately with gossip and speculation as to my location and my standing in relation to my famous benefactor and my rumored young lover. The fact that people are watching us now puts me on edge.

Stan is staring in silent fury at Art, and he says only, "You're a cad."

Art responds quietly, "She's accepted my proposal. We've already begun to consider arrangements for the wedding."

"It's true," I say, stepping between them but looking to Mamma. "I wrote you immediately. I left word at your hotel, too. I'm not doing anything shameful. I only wish for you to—"

"*My* hotel?" Mamma speaks to me for the first time.

"Yes," I reply, shifting on my feet, pointing toward the building behind her. "I live here now, with Art."

"Oh, Florence, what have you done?" Mamma's face crumples. "Why must you ruin us all?"

But I don't understand why she sees this as ruination. I'm happy. Art is a wonderful man; he's offering me a beautiful life. Why would my mother not see this as a happy development?

Nor do I understand what she means when she goes on, repeating what Stan said: "We must get you to a doctor."

"Why?" I ask.

Stan steps toward me and whispers as he closes his grip around the top of my arm, "Do you really want to discuss this here, with so many people looking on?"

"Discuss *what*?" I look between the three of them, and in my frustration, I feel the tears beginning to burn my eyes.

Stan is muttering to Mamma, loud enough for me to hear: "She needs to be seen, sooner rather than later. I have a fellow who will be quiet about it."

To my surprise, Art does not voice any disagreement, but I see how his face has gone unnaturally pale. Stan tosses his chin toward the street. There waits his gleaming car, as always, with his driver.

Now the folks all around us are whispering—I see the interest building, along with the size of the crowd. I don't want a scene here. Another article, a gossipy column outlining this street-side showdown between my lovers past and present. A scandal that could further upset Aunt Alice or perhaps even scare the Broadway theaters off from working with me in the future.

I look from Stan toward Art, then toward my weeping mother, and something cracks in me. I don't know why Mamma feels this way, but I don't want to speak with her here, not on the crowded street like this. Perhaps I should simply see their senseless doctor, who will undoubtedly tell Mamma that I am fine. More than fine—happy, for the first time since I can remember. And then I can return here to be with Art, whether Mamma gives her blessing or not.

So, with an exhale that sounds like surrender, I agree. I throw my lover an apologetic look and walk like a prisoner into Stan's car, where I'm wedged in between Mamma and Stan. As we drive away, I see through the back window that Art is running after the car. I raise my hand toward him, press my palm to the rear glass, and I hear his voice follow us down the street: "Evie, we'll be married! When you come back, we'll marry!"

Chapter Thirty-Three

The doctor's office on West Thirty-seventh Street is small and quiet, and mercifully we are the only people inside. As soon as I'm ushered into a private room, with just Stanny taking his seat in a wooden chair beside a sterile examination table, I turn to him and whisper: "What are we doing here?" My words are hushed, but the rage is evident. "And why didn't you allow Mamma to come in with me?"

"You're welcome, Evelyn." Stan folds his hands across his lap, an infuriatingly placid expression settling on his face. "It's been a while. It's nice to see you, as well. I'd ask you how your summer has been, but I suspect that you've found ways to keep yourself . . . entertained."

"Oh, enough. This isn't some Broadway stage, and you can drop the act. You knew things were never going to be the same between us since—"

"To answer your question, Evelyn, your poor mother has been through enough. I've had my driver bring her back to the hotel so that she may rest. She need not endure this ordeal, on top of everything else you've put her through."

My cheeks flush with fury. "Why did you even drag me here in the first place? What are you getting at?"

Stan maintains his unnaturally bland mien as he says, "You're lucky I have a friend who could see you immediately, Kitten. Dr. Porter will be discreet."

"Discreet about *what*?"

Stan laughs, a joyless sound, and looks down at his hands with a woeful shake of his head. Then, peering back up at me, he asks: "In your utterly reckless behavior, did it never occur to you to protect yourself?"

Why would I have to protect myself from a man like Art? It's *Stan* from whom I should have protected myself.

"Evelyn, for heaven's sake, you really are just a kid." Stan exhales. "How do you think babies are made?"

My stomach feels as though it could drop out of my body, and I tip back, sitting down on the sterile medical table. The pieces click into place: Stan's words about the doctor, Mamma's concern, even Art's mute acquiescence. Stanny always used a device—he told me it was made of lambskin—when we were together. He told me it was to protect me, and I never inquired further, given how much more experienced he was. But now that I think of it, Art took no such precautions.

My entire body has gone cold. Have Art and I conceived a child? Now I see why Stan told Art he might have ruined my career—I would certainly have to leave the stage if I were with child. And my modeling work would be over. Am I ready for that? Am I ready, at eighteen, to be a mother?

But before I can make sense of any of this, a man in pince-nez spectacles and a long white coat enters the room without a knock. Dr. Porter. He does not ask for my name, but already seems to know it as he reviews the papers in his hands. "Miss Talbot, would you please remove your clothing and recline on the examination table?"

Horror washes through me. Total and complete mortification. Stan excuses himself, quitting the room as the doctor averts his eyes. When Dr. Porter uses a key to lock us in and then says, "Let's begin, Miss Talbot," I feel as lifeless as stone. Staring at the locked door, I refuse to move for a long moment.

An impatient clearing of his throat tells me that the doctor is waiting. His face betrays no emotion—perhaps it's even boredom that crosses his features. I feel that familiar void of nothingness opening deep in my core. Longing only for this to be over so that I may escape, I rasp out a breath. And then, moving like I am in the grip of a trance, I slip my skirt off, slide my stockings and bloomers down, and recline on the table to undergo the most degrading of physical examinations. He pokes and prods, but I resist the urge to show my pain or my shame. Instead, I slide inward to that quiet place in the back of my mind. That place behind all thoughts and feelings, that vacuum of deep numbness.

I don't know how long it lasts. Once dressed, I am forced to slip out of my trance to endure the doctor's mortifying litany of questions. I land back into myself, seated upright on the table, as Dr. Porter asks me whether I had "physical relations" with Mr. Arthur Darrow. I remain silent. "Did Mr. Darrow force himself on you?"

Given that the doctor has already had access to far more of me than I would have ever liked, I refuse to answer any of his vile questions. Eventually, perhaps seeing that he'd have more luck with a pile of bricks, the man leaves the room with a scowl.

He returns a moment later with Stan on his heels. "The girl is not answering," the doctor says, looking only at Stan.

Stan nods, a look of paternal concern plastered on his features as he steps slowly toward me, moving like he's approaching a trembling animal. An animal caught in a trap, which is precisely how I feel as Stan places his hand softly on my leg and entreats: "Evelyn, you must answer Dr. Porter. He will help you. Did this rake, this Darrow fellow, seduce you?"

I cross my arms and look out the window. Tense silence pulses in the room, and it's the doctor who breaks it. "Well, she does not appear to be with child."

With a conspiratorial tilt of his head, the man adds: "But whether or not she's intact, that's for you and the young lady to discuss." A quick glance passes between them, then a small shake of the doctor's bespectacled head.

I look to Stanny, astounded. He knows I'm not intact! It was he who broke me. But without any further discussion, he thanks the doctor and ushers me out. It's not until we are back in his motorcar that I hiss: "It was not Art who unvirgined me, and you know it better than anyone."

Now I see why he excused Mamma from this unholy errand!

Mamma who still, to this day, has never inquired about the true extent of my relations with Stan. Even as she appeared so eager to bring me to the doctor when Art was involved.

"I suppose now you're relieved, Stan," I say, my voice chilled with sudden clarity. "Now you can blame my besmirchment on another man and wash your hands of your original sin. That's why you brought me to that hoax of an appointment, isn't it?"

Stan ignores my question, but I see that his face has gone unnaturally pale. "So, did you . . . did you let him in?"

I'm so disgusted by him, by the charade he wishes to maintain of being my protector, when all along the opposite has been true. And now he can't allow me to be happy with the man I love. My rage and my hatred fuel my response. "Stan, I didn't *let* him in; I invited him in." Looking him squarely in the face, I add: "Which is more than you can say."

Stan lets out a slow whistle. I'm repulsed by the sight of his orange-silver mustache when his lips curl into a wry sneer and he says: "I gotta hand it to him, the kid is good. Got you to open up much quicker than I did. And for a pittance of the price."

I can't look at him a moment more. I turn, stare out the window as I mutter, "You couldn't possibly understand what Art and I share."

"You know the pup is penniless?"

This catches me off guard. "That's ridiculous. He's a very talented sketch artist."

"More like a con artist."

I turn my eyes, which are blazing, back onto Stan, hoping to burn him with my heat as I rasp: "You'll do anything you can to break us apart. To keep me in your control. But I won't listen to this."

"Oh, grow up, kid. You're acting your age. In addition to being impetuous, foolish, and reckless, you've also been incredibly lucky that your frolic with that stripling didn't leave you in the family way. But you still can't seem to see reason. Even after your mother and I pulled you back from the cliff just in time."

The motorcar has arrived outside the Audubon. I look through the window, then to Stan, sitting back against the seat. "What? No, I'm not staying here. Take me back to the Algonquin."

Stan has recovered his equanimity, and his tone is steady, even a bit frosty as he says, "Kitten, you're a mess. Go inside and take a bath. Talk to your mother. If the pup really wants to marry you, he'll keep till tomorrow. But just do me one final favor, and then you never need to speak to me again. Just sleep on it, would you?"

"You're a fool, Stanley Pierce," I hiss with quiet venom. "You think one night apart would change our minds? We are going to marry."

"Maybe you will," Stan says with a shrug. The chauffeur has arrived at my door, which he opens, letting in the noises of Midtown all around us as Stan stares at me but doesn't rise. "Then at least go have a conversation with your mother. It's the least you can do."

I step out of the auto and stride toward the hotel without a look back. My mind is battered, and I can feel the beginning of a headache as I trace the familiar route to our suite. I'm back in a place that I was once so elated to call home. But now, as I enter the apartment, I notice how the place that once felt like my luxurious haven has come to feel like a prison.

Chapter Thirty-Four

Mamma won't hear me, won't accept the fact that Art and I plan to marry. She keeps peppering me with frantic questions. "How could you be so ungrateful to Mr. Pierce? Did you forget all he's done for us? You'd throw it all away for some reckless frolic? How could you run away like some fallen girl? Don't you know better?"

But I do know—perfectly well—what I'm doing. I'm not a fallen woman. I've fallen in love. This "reckless frolic" is the first time I've been treated with actual love in years. But Mamma merely insists over and over that Art will be our ruin. My headache worsens, and it's been a long day, so I flop into bed. Tomorrow will be a new day, and I'll slip out early to return to Art.

I wake with the sun and dress in the lilac light of the early morning. Mamma's bedroom door is shut—a relief. I slip a note under her door, telling her I love her. That I am still her good and loyal daughter. That I wish her to be at my wedding and in my life with Art. And then, with my biggest garment bag stuffed with clothing, I tiptoe out.

The doorman stationed outside the Algonquin on the early-morning shift asks me if I have a reservation. This gives me pause—I'm not used to being stopped outside of doors and certainly not here, where I've been living for the past week. Why, this young man must know that I'm staying here with Art. Surely he's seen me entering and leaving on my fiancé's arm.

"I am Mr. Darrow's fiancée," I say, squaring my shoulders, a touch of pique in my voice.

"Mr. Darrow is no longer staying with us." Now the lad meets my eyes, and he does not match my irritation; in fact, there's something else I see in his gaze. Pity?

"What do you mean?" I ask, laboring to keep my posture firm and upright.

"Mr. Darrow has gone." The young man's eyes float to the ground. "Late last night."

"Gone? To where?"

"He didn't say. Simply left in a rush, after his visitor came by. Didn't even settle up his bill. Luckily Mr. Pierce saw to it on his way out."

My heart could drop into my stomach, then keep tumbling, splattering on the street below me. But I don't allow myself to crumble. No. Instead, I thank this man, and I turn on my heels, hailing the next hansom that speeds by and giving the driver the address of Stanny's townhouse on Twenty-fourth Street.

I storm in, unannounced, catching Stanny in his god-awful parlor, surrounded by the nauseating dark red hues he loves so dearly. He's sitting on the upholstered settee smoking a cigar. He looks up at me with a bemused expression, face relaxed and yet somehow expectant, as though he's been awaiting this visit. "What have you done?" I demand.

He puffs out a lazy exhale, his face wreathed in horrid cigar smoke. "In all honesty, Evelyn, I didn't have to do much at all. A huckster like that knows a good deal when he sees one."

I yearn to slap the half smile off his features. "How dare you?"

"How dare I what?"

"Whatever you did to run Art out . . . like you're some crime boss."

He throws his arms out wide, affecting a look of exaggerated innocence. "All we did was talk! Last night, I paid Mr. Darrow a visit at his nice hotel, and we had a frank conversation. Man-to-man." Another puff on his cigar. "He showed particular interest when I ran through the list of expenses necessary to keep you."

"This is preposterous!" I shake my head, refusing to allow Stan's vile words to take root. "Art does just fine for himself. We will be fine."

"You really believed that?" Stan shrugs, gumming his cigar. "So he gets a dollar here and there for his little scribbles? Pin money for you, Kitten."

"I've seen his family home. I've met his aunt."

"Ah, yes. The aunt who has a son of her own and not much to leave for her little nephew Arthur? You know how much debt your guy had? Why, he hadn't paid his hotel bill in over six months. You should have seen his relief when I offered to help him out of that hole."

"I don't care about any of that," I say, my words sharp. I refuse to think of all those nights we ordered room service on credit—filet mignon and champagne. I refuse to hear—or accept—that Stan picked up that bill. "I don't care about money."

"Well, he does," Stan replies.

"No, he cares about *me*. He loves me." I say it with all the conviction I can muster.

But Stan's straight, direct stare causes my heart to clench. And the words that he lobs next are even worse: "Kitten, when I offered that stripling first-class passage to Europe, some dough to take a few drawing lessons in Milan, why, he hopped on my offer quicker than he hopped on . . . Well, let's just leave it at that." Another exhale of putrid smoke as Stan's eyes glow with satisfaction.

My legs give out beneath me, and I sit with a plop on the red armchair. "You are vile."

"Evelyn, you should be thanking me."

I shake my head again. This is all wrong. "Art wouldn't just leave me."

"Yeah? Then where is he?"

As I fumble to make sense of all this, Stan hits again: "Where's the ring?"

"The ring?"

"Your engagement ring, Evelyn. Where's your engagement ring?"

"It all happened so fast. We haven't had the chance to—"

"That's the first smart thing I've heard out of your mouth all day," Stan says, his words as hard and direct as bullets. "*It all happened so fast.* Almost like you were, say, perfect strangers?"

"No," I reply. "I know him."

Stan arcs an eyebrow. "What do you know about him?"

"I know that he loves me. That he's an artist. That he was there for me, and kind to me. . . . He told me that he fell in love with me the first time he saw me."

"Of course he did, kid! Every man in Manhattan is in love with you. But that doesn't make a fellow marriage material." A shake of his head. "I don't doubt that he fell for you, kid. Nor do I blame him. Trust me, honey, he wasn't up to the task of keeping you happy, and even he came around to seeing that. Naw, that isn't the sort of fellow you want to throw your lot in with. I offered you both a good way out. I'm glad that at least he saw reason."

I can't stand a moment more of this, and I force myself to rise from the chair. "I'm not staying here. I'll never go back to you . . . to—"

"I'm not asking you to." Stan, for his part, does not make a move to rise. His posture is still one of total ease.

"You ruin everything," I say, hoping it will hurt, though I doubt it will. I don't think a man like Stanley Pierce can feel pain, only inflict it.

"Listen, in spite of what you may think, how you may feel, I have always cared for you, Evelyn. I've promised you from the start that I'd never let anyone hurt you."

"Because only you are allowed to do that, right?" I turn to leave the room, storming away from Stan.

But his words follow me: "On the contrary, I've always taken care of you, doll. And I always will. Listen, you don't need to stay in New York for me. But you can stay in New York for another reason. Something I think you'll want."

I pause at the doorway, in spite of myself. Without turning to look at him, I ask, through gritted teeth: "What are you talking about?"

From his reclined position, Stan declares, "Your mother wants to bundle you off to boarding school. Some place in the country."

I laugh, a bitter rasp. "Mamma, who never lost a minute's sleep over pulling me out of school and putting me to work. *Now* she cares about my education?"

"Not so much your education, I think, as your safety. She doesn't want you . . . *falling in love* again. But I told her we should give you a choice."

Now I can't help but turn to see what he means. "What choice?"

Stan places the cigar down in the nearby ashtray. "You have two options. You can do as your mother says and go to boarding school. I would pay your tuition, if that's what you want. Or you can accept the role of a lifetime."

I cross my arms, staring at him. He has that look I know so well, that expression he makes when he's about to offer me something he knows I'll like. "Miranda, in *The Tempest*," he says.

In spite of everything, in spite of the white-hot hatred I feel for Stanley Pierce, the confusion and heartbreak I feel over Art, Stan's words do something in this moment that cause my heart to lift with the surprising but undeniable stirrings of hope. *The Tempest*! My work. It's been a fever dream of a summer, but it all comes back to me: I have long wanted to be a serious actress, and it doesn't get more serious for a girl than to land the lead in Shakespeare's beloved masterpiece. This role would prove that there's more to me outside of this room. So much more than merely being Stan's plaything or Art's jilted lover.

I want the role. I want the opportunity. I won't tell Stan right now. I won't give him that immediate satisfaction. But I know I'll say yes.

I turn to leave without a word. But as I'm slipping through the doorway, Stan calls out: "Someday you'll see, Kitten, I haven't ruined your life. I've just saved it."

Chapter Thirty-Five

Autumn 1903

MIRANDA IS MY KIND OF GAL. NOT ONLY DOES SHE SURVIVE, making it to dry land after her abandonment at sea, but she's clever enough to come out on top, even with the horrid men all around her trying to tell her what to do. I pour all my focus that autumn into Miranda because, like hers, my life has been a stormy journey with men who have let me down, each in his own way. And perhaps this pain hurts worst of all.

If viewed in the most favorable light, Arthur Darrow was simply too weak and feckless to stand up for us, the promises we'd made and the life we'd envisioned together. He gave in to whatever threats and enticements Stan lobbed at him—and I don't doubt that there were many.

If viewed in a less forgiving light, Arthur Darrow lied to me, seduced me, and then abandoned me. But no, I cannot allow myself to believe that. What we had that summer—that was real. It was real for me. I have to believe it was real for him, too. Because if it wasn't, it's both too shattering and too frightening to think just how foolish I was. *"Sweet lord, you play me false."* I memorize my lines before the mirror in my bedroom, swearing I'll never be a fool again.

I throw myself into my work, allowing my heart to scab and then harden. With Art gone, I have no choice but to move back in with Mamma at the Audubon. Stan doesn't mention anything about cutting off his support—our hotel bills, our food, even the allowance I know he gives Mamma for our wardrobes and other expenses. When he does come to visit Mamma, I maintain a cold and distant cordiality.

My wages from *The Tempest* are a pittance compared to our monthly bills. As much as I loathe him, we do depend on Stan. But I'll never again touch him. Nor will I get into the back of his auto. Or visit his brownstone. Or the tower. For now, while I'm busy with rehearsals and out of the suite as much as I can be, this flimsy and odious truce appears to hold.

When the curtains go up and I begin my run as Miranda, all the papers give me begrudging praise. The showgirl who has turned to Shakespeare. I relish the opportunity to win over the audience each night—to show them there's so much more to me than just my pretty face and high-kicking legs.

The Tempest plays through its limited run. For my next role, I decide I want something a bit more energetic, to get back into singing in a company with other young gals. Penny is auditioning for a part in the chorus of a new show, so she tips me off. I decide I'll try for the lead.

While the show may seem a bit frivolous after Shakespeare, I am desperate for the part—it would be the first role in years that Stan had no part in getting for me. I decide to get it for myself.

The play is called *Sweet Cherri Pie,* a musical, far from Shakespeare's caliber, but it's bound to be a packed house each night, and the pay would be steady. The high point of the show comes when the leading lady, Cherri, pops out of a pie with live birds flying all around her, just before the curtain falls for intermission. Variety will keep me entertained, and the work will keep me from getting pulled under by grief.

The audience falls in love with me all over again as Cherri. With Penny in the chorus, work feels enjoyable, and my melancholy loosens its hold. I no longer crave nights on the town, dancing and reveling like a young chorus girl, but Penny and I do step out occasionally, and her friendship provides a light with which to fend off the loneliness.

Now that I'm the lead, the attention becomes even more glaring than what I experienced as the Spanish Maiden or Lakshmi. I receive letters every day, piles of mail. But even more than that—invitations and offers. Offers of jewelry and other gifts, invitations to dinner, to dances, to marriage. I know how this goes and take little notice of the mail that keeps coming to the theater and the hotel. I don't need any more empty promises.

There is, however, one delivery that catches me off guard. It's a bouquet of blood-red roses. My first thought is that it must be from Stan, but then the concierge offers me the envelope that accompanies the delivery. I study the unfamiliar handwriting a moment before I notice that the flower stems are wrapped in a fifty-dollar bill. I peel the money off and stare at the curled, soggy bill, and then I decide to write to whomever the sender is to tell him I cannot accept. But when I look down at the envelope and see the name, my blood stills in my veins.

Thorne.

Mr. Hal Thorne.

I know that name. Is this Mr. Thorne related to the Pittsburgh family, with their railroad millions and mansion on Beechwood Boulevard? That sour matron who turned us away on that frigid Christmas Day, all those years ago? I decide not to write but instead slip the fifty to one of the maids who cleans my suite each morning.

The next day, the same delivery arrives at my suite—blood-red roses wrapped in money. This time I ask the hotel errand boy to return the money with a terse message saying that Miss Talbot is thankful for the generous gift, but she cannot accept. I hope that will put an end to the matter.

It does not. The next day, the same red flowers from Mr. Thorne, without the money this time. By the end of the week, my suite looks like a rose garden, all the flowers the same shade of deep red.

On the seventh day, the roses arrive with a handwritten note from Mr. Thorne, asking if we can meet.

"You know anything about a Hal Thorne?" I ask Penny on a Monday night that winter. It's our one night off, and I always look for reasons to be away from the suite in case Stan calls. I usually drag Penny with me on my outings. Tonight we have bundled up in furs and walked for over an hour, so far south that we are now nearly to the bottom tip of the island.

"Hal Thorne?" Penny has her arm woven through mine, and I throw her a sideways glance. "Why, of course I do. He's all over the papers. He's one of Comstock's big supporters."

Now, *that* name I also know. Mr. Comstock, the self-appointed vigilante of virtue in New York. Mr. Comstock is the gent who is always getting people in trouble if they do something he considers a sin. He was an ever-present thorn in Stan's side, always coming after him.

"I heard Hal Thorne is richer than royalty," Penny says.

"Is he from Pittsburgh?"

"I don't know that one," Penny answers. "But I can find out. Say, would you look at her?" Penny has paused her steps at my side. We have made our way to Bowling Green, with its sweeping view over the water and Lady Liberty rising up from her island perch beyond that. She's illuminated against the crisp, clear winter night, proud and steadfast.

"Ev, do you think it's all bunk?"

I turn to Penny, unsure of her meaning. "What?"

"Life, liberty, the pursuit of happiness . . ." Penny is still staring at Lady Liberty with a thoughtful expression. "Does a fatherless romantic like you or a scrappy orphan like me stand a chance? Or do those dreams of freedom and happiness only apply to the men?"

"Ah," I say, grasping her meaning. "Certainly not." My voice is low, but tinged with defiance. "I think we have just as much a right to it as anyone else," I declare, and I know I'm saying it not only for my friend to hear, but for myself. "Pen, let's make a promise."

"What kind of promise?"

I face Penny, dropping her arm but grabbing her hand and raising it up so that our grip is clasped between our two hearts. "We are going to live free, just like that lady in the harbor. Deal?"

"Evie, my friend"—Penny leans her face toward mine, catching the reflected lights of lower Manhattan in her gaze—"you got yourself a deal."

THE NEXT DAY, Penny bursts into my dressing room half an hour before our curtain call. "Mr. Thorne *is* from Pittsburgh. Steel and railroads. Like I said, rich as a king."

I swivel around in my chair, my rouge brush grasped in my fingers. "Well, then, he's part of that family."

Penny leans over my shoulder and takes a quick glance at herself in my vanity mirror. "Which family?"

"The Thornes in Pittsburgh. You could say that his family started . . . well, everything for me."

Penny throws me a confused look. "What do you mean? You and the Thornes were friendly down there?"

"Hardly." I sputter out a laugh. "The Thornes were why we left Pittsburgh," I clarify, my mind traveling back to that cold Christmas night. The Thorne mansion appearing bright and warm, huddled back from the quiet boulevard, a forbidden domain. "That must have been his mother, Mrs. Thorne."

"Ev, I haven't a clue what you're talking about."

"It was her snobbery, and her five-dollar bill, that started our whole trip."

"Trip to where?"

I meet my friend's eyes as I say, "We went to Philadelphia first. And then came here, to Manhattan."

"Ah," Penny says, crossing her arms. "Well, he must have wanted to leave Mother Dearest as well, because he's set up here in Manhattan now. He's a fixture in the society pages. Oh, but get this: your sweetheart Mr. Thorne—"

"He's not my sweetheart! He's sent me some roses."

"Fine, fine. Your *admirer,* then . . . He's been denied entry to every gentleman's club in town—the Union League, the Metropolitan Club, which of course, your Mr. Pierce will let us all know *he* built."

"Where did you find all this out?" I ask, studying my friend with appreciation and a fair bit of awe.

Penny's face drops. "I got the scoop from Dinah and Dolly. They know everything, as you are well aware."

I nod, my stomach taking a slight dip at the mention of their names. They still don't speak to me much, when I bump into them around town. Then a question pops into my mind. "Did you tell Dinah and Dolly that you were scoping out details for me?"

"I didn't. But I'm sure they guessed."

"How would they have guessed?"

"Because they know you're my best girl," Penny says, giving my rouged cheek a playful pinch. "And who else has a face pretty enough to have royalty banging down her door?"

I roll my eyes and look back into my mirror. But my friend chatters on: "Come on, Evelyn. They ain't cross with you. We girls gotta stick together, right?"

Penny's words give my spirits a small lift. Perhaps, in time, we can all be pals again. I'd like that very much. Stanley Pierce isn't worth losing a single friend over, let alone two.

"Dolly and Dinah had some other good gossip, as they always do," Penny continues, as she hops up onto my vanity and crosses her stockinged legs. "Seems for as virtuous as this Mr. Thorne may be, helping Comstock to fight against sin and whatnot, he's been known to display some bad behavior of his own. He once crashed his auto into a shopfront because they didn't have the gloves he wanted."

I cock my head to the side. "Come now, that sounds made up. You can't trust the newspapers as far as you can throw them."

"Maybe so." Penny shrugs. "Or that may be part of the reason why Mr. Thorne has been banned from the gentleman's clubs. That, and the fact that he and Stanley Pierce despise each other."

This is the most interesting morsel of gossip she's shared yet. "They do?"

"Think about it." Penny hops down from my vanity, gives herself a final once-over in my mirror, then holds my eyes in its reflection. "Thorne funds Comstock. Who does Comstock take aim against most often? Your friend Mr. Pierce."

"Mr. Pierce is not my friend," I respond, my tone brittle.

"He ain't Mr. Thorne's friend, either, from the sound of it."

In fact it sounds like Hal Thorne and Stanley Pierce loathe

each other. Which is very interesting indeed. "Penny," I say, taking my friend's hand and giving it a squeeze, "I think I'll accept Mr. Thorne's invitation to meet."

"I think that's a bully idea." Penny nods. "What harm could there be in one little meeting?"

Chapter Thirty-Six

Rector's is in the full throes of afternoon high tea, and almost every head in the crowded space turns as I waltz in, sheathed in a snug-fitting bodice of pale rose silk, a layered skirt frothing out from my narrow waist with a row of pearl buttons lining the length of my derriere. My dark hair is swept up and tucked into a pink hat with one long ostrich plume. But my favorite detail about my attire, the detail I selected with the most care, is the gauzy netting that falls down the front of the hat to throw the top half of my famous face into shadow. I think it gives me not only an air of chic sophistication but also privacy. I need not reveal my feelings to Mr. Thorne should I decide I don't wish to. For some reason I have not fully puzzled out, this option gives me a much-needed bit of comfort going into today's meeting.

"It's Miss Talbot!"

"Is it really her?"

"I told you she comes in here!"

Whispers behind gloved hands, curious stares, but I keep my gaze straight ahead and walk steadily through the fray. I don't pause until I've arrived before the gentleman at the linen-draped table set for two in the back of the crowded restaurant.

He hops up from his chair, his back going straighter than a general's, his eyes fixing attentively on me. I stand a few steps from the table. Mr. Hal Thorne is not what I was expecting. Knowing what I do about his sanctimonious family and having heard from Penny what a killjoy he can be alongside Mr. Comstock, I didn't expect him to be so, well, attractive. Or well-built. He is tall, well over six feet, but unlike Stanny, who always reminded me of a bear, Mr. Thorne is slim, his entire appearance impossibly elegant.

My veil affords me the discreet opportunity to take a quick study of his full appearance. He has nothing in his appearance of the dour spoilsport—in fact Mr. Thorne appears youthful and quite dapper. He's dressed in a fashionable three-piece suit that fits well around his slender frame. A black top hat rests on the unoccupied chair across the table, his glass-topped cane tipped against it. He has full lips and a clean-shaven face, without a hint of a shadow.

Mr. Thorne parts those lips now in a smile of greeting, an expression that strikes me as a bit timid. And then he speaks, and his velvety voice is soft as a whisper in the noisy restaurant. "Miss Talbot, at last." His words are so quiet that I have no choice but to take a step closer as he adds: "Up close, oh my. Even better than I had imagined."

This makes my cheeks fill with heat, and I'm thankful yet again for the netting that obscures my face. "Mr. Thorne, it's lovely to meet you."

"And you. Please, will you sit?"

I accept his help into the offered chair, and he flies to take the seat opposite me but not without throwing a look around the entire restaurant as if to query whether all who are staring—and they are all staring—are seeing this play out. I try to ignore the inquisitive eyes as I unfold a white linen napkin and drape it across my lap.

"Thank you for the flowers," I say, launching straight in, in an attempt to keep up a façade of cool and breezy sophistication.

"Oh, I hope you enjoyed them." Mr. Thorne's eyes tilt down to the table, a bit bashful. Just then the tuxedoed waiter approaches, and Mr. Thorne orders a full tea service. "Jasmine for you, Miss Talbot, yes?" I nod, wondering how this stranger could possibly know my tea preference. Mr. Thorne makes sure to ask for extra cakes and cookies. "I hear you are a great enjoyer of sweets, Miss Talbot."

"How do you know all of this?" I ask.

Mr. Thorne beams. "Miss Talbot, I always arrive to my meetings prepared."

I can't help but grin at Mr. Thorne's frank eagerness to please. It's refreshing, especially when I know that his pedigree and wealth give him plenty of boasting rights. Hal Thorne is the only son of the Pittsburgh Thornes, and as such, he's the scion of a railroad empire, plus coal mines, a transcontinental freight operation, and properties making up a fortune that exceeds forty million dollars. This according to my own personal sleuth, Penny. With his own father dead and just one sister, married and living abroad, Hal Thorne is now the patriarch of the Thorne holdings in his late twenties.

And yet, I note to myself how his unlined face appears entirely boyish. Is that the face of a man who has never had to fret or worry? Not just his face—when the waiter arrives and Mr. Thorne hastens to pour me my tea, I see his hands are marble white and smooth, the hands of a man who has never done hard physical labor.

His demeanor is pleasant, and his chatter comes easily and affably, so I find myself settling in to enjoy the sumptuous spread he's arranged. "I must say how grateful I am that you agreed to meet me," Mr. Thorne says, stirring his own tea once he's served mine. "I've come to your show any night I can make it. I think my tally is at fifty-one performances as of this week."

"Mr. Thorne!" I exclaim, clutching my teacup. "Then surely you must hold the record. Why, I think I've only sung in sixty so far."

"Sixty-three last night," he corrects me, his face entirely guileless.

I tilt back in my chair. "Is that right?"

He nods. "I checked with the box office, and they confirmed that I've seen more of your performances than any other gentleman."

I shift in my seat, rearranging my silk skirts, not entirely sure how to respond to this, or to the frank directness of his pale-eyed gaze. But he fills the silence, leaning over the table. "I am nothing, Miss Talbot, if not a loyal man."

Just then the waiter reappears, this time delivering a tower of white porcelain plates loaded with tasty-looking treats. I am glad to have the distraction. "Oh, look," I say approvingly, studying the tiered feast. Even with my nerves, I'm suddenly quite hungry for the strawberries covered in chocolate, the finger sandwiches with smoked salmon and cream cheese, the miniature lemon tarts, and the macaron cookies that I know will melt on my tongue.

Mr. Thorne thanks the waiter and dismisses the fellow, offering to serve me a plate himself. "May I?"

"Please," I say, and gladly accept the heaping dish.

"You are from Pittsburgh, are you not?" he asks as he helps himself to the smoked salmon.

Given everything else he seems to know about me, I'm not surprised he's unearthed this fact. I swallow my bite of the lemon tart, the flavors rich and floral on my tongue, and answer that I am. But I say nothing of my meeting with his mother on a cold Christmas Day—a memory that feels like a lifetime ago. That forbidden castle must have been his childhood home.

"You know that I am, as well?" Mr. Thorne asks.

"I do know that," I admit.

"And like me, also, you lost your father at a young age, Miss Talbot."

I nod, lowering my eyes.

"And you moved to Manhattan with your mother?"

"Yes," I say, taking a small nibble of a pale pink macaron.

"May I meet her?"

I pause my chewing, blinking my eyes open to meet my companion's stare. "Pardon?"

"May I meet Mrs. Talbot, your mother?"

I swallow, look down at my plate. I haven't told Mamma where I am, or with whom I'm dining. I know how my mother would react—the memory of Mrs. Thorne is enough to make her scowl, all these years later. *The snobbery of that woman. The cold, hard hypocrisy of her high-and-mighty self-righteousness!*

And yet Mr. Thorne appears to have nothing of his mother's cold snobbery. Why, he is perfectly cordial. Even solicitous, I might say.

But he has seen my hesitation. "Miss Talbot, I am a frank man. In my line of work, one must be, or one would not survive from sunrise to sunset."

His line of work? So then, does he work for his family business in railroads? Or coal? I had presumed Mr. Thorne to be a passive heir, gifted with such wealth that he never need toil a day in his life. But my wondering is interrupted as he carries on: "I shall speak plainly, Miss Talbot, if I may. I wish to court you. With your permission, of course. But I cannot do so without first paying my respects to your mother, so that I may express my admiration to her for raising such a daughter as yourself, and humbly requesting her blessing that I may call on you."

My mouth falls open before I remember myself and pull my features back into a look of some composure. But I'm finding it hard to stanch my grin. This whole thing is so proper! The flowers, the invitation to tea. Now this formal request to call on Mamma. Why, Art did no such thing. And Stanny, well, nothing about his predation was proper.

It's in this moment that I realize: I find Mr. Thorne to be adorable. In truth, I'm not at all certain whether I'm interested in him in any sort of romantic way. But he's a gentleman. Almost as though he hails from a different era when men were gallant and respectful, entirely unlike the rapacious and self-serving swashbucklers of today's Manhattan.

His refreshing candor prompts me to respond with a frankness of my own. "I must confess, Mr. Thorne, it's a bit complicated." I lift the delicate veil that's been hanging over my features and meet his earnest gaze. "Our mothers are already acquainted."

"They are?" His smooth face crumples in thought. "But I never forget a face, or a name. Surely if Mother had spoken to me of a Mrs. Talbot in Pittsburgh, I would recall."

My gaze slants downward. "I'm not entirely certain that your mother would recall the introduction, Mr. Thorne." She did, after all, tell us that we were just the latest beggars to show up at her doorstep on a busy day of bothersome petitions. I leave that bit out. "But *my* mother certainly remembers the encounter. We visited your home on Christmas Day, years ago. Shortly after my father died. Before . . . before all this." I gesture around the rarefied space that surrounds us, the potted palms, the tinkling silver, the well-heeled patrons enjoying their teas and canapés. "We barely had any food to eat when we knocked on your door."

"Ah." Mr. Thorne's eyes hold mine. He nods once. "I see."

I look down at the spread between us, chewing on my lower lip, no longer feeling hungry. Feeling, instead, how it was to be shooed off the doorstep and out onto the dark, cold street. More so than any indignity I felt, it's the recollection of Mamma's shame that burns like a coal, still, in my gut.

Mr. Thorne's voice is velvet as he asks, "Was Mother . . . was she charitable, at least?"

"Your mother did give us some money. Five dollars."

Mr. Thorne makes a noise as though he's clearing his throat, but I continue. "It was the money with which we booked our travel to Philadelphia, in fact. And that is no small thing. But the meeting itself was not . . . Mamma does not remember the exchange with great fondness."

"I knew it, Miss Talbot."

"Knew what?" I meet his gaze once more.

"I knew that you and I were connected in some way," he says. "I felt it deep in my heart. My mother's cold hauteur is what drove you and your own mother to begin your journey. A journey that would bring you here. No, but you must let me put this to rights."

"There is nothing to be settled, Mr. Thorne," I hasten to reply, shifting in my seat.

But he shakes his head. "I *must* apologize," he says. "Mother's demeanor at times, well, trust me, no one knows what she can be like better than I do. I completely understand your misgivings. But I beg you: give me the chance to rectify this. You see, I would bring you home—I would bring you anywhere—and seat you in the place of honor."

"Mr. Thorne, really, I don't wish for you to feel in any way that—"

"Then please, just grant me one request. Would you do me one small mercy?"

"What is that?" I ask.

"Please, allow me to take you out one more time."

"Oh, well."

"Perhaps something a little less formal," he says, waving a hand through the air. "A costume party. Do you enjoy costume parties? The Hoffman House, this Saturday evening. You may bring as many friends as you like. How does that sound?"

It sounds just fine. Swell, even. I can bring Penny. I know she'll be excited to dress up and join me at the Hoffman. And so, seeing no reason to object, I agree to meet Mr. Thorne one more time.

Chapter Thirty-Seven

The Hoffman is packed, the costumed crowd in the full swing of merrymaking as Penny and I saunter through the entrance from Broadway, giggling to ourselves as we step through the marble columns and take in the scene. We've just wrapped up a show for a full house and managed a quick costume change ourselves. Penny had the prop boy backstage transform her into a cluster of grapes, and she looks ridiculous beside me. I'm sheathed in a simple robe of celadon, a prop snake wound around my shoulders, a gold diadem resting atop my hair.

"As a bunch of grapes, I feel it's my bounden duty to drink many glasses of excellent champagne," Penny practically shouts over the din of the hundreds of patrons and the string notes of the orchestra playing in the corner of the room.

"Did Cleopatra drink champagne?" I ask, noticing how many in this colorful crowd have turned their eyes toward us. It seems I can't walk into a room these days without having that effect.

"I think Cleopatra was more the drinking arsenic sort of gal," Penny responds.

"Shame." I sigh. "Another beautiful gal meeting an ugly ending."

"Not us. We're going to enjoy this party. Now, back to that champagne."

We giggle and link arms, making our way intrepidly toward the bar. It's as we are shuffling through the close-packed bodies that I hear a velvety voice at my shoulder, the words quiet yet close. "A queen, of course." I turn, startled. There is Mr. Thorne.

While I'm not surprised to see him, as the invitation to this evening's costume party came from him, I am taken aback as I notice his garb. He is dressed in a white Roman toga with a wreath of laurels resting atop his head. "Why, Mr. Thorne, this is a surprise," I say. "You could be the Julius Caesar to my Cleopatra!"

But Mr. Thorne shakes his head. "No, Miss Talbot."

I tip my head to the side.

He goes on, "Caesar abandoned Cleopatra. It was Mark Antony who won her and remained faithfully at her side, even till death."

I lower my eyes with a bashful smile, taking a moment to collect myself. Men flatter me all the time—but there is something so earnest, so ardent and direct about Mr. Thorne. Penny gives my arm a gentle squeeze, and I turn to my friend to make introductions. "Delighted to meet you," Mr. Thorne says with an affable smile. Then he turns his gaze back on me. "You both just finished a show?"

"Yes," I reply.

"Then you must be starving. Shall we have some supper? Please, I have everything arranged at my preferred table." He gestures across the crowded room to an empty table that bears a placard marked "RESERVED." We gladly accept and follow him to the table, where he helps us both into our seats.

Before I have glanced at a menu, a legion of tuxedoed waiters appears as if summoned by magic, and a feast is spread before us. Mr. Thorne, tipping his laurel-crowned head and very much looking the part of the distinguished Roman ruler of antiquity, names each plate: halibut, filet mignon, foie gras, almond cakes, mushroom croquettes, green beans with lemon and butter, creamed spinach, fresh bread still warm from the oven. And several bottles of champagne chilling on ice. Penny gives her hearty approval.

Mr. Thorne sends the waiters away and fills two plates for me and my friend, then pours us each a flute of champagne. "We must eat and drink as the ancients did. What say you?" He winks and clinks his glass against mine. "The nectar of the gods."

"Cheers to that," Penny agrees.

"How was the performance this evening?" he asks, spreading his linen napkin across his lap and fixing his gaze on me.

"It went well," I say, taking a bite of the filet.

"I am sorry I couldn't be there." I notice Mr. Thorne isn't much interested in his own food, but he appears interested to speak with me. "I am sailing for Paris in the morning, so I've been quite preoccupied. It was either this or the show, and I felt this supper would give me a greater opportunity to visit with you."

This makes me feel warm, as does the delicious food and the few sips of champagne I've had. As I'm chewing my steak, Penny happily interjects, "Gee, Paris in the morning. Must be nice!"

"I've always wished to see Paris," I say.

At this, Mr. Thorne turns from Penny toward me. "Have you, Miss Talbot?" he says, his voice thoughtful.

"Yes."

Mr. Thorne folds his hands before him on the table, and when he speaks next, it's as though it is just the pair of us in this packed and noisy room. "It is a place you must see, to be sure. I wish you could come this time. I plan to give a smashing party—I have made arrangements to go up in a hot-air balloon and land on the Eiffel Tower, where I will have John Philip Sousa ready to serenade my guests. Are you familiar with the music of Mr. Sousa?"

"Of course I am." Everyone knows his music. My mind spins from the descriptions of this adventure; it hardly seems real.

"I hope my French guests appreciate Mr. Sousa as we Americans do," he adds. "One of my guests shall be Cléo. So I shall go from Cleopatra to Cléo."

"Cléo?" I repeat, feeling a bit self-conscious about asking for clarification as Mr. Thorne clearly presumes I'm familiar with the name.

"Ah, yes, Mademoiselle Cléo." He smiles kindly. "She's like you—except in Paris. A ballerina."

What is that unpleasant sensation I feel as Mr. Thorne utters these words—a twinge of jealousy? But then he goes on. "The King of Belgium has asked Cléo for her hand in marriage. Has any king asked to marry you?"

"No," I reply, letting out a puff of air, entertained by how highly he thinks of me.

"Not *yet*," he says, leaning his body toward mine. "You know, Miss Talbot, I meant what I said before. Mark Antony and Cleopatra. When I believe in something, I am loyal to the end."

I stare at Mr. Thorne, my heart knocking against my ribs. I don't move. I don't touch my food or my champagne, this nectar of the gods that he has arranged for me with such thoughtfulness and care. I'm too busy digesting our brief but remarkable acquaintance. To a girl who has been betrayed or abandoned by every man she's ever loved, his words feel like nectar indeed.

• ◆ •

BUT THEN HE'S GONE. The morning after the costume party at the Hoffman, Mr. Thorne sails for Paris, and he told me it would be at least a month before he returned.

"May I write to you while I'm away, Miss Talbot?" he asked as he escorted me and Penny into his waiting auto after supper, dispatching his chauffeur with orders to see each one of us safely home.

"You may, Mr. Thorne," I'd replied, realizing that I *wanted* him to write. Not only because I wished to hear all of his colorful details from Paris but also because I wished to carry on this fledgling friendship.

His red roses keep coming, but now I have no desire to send them back. The daily arrival of these bouquets now fills me with a warm and pleasing glow, the reminder that this chivalrous and generous man is thinking of me, even as he travels the world.

Within a few days I am surprised to find that I miss Mr. Thorne. This gentleman whom I've only just begun to know. This realization crystallizes for me when Stan arrives at the door of the suite. I can barely stomach the thought of seeing him, but Mamma insists we allow him in.

It seems as though Stan also has Mr. Thorne on his mind. It catches me by surprise when he takes a seat opposite Mamma and me in the parlor and declares: "I hear you've been gadding around town with that Thorne character."

I shift in my seat, looking down at my hands, toward the window, anywhere but at Stan. Trying to affect a mien of cool disinterest, but feeling a jangle of nerves, I sigh. "Stan, it's really none of your concern."

"It's entirely my concern," he retorts. He throws a look toward Mamma, then turns back to me. "There are all sorts of unsavory reports about him, Kitten."

His use of the nickname feels like fingernails slicing my skin, and it's all I can do to suppress a full grimace. Drawing in a slow breath, I take a moment. "There are always rumors."

"Reports that he's got some sleazy inclinations."

That's rich, coming from you. I don't say it aloud, not with Mamma sitting beside me, but I hope that Stan can see the ire in the look I give him.

His eyebrows hitch together. "Girls in the Tenderloin, they talk. A man who looks an awful lot like your Mr. Thorne pays for their services. I won't tell you more than that."

"Preposterous," I say, shaking my head and turning away. Stan sees the worst in others because he himself is made of the worst stuff. I say, "I saw how you treated Art." He'll do anything to keep me away from other men.

Then I add: "Mr. Thorne is so recognizable; if he were some sort of unsavory rake, everyone would know without a shred of a doubt. It'd be all over the papers."

Stan's voice is suggestive when he replies. "Unless he uses some of that eighty-thousand-a-year allowance to keep the reports quiet."

I let out a puff of air. "There's no such thing as keeping reporters quiet, and you know it."

"Listen, Kitten, even if he's not the monster of the Tenderloin, he's a playboy. A cad."

"Name-calling is beneath even you, Stanley Pierce."

"Florence Evelyn!" Mamma rasps, her tone biting as she pipes up for the first time.

I can't help but roll my eyes; I realize exactly what is going on. Stan has money, to be sure, but Thorne has more than a royal. And he's a backer of Comstock, who is a daily barb in Stan's side. *And* on top of all of that, Mr. Thorne has gotten my attention. Which means he is a threat, on every level, to Stanley Pierce. I relish this moment of watching Stan squirm as he sees all of this as plainly as I do. "You're scared of him," I say, a smile tugging on my lips.

"You will remember yourself!" Mamma hisses, but I don't turn to face her. Stan's face has gone pale. I've gotten to him—or Thorne has. Or we both have, together.

When Stan speaks next, his voice sounds thin and quiet, but his gaze is intense. "Evelyn, take care. I'm warning you, you're playing with fire, and I'm trying to save you before you get burned."

"Don't worry, Stan," I say. "I know how to rise from the ashes. I had to learn as a girl, when someone I loved set fire to everything I thought I knew."

Among all the things Stan has tried to pull over the years, his claims of Mr. Thorne's depravity are a new low. Predation of young girls. Sexual promiscuity. Insinuations of depraved morals or closeted abuse. Why, Stan is hurling the precise insults that *he* doesn't want sticking to his own face. All this when Mr. Thorne is a well-known benefactor of the Society for Prevention of Vice. The man is a choirboy beside Stanley Pierce. It would be far cleverer for Stan to take the tack that Mr. Thorne is too *boring*, rather than trying to convince me he's a lech.

But he's not boring, not at all. From the letters Mr. Thorne writes from Paris, I see what a grand time he's having. Tours of the Tuileries Gardens, the finest meals beside the River Seine, shopping sprees along Paris's chicest boulevards. Not only does it all sound grand, but he continues to amaze me with his thoughtfulness and care. Mr. Thorne writes of the gifts he's purchased for me: chocolates, silk kerchiefs, elegant baubles like ivory combs or fans. All this emboldens me to write to him: "*I wish I were there with you.*"

He responds to this with boyish glee. "*I wish you were here, as well, Miss Talbot. Your presence would be the one thing that would make this trip even more enjoyable. May I be bold in making a request? Would you please do me the honor of calling me Hal?*"

I smile as I read his words, and then I write back: "*If you say so, Hal. And you may call me Evelyn.*"

"*Evelyn!*" He writes back in his next missive. "*Your invitation filled me with the greatest joy. Evelyn, the most beautiful name ever uttered. Oh, but I would call you Angel, if you would allow it.*"

An angel, I think, pondering his words as I lower Mr. Thorne's most recent letter, posted just after his visit to the country estate of the famed painter Mr. Claude Monet. The letter swirled with colorful descriptions of the painter's fragrant gardens, his studio filled with priceless tableaux, his cozy rustic kitchen stocked with crockery and blue dishes. But only one word grips me, and I could weep as I stare at it. *Angel.*

Hal would call me Angel.

A fallen angel, that's what I was for Stan. But Hal Thorne sees me as good. I can be good with him. Hal makes me feel good.

As I devour his daily notes, as Penny and I delight in his delicious packages of chocolates backstage before the show, as I admire his daily bouquets in my hotel bedroom, their arrival as predictable and steady as a clock, I realize that I can also feel safe. Life with Hal could be safe in a way I have never been allowed to imagine.

This spring, I've been thinking more and more about how shaky the ground is on which Mamma and I currently tread. Yes, I'm employed in *Sweet Cherri Pie* for now, and my salary as a showgirl can support my mother and me well enough. But it would never sustain our lifestyle. No, as much as I hate to admit it, the funding to maintain all of that still comes from Stan.

But I would be a prize fool to assume it will continue forever.

I've seen Stan's book, and he's seen my coldness. As much as Mamma insists that we continue to visit with him and allow him in when he calls, Stan knows that I can no longer bear to look at him, let alone think of touching him or carrying on the way we once were.

I'm no longer Stan's pliable or innocent plaything. He'll find his fresh new prey, and soon. He'll move on, and so will his money.

The theater will move on, too. Showgirls shouldn't be much older than twenty—I've known that from the start. I'm almost twenty now. I was young when I began, but now I'm one of the oldest girls backstage. I've seen the story play out so many times at this point, I know there is only one happy ending: a showgirl marries and moves on as soon as the opportunity presents itself.

I've had a few good years, but how many more can I expect? There's an inexhaustible crop of fresh young things knocking on the stage doors each and every day, girls with big dreams and hungry hearts, girls who will kick higher or sing louder—because their lives depend upon it. I know, because I was one of them. I know how motivating their desperation is, because I carried it in my own broken heart and empty belly.

The theater and the audience, do they love me? For now. But just like Stanley Pierce, Broadway will eventually find my replacement and show me my exit. And then I'll be hungry and desperate, just as I was before.

Unless I have my next role lined up. Unless I have a friend like Hal, a man who will love me even after the theater lights have gone dark.

That spring, with Hal gone but paying earnest and attentive court, even from an ocean away, I begin to seriously consider: Could my next role be Wife?

Chapter Thirty-Eight

Late Spring 1904

"Goodness, Evelyn, you need not fear they'll come take your plate." Hal looks at me from across the table, amused, as I shovel a silver fork full of filet mignon into my mouth. A beat later I bite into the softest mushrooms from the steak's gravy and close my eyes in a moment of appreciative rapture.

"It's just . . . sinfully good," I say in breathy reply. "My favorite steak in this city." In truth, when I dine here at the Waldorf, I enjoy everything about the meal. The sumptuous surroundings, the rich food. The space in which we sit is sprawling, with stately marble columns that rise up like a forest to reach the elaborate ceiling of Greek friezes and colorfully painted birds. Generous sunlight streams in through the spotless floor-to-ceiling windows, illuminating a sanctum of privilege and comfort—elegant diners gathered around the circular tables, Wall Street businessmen hashing out deals, society ladies meeting for a midday meal and morsels of gossip. And Hal and I, happily reunited after his recent return from Paris.

"So you've been here before?" he asks, drinking from his cup of black coffee.

"Oh. Yes, loads of times. With . . . Well, Stan worked on the place. When it was being built."

Hal's face hardens, and he lowers his coffee cup into its saucer. My body tenses. Have I ruined this lovely moment of our warm and happy reunion? When he speaks, Hal's expression remains clenched. "Well, let's hope our paths don't cross today." Then he attempts a smile, though his face still looks taut.

Of course I've seen how, the few times that the name of Stanley Pierce has arisen, Hal's entire demeanor has changed. I've known from the start that Hal loathes my former lover. But the words that come from his mouth next catch me unprepared. "You know, Evelyn, I'd do anything for you."

I clear my throat, finding no easy words with which to respond. What, exactly, is he saying? But Hal carries on, his words sounding gruff but earnest: "To save you from him. From *them*. Not just him, but all of it. The life of toiling in the lights. Popping out of a pie."

I hesitate, my appetite for the steak suddenly gone. This is a lot to digest. "Thank you, Hal . . ." I begin. But I can find nothing else to say. I think, not for the first time: *It's as though Hal Thorne is out of place here in Manhattan, a gallant gentleman born in the wrong century.* And I, who have never had a suitor treat me decently, find myself ill-equipped to even respond. Are we sweethearts? Is he paying court to me with intentions for something more? It certainly seems that way. And yet, in all the times that we have stepped out together, Hal has never even touched my hand in a lingering way. He's always maintained a bearing of perfectly respectful distance and courteous but detached admiration.

Hal interrupts my brooding. "At least come traveling with me."

Once more, he has caught me unprepared. I look up at him, my confusion surely showing on my face. He hastily adds, "We could travel as friends. You always say you'd like to see Paris. I could bring you. Or would you prefer London? We could do both. Or Rome? Everything quite aboveboard. . . . You'd bring your mother along, of course. And as many attendants as you require. Everything would be my treat."

"Hal!" I can't help but laugh, a small exhale of shock. "You're so kind."

"I'm not being kind; I'm being serious."

"But . . . Hal . . . you've only just returned from a trip."

"Yes, but I intend to travel more this summer. Before I met

you, my hope was to be gone until autumn, touring the Continent. The only thing giving me pause about leaving again is, well, I don't wish to be apart from you. But perhaps . . ." Now his manner is boyish, even timid, as he flashes me a searching look with his pale eyes. "Perhaps you might consider joining me. Wouldn't you like to get away?"

"I don't even know how to respond," I say honestly, my voice quiet.

"Don't respond. At least, not yet. But promise me one thing: Will you consider my offer?" I promise him I will, and we tuck back into our meal together without revisiting the topic.

Sadly, I know that I must demur. Not that I wouldn't like to jump at the chance to tour London, Paris, and Rome, and here Hal is offering to bring me anywhere I'd like to go. With a full fleet of attendants, no less. Why, it sounds like a dream.

But there's something that stops me from being able to accept his generosity.

When luncheon is over, I decline his offer of a ride in his motorcar. I tell him I crave some fresh air and a bit of a walk. What I don't share with Hal is the fact that I need time alone to think all this through.

As I walk alone along the busy streets of Manhattan, I can feel my frown deepen as I plunge into my fretful brooding. Hal is kind in a way I've never known a man to be. He is earnest and forthright. And generous. And apparently he is eager to give me the world, quite literally, and he possesses the means to do so. What, then, is giving me pause?

Why do I feel as though I cannot fully give myself over to Hal's generosity? This invitation to travel together, though extended with all propriety, is a demonstration of his clear interest in pursuing a deeper connection. Why do I feel this niggling sense inside of me that I should keep him at arm's length?

I realize, on that gloomy walk home from the Waldorf Astoria, that it's because I feel I must keep my secrets hidden from Hal Thorne. He who calls me his angel. He who wishes to be the knight that guards and keeps my honor. Hal doesn't know: I'm no angel. I have no purity left to preserve. He doesn't know the truth about me, that I've been tainted, ruined, and that it was the man he loathes more than anything, Stanley Pierce, who ruined me.

The further along Hal and I go in our relationship, the more I feel as though I've been lying by neglecting to disclose this, as though I've betrayed Hal by allowing him to court me when he doesn't know the full truth of me. I can't quite stifle the unpleasant feeling that I'm not worthy of his kindness, nor can I silence the voice telling me I should not accept his generosity when he doesn't in fact know the true *me*.

Had I met Hal before Stan, had I been able to follow a straightforward courtship with him, I could have been a respectable girl and an unhesitating bride. If not a smoldering passion, I do feel a fondness for him bordering on warm affection. In time, my feelings of friendship for Hal could certainly deepen to devotion and attachment.

But Stan has ruined that chance for me. Because if I were to share the truth of who I actually am with Hal, he would likely not want me.

I'm still frowning, still in a lather over all of this when I barge into the suite. I don't even notice them until I've swept inside and shut the front door: there, on the couch, seated with my mother, is Stanley Pierce.

But Mamma is not on the couch. Mamma is on Stan, on his lap. They both scramble at the disturbance of my entry, both turn toward the doorway, and me before it, at the same time. And then they freeze, a most unseemly tableau. I feel a noose tighten around my neck.

"Oh, Florence . . ." Mamma hops off Stan's lap, rustling the folds of her skirt around her legs. "We weren't expecting . . . You're earlier than I thought."

"I can see I've disturbed you," I say, my voice toneless, body unmoving.

"Oh, don't let's have a scene. . . . Must you . . . ?" And then Mamma does what she does best: she takes her skirts into her two fists, and she flees. She hurries into her bedchamber and slams the door, leaving me behind with only Stan and the torturous thoughts whirling inside of me.

My eyes bore into him. "You are carrying on with my mamma?"

Stan retrieves his pocket watch, as though bored. "No, Kitten."

His disinterest only sharpens the blade of my fury. I walk farther into the room, slowly. "Funny, ain't it, how I have a hard time believing you?"

Stan shrugs. "Too old."

I narrow my eyes. "Begging pardon?"

He meets my stare now, his own gaze direct, even a bit defiant. "Believe me, I could have. She was interested long before you were. But she's not the right age for me."

I rasp out a laugh, a hollow, gravelly sound. "Well, she certainly isn't the right age to be sitting on your lap for a bedtime story. So then I'm wondering what it is that I just saw."

"I'm throwing her crumbs. She's so lonely. And she's no idiot—Mother knows you're playing a terribly risky game, taunting me to throw it all away, everything the two of you have. So I suppose your stalwart mother simply wanted to make sure I was, well . . . satisfied."

"Get out." I walk back to the door and open it, looking away from Stan. I can't bear another moment of this. I doubt I shall ever be able to look at him again. The clarity hardens within me: I need to be done with this man. I need both of us to be done with him. Stan, Mamma, me—this unholy trinity that I've allowed to linger on for far too long, it's rotten and it reeks more with each day. Whatever we once had that worked, it's ruined. I need to rescue Mamma—and myself.

And suddenly, the proposition that seemed so impossible merely an hour ago—and my certainty that I had to decline it—has shifted, and I'm willing, in spite of all my hesitations and fears, to take a leap. Even to cross an ocean.

Chapter Thirty-Nine

*The North Atlantic
Summer 1904*

THE FIRST DAY OF OUR CROSSING IS MILD, WITH SHIMMERING blue waters that break before the bow of the HMS *Perdita* as the sun dips toward my first ocean sunset. I hope this clement weather bodes well for the remainder of our six-day crossing. I breathe deep of the salty air, taking one last look at the open waters of the Atlantic, and then I step away from the railing to make my way belowdecks. I move slowly toward my stateroom, still a bit wobbly on my sea legs, though I'm told I will adjust to the ship's sway in no time. But will Mamma? I decide to check on her, as she has spent most of the day in bed, complaining of seasickness.

Hal, through a private secretary by the name of Mr. Brion Ballard, has seen to it that Mamma and I have the finest staterooms on board. And what's more, Mr. Ballard is traveling with Mamma and me to ensure our every comfort is achieved. "No matter the time of day, ladies, your wish is my command," Mr. Ballard keeps telling us in his fine English accent that's as crisp as his manners. Hal isn't even with us for the crossing, as he left for London a few days prior, in order to secure our accommodations and finalize all the details before our disembarkation.

The carpeted corridor is hushed, the other first-class passengers ensconced in their suites to dress for the formal dinner this evening. When I arrive back at my staterooms, I notice I've had a delivery. There on the marble-topped table is a huge arrangement of red roses. *Hal*. Though how he managed to send fresh-cut flowers to the middle of the Atlantic, I have no idea. Beside the vase rests a small blue box. The handiwork of Mr. Tiffany, I see. I throw a look toward Mamma's closed door, then open the parcel. My hand flies to my mouth. On the plush cushion sits a diamond brooch the size of a small plum. It's too much! I read the note that accompanies it:

> *Welcome to your maiden crossing, my dear.*
>
> *I hope you enjoy this small token, though it will appear dull and dim in the moment it is placed beside your face, as you outshine the most brilliant of diamonds.*
>
> *While I cannot control the weather or the conditions of the sea, I do vow to arrange every other detail that I can, in order to ensure that your trip is all enjoyment.*
>
> *Yours,*
> *Hal*

And he does. Even from afar, the man's generosity knows no bounds. Each morning he's seen to it that my favorite fruits—peaches and strawberries—are brought fresh to me in bed on a tray bearing cut crystal with sugar and cream. Each evening before dressing for dinner, I find a warm bath prepared in my powder room, perfumed with lavender and crushed rose petals. A fresh new pair of silk pajamas lies folded on my bed each night. Mr. Ballard informs me and Mamma that a masseuse has been hired for us and is available at any time. Hal has a milliner visit us to make several new hats and a seamstress to spiff up our gowns. On the third night of our crossing, Hal arranges a private dinner with the captain. The next morning I learn that he's arranged a tour of the entire ship with its first mate. Hal does not overlook a single detail, nor does he let pass a single chance to pamper or spoil me, so much so that the passage flies by in a flurry of excitement and heady anticipation for all that is to come.

And then it's been almost a week. On the final night of the crossing, I find I'm most eager to see Hal again. To thank him for his gifts and to speak to him about my time at sea, and to embark on whatever new adventures he has planned for our first stop in London. Yes, though it's only been a week, I truly do yearn to be reunited.

As if sensing my thoughts—as he so often seems to do—Hal responds to my longing in that very moment, as Mr. Ballard knocks on my door. "A letter for you, Miss Talbot." I thank the man and then look down at the envelope in my hand. I don't even attempt to stanch the smile that spreads across my face as I see Hal's now-familiar cursive. I tear it open.

> *My dear Evelyn,*
> *You know I love you. But if it is only friendship between us that you desire, then we can be dear friends.*
> *Your happiness is my happiness.*
>   *Forever yours,*
>   *Hal*

To my surprise, I see the words begin to blur and dance before me, as a thin misting of tears fills my eyes. My happiness is his happiness. Hal. Ever thoughtful, ever kind. He is a true friend, indeed. In all this time, as he's poured out his care and his riches on my behalf, he's never asked for a single thing in return. He is a most singular man.

That fact is driven home with a harsh clarity when, on our final morning at sea, I ask Mr. Ballard to bring me the latest news bulletins. I've spent the week of our crossing deliberately avoiding all news, blissfully relishing the isolation that the sea voyage offered, but now that we are set to step our feet back onto land, I figure I ought to know at least a bit of what is happening in the world.

Mr. Ballard promptly delivers to me the ship's latest news dispatches along with breakfast. I sit upright in my bed and look over the pages in turn. My giddy prearrival exuberance quickly dissipates when, as I scan each article, I see several tawdry reports that make mention of me. The first report declares that my absence from Broadway has given fuel to the flames of rumor, and many wonder if I've fled in order to have an operation. "*Perhaps*"—the words drip with their dirty ink—"*Broadway's favorite star has found herself in the family way.*" I swallow my half-chewed bite of pastry and note that it tastes dry as paper. I throw the page aside.

The second report is hardly better: "*We have it on good authority that the star is traveling with a lover, unnamed, though he's described with looks quite similar to a description of one Mr. Arthur Darrow, lately of New York City.*" I roll my eyes and push the paper away.

The third gossip column comes closest to the mark, claiming that I've sailed for Europe because my mamma was so concerned about my intimate relationship with an unsavory gentleman suitor, she's removed me from Manhattan. Who of all people but *Stan* is quoted in this one: "*I've always cared for Evelyn, and I continue to want what is best for her.*" The nerve! Surely he knows his words will only prompt further speculation. I toss the paper to the floor.

Scavengers and predators, I seethe, pulling my knees up to my chest, wishing I'd never even looked. All of the newspapers feed on me, as if my purpose in life is to make them money. And their millions of readers—is my role to provide entertainment for their colorless lives? With no thought ever spared for the fact that I am also a human being.

This past week I've been so happy to be away from it all. To look ahead and think of new adventures. Perhaps I ought to leave it all forever.

As I rise from bed and prepare to face the day, to disembark at last in London, I put on not only one of my fabulous new gowns but also a grim determination—a steely resolve to embrace all that this novel experience with Hal shall offer. I won't let the past, or the demons who fill it, haunt this fresh new soil. Nor will I allow the future, with its many unknowns, to frighten me. I will enjoy myself, here and now, along with my good friend. My friend who has one final note delivered to me as I prepare to step off the ship: *"Welcome, my Angel."*

Hal sees me as pure and good. Perhaps I can truly be just as he sees me.

Chapter Forty

London
Summer 1904

The salon in Claridge's hotel is full for afternoon tea. Prim ladies nibble on cucumber sandwiches and caviar canapés as I follow the tuxedoed attendant past an assortment of potted palm trees to take the proffered seat at the center table, set for two. There I await the arrival of the Right Honorable Countess of Fairmont. That's how Hal's older sister is to be addressed. Anne Thorne, the American heiress who made an exceptional match, marrying the much older Earl of Fairmont, moving from Pittsburgh to London, where she now lives as a widowed aristocrat.

I settle in at the linen-draped table and glance around. The bright space smells of cakes and lemon, as well as a medley of fine perfumes. There's been a break in the rain; sunshine now pours in through the windows, while outside the Mayfair streets teem with midday carriage and foot traffic. Every few minutes I hear the braying of a motorcar's horn or a clamor of chatter, but inside here it's all decorously restrained conversation, the tinkling of silver and porcelain, the soft strains of the string quintet floating through the gracious salon.

I'm grateful to have this brief moment to catch my breath and prepare for the upcoming meeting. It's been a whirlwind first week since Hal set us up here in this posh hotel, in a sprawling suite of rooms with grand views looking out over London's exclusive

Mayfair neighborhood. He was not exaggerating when he said he'd planned a full itinerary. So far we've had two shopping excursions to Harrods, private guided tours of both the National Gallery and Westminster Abbey, a chartered boat ride up the Thames, a walk through Hyde Park, a picnic luncheon, and a performance of *Romeo and Juliet* in the West End.

Just this morning, we had a coach ride across the city to drive past St. James's Palace, Kensington Palace, and Buckingham Palace. It was at the third palace, while Hal was pointing out the Union Jack flag bearing the royal standard, that he remarked: "That's an indication that King Edward is in residence—when the royal standard flies above one of the royal residences."

I'd nodded, happy as always to have Hal point out these new and exotic details of life abroad. I'm learning so much from him. But then Hal had added one more detail: "Evelyn, do you know that my monthly allowance is greater than his? The king's?" He'd flashed a smile as he said it, and I wasn't entirely certain whether it had been said in jest, so I simply returned his grin and turned my gaze once more out the window.

It's too bad he's not able to join me now in the busy salon of Claridge's for tea with his sister. "Why can't you?" I asked, and he sighed, telling me only that he had to go out of the city with Mr. Ballard for the afternoon. Something came up, some sort of urgent business. Mamma, too, has declined to join me and instead sent me down to the salon with her regrets. "A splitting headache, Florence," she lamented, unable—or unwilling—to rise from bed. So here I am, quite alone.

Mamma's attitude toward Hal *has* evolved over the course of our first week in London. It's not the honeyed warmth she's always offered Stan, but her frostiness has thawed to a cool sort of gratitude. When I told Mamma back in Manhattan that I was taking a hiatus from the stage, accepting Hal's offer to travel for the summer, I offered absolutely no hint of equivocation. Seeing my resolve, she'd begrudgingly agreed to travel with me. It would have been too scandalous to let me go alone, though she'd evidently seen that I did not care and was going either way.

"I'll come along," she sighed. Really, how terrible of an offer is it to travel throughout London and Paris with Hal Thorne treating us to deluxe accommodations at every stop?

Hal has indeed spoiled us like aristocrats, while keeping a courteous sort of distance, staying in a separate suite on a different floor of this hotel. And now he's facilitated this introduction to a true aristocrat, his sister, who has deigned to leave her townhouse in Berkeley Square to call on me for tea.

Truth be told, I'm not overly enthusiastic about this meeting. As Anne has lived in England for the past decade, she was not present in Pittsburgh on that evening when her mother turned us away in disgust, but no doubt she knows of my career on the stage. She's likely heard, too, of my humble origins.

My fretting is interrupted as Her Ladyship sweeps into the salon. A server guides the countess toward our table. She's a tall woman, and her plumed hat soars so high that its cream-colored feathers almost graze the chandelier overhead. The patrons all around the room throw furtive glances toward me as I rise from my seat; I don't believe anyone in this crowded salon knows who I am, but surely they wonder who has the privilege of taking tea with the Countess of Fairmont.

I've dressed with care for this meeting. I'm wearing one of my chic new gowns, a beaded tea dress of lemon-yellow silk, the expert tailoring snug and flattering, thanks to Hal's largesse. My hands are gloved, and I fold them before my waist, affixing a mild smile that says I am happy to meet her but not excessively so. *Play the part.*

The Countess of Fairmont comes to a halt before me and offers a tight smile in return. I see the family resemblance in her full lips, her pale eyes, though she looks more like her mother than her brother. As Hal is ten years older than me, and she is older than him, I suspect she may be in her late thirties, perhaps early forties.

And she seems to take almost a maternal demeanor with me now, as though I'm some charity case to be taken in hand as she leans forward and brushes my cheek with the faintest hint of a kiss, a cloud of rosewater wafting around her. With the charming trace of a faint English accent, she dismisses the server and turns her gaze back on me. "My dear Miss Talbot, he certainly didn't lie. Why, you *are* a pretty thing, aren't you? It is good of you to invite me for tea." We settle into our seats, and the countess launches a flurry of questions, showing none of her mother's cool reserve. She asks how I have liked London. I tell her that I particularly enjoyed my night at the theater. She asks if the hotel has been to our liking, and I tell her that it has been lovely.

As a full service of black tea is brought to us by a pair of white-gloved attendants, followed immediately by a tower of plated pastries and finger sandwiches, I can't help but think back to my first meeting with Hal. A table so much like this one for high tea at Rector's.

It's enough to make my head spin, how far we have come—that I am now here in London, traveling with Hal Thorne, sitting down to nibble on lemon cakes with his sister, an aristocrat, who interrupts my musings by asking, "Paris is next?"

"It is, ma'am," I respond, accepting an offered cup of tea from the server. "Though I will confess, I know little of the details."

The countess stirs a small drop of cream into her own tea. "Why is that?"

"Your brother has been so generous, seeing to every detail."

She considers this a moment, stirring the murky brown clouds of her tea. Then, lifting her silver spoon aloft, pointing it like a schoolmistress would wield a ruler, she says, "Be that as it may, I still feel it's always best for a lady to act as her own guide on any expedition. Or, at the very least, to know where she's going next."

I shift in my seat, my hand gripping the delicate bone china handle of my teacup. Not sure how to respond to her remark, I blow on my tea softly. I notice Anne is eyeing me intently over the rim of her own cup. Before she takes a sip, she asks, "You were close with that architect back in Manhattan, were you not?"

I tip back in my chair, my back stiffening.

Anne narrows her eyes, as if studying me. "Hal told me the name. . . . Goodness, where is my memory? What's he called?"

"Stanley Pierce." My voice is little more than a whisper.

"That's it! Yes, that's the one."

"He was a supporter of . . . my theater company," I say, lowering my teacup into the saucer.

"They always are, aren't they?" Anne plucks a scone from the plate between us, her pincer grasp a fluid movement of implicit gentility and assumed privilege. She is a woman who has never known hunger. Rather, she has had a plate of delicacies to sate any craving she has ever wished to indulge. She takes a small bite before saying, "Hal tells me he was positively beastly. That you were in need of rescuing. Am I remembering that correctly?"

I look down at my tea, fumbling to form some reply. But she goes on: "And now here you are. So then you *do* know how to get where you need to go, in any event. You're no helpless damsel." She scoops a small dollop of clotted cream onto the scone, muttering, "There, now, that's more like it." Turning her too-direct gaze back toward me, she adds: "Isn't that so?"

I bristle at this, at all of this. Is the countess implying that I am some artful woman with designs? That I've ensnared her brother? Why, I did not seek out Hal. Or Stanley Pierce, for that matter.

But she goes on, apparently oblivious to the offense she's caused. "Still, I hope it's not a case of leaping from one disaster to another." Her Ladyship arcs a thin eyebrow, takes a slow sip of tea. "Tawdry, sordid stuff, if I remember correctly. Let's hope everyone minds their manners this time round."

My head whirls. She is speaking in such vagaries and snippets, and while I find it hard to follow the disjointed train of her blunt thoughts, I do see one thing quite clearly: she is her mother's daughter after all. A snob—and so far above me.

But even worse, on top of her snobbery, she has the noble's complete lack of restraint. Lady Fairmont is brusque and abrasive; so accustomed is she to being deferred to and obeyed, she's insulting me now and smirking as she does so.

Well, I need not take this offense with a smile of my own. In fact, I'll do the opposite. I don't attempt to mask my scowl as I sit across from her, allowing my tea to go untouched. Keeping my voice restrained, yet tinged with frost, I answer her: "I assure you, I'm minding my manners."

For the first time, I seem to have caught Lady Fairmont speechless. Her blue eyes go wide. She surveys me curiously for a long moment before she raises a gloved hand to her chest and declares,

"Oh, my dear girl. You thought I meant *you*?" She titters a high-pitched laugh. "No, but you misunderstand me! The disaster. The minding of manners." She leans forward, tilting over the table, and then to my fresh shock, she places her hand on mine. Her voice goes low, confiding, as she says, "You pretty little thing. It's not *your* manners about which I worry. It's my brother's."

Chapter Forty-One

Paris
Summer 1904

Even with all that I've heard, read, and imagined, nothing could have possibly prepared me for Paris. Nothing could have fully painted the picture of what I would find upon my arrival to this jewel on the Seine, which meets my high expectations and then soars even higher.

Oh, but of course that is helped by the fact that Hal has spared no detail or expense in arranging the best of stays in the City of Light, starting with Mamma's and my massive suite at the Ritz, with its two grand bedrooms, each with a gracious en suite bathroom, and a shared salon in the middle. Most of our prior apartments could have easily fit in just one of these vast marble and gold bathrooms. But the best part of all is the view, our floor-to-ceiling windows and lovely terrace that look over the historic Place Vendôme.

Hal, who has taken a suite for himself on a different floor, presents a breathtaking new itinerary each day, and I eat it all up with the same delight with which I sample *les macarons* and chocolate nougats.

Mamma, in spite of the splendor, is out of sorts and less pleasant with each passing day. "Overseas travel disagrees with me," she declares over breakfast, a week into our stay in Paris. She does not like that she cannot read the menus or make herself easily understood by the hotel staff. The rich foreign food has worsened her digestive complaints, and her body has yet to acclimate to the change in hours, which has caused several weeks of fitful sleep. "Oh, and the heat! Too blistering to be out there hoofing it in the streets." She declines most of Hal's outings, preferring to stay in and rest. By our second week, it has turned into Hal and me exploring Paris as a pair. I don't mind, and neither, it seems, does he.

The Monday evening of our third week, Hal has arranged a private after-hours tour of the Louvre museum. Of course I recall how Stan used to speak about the sculptures from antiquity and the rich oil paintings done by the Renaissance masters. Recollections that I do not share with Hal, though I do go into our private tour with the highest of hopes for what I shall see. Once again, Paris does not disappoint.

The empty corridors of the erstwhile palace are cool and candlelit as we make our way through the gracious salons, accompanied by a curator who serves as our dedicated guide. I linger to gape at the winged statue of the goddess Nike, marveling over her dynamic strength, the latent power of her marble muscles and limbs. David's massive tableau of Napoleon crowning Joséphine also takes my breath away. "I hadn't expected the canvas to be on such a vast scale."

But when we arrive to the legendary masterpiece by Leonardo da Vinci, his *Mona Lisa*, it is Hal who seems overwhelmed, frozen in place. After a reflective pause, he says, "I can't figure it out."

I pull my eyes from da Vinci's painting and turn toward Hal. "You can't figure out what she's thinking?"

"Not that." Hal shakes his head. "I can't figure out why she's stirred up such a frenzy." Then he meets my gaze, and his expression is open, earnest. "Any one of your images is infinitely more appealing than this."

A small laugh spills from me, and I throw him a wry smirk. "Only you would compare me to an incomparable piece of art."

"You have it backwards," he says, holding me with his intense stare. "*You* are the incomparable one, my dear."

At the world-famous couturier House of Worth, dressmaker to queens, empresses, and heiresses, I am welcomed as a treasured client. Hal has arranged a private fitting with Clothilde, whom he assures me is their most sought-after modiste. "She was the personal favorite of Empress Sisi of Austria," he declares, and it strikes me as almost comical, how outlandish that sounds. Me, the hungry girl from Tarentum, dressed like an empress?

Clothilde escorts us into a private room walled in mirrors with a sitting area of plush couches beneath a crystal chandelier. There Hal takes a seat and an offered flute of champagne as Clothilde sets me up on a raised platform in the salon's center. Unspooling her measuring tape, she examines me with military precision, cinching and squeezing until she's investigated every inch of my figure, muttering in quiet French as she jots down her notes. She slips me in and out of several styles, a variety of lush fabrics in various states of completion.

Next she brings me to a wide mahogany desk covered in a sprawl of pencil sketches. I look down on an endless array of chic ensembles—traveling suits, day dresses, evening gowns, skirts, jackets, dressing gowns. I stare at the designs in wonder, recalling my first day in Wanamaker's and the ten-dollar dress that stunned me.

Clothilde turns from her sketches back to me. "This shall be your trousseau, mademoiselle?"

I frown, confused by her heavily accented words. "Your bridal wardrobe, *oui*?" she hastens to clarify. "For the honeymoon travels?"

Before I can say anything, Hal interjects, rising from the sofa and striding toward us. "Clothilde, she has to agree to marry me first," he says, his tone casual.

Then he throws me a wink, and I offer him a playful smile in return, even as I feel my cheeks flush. It's only a quip, his manner tells me. But then my eyes tilt downward, taking in the elegant stitching of the new plum-colored gown that sheathes my figure, its silk shimmering as it drips to the floor. And for the first time, the topic of marrying Hal strikes me as something I'd like to keep considering.

At Marie Antoinette's picturesque folly in the Bagatelle gardens, Hal once more approaches the subject that we've spent weeks dancing around. We are walking along the lake, through the dead queen's former playground, where I pause to admire a colorful cluster of roses. Hal is not looking at the flowers, however. He's looking only at me. "I could give you the life of a queen, you know."

I step back from the flowers, suddenly a bit dizzy, and I know it's not from the petals' perfume. I meet Hal's direct gaze, and he goes on, "If you would have me, I would see to it that every day felt like a fairy tale for you. Whatever you wanted, I would provide."

I look down, taking in these words of his. "I know you could," I reply, my voice quiet. "I know you would." But there are still the hidden parts of me that I'm too ashamed to pull into the light. The secrets of what Stanley Pierce did to me, made me into. Aren't I unworthy to be Hal Thorne's beloved and coddled bride?

The day is warm, and now my entire body feels unpleasantly flushed. "Hal, I wish to return to the hotel," I say, turning to tromp up the garden path. "I have a headache."

We return to the hotel an hour later, after a quiet carriage ride in which I closed my eyes and pretended to rest. All of me feels closed, in fact. The truth is that my mind is knotted and I need some time alone to sift through my tangled thoughts. But when Hal escorts me back to the suite and I open the door, stepping into the grand salon, we see Mamma seated on the sofa, a sprawl of money before her. American money, bills of every denomination.

I halt my steps, and Hal halts his, too. When Mamma looks up, her face goes white, and it's her expression—as though we've just caught her in the act of something most unseemly—that puts me even more on edge.

That, and the simple word she lobs at us both: "What?" She looks down at the money, then back toward us. "You're hours earlier than . . . You said . . . you said evening."

"Mamma, what are you doing?" I ask. "Where has all of this money come from?"

Mamma stuns me further when she replies, her voice an angry snarl: "It's none of your concern where I get my money!"

This catches me entirely off guard, the ferocity of her words. What has she done?

Hal strides into the room. "Have you stolen from me, Mrs. Talbot?"

My eyes cut toward him. His tone is icy; there's an expression on his face that I've never seen before. But Hal seems to remember himself in an instant. When he speaks next, his voice is calm and measured. "You know I would have given you whatever you desired. If you needed money, you had only to ask. Have I ever told you no?"

"I didn't steal it," Mamma growls, her bearing like that of an animal pinned in a corner.

"Then where did it come from?" I ask, frowning.

"Stanny gave it to me." Mamma's voice is petulant. "Before we left. He said you couldn't be trusted," she declares, looking directly at Hal. "He wanted me to have my own cash, said it was *he* who has always been there for us."

I don't look toward Hal, but I can sense that he has gone rigid. Keeping my eyes fixed on my mother, holding my voice as steady as I can manage, I say, "Mamma, please. Is this called for?"

"I'm leaving. I want to go home. I don't like it here." Now she flops backward on the couch and crosses her arms before her chest, looking very much like a child who has just told us she no longer wishes to play our game. But in fact, what she's just told me is that she wishes to leave me here, in Europe. Alone and unchaperoned. All because she doesn't like the food or the foreign language? We aren't set to sail back to New York for another month. We have a trip planned for a week from now to Orléans, a medieval city Hal has told us we will adore. "Mamma, why would you . . . ? You can't be serious—"

"I think it's for the best," Hal interrupts.

The words land with a thud between us, and then the room falls into a tense silence, the only sound the rhythmic ticktock of the ormolu clock on the mantelpiece.

I don't know what to say. Mamma looks as though she has nothing more to add. But it's Hal's silence that most troubles me.

I know how he loathes Stanley Pierce, and how he seethes now to hear Mamma refer to the scoundrel as our protector, even while sitting in this sumptuous suite that Hal has so graciously provided for us. Hal has every right to feel hurt after everything he has done.

But do I wish for Mamma to leave, for us to part ways? Do I wish to remain here, in Paris, with only Hal and his secretary, unchaperoned? It would be a scandal, to be sure, if the papers caught wind.

Suddenly my muddle of an hour earlier feels even more complicated. But before I can rein all these thoughts into some sensible response, Mamma, without another word, leans forward over the table and pulls the banknotes into a pile. Flashing me a pouty scowl, she rises from the couch, crosses the salon, and storms out of the suite. I know not where she is going.

But even if I did know, I wouldn't follow. Walking out on me like this, without a word, is perhaps her greatest act of betrayal. I'm disappointed, but sadly, I'm not surprised. And I do not wish to follow her. No more.

I will not leave—Paris, or this suite, or Hal. Hal, who has never treated me with Mamma's mercurial moodiness or displayed such a willingness to disregard my well-being. Mamma has abandoned me, I realize, time and again. And it will be the last time I allow her to do so.

That night, Hal sleeps in Mamma's room on the opposite side of the suite. He tells me he doesn't feel right leaving me alone. It might not be entirely conventional, or even proper, to be sharing a suite like this, but there is nothing uncouth about his behavior. If I'm being truly honest, this is hardly the first unconventional thing I've done. And it's not as though Mamma's presence has ever translated to my protection or well-being. To think of all the things I've done, right under her nose. Sometimes at her urging. Or with her complicit negligence, at the very least.

No, there's nothing indecent about this at all. After a quiet supper Hal retires into the far bedroom and shuts the door, and I don't hear another peep all evening.

I lie in my own bed, but sleep evades me. My thoughts keep me agitated and awake: I don't know where Mamma is. I know she has enough money for whatever it is that she decides to do. My guess is she'll book passage and return to New York. Which means she'll be farther away from me than ever before. I nestle my head deeper under the pillow, just as I did on so many nights as a girl, when I sought refuge from Mamma's wailing at my side. Now I seek refuge from my own thoughts, wishing that sleep would take me, give me a reprieve, even if for only a few hours.

I force myself to exhale. Just knowing that Hal is there, in the room across the way, is a comfort. Hal is the only person I have left in the world. The only person I know who has vowed to care for me and then has not left me. I am with him now.

Chapter Forty-Two

Orléans

"Joan of Arc would have been no virgin, had she met Stanley Pierce."

I slide my gaze from the view before us, Joan of Arc's narrow home in the heart of this ancient city, and turn to look at Hal. I don't conceal the fact that I'm perplexed by his comment. Since we left Paris for Orléans, he's been increasingly inclined to bring up the man's name. Is it because he's still wounded that Mamma left, choosing Stan as her friend and provider?

Or, a worse thought, does Hal know more than I've told him—that Stan was not only a friend to me and Mamma, but also my lover?

I shrug, looking back toward the saint's home, a structure of brick and stone ribbed in timber. Managing what I hope is a disaffected tone, I say, "Hal, I wish you would not bring up that name."

"The man's a devil, Eve. If only you knew."

If only you knew, I think. Still, Hal's comment makes me suspect that he might not in fact know the full truth of my past, and that gives me some measure of relief. So I say, "But he's not here, mercifully, and I'd rather not think of him."

We are standing together in the broad square of Orléans, the famously besieged city of France's beloved virgin warrior, on a pilgrimage that Hal had been most enthusiastic to make. While I'm happy to see the fabled city, to visit the site where the saint held out against a conquering army, to hear Hal tell of her virtue, I can't help but feel that this stop does not compare to Paris.

Traveling, of late, has lost a bit of its luster. Hal's mood has taken a noticeable dip since that day we visited the Bagatelle gardens, when he raised the idea of marriage and we returned to the hotel to find Mamma intent on departing. Perhaps we should return to Paris, where we were so happy. Perhaps, back there, we can recapture the magic that was swirling between us before Mamma's retreat threw everything off-kilter. Or maybe it was my refusal to acknowledge his proposal of marriage; perhaps Hal's patience with me has finally expired.

That evening, back in our inn overlooking the main square of Orléans, Hal and I sit down to a private dinner in the sitting room of our suite, a sprawl of rooms with separate bedrooms and this salon between them. We have barely been served our entrées before he confirms my suspicion: he has in fact run out of patience. "Why won't you marry me, Eve?"

I swallow the bite of lamb I've just begun chewing. Of course I knew he'd ask me again. But I don't feel ready to address this, not in this moment.

"Do you not care for me?" he asks, his voice low.

"I do care for you." And it's the truth. But perhaps now I need to tell him the whole truth.

"Then what is wrong with me, Angel? What failing of mine prevents you from taking my hand?"

His vulnerability softens me, and a sigh slips out. "It's not your failing, Hal, but mine." *There.* The words are out. I look through the window at the square below, unable to bear the earnest intensity in his eyes. "I'm not . . . precisely . . . all that you think I am."

"What do you mean?" he asks, confusion apparent in his voice.

I look around the room, ensuring the attendants have all gone. Then I turn back to him and force myself to meet his stare. Drawing in a fortifying breath, I begin. "There was a night, years ago, when my entire life changed."

I tell him. I tell Hal all about what happened when I was sixteen and Stan yanked me from the innocence of my girlhood into the realm of womanhood, without my ever knowing it was happening. I describe the darkened stairwell with the doors that opened from within. A room swathed in crimson. My belief that we were returning for a late-night dinner party and how I found instead a table set for two. Champagne, oysters, a mysterious midnight phone call pulling Stanley from the room. More champagne, his urging that I keep drinking. How my head became a cobweb. A swing through the air.

And then, nothing.

A black void without feeling or memory.

Before I startled awake, naked and in pain, back into the world of red.

Feeling returning, but still no memory.

And everything, including me—especially me—broken.

It's the first time I've ever spoken the words aloud. It's the first time I've ever even allowed my mind to move through the events of that night in such vivid detail, revisiting the pain that still aches within, even as so many of the memories remain out of reach.

"He drugged you, Evelyn," Hal says, after considering all my words in a glowering, brooding silence. "That much is clear. Stanley Pierce drugged you so that he could rape you."

I wince, my heart clenching at his unvarnished words, words that I've never voiced, even to myself. Then I say, "In truth, I've never understood what happened. The memory is so hazy. All I knew for certain was that I was never to tell anyone."

Hal reaches his hand across the table, taking mine in his. The press of his skin on mine, in this moment, is jarring. But his tone is soft. "Well, you've told me. And I can see how painful it was to speak. But you're safe with me. I shall protect you."

I could cry, I'm so relieved. I hadn't even realized what an unburdening it would be to speak the words aloud. To share the truth that only I have had to carry. So I decide to share even more. The hours pass, and we remain together at the table, and we talk and talk. I tell him everything as it comes to my mind, going back ever further in time. I tell him about Stan and his lavish spreads atop the Madison Square Tower. The private elevator. The chauffeured motorcar. The photos of me he had taken privately. Mamma's going away, leaving me in Stan's care.

"You have been a victim of them both," Hal says eventually, his voice heavy. "He's a viper, to be sure. But you've also suffered at the hands of your mother. Look at you, only sixteen at the time and left alone in the hands of a beast. Now not even twenty years old, and already you've endured a lifetime of misuse. And see how she's abandoned you yet again. Only this time, I shall keep you safe."

Hal rises from the table and comes to my side, kneeling before me. "You are still my angel." He takes my hands in his, his voice tender as he looks down at our intertwined grip. "You are trembling."

"I know." I can't make myself stop.

"You do not need to be afraid, not anymore."

Tears burn behind my eyes. In that moment, I make a decision. I give his hands a squeeze. "Hal?" My own voice sounds hoarse.

He lifts his gaze to meet mine. "Now there are no more secrets between us," I say. "Now that you truly know me . . . if you'll still have me, I will marry you."

At this, his pale features break open in a wide grin. Hal looks happy, so very happy. He knows the truth of me, and yet he still adores me. He still wants me. He still wishes to give me a life more beautiful than anything I could have ever dreamed of.

So I can't help but wonder in this moment: If *he* can be so happy—if *we* can be so happy together—then why can't I stop shaking?

PART 4

A real escape is possible when all eyes are on you. That's how it's always felt to me. When I'm up there on that stage, or in front of the camera, or posing before the canvas, I can become whatever it is they wish to see. My greatest power as a performer came from the fact that I knew how to make my Self disappear.

> —Evelyn Talbot, in a letter written to Mr. Anthony Comstock, published after her death

• ♦ •

Was it a blessing or a curse, this knack I had? The knack for knowing how people saw me. What they saw and what they didn't—even when they were looking right at me.

Twinned with that knowing was my ability to give them what they wanted.

Until I realized: *I've had enough of doing that. What about what I want?*

If I could find a way to answer that question, then the much harder question would follow: How am I going to get it?

Chapter Forty-Three

Pittsburgh
Autumn 1904

I scowl at the pile of newspapers sprawled before me. Each sheet has been meticulously ironed by the Thorne butler and brought to me like some savory dish on a platter of polished silver. The newspapers come from Pittsburgh and Philadelphia, New York, too.

And I'm featured in every single one of them.

I, Evelyn Thorne, am "*the Mistress of Millions, America's living Cinderella.*" Having begun as a penniless artists' model, I've now won and married my prince. I've left the bright lights of Broadway behind to take up my plush perch in Stonehurst mansion, the grandest castle on Pittsburgh's Millionaire's Row. I'm Mrs. Thorne at the age of nineteen, the luckiest girl in the world.

Then why does each article I read bring a frown to my face?

I suppose that, in large part, it has to do with my company at the table—the fact that I'm not the only one at breakfast scowling. Nor am I the only Mrs. Thorne presiding over this meal, or this castle. "I've told them not to show me that filth. I don't understand why my son insists on seeing the papers each morning." My new mother-in-law, Mary Thorne, deepens her glower as she turns her gray eyes from the headlines toward me. "It'll only stain his soul. Or, rather, further stain."

Known as the pious and venerable Widow Thorne throughout her hometown of Pittsburgh, Mary has instructed me to call her

Mother Thorne. And thorn in my side she is. Though she'd undoubtedly aver that the roles are reversed and that I'm nothing short of a crown of thorns that she, like the suffering savior, has been forced to wear ever since her darling boy returned home from his European summer travels and announced that we'd married while abroad.

It was all done in a whirlwind of haste and practicalities, if not necessarily romance. All at Hal's direction. "I'd like to see it done here and now," he'd told me that evening in Orléans when I unburdened my soul to him. To my immense relief, it hadn't pushed him away; in fact, it had seemed to fuel his desire for us to be together.

"If we wait to do it back in New York, Angel, you'll have to invite your mother. And possibly *he* would show up, audacious as he is. No! There's no way. Let us sanctify our union here. And then we may be truly bonded in the eyes of God. And no one may cast aspersions on our traveling together. Let no one dare to taint what we share."

He dispatched the hotel staff to summon the nearest priest. He made arrangements for us to be married in the sanctuary where Joan of Arc's sainted feet had trod. He even selected the outfit for me from my traveling trunks—black satin with onyx beading, a veiled hat to accompany it.

"I thought I might wear white," I said, dashed with disappointment when Hal placed the gown before me. In truth, I hadn't envisioned with any specificity *what* my wedding dress might someday look like, as matrimony had always seemed like a vague and distant destination. But a black gown more fit for mourning? That had never featured in my fantasies.

"You don't like this one?" Hal balked. "It's brand-new. We just ordered it in Paris. From Worth."

"It's lovely," I quickly replied. "I only mean, white is the fashion now for weddings."

Hal's face furrowed into a thoughtful frown. And then, still looking at the dress, he said, "Don't you think that would be a bit hypocritical? We are in the hometown of Joan of Arc, of all places. She who never allowed her body to be defiled."

So I'd donned the black onyx to meet the priest, who married us in the hometown of Hal's favorite saint. And now I've returned to the United States as Hal's wife, my head very much in a spin, and not because of the rough sea crossing. I'm still trying to catch up with all that has happened, and changed, in my life as the newlywed Mrs. Thorne.

Speaking of saints . . . suffering in saintly silence does not appear to be Mother Thorne's preference. On the contrary, she's made it abundantly clear that she disapproves of the hasty marriage her hapless son entered into while abroad. That she now sees it as her divine purpose to save my ruined soul. Or perhaps to save her son after his grievous mistake of attaching himself to me.

"Ill-made match," she'd groaned when her son and I had appeared together at Stonehurst, weary from the trip. She'd whisked Hal into the study and closed the door but did little to lower her voice as she shrieked her thoughts. "This is a tragedy! You are a scion of steel and railroads, my poor, darling boy. A showgirl? If you wanted a dalliance with a pretty skirt, you could have walked into any of the boardinghouses in Pittsburgh."

"Please, Mother," I'd heard my new husband attempt to interject on my behalf, but she gave him no space, railing on: "Why, my daughter went to Europe and became a countess!"

"Mother, if you would only give her—"

"You went to Europe and came home saddled with a vulgar dime-novel character!"

Eventually he'd stopped trying, letting the storm of her furious disapproval run itself out. I was treated to the whole litany of her horrors on Hal's behalf. One thing that was immediately clear to me from my eavesdropping: she's a mother entirely unlike the detached mother I have, a woman willing to leave me alone on foreign soil.

As much as Mother Thorne may dislike me, I do have to give her credit for adoring her boy. Seeing the extent of her maternal adoration, I have the strong suspicion that *no* bride would have been good enough for her beloved son. I only hope that, with time, I'll be able to show her that I am not the tawdry character she believes me to be.

In fact, now that I've agreed to be his wife, I want nothing more than to be worthy of Hal, to make him happy—and his family, as well. Why, I agreed to the hasty wedding he wanted in France, didn't I? And then when Hal told me he wished for me to leave the Broadway stage behind, when he told me being a showgirl wasn't proper now that I was a member of the Thorne family, hadn't I complied without a quarrel? When he said he wanted us to settle as a family in the Thorne estate in Pittsburgh, quitting Manhattan for the quieter life he'd always envisioned with his bride, didn't I agree?

So here we are. Living as a new family, folded into the larger family that has presided over the Thorne estate for generations. In marrying Hal, I've gotten his mother, too, and so I'm trying my best to make peace. She's the only mother either of us has got now that my own mother no longer speaks to me.

Mamma did leave Paris abruptly, as I had expected, and she's thrown in her lot with Stan. I did write to tell her that I'd married Hal, but she never replied. I believe she still lives in the hotel, supported by Stan. New York is his town. He built it. Any relationship I might have with Mamma or with Manhattan would now come with a price I am no longer willing to pay, if it would mean Stan would be involved. Perhaps Mamma and I will find our way back to one another in time.

Cut off from New York and isolated here in Pittsburgh, I've got no hope of seeing my girlfriends from the stage. Penny is the only one who still writes regularly. Trixie got married and Annissa moved away, I heard to Chicago. Dinah and Dolly wrote one letter to congratulate me on my wedding news, but that's all I expect to hear from them. That's just as well; they are also too closely intertwined with Stan for my—or Hal's—comfort. He's asked me to leave the stage, the artists' studios, the late nights and frenetic days, all behind.

"How about I invite Penny for a visit here?" I suggest. "Or maybe I could make a trip to Philadelphia, if not New York?" The truth is, I'd love to see Leah and Rachel after all this time. To show them how far I've come, and all because of their support and friendship at the very start.

"In time, in time, dear wife," Hal responds a touch dismissively.

"Pittsburgh is your home now. Let's settle here after our wayward travels. It takes time, but we will introduce you around," Hal tells me often during our first weeks in this new, quiet life. I've confessed to him how overwhelming, how *different* it all feels—more foreign, even, than Paris or London. And the loneliness. Without the distractions of the packed days that I had in foreign cities, I am aware, suddenly, of just how alone I am here in this new place.

"You'll make friends," Hal says. "And when we have family news of our own, you'll be busier than ever, beautiful wife." Does he mean . . . a baby? The thought lands in my gut like a brick. Do I want a baby? So soon? I'm nineteen, about to turn twenty. I've only just become a wife and have not yet adjusted to the hastily taken role. Am I prepared to also become a mother?

These questions give me a headache that sends me to bed for the rest of the day. I have my own bedroom suite in our wing of the mansion, and as I shut the heavy door and look around the vast space, I can't help but note how the room resembles the quarters of a princess. And yet, it's cold. It's cold everywhere inside this massive house, and since we moved here in the autumn, there's been an ever-present damp, a moist and cloying chill that lurks throughout, just like the heavy dark drapes. Drapes that I constantly want opened, because it is dim in this house also. Both day and night, the shadows stretch long, and I wish to welcome any spot of sunshine that is willing to push its way through the ivy that wraps this castle.

When I confess to Hal that I feel cold quite often in my bedroom, he scolds the servants. "Keep Mrs. Thorne's fire blazing at all times!" I hear him censuring a chambermaid. *Mrs. Thorne*. It gives me pause to hear him speak the name. Does this poor maid find the new title as confounding as I do?

After that, there is always a hearty fire in my hearth, and gleaming new silver candelabras appear atop every empty surface in my bedroom—that helps with both the damp and the gloominess. Hal is trying to make me happy. And I am trying my best to settle into my new days as Mrs. Thorne with as little disruption to the household as possible.

The evenings, I find, are more tedious than the days. After dinner the three of us kneel in the parlor to say prayers as a family. I gather this was a mainstay of Hal's childhood, this nightly vigil that lasts over an hour, all of our hands clasped, heads bowed.

The first time I joined Hal and his mother for this Thorne evening ritual, I was stunned when, as Mother Thorne prayed aloud for the "list of sinners," she included my name. Stung, I threw a pointed look toward Hal, but with his eyes shut and head tipped, he didn't see me. So I pulled him aside later that evening, after his mother had gone up to bed.

"What was the meaning of that?" I asked, my anger outpaced only by my hurt.

He sighed, throwing a look down the dark corridor, before he answered: "The thing is, Mother tells me that *she* has forgiven you."

"How kind of her." My tone is wry, but from Hal's distracted expression, I can't be sure he's heard that.

He goes on. "But she feels it behooves us all to continue to pray for you. And in exchange for her forgiveness, she's asked that we never speak of your past again."

"Haven't I already agreed to leave my past behind?" I ask, wounded afresh. And not a little bit irked that my husband is submitting to this ridiculousness from his mother. When it's just the pair of us, my Hal is still as kind and thoughtful as ever, but the problem is, in this house, it's rarely just the pair of us. And I'm under no illusions as to who is in charge, running this household. *That imperious, disapproving, marble-mouthed . . .* I catch myself. And before I can say anything too disrespectful aloud, something that might offend my husband, when he's only ever tried to defend me, I excuse myself, telling Hal I'm tired.

But back in my massive bedroom and plush bed, sleep evades me, my body as uncomfortable as if I were lying on a slab of stone. I've been the model daughter-in-law, obeying her ridiculous list of house rules without protest. When Mother Thorne told me she wished for me not to read novels, only the Bible, I agreed silently, doing my best to block out Daddy's face.

When I asked her why her beautiful home didn't boast any art besides portraits—they could afford original Monets, after all—she explained to me that the endless rows of drab portraits were of deceased Thorne family members and that it would do well for me to reflect on their examples if I ever hoped to be worthy of them. I bit my lip and offered her a respectful nod. Insufferable woman. She's as dull as the dead family members that darken these walls.

The worst painting of all—one of the main reasons I find sleep so elusive—is a portrait that hangs in my large marble bathroom. Right over the bathtub. The sallow face of some long-dead Thorne lady. I can see from the plaque on the frame that her name was also Mary.

"She hanged herself with a towel, in this very room," my mother-in-law told me when she first helped me settle into my suite. "While her family thought she was taking a bath. Can you imagine?"

And then, with a quiet "tut-tut," my mother-in-law simply walked on as if she'd commented on something as banal as my bath towels. But I remained fixed, staring up at the portrait, at the yellow hue of this Mary Thorne's sickly, unsmiling face. No, I could *not* imagine. Either what would make this woman wish to end her own life or why the Thornes who came after her had thought it a nice idea to hang her portrait in the very room where she had hanged herself.

A month into my new life here with the pious Widow Thorne, I wonder whether it is the tragic Mary Thorne of long past who haunts my sleepless nights. Or is it perhaps the *other* Mary Thorne, the living woman who gave birth to my husband and now prays just down the hall for my fallen soul?

Chapter Forty-Four

"How was your morning, Mother?" I do my best to summon a chipper tone, looking up as Mary Thorne struts into the gloomy family parlor where I have been sitting alone.

"Fruitful," she replies, lowering herself with a swoosh of her skirts into the uncomfortable mahogany chair opposite me. She's turned out in black and white pinstripes, reminding me of a peppermint stick that's been sucked of all its color. "We were preparing food baskets at the church."

"How good of you, Mother." I splay the leather-bound Thorne family Bible across my lap, intent on her noticing my selection of such suitable reading material, and fix the most benign smile I can muster to my face as I sigh.

"Yes, well . . ." She waves an imperious hand across the room, and a well-trained servant slips from sight to fetch her beloved brew of warm water with lemon; nothing so sinful as caffeine would cross her pristine lips. She'll take this hot drink with me for a few minutes and then be off again.

I've come to learn that Mother Thorne's days are usually occupied with a full agenda of good works: organizing the upcoming parish bazaar, raising money for the new organ, meeting with the minister, or, as she was today, collecting and arranging foodstuffs. Otherwise, if she's not gadding about with her clique of fellow Presbyterian goodwives, she's off by herself, closeted in her drab bedroom, praying on her knees beside her massive bed.

While Hal works, or takes meetings, or goes out to join the

gentlemen at the club for golf or drinks, Mother Thorne is my one companion. I see my husband in the early morning and in the evening if he gets home before I've retired. I receive the occasional letter from Penny with her seemingly unenthusiastic updates on yet another show she's singing in. But the gaping maw of my day is otherwise unfilled.

The footman reappears, carrying Mother Thorne's hot drink on his tray. He strides briskly into the room and lowers the cup onto the table before us, and Mother takes a napkin in her lap without acknowledging the fellow. As he is turning to go, I thank him and flash a smile. He nods, but does not meet my eyes, leaving us without a sound.

I cannot get the household staff to speak to me or even look me in the eye. Not even the chambermaids, who appear to be about my age. Why, couldn't one of them be a friend? But no, it's as though they've been ordered not to make a noise, let alone initiate any communication with a member of the exalted Thorne family. So, no hope of making any friends there.

As my mother-in-law sips her drink, I drum the wooden arms of my uncomfortable chair. I could cry, I am so bored. *This cannot go on; I simply must find ways to fill the hours, or I will go numb from the dreariness of it all.* "Mother, I was wondering . . . one of these days, when you go to the church, may I join you?"

Mother Thorne sits up even straighter in her seat, staring down at me over her thin, patrician nose. Pinching her cup of hot water between her fingers, she asks, "You feel that you are ready?"

"To help you with . . . with your food baskets and such? Yes, I'd like to join."

Hal's mother tips her white-haired head to the side, still surveying me. "Would your soul be in the work?"

Would my soul be in the work of stuffing food baskets? Why, I don't see why not. What my soul longs for, more than anything, is to see people. To get out of this quiet, cavernous house and break up the dull and dreary monotony. What I can't tell Mother Thorne is that being plucked from my life on Broadway to end up here, where there is no color, no sound, no art, no company of any kind—why, it's like my soul is being starved. But I say only, "I wish to be worthy of the Thorne name."

This remark lands well enough, in spite of the fact that it's my sinful lips that utter it. I can see that my mother-in-law is pleasantly surprised. She tilts back in her chair, thinks for a long moment, then seems to land on a decision, declaring: "I shall host a series of at homes."

"I beg your pardon?"

"*At homes.*" Mary doesn't even try to conceal her disdain as she rolls her eyes. "Honestly, where did he find you?"

Broadway, I wish to say. *Your son found me on the stage of Broadway.* And find me, he did. He came for me, a relentless pursuit. But I bite my lip because this feels like perhaps some progress, minuscule as it may be.

"I shall inform the town that I will be at home for an allotted day and time and willing to receive," Mother Thorne explains, making plain her displeasure at having to do so. "At least, I shall be willing to receive those to whom I send invitations."

• ◆ •

THE ALLOTTED DAY and time arrive, Wednesday at three o'clock, and I sit beside Mother Thorne on our hard-backed chairs of carved mahogany. Outside it's a gray day, with steady raindrops slapping her tall windows, but I don't doubt that her crowd of Presbyterian goodwives will turn out to answer the Widow Thorne's summons, in spite of the inclement weather. Hal has made himself scarce, fleeing for his club with a quick kiss atop my head and the words "Have fun, beautiful wife." He was hopeful for me, knowing how lonely I've been feeling of late.

"Good posture, remember," Mother Thorne chides me as the clock strikes three and the butler presents her with a silver tray already bearing the cards of her first callers.

"Your friends are prompt," I note.

"Why shouldn't they be?" She scowls. "Tardiness is for the slothful and indolent."

I manage to sit up even straighter, as if the corset she's had me laced into would allow me to slouch for an instant. She's picked out my entire outfit: a cream-colored day dress with black frogging along the neck and sleeves, gloves, white boots, not a drop of perfume or makeup. My only jewelry is a pair of tasteful pearl earrings, a gift from her son, and my wedding rings.

Mother Thorne and I sit side by side, presiding over a dull spread of bland tea sandwiches on white bread, as dry as the white shirtwaist she wears, which has been starched to the texture of flint.

Today *I* am her charity project. Her philanthropic burden. In spite of the mortification she clearly feels at having to tolerate me in her home, today she will show me off to her dozens of church friends. The bride whom her prized son, who could have had anyone, has taken on. And I can see that that's precisely how she's going to spin it—I am yet another charity case that she, in her boundless piety, has been willing to take in hand.

Her first guests enter, prim ladies who look as though they've plucked their own stiff shirtwaists right off of Mary Thorne's ironing board. *Is it some sort of Presbyterian uniform?* I wonder. *Does it come with a hair-shirt lining?*

"Ann, Ruth, Helen, welcome," says my mother-in-law. In they stride, reminding me of the pigeons in New York City who all move together, bodies coordinated in wordless collaboration. "May I offer you some juice or tea?"

I can see their eager stares. All three of them, in spite of their better judgment, are simply desperate to take in the sight of me. My mother-in-law has warned that I am never to speak of my past; it's been washed clean, like my soul. But as the hour wears on, as more and more of Pittsburgh's finest ladies file into this parlor, helping themselves to tea and finger sandwiches and furtive glances at my face and figure, I come to suspect that every single one of them knows about me. Not only me, but my past. Dancing on Broadway, posing for artists. And perhaps, given their lingering, inquisitive stares, perhaps even Stanley Pierce.

My suspicion is confirmed forty-five minutes into our "at home" when I overhear a snippet of Mary's conversation a few feet away from me. "My son believes he can save the girl," Mary says, her voice low but dripping with displeasure.

"He's always been such a good boy," the friend replies, her own tone sugary, if a bit sorrowful.

"That may be so, but the poor girl . . . As I told my Hal, some people are simply beyond salvation."

My entire body clenches as I feel my heart hammer angrily against my ribs. It strikes me as I look around the room that I now feel even lonelier than I did when all the rooms in this house were empty.

As the ladies depart at the end of the afternoon, making their obedient reverences to Mother Thorne, each one quits the room with parting words that indicate just how much they fear for my soul, or pity the Thorne family that has taken me in.

"We are praying for you."

"Your mother-in-law is a fine lady."

"We shall keep you in our prayers."

I hear these words of woe and concern over and over, from each lady who departs. And as I glide back up, alone and drained, toward my bedroom, I feel further than ever from my hopes of making a new friend or feeling at home.

Chapter Forty-Five

Christmas 1904

Christmas morning breaks over the city, cold and clear, as Hal stirs in bed beside me. "Our first Noel as newlyweds, beautiful birthday wife," he says, his voice still fuzzy from sleep. He rises and draws open the thick velvet drapes. He must have slipped in late, after I was asleep, for I didn't hear him enter. I'm glad to have this warm and tender moment, just us, before we must inevitably join his mother.

"Merry Christmas," I say, flashing him a sleepy smile as I look out the window over the snowy grounds of the estate and, beyond that, Beechwood Boulevard. As I stare at the wintry scene, I can't help but reflect that it's not in fact my first Christmas at Stonehurst, though it is certainly the first Christmas Day on which I have been invited inside. I blink, pushing the vivid memory of Mamma and Kit and the cold front steps from my mind. I need to dress, for his mother has warned us we are not to be late to the front pew at church for the early service.

By the time we are back at Stonehurst, where the hearths are blazing and the candles are lit, it's time to sit down to Christmas dinner. "Not just Christmas dinner," my husband remarks, helping me out of my furs. "Also the birthday dinner for my booful."

Mother Thorne is visibly irked—she hates this affectionate name her son uses for me. Or maybe it's the fact that she now has to share the birth of the savior with my own birthday, for my husband insists on celebrating me.

We sit down in the dining room, the three of us, at the table laden with enough food for a crowd of twenty. But with Anne in England and Hal's father gone, we are a small party. This day is filling me with unpleasant nostalgia, the thought of another party of three. *Kit.* I miss him with a deep, hollow ache. And Mamma—well, there's no hope of seeing her this Christmas. I wonder if she opened the Christmas card I sent her, written on my thick new Thorne stationery. Or the new silver candlesticks I sent with it.

"Booful?" The sound of Hal's voice pulls me from my gloomy reverie.

"Sorry," I stammer. "Yes?"

"I asked if you were ready for your present."

"Now?" I shift in my seat. "Before we eat?"

"Yes," he declares animatedly. "I can't wait another minute to spoil you."

"Hal, you've already spoiled me." How many pieces of jewelry has he lavished me with? There's not a single item I can think of that I need; even just the thought of another thick necklace around my neck feels heavy. But seeing his eager anticipation, I tell him, "How nice," attempting to summon some delight.

Hal waves toward the dining room doorway, and a young male servant materializes with a large basket draped in a blanket and wrapped in a big cherry-colored bow. "What's all this?" I ask, seeing that the parcel is not going to be another diamond or strand of pearls.

The servant gently lowers the large basket onto the floor at my feet and, with a flourish, pulls aside the blanket to reveal a small mound of fur.

I gasp, my hand flying to my heart, and now I do not need to pretend at happiness. "Is it . . . a puppy?"

Hal nods, looking thoroughly satisfied, as his mother makes a sound in the back of her throat.

I ignore her. "Oh, Hal, I love her."

"Do you really?" Hal is eyeing me as I lean forward and take this adorable creature in my arms.

"How could I not?" I coo, breathing in her powdery smell. "Oh, hello, my darling girl." This close, I feel her tiny heartbeat, its rapid pace telling me that she's scared. "There, there, my dear. Nothing to fear. This shall be your new home. And I shall be your mamma."

"So then, you *are* pleased, booful wife?"

"Oh, Hal." I pull my eyes begrudgingly from the dog's precious face and look to my husband. I feel as though I could cry. "This means more to me than any gift I could imagine." In fact, she's the *only* gift that I could imagine making me happy in this moment, short of a revival of Kit or maybe an erasure of some of the memories of the past few years. What I needed was some salve for my constant loneliness. A companion. And my husband saw it and delivered. "Your thoughtfulness, my darling," I say, taking his hand in mine, giving it a thankful squeeze.

This tender moment is interrupted when another footman peeks his head into the dining room. "Pardon the interruption, Mrs. Thorne. Mr. Thorne."

Both my husband and his mother turn to answer. Only I don't, not even realizing until too late that I, too, am Mrs. Thorne.

The footman takes a tenuous step toward us, folding his gloved hands before his waist. "We've just received a rather large package. From the Carnegie family." The name causes all three of us to sit just a bit straighter in our chairs. The Carnegies are another wealthy Pittsburgh family—steel. "Shall I have it brought in?"

"Yes," Hal answers with a wave of his hand. A few moments later, two young fellows are hauling in a massive wooden crate branded with the lettering and art of Haudenshield's Butcher. A place I know well.

"It is sausages, salami, sweetmeats, and cheeses, they've told us," the footman announces, as all three of us admire the gift. And that's when I see it—the image emblazoned along the front of the crate. A girl in a German dirndl, her glossy dark hair falling in two thick plaits over her otherwise bare shoulders. Her head tips back, red lips parting in an impish smile.

It's me. I remember posing for the advertisement, years ago.

Mother Thorne gasps, noticing the image at precisely the same moment. I look to her and see that her face has gone sheet white.

Then she turns to her son, speaking as though I'm not even in the room: "How can you bear it?"

Hal rolls his eyes, but I can see the scarlet flames that now tint his cheeks. "Mother, please."

"In our home!"

"Mother, I'm warning you, watch your—"

"Evidence of her pollution in plain sight."

"How dare you!" Hal roars, pounding a fist on the table, sending several crystal glasses tumbling sideways as he does so. I wince, and so does the puppy in my arms. I've never seen my husband yell like that. And over me, no less. All in the name of my honor. Or, as my mother-in-law would surely say, my dishonor. All three of us fall silent at the table as, in my lap, the puppy lets out a small whimper.

It's all too much. I can't stay here, in this room, with my face smiling up from the wooden crate, my mother-in-law's pale horror, my husband's flushed rage. I cling tight to the puppy in my arms, rise from my seat, and flee the room without a word.

Back in my bedroom with the door shut, I pace the large space. My heart races, but my mind goes even faster. I'm thinking back to that day when I posed for the Haudenshield's advertisement. How much it had meant to me, as I could remember only too well the days when I never would have been able to afford a cut of meat from Pittsburgh's most popular butcher. Posing for their advertisement felt like a triumph. And now my image is being used on Christmas gifts from the likes of the Carnegie family. It would be considered by so many—including me, until only recently—to be a stunning rise.

But Hal's mother will never see me as anything but fallen.

H<small>AL COMES TO ME</small>, hours later. I'm in bed, clutching the puppy. I hear the groaning of the heavy door, my husband's footfalls on the carpet, and I pretend to be asleep. But he doesn't take note. Or else, he doesn't care. Instead he approaches the bed and yanks on the bedcovers, rending them from the mattress. "Evelyn?"

I groan as though still half-asleep. "Evelyn?" he repeats my name, more insistently this time.

"Yes?" I turn to face him, squinting in the dark. I can make out his outline as he places a nearly empty glass down on the bedside table and climbs into bed, his movements clumsy and graceless. I can smell the wine on him. I realize, with a mounting sense of unease, that he's reaching for me. He intends to make love.

I wish to grimace, to push him away, to tell him no, but his movements are less than tender. Earlier he was angry with his mother at the dining room table, but now it seems he's angry at me. And yet the anger only seems to fuel his desire, for he pulls me toward him with an urgency I've never before seen.

Mercifully, it is over quickly.

After, as he lies panting beside me, he's still angry; I can feel the anger seeping off him. As though our lovemaking has sated his desire but not his rage. He gets up to go, I know not where. And I do not ask, because the truth is that I'm relieved to have him leave me.

Once he has shut the heavy door, I pull the puppy back toward me and I cry. I weep into her soft fur, feeling as though she is the only thing anchoring me to this world.

I've had some terrible birthdays on wretched Christmas Days. My mind spins through many of them now—memories of missing Daddy, crouching in the alleyway, starving, hunting for the butcher's scrap droppings. Begging outside this very house, seeing the rich red drapes through the windows, imagining the rooms inside, so grand and warm.

Here I am, inside this house now, being gifted crates of sweetmeats with my own image on the box, never again at risk of having to go hungry. Just as I once clutched the stray cat, now I clutch my puppy. And I ask myself, as I lie tucked into my warm bed on Millionaire's Row: Why am I wishing I could be back in that cold alleyway?

Chapter Forty-Six

Spring 1905

I'VE ALWAYS BEEN GOOD AT PLAYING MY PART, LEARNING THE role that has been assigned to me. Modifying who I am and how I appear in order to give them all what they want to see. More times than I can count, it's been the difference in my survival. As we showgirls often quipped backstage, with a bit more world-weariness than our tender ages should have afforded us: "It's either learn the ropes, sweetie, or else hang."

But this is the hardest role I've ever had to play. I'm trying my best, every day. To be a respectable Thorne, a pleasing daughter-in-law, a good Presbyterian wife. If I can convince Mother Thorne that I've seen the light, that I've left my Broadway past behind and am now a good girl, perhaps she'll stop loathing me; perhaps she'll stop disparaging me to my husband. Perhaps we might be able to settle into some sort of peace in our home. And peace is what I need.

To that end, I ask my husband for a favor. "I wish you would build me a pool," I declare. "They're all the fashion now, indoor pools." As I'm no longer permitted to dance or sing or really do *anything* diverting, I need something to occupy my hours and utilize my energy. I'm only twenty years old, and I'm bored stiff.

Hal quickly complies. "Some men build their wives gardens, others temples. I'm building you a pool."

He covers it with a glass greenhouse so that I may use it all year long, regardless of weather, and when it's completed that spring, I am delighted. The pool, set apart from the main house, becomes a much-needed refuge. I swim every day—half a mile at first. Then a mile. My body responds well to it. I've always been strong from my youth and the dancing, but this is new. Soon I have lean and taut new muscles on my legs, my arms, my midsection.

But it's more than my body—the laps lull me with their rhythmic movement, and I find that, gliding through the water, I can quiet my spinning mind. It does give me some measure of peace. *Learn to swim. And then you'll survive.* It's what Charles Dana Gibson told me years ago. I didn't fully understand it then, and I don't fully understand it now, but I know that swimming is the one thing that soothes me on some desperate days, when otherwise the gloom threatens to pull me under.

As spring turns to summer, Hal and I begin to speak about traveling again. It's hard to believe we've been married almost a year. I ask if we can go to New York around the time of our anniversary. "The place where we met, Hal." And, I neglect to add, the place where I might be able to visit Penny.

But my husband immediately rejects the idea. "Then how about Philadelphia?" I suggest. If I can't see Penny, it'd be nice to see Leah and Rachel.

"I was thinking farther afield," he responds. "Germany?"

This catches me off guard, but not unpleasantly. *Germany.* I tell him I'll think about it. The thought of a trip, anywhere, does fill me with glimmers of hope.

Shortly after that Mary prepares to host a tea at home with several dozen of her church ladies. When the morning of the gathering dawns, I rise early to swim, then I find her in the parlor as she's overseeing the final arrangements. Offering my blandest smile, I ask, "Mother, I was wondering if I might join you in the parlor for tea?"

With a sigh, she begrudgingly assents. "Thank you," I say, and then I excuse myself from the room before she can change her mind. If there are some new faces in the crowd, I might meet a friend or two. I try my best to keep hope alive.

The appointed hour arrives, and we sit in the sun-filled parlor as the ladies file in. There is a full tea service set before us, with small plates filled with almond cakes, finger sandwiches, lemon biscuits. The chitchat is quiet and bland, all talk of weather and children and pious church business. Mother has gathered her coterie together today to speak about some much-needed repairs to the church's roof, and as we are all finishing our tea, she reminds us that we must start thinking about how to raise the funds.

Mrs. Fletcher, a matron in a feathered hat, suggests a variety show. "Wouldn't that be amusing?" And then, with an earnest smile, the woman looks to me. "A night of entertainment. Folks could read a poem or play an instrument. What do you think?"

"I think it's a grand idea," I respond, instantly excited. And surprised, too, that this lady has looked to me, seemingly to seek my opinion. Delighted, as well, to be spoken to. Perhaps responding to my animation, Miranda yelps in my lap, so I lower my squirming dog to the carpeted floor and then carry on. "You could sell tickets, perhaps even put on a supper at the show."

Mrs. Fletcher nods, considering my suggestions. "I like that." Murmurs of tepid assent fill the room as Mrs. Fletcher goes on. "We could decorate the space. Should we call it *Broadway Comes to Pittsburgh*?"

"That's enough for one day, ladies," Mother interjects, and when I turn to her, I see that her features have gone startlingly pale, even whiter than usual. With a pinched smile, she rises from her seat. The tea party, and all talk of the fundraiser, has reached its conclusion.

Mother's postulants dutifully file out. After we've seen our final guests to the door and Mother has graciously accepted more than twenty servile murmurs of thanks from her friends, we remain, the pair of us in the quiet foyer. Miranda, agitated by all the visitors, runs in small circles at my feet, nipping at my skirts in her puppy playfulness.

But Mother doesn't move from the door. In fact, she appears fixed to the spot, lifeless as a statue while she holds me in her gray gaze. And then, with her voice thin as a reed, she speaks the words so quietly that I barely hear her: "I suppose you think you'll get up there?"

My heart could fall into my stomach. She's displeased with me, even more than usual. "Up . . . where?" I ask.

"Come now, I'm no fool." She folds her paper-white hands primly before her waist. "*Broadway Comes to Pittsburgh*?"

"I didn't make that suggestion," I say. "Nor did I suggest the variety show. I suggested ticket sales and a supper. This is to raise funds for the church, isn't it?"

"Why do you suppose the ladies even thought of the Broadway idea? If not for being swayed by your . . . influence."

My *influence*? Now my mere presence in a room has the power to stain these poor women, polluting their minds and souls? I resist the urge to scowl, or to jump to defensiveness. I remind myself to stay calm, and I try a different tack. "Mother, if we are raising money for the church, and we find a way to get the ladies excited to plan and the congregation enthusiastic to attend, that's a good thing, is it not?"

Her features clench. I hear an exhale before she says, "Ill-gotten money can do no good. I'll not have my own daughter-in-law standing up on the stage like some painted lady for all to gawk at."

"I never said I would go up on that stage," I hasten to clarify. "I can help plan; that's all." Miranda is trying to play with me, to grab my attention, and I shift on my feet to keep her from pawing my skirts. I don't need anything to further upset Mother, especially not my puppy.

"I'm not so easily deceived." My mother-in-law arcs a gray eyebrow, ignoring the bouncing puppy at her feet, pinning me with her stare. "You could barely hide your delight in talking about the stage."

"The stage is diverting to speak about, perhaps, but I never—"

"You're still the chorus girl," she spits, her gaze as cold as the steel that has made her rich as a queen. And I see how, also like her steel, which can be used to forge the sharpest of blades, Mother wishes to cut me. She scowls down at the floor where Miranda is prancing around, trying to play with us both. In the next instant my mother-in-law hitches up her skirt and lands a decisive kick on my puppy's head. It's not a hard kick, but Miranda is not a big dog, and it sends her stumbling with a yelp of startled pain.

This is more than I will stand. I lean over and grab Miranda and storm from the room. I don't stop until I've slammed my bedroom door shut, my puppy and I alone inside.

White-hot anger writhes within me. The dog is fine, but I am not. Oh, I've learned to act my roles, all right. But do I wish to continue playing this part? This role that will drain my soul, rather than save it?

· ◆ ·

HOURS OF PACING and brooding do little to calm my anger, but then my bedroom door opens without a knock. "Hello, booful wife." My husband waltzes in to find me clutching Miranda and walking a straight line back and forth before my fireplace.

"How was your day?" he asks, his own mood light and unburdened. It's the first time I've seen him since morning.

"Horrible," I reply, doing nothing to mask my frown. I feel a twinge of remorse about bringing down his mood, but he must know what his mother has done. I can no longer keep it in.

But Hal, to my surprise, doesn't seem to notice my stormy mood, nor does he ask for more information. In fact, he doesn't even appear to have heard me as he walks to the tall window and peers out over the darkening gardens. So I ask: "How was yours?"

"Good, good," he answers, nodding distractedly. "Every day is a good day when I have my booful wife." And then he begins to hum some childish, jingly sort of tune, still staring out the window.

I narrow my eyes, taking a moment to study him a bit closer. That's when I see him slip his hand into his trouser pocket and I catch a glint of something sparkling. My blood stills in my veins. "Hal?"

Now he's whistling the tune, acting as though he hasn't heard me. Perhaps he really hasn't.

"What is that in your pocket?" I ask, speaking louder. Hal looks at me for the first time, and his pale eyes appear vacant, confused, even. I point in the direction of his trousers, and he glances down, opening his pocket wider. My horrible suspicion is confirmed. "Why are you wearing a gun?" I ask, my voice strained.

"This? Yes, my trusty little toy."

"Oh, it's a toy?"

"Of course it's not a toy," he says, nearly laughing. "Though I have many toys that look just like this one. Such fine quality. You would not be able to tell the difference, booful girl." He titters, and I resist the instinctive urge to wince.

He pats his pocket affectionately. "Oh, but no, this beauty here is as real as they come."

"Then why . . . Hal, why must you wear it around the house?"

My husband meets my gaze again, and I'm struck by the icy, blank expression behind his pale eyes. Something inside me hitches. Then he gives me an unbothered shrug. "Never know who might be following, right?"

I swallow, saying nothing, though I'm confused by this remark. By his entire demeanor. Do I even *want* to know more? Before I can decide, he asks: "Coming to dinner, booful girl wife?"

"No," I say, breaking from his stare.

"Why not?"

"Your mother"—what do I even say?—"kicked Miranda."

Hal glowers at this, finally seeming to follow at least a thread of my distress. "She did?"

I nod. "After tea with her friends. I'm not up for a family dinner."

"My poor booful wife." Hal's voice turns soft, the off-putting iciness in his expression from a moment ago suddenly replaced by tender warmth. "I shall speak to her. An affront to you is an affront to me, and I won't stand for it."

HAL DOES NOT come into my room after dinner, so I decide to go to bed. Settling in, I hope that he's spoken to his mother on my behalf. Perhaps she might even feel a small touch of penitence, if not for her behavior toward me, then at least for hurting the poor pup who committed no offense. I fall asleep, allowing myself the dim hope that perhaps we have finally reached our lowest point. Surely, it can't get worse. Maybe now we will all be able to move forward into some sort of détente.

But then, in a deep slumber, I'm roused. "Evelyn?"

This time I don't need to pretend at sleep. "Yes?" I respond, my mind and my voice fuzzy. I lift my head from the pillow, squinting.

It's Hal, holding a candle. "Are you awake?"

"No . . . I wasn't. What is it? Can't it wait until morning?"

He plops down on the bed beside me, clutching the lone candle up near his face. He seems erratic again—I don't know if it's wine, or something else. "What is it?" I ask again, eager for this to be over.

"She said terrible things."

My mind spins, trying to make sense of this as he goes on. "She told me that you were being indecent. Talking about the stage in front of a large crowd of her friends."

Ah. Mother Thorne. I exhale a long breath, steeling myself, feeling the last wisps of sleep fly away. "Hal, I had no interest in getting on the stage." It's a lie. In truth, some very real part of me *was* excited, simply by Mrs. Fletcher's one mention of Broadway. And something deep inside me *had* thrilled at the thought of participating in such a festive evening. Just a few hours of diversion, one last chance to experience the feeling of an audience held in thrall before me. But once I saw my mother-in-law's horror, I meant it completely when I said I would merely help with the planning. And I explain to my husband now, "The ladies were speaking about a charity event, a church supper with a variety show. I merely hoped to help plan."

Hal's response is sharp: "You won't ever mention his name again."

My entire body tenses, and I sit up taller in bed. "His name?"

"*If,* for some reason, you ever need to bring him up, call him the Beast."

"Are you referring to Stan?"

"What did I just say? I don't want to hear that name!" Hal puts his hands over his ears like muffs. In the glint of the flickering candlelight, I catch sight of that sparkling shape again: the revolver is still tucked into the pocket at his waist.

I lean back, away, feeling as though I'd like to melt into the bed. Disappear from here. I glance around the vast, dark space, seeing only shadows and glimpses of dead Thornes hanging on the walls. The doorway is so far away. Summoning everything I have, I attempt a calm, conciliatory tone. "My dear, there's no reason why I'd ever bring up his name."

"The Beast," he says, his words like a hiss.

"The Beast, yes. Let's not even speak of him."

"Good, good." He's looking directly into the flame of the candle, which he holds only a few inches from his face, making it appear as though his pale eyes are ablaze. "Good girl," he says, nodding. "But you must tell me once more what happened."

"What happened?"

"What the Beast did to you, booful."

I grimace. "You just told me never to bring him up."

"But I'm asking you now to tell me the facts!" The candlelight quivers in Hal's grip as I notice how I, too, am trembling.

There's no reasoning with him, no placating him, not when he is in such a state. So, with a feeling akin to a choking cord at my throat, I do as he orders. I tell my husband about the night Stan unvirgined me. I tell him the facts that I've already said aloud to him on multiple occasions, at his request. I revisit the moments with a rote, toneless voice, but Hal clings to my every word, rapt. As though hearing it for the first time. When it's all done, I feel exhausted and like I might be sick. But Hal, energized, rasps: "Don't you see what a wicked beast he is?"

"I do," I answer woodenly.

"I should have killed the bastard while I had the chance."

"Hal." I shudder. I study his face, hoping to see that he meant the remark in jest or at the very least as an exaggeration, but I find his feverish expression hard to read.

"It would have been a service to society. Think of all the girls he's hurt. All the girls he still will hurt. And you, worst of all. He was wicked to you, girl wife."

"He was." My throat still feels painfully tight. "And that's why I'm not with him. I'm here, with you."

"Yes, yes. That's right." That manic glint still kindles Hal's gaze as he leans close to my face, and I can smell the booze on his breath. "I saved you from him, booful."

I cannot bear this a moment longer. Kicking my legs over the side of the bed, I make to rise, saying, "Hal, I'm sorry, but I have a headache."

"Oh!" he exclaims. "Just thinking of him makes you ill."

"That's correct."

"Poor wife."

"I need a bath."

"You do," he says, agreeing heartily. "You need to get clean, booful."

I can't help but grimace at this, but I make my way across the room without another word. Hoping, desperately, that he will leave. Once inside the bathroom, the space wrapped in darkness, I close the door and lock it. I'll stay here all night if I need to, until Hal has left.

And that's when I remember her. Mary Thorne. The eerie portrait I take such pains to avoid at night for fear of her haunting visage, her haunting story.

Tonight, it turns out, I prefer her company. I'd rather hide here in this room where the tragic woman ended her own life than face my husband on the other side of the door.

I turn the golden knob and let the water pour into the marble tub. I lower myself in, and I sit, motionless, as it fills around me. I can't help it—my eyes are drawn up toward the oval visage of dead Mary Thorne. When the water is high enough, I slip down and submerge my head, finding that blank and quiet oblivion that water alone can give me these days. I pop up only once I need a breath, then sink below the surface once more.

When my aching lungs can bear it no longer, I pop up again, catching Mary's unblinking gaze. *She hanged herself with a towel, in this very room. . . . Can you imagine?*

I stare back at the Thorne lady, as the water drips down my

face, hair, eyelashes. She who felt she had no choice, no other way to leave this house. What have I done? *Learn to swim. And then you'll survive.* Slipping down once more into the water, I close my eyes as the image of Mary's face dances through my imagination. And, along with it, something that feels akin to an idea's ember. Or, at the very least, a primordial desire—a glow, weak, yet unwilling to go out—the deepest desire of my soul, yearning simply to survive.

Chapter Forty-Seven

Summer 1905

"Hal, can we please go back to New York?"

"No," he replies, quick and decisive. We are out for a walk with Miranda on a mild summer day. The well-heeled neighbors we pass at regular intervals flash us friendly, inquisitive smiles; the Prince of Pittsburgh and his Broadway beauty, that's how they see us. We nod, returning their greetings, but I'm grateful that the puppy serves as a distraction, her wayward exploration pulling us along.

I had been hopeful that the pleasant weather, the lovely walk, might present the right opportunity for me to raise the topic I've been ruminating on. I'm not going to give up on this easily, so I press on, my tone delicate but steady. "Not to stay, dear. Just a visit. Summer in New York. Don't you miss it at all?"

"*Miss* it?" Hal flashes me a scowl. "Why, it's a den of beasts. A modern-day Sodom. The only good thing to come out of it was you, booful. And I got you out just in time."

I can see the clenching of his jaw, can hear the unyielding tenor of his determination. Fearing that he might bring up Stan's name, I quickly pivot. "Fine, then London? Even if only for a visit?"

Hal pauses his steps now, and I can see the faintest pearls of perspiration on his temples as he leans his head to the side and asks, "Why are you so desperate to leave Pittsburgh?"

Miranda, unhappy with the pause, tugs on her leash in my

hands. But I stand still, facing my husband and fixing a bland expression on my features. "I need a change . . . of scenery."

It is perhaps the most watered-down understatement I have ever uttered. The truth is, I need a change—of all of it. His mother. The dark and dreary mansion, which has come to feel more like a haunted castle. His erratic behavior, the frequency with which he now struts around with a revolver at his waist. The nights when he reeks of booze or, worse, behaves as if he's taken his god-awful morphine. This town where I have not a single friend. My endless days of monotonous solitude, during which I can only find *some* small measure of peace in the hours when I swim my morning laps or walk Miranda. No, it cannot go on; I'm twenty years old, locked up in this castle, finding it more unbearable with each passing day.

Hal looks around, surveying this gracious stretch of Beechwood Boulevard, its grand and well-groomed mansions lined up like a row of society brides on display at a debutante ball. And then, with a disinterested shrug, he resumes his walk. "I think this scenery is just fine."

Frustrated by his certitude that it's his decision alone to make, I answer: "Then I'd like to invite Penny here for a visit."

My husband throws me a horrified look, as though I've just told him that I've taken a lover. I clench my hands into two fists at my sides and forge ahead, steadying my tone as much as I can manage. "Hal, you know Penny well. You know she's a nice girl. Why, we were always together, surely you remember. And I deserve to see a friend, don't I?"

"Mother will say no," he says, his eyes pointing straight ahead.

"This time, I'm not asking. It's our house, too, ain't it?"

He halts his steps again, heaving a sigh. And in that, I allow myself to hope that perhaps he's softening. Perhaps he's considering my perspective. I press on: "Hal, I'm lonely. I'm so very lonely. We've been here for a year. I've been the good wife you asked for, haven't I? But I wish to see a friend. I've got no one but Miranda."

"And *me*," he retorts, wounded.

"Yes, you," I hurry to agree. "Of course I have you. But you have your time with your fellows—dining out, drinks at the club, shooting parties. Hal, I have—"

"Booful, I had no idea you could be so stubborn."

Stubborn? I've been quite the opposite. Unendingly compliant, more like. It feels as if I've been so willing to bend for him—and Mother—that I'm now in danger of breaking if I don't come up for a gasp of air in the immediate future.

But hearing my pet name, I get the sense—and very much hope—that he is warming to my point. And I dare not argue. Not if I'm so close to my goal.

Flashing me a benevolent smile, as though he's the indulgent adult who has just told me I may have a sweet before my supper, he says, "It's fine by me. To invite Penny for a brief visit."

"Oh, Hal, thank you! I am so very—"

"But Mother won't stand for it."

His words land like rocks in my belly. He's right. His mother would be outraged by the very thought. Why, I'm not even allowed to speak of my former days on the stage, but to think—hosting a Broadway showgirl under her very roof! "No," I say, breathing out. "No, she'd spoil the whole thing."

Another one of those indulgent grins, and Hal raises his hand to stroke my cheek. I force myself not to recoil from his touch, but instead to meet his pale gaze. With his stare direct and intense, he says, "Booful, you know I only wish to make you happy."

I swallow, saying nothing. I remind myself to nod.

"If this is what you really want, then I shall see to it," he says. "I'll spirit Mother away to Hot Springs. I'll tell her it's for her health, a quick trip to take the waters, just the pair of us. So that Penny may come to visit."

"Really?" I'm surprised—and so deliriously happy. "You will?"

"But only for a weekend, wife. Do we have a deal?"

For the first time in weeks, perhaps months, I feel as though I'd like to kiss him. With my heart leaping against my chest, I say, "Oh, yes, we do! Thank you."

• ♦ •

I AWAIT PENNY at the depot on a chilly December day. It took us months to find a time for her to get away from New York, given her busy schedule of performances, but around the Christmas holiday—and my birthday—she's taking a few days off.

Mother Thorne was delighted to think her son was so thoughtfully devoted as to whisk her away somewhere warm and curative, just the two of them. She certainly did not invite me to join, nor did she lament the fact that I was not party to their plans. Does she suspect I'm up to something in her absence? I don't know, but neither do I care. For here I am, standing alone, ready to embrace my friend for the first time in over a year. And we will have two whole days to ourselves!

When I spot Penny stepping off the train, her lean body wrapped in a thick and stylish coat of caramel-colored fur, my own body unclenches, as though the mere sight of her does something curative for me. I hadn't realized I'd been so tense.

"Pen!" I call out to her through the jostling crowds. She turns at the sound of her name. I can't help but laugh as I take her in across the platform, her figure standing out among the throng of gray-and-black-clad travelers. With her chic sable coat and matching hat, her stylishly tall pumps, and the slash of bright red across her lips, she's the very image of a Broadway starlet. And here I stand, feeling downright dowdy before her in my matronly coat of charcoal wool. It's as though she's bringing me the fire of Broadway's sparkle and song on this frigidly cold Pittsburgh day. I am desperate to warm myself beside her. "Oh, Pen," I say happily, "you are a sight for my sore eyes. Thank you for coming."

"I'm your lucky Penny, Ev! I'll always show up." We fall into a hug, and I nestle into her, breathing in the familiar scent of her hair and perfume. Before I realize it's happening, I begin to cry.

"Mrs. Thorne!" She leans back, holding me at arm's length. With her appraising gaze resting on my tear-slicked face, she cocks her head to the side. "What is the meaning of this?"

"Pen, I'm just so happy to see you. Tears of joy." That's all I say. That's all I can say; otherwise, this dripping of tears might build to a full deluge right here on the cold platform.

Penny, for her part, seems lighthearted and gay as her eyes take in the crowded scene. A porter appears with her luggage on a small trolley, and I guide us all toward the waiting motorcar. "Just like old times, Ev," Penny says, slipping her arm around my waist. "Little ol' me hitching a ride alongside you in your sweetheart's chauffeured auto."

With her arm looped through mine, the solidity of her body at my side, I allow myself to savor her smile, and some of the faded memories of the old times. What it felt like to have my best friend with me. For now, that's all I want. And it's what I very much need.

THAT EVENING, I order supper on trays, and we eat together in my bedroom. I don't want anyone to listen in or spoil anything. I want my lucky Penny all to myself. Just as true friends can do, we slip back into the rapport of our younger selves, no closeness lost in spite of the distance that has kept us apart for so long.

Penny tells me about the new show she's in, a musical production set in California during the Gold Rush. I tell her, in response to her questioning, that I don't dance or sing much these days, but I have taken up swimming with great enthusiasm. She plays a bit with Miranda, feeding her small nibbles of our cheeses and steak. And then Penny's voice grows serious, and her smile slips as she says, "I saw your mother."

My heart leaps into my throat. I say nothing, but Penny continues, "I was dropping off your Christmas card last week, with the concierge in her building, like you asked."

"And what . . . ?" I shift on the bed. "What did she say?"

"It happened so fast."

"Did she open my card?"

"I'm not sure," Penny says, with a look like sympathy in her eyes. "But I did tell her that I was coming to visit you."

"Did she give you . . . any message?"

Penny shakes her head, then lowers her gaze. I nod once, no longer hungry for the supper spread before us. "How did she seem?" I ask.

"She seemed all right."

"You think Stan is still supporting her?"

"Must be, right? She's still at the Audubon."

I bite my lower lip. "Well, then . . . I guess she doesn't need anything from me." Will she ever speak to me, if she doesn't need anything from me? My heart feels freshly bruised, and I let out a long, heavy breath. "I miss her," I say. "In spite of it all, I do. I miss having a family."

"You've got a family right here, Ev. One of the top families in America."

I can feel my face drop at this remark, and Penny must notice because she changes tack. "I'm sure she misses you, too, Ev." Penny puts her hand on mine, holding me in a searching gaze.

I shrug at this, pulling my eyes from my friend's stare, not willing to let her look too deeply. "I suppose she'll come calling once Stan finally stops paying the bills," I answer.

"Do you ever speak to him?"

"To *Stan*?" I ask, hitching an eyebrow. Penny nods.

"Absolutely not," I respond. I don't even want to envision what Hal's reaction would be if he were to hear Penny ask such a question.

"Well, she's a prize fool," Penny says, lightening her tone. "To miss out on all this. Why, you live in a palace! You're married to a millionaire. This is the tiger's stripes right here. It's her loss."

"You're right," I say, trying to match her cheery tone.

But Penny is still staring at me, and she narrows her eyes, as though not entirely satisfied with my response. After a pause, she says, "Ev, it *is* the tiger's stripes, right? Happily ever after for America's Cinderella and all that bunk I'm always reading in the papers about you?"

I can't bear to meet my friend's too-observant gaze, so instead I wrap my arm around her shoulder and pull her in for an embrace, burrowing my face into her hair so that she can't see the pain in my expression. "Penny, it's a regular old fairy tale."

· ◆ ·

THE NEXT MORNING is cold but sunny, and Penny and I take breakfast together in my bed before we set out for a walk along Beechwood Boulevard, Miranda bounding happily between us.

"You must tell me everything, Penny," I say, weaving my arm through hers. I'm like a starved person, I realize, desperate for news of Manhattan and her life and the Broadway gossip, all of which feel entirely foreign to me now.

But Penny doesn't seem to think she has anything all that exciting to report. "I don't know what to tell you, Ev. Broadway, well . . . it's not the same. I mean, sure, in some ways it is. The bright lights, the new shows. The parties at night, the Stage-Door Johnnies. But, well, it all feels less glittery now. Maybe because I miss you. Maybe because I'm so old."

"Hardly old," I say, smirking at her.

"Maybe not by your standards, but for a showgirl? You're about to turn twenty-one; I'm about to turn twenty-five! I've got a couple more years, at most. I'm already the oldest gal in the chorus at *Hearts of Gold*. If I try out for another show, I'll have to lie about my age."

This makes my head spin. To think about how we were so young when we started that we had to lie about our ages for the opposite reason. "What would you like to do next?" I ask.

"Suppose I should settle down," Penny says, staring at a colossal estate, with its wrought iron fence and stately old trees, as we walk past. "If I knew what was good for me, I'd have snagged myself a rich husband years ago, when I was still one of the shiny new things."

It's not like Penny to sound disheartened. "Well, have you got a sweetheart?"

"Not a serious one. You know how they are. Champagne Charlies, promising the world at midnight, offering much less come sunrise."

I glance downward, nodding. Of course I know. Why, Penny was one of the friends who first warned me to stay away from them. I sigh, preparing to tell her that she's the greatest catch on the island of Manhattan, and not to lose heart, but before I can say anything, she interrupts my thoughts: "There was one fellow, a year ago. . . . I thought . . . I hoped . . . Oh, but I can't even stand to think of him." She heaves a sad exhale, her breath misting the cold air. "We can't all be as lucky as you, Ev."

I freeze mid-step. Struck, in that moment, by the fact that Penny is just as disillusioned with her life as I am with mine. Which one of us feels more trapped? While I've envied Penny the freedom and excitement of her days and nights on Broadway, she looks at my life and believes I've landed myself the storybook ending. Safety, security, a husband, and a grand home. My friend is tired. She doesn't know what comes next, and it'll fall on her, alone, to figure it out. She's lonely, too. Broadway will never be her happy ending.

Does anyone truly get the happy ending? Didn't I learn long ago that all fantasies crack at a certain point? I faced that truth as a sad and lonely little girl, and then I've learned it again, many times since. Happy endings can turn into tragic stories, in the blink of an eye.

I'm thinking through all of this, ready to get downright philosophical, but Penny interjects: "Speaking of sweethearts, I'd say you've got yourself yet another admirer, Ev." I'm confused by this, but she goes on. "I swear that man has been behind us the entire time." Penny tosses a look over her shoulder, whispering, "Who is he, some local gent who holds a candle for you, hoping to try his chances while Mr. Thorne is away?"

I turn in the direction she's indicated and see a man about twenty paces behind us, in a dark greatcoat and a fedora that throws his face into shadow. When he sees us staring, he, too, ceases his steps and suddenly becomes preoccupied with the wrought iron fence at his side.

I frown; it's true that the man appears familiar. I have seen him around town. But is he following me?

Never know who might be following, right? Hal's odd words. He is so convinced that men are following him. Does he now have men trailing me?

Later, after I've sent the staff to bed and Penny has retreated to the guest room, I pad down the darkened hallway, and I knock on her door.

"Yes?" she says.

I step in, find her tucked under her covers, her hair pinned back, a lone candle lit on her bedside table. "Can I come in?"

"Why, it's your house," she quips. "I'm only here until you throw me out."

I don't return her smile. Instead, I plop down onto the bed, and I take her hands in mine. Unable to fight it an instant longer, I crumple. The tears come out, hot and urgent, and I close my eyes.

"Oh, Ev!" She pulls me into a hug, and I'm so weepy that I fall into her arms, all resolve and fortitude gone. "What's the matter?"

"I don't want you to go, Pen," I manage to gasp out.

She hugs me tighter, patting my back.

"I wish you could stay."

"Trust me, I'd stay if I could."

But we both know she can't. Hal will be home, with Mother, tomorrow. And Penny's break from work has reached its end. We each have to return to reality. Though it seems that neither of us is ready to do so.

Chapter Forty-Eight

Hal returns the next evening in a foul mood, escorting his mother to her bedroom before I hear him bumbling and banging around downstairs. Pouring himself a drink, or mixing up some morphine—or both.

I glower in my seat before my vanity mirror. I'm not in the happiest of moods myself, having escorted Penny to the depot just a few hours earlier and feeling as though a large part of my heart left with her on the train bound for Manhattan. Now, with no idea when I might see her next, I'm back to my solitary existence.

Adding to my gloom are the two letters in my hands, which arrived this afternoon by post. Mercifully, they were delivered to me before Hal returned home, and I've had this stolen chance to open them away from his covetous eye. He told me several weeks ago to stop sending letters without showing them to him first, but I've disregarded his order, and he has yet to notice.

These two letters will have to stay secret. The first is from Mamma—it's my Christmas card, returned, after Penny hand-delivered it to her. She didn't even write to explain why she couldn't bear to look at it. I toss it into the fire.

The second note is postmarked from Philadelphia. Chestnut Street. I close my eyes for a brief moment, and I can see it: the studio with its familiar smells of turpentine and coffee, its big windows that let in the ever-changing light. But when I blink my eyes open and look back down, I see that this letter is not from

Leah or Rachel. It's from a Mr. Ralph Perkins. He informs me, briefly but cordially enough, that Rachel and Leah no longer live at the address to which I've written. I'd sent, on a lark, my Christmas card showing myself as a newly married resident of Pittsburgh. They have moved abroad, to France, and he includes some address that's a series of numbers and foreign words.

They did it. They went to France. I smile to myself, but feel a pang in my belly. Happy as I am for the pair of them, that they've realized their long-held dream, this news does spotlight the dismal fact that I am stuck here, in this haunted mansion, living with nothing more than the harrowing ghosts of my own unhappy ending.

A knock on my door, and I slip the letter under a tub of rouge powder, rearranging myself before the vanity. I see Hal's reflection in the mirror and summon a smile, endeavoring to greet him pleasantly as he comes barreling into my room, walking stick in one hand, top hat in the other.

"How was the visit, then?" he asks, catching my reflection in the mirror.

I hope he sees that I was preparing for bed. "Oh, Hal." I finger a nearby pot of cold cream, turning to face him. "It was so good to see Penny." I decide to leave it at that, hastening to ask, "And how was Hot Springs?"

"Taking Mother away like that . . . I hope you appreciate what I've done for you." His eyes rove around my bedroom as though cataloging every detail to see whether anything has changed.

"I do, my dear. Thank you so much." And I have no doubt that Mother Thorne derided me with most of her breath while they were away together. "Did you have a nice time?" I ask, my voice falsely bright.

He ignores the question, his gaze still intense, as though searching for something. "Leaving the entire house to you and that girl. I hope you both behaved."

"Of course we did." I stiffen. "Hal, it's Penny. You know her. She's like me."

"She's *not* like you," he says, eyes cutting back toward me. "You're reformed. She's still living that life."

"That life," I say, my voice quivering, "was what led me to you. You came to my show every night."

"I swear, Evelyn, sometimes I feel as though you still don't understand how lucky you got." He's spinning his walking stick in his hands, and I'm afraid he might knock something over with it. But I say nothing. I do not move from my seat. He sweeps my appearance one more time with his blazing blue gaze—taking in my dark hair falling loose over my shoulders, my thin silk wrapper cinched at my waist, the bare skin of my calves and ankles. I want to recoil, but I resist the urge to fidget, for fear that any movement might set him off further. He takes a step toward me, barely whispering the words: "I saved you. From all of it. From *him*."

"Do you have men following me?" I lob the question at him, the words escaping before I've had time to fully think it all through. I suppose I am just trying to catch him off-balance. To change the topic. It works; he pauses mid-step. And as his face hardens, I can see he does not know how to respond. So he doesn't. Instead, he turns on his heels and stalks out of my bedroom.

I nearly collapse in relief. Flying to the door, I lock it. I check three times to ensure it's bolted before climbing into my bed. And yet, as I crawl under the covers and blow out the candle, I'm still trembling. I tremble until, somehow, merciful sleep takes me into its embrace and pulls me into black.

BUT I WAKE, I know not how much later, to a sliver of light. And a clicking sound—the turn of a key. The soft padding of slippered footsteps. I stir. "Hello?"

I see Hal's outline. My husband doesn't answer but plods directly toward my bed.

"Hal, I'm sleeping. I'm tired." But I can see it plainly, that he's not himself. He might not even be hearing my words. He is certainly not listening to them as I plead, "Can't we please speak in the morning?"

But then he's right beside me, hulking over me in the dark, his whiskey breath enough to make me sick. Before I understand what is happening, he is pinning me down. Something hard and unyielding presses across my shoulders. It's his walking stick.

"Please!" I'm begging now, afraid he might strangle me.

It's so dark in the room that I can't see his face, but I know how his features must be writhing in fury because I can hear it in his voice as he hisses: "Deceiver!" His face is so close to mine that I feel the spray of spit that lands on my cheek. "Whore! You wanted him, didn't you? All that flam about Stan Pierce robbing you of your virtue. You were willing the entire time!"

"No!" His cane is still boring into my chest, and when he puts the entire weight of his body on me, I truly don't know whether I will survive. "Please," I try again. "You're hurting me."

"You're lying!" he growls. "You've been lying to me this whole time! You invited that tart into our home; you wish to return to your old ways."

I protest, struggling to push him off. But this only seems to enrage him further. "I heard from the staff. I know! I know that letters have been arriving for you, two while I was away. From Philadelphia. And New York! From him! After everything I've done for you!"

"Hal, please!" I beg. He's yanking on me, his hands rough. Intent on pain. So I close my eyes. I can't breathe. Does he intend to kill me? In that moment, I decide, death might come as a welcome reprieve.

• ♦ •

I DO SURVIVE. Somehow. The memories are patchy and black in places, and that comes as some small mercy. But as wretched as the night was, the morning proves even more terrible. In a different way. The horror of the daybreak is in having to face him. In having to face another day with him.

Hal seems to dread our reunion almost as much as I do, as he comes slinking into my bedroom, everything about his demeanor reminding me of some sort of penitent serpent. But I do not wish to hear anything from him, not even his best apology. My entire body hurts. I already have the purpling prelude to bruises across my chest and shoulders. My lips taste like blood; my neck is scratched red and raw. But the cruelest pain lurks in the deepest parts of me, an ache far worse than the physical.

He doesn't knock, nor do I welcome him in, but here he comes. All pretense of genteel knocking is gone after last night. He hovers a few steps away from where I sit in bed, my knees pulled up toward my chest. "I'm sorry, my booful." I won't look at him. He goes on, his voice hoarse: "I wasn't well."

A shudder escapes me.

"I had taken some morphine after the long day of travel," he says. "I felt terribly out of sorts after the journey. And Mother had been . . . Well, you know she can be tedious."

"Yes, I do know," I say, my tone icy. It's one thing that I can agree with.

But the fact that I've spoken seems to give him a drop of hope, because he asks, "Will you forgive me?"

I still can't look at him. "See this?" I gesture toward the bruise that's seeping across my neck.

He takes it in, and I force myself to meet his gaze for the first time. I see he's horrified, and he puts his hands to his own throat, looking as though he may cry. And then he falls to his knees, groaning like a penitent as he rasps, "I'm so sorry!"

Looking down at him in disgust, I try to make sense of everything that's happened. Of how to proceed. My mind is swirling. "You weren't well last night, Hal. You said it yourself."

He's rocking on his knees. "You're right, booful."

I feel as though I have just the narrowest of windows in this period of his contrition, in this fleeting moment when he is the repentant worshipper—desperate for absolution and reconciliation—and the penance is mine to dole out. So I make a decision. "I've told you for some time that I need a change of scenery."

I can see he's in a conciliatory mood, an obliging mood. I must act. So, with my voice hard as steel, I say: "We are leaving. We must get away, you and I. We will take a trip."

"Fine," he says, nodding vigorously, making as if to rise from his knees. "Once the weather is mild, booful, we can travel. We'll take a nice, long summer voyage. England?"

"But New York first," I say. I see the shift in his eyes, the wavering in his willingness to agree. So I press on before he can say no, before I lose my resolve: "Before we sail, Hal. Even if we stay for only a couple of days. I wish to see the city one more time."

Chapter Forty-Nine

New York
July 1906

MANHATTAN'S FAVORITE GIRL IS DEAD!

I stare down at the newspaper headline, saying, "Hilde the hippo has replaced me as Manhattan's favorite girl." Or at least, she *had* replaced me. Poor thing. She collapsed in the Central Park Menagerie because of this ungodly heat. "Ah, and look here." The column just below bears the headline:

AMERICA'S EVE RETURNS TO THE BIG APPLE!

"Yes, the hippo bumped me down." I fold up the newspaper and use it as a fan, as the heat hangs all around like a thick soup, wet and sticky.

"At least the heat will mean thinner crowds," Hal grouses, tugging on his shirt collar. "Everyone with half a nickel between their ears will have fled. And yet here we are."

I ignore his complaints, refusing to let anything dampen my mood or distract me, even as I, too, can feel how the sweat has begun to pearl along my temples.

"This heat makes me crazy," Hal gripes. *Oh, it's the heat, is it?* I quit the room, in search of a lady's maid.

We are staying in the grandest suite in the Hotel Lorraine, and one of the staff is soon drawing me a cool bath as I shed my sweat-damped silk.

"Make it as cold as can be," I say, eager to slip under the water. Even more eager for a few minutes to collect myself and run through my plans for the next few days.

As I close my eyes and slide under the water's surface, the rowdy noises of Fifth Avenue below our windows dissipate, muffled by the cool embrace of the marble tub. I float in that suspended silence, forcing my mind to calm itself. To focus. To recall how it felt all those times I slid into the massive bathtub back in Pittsburgh, staring up at the harrowing image of Mary Thorne. How her ghost had first haunted me and then inspired me—that glowing kernel of desire her story had kindled within. I can feel the resolve hardening deep in my core now. I rise above the water and draw in a long breath.

I blink my eyes open and grab the fresh, unopened bar of soap. I can't help but grin: there I am. The Fairy Soap wrapper has my image on it. What was I, sixteen, when I posed for this campaign?

It all started with fantasy, I suppose. Stanley Pierce telling me I'd dropped from heaven just for him. And me, for a while, I fell for it. But like all fairy stories, it had only ever been an illusion. A glittering but fickle mirage that kept shifting all around me. I've never had any choice but to learn how to kick higher, put on the next costume, recite the new words, and then, even when it was darkest, find the light.

Tonight shall be my grandest performance of all. Regardless of how the story may end, this I know: tonight, America's Eve performs her finale.

I take my time in the bath, knowing that this may very well be my last peace for quite a while. Drying off, I step into my outfit for the evening. Costume, more like it. Beige slip, the color of my skin. Then floor-length white satin, also light, for the heat, with a cinched waist and pearl and crystal trim, a bolero frothing with wispy white ostrich feathers draped over my shoulders.

Sinners don't wear white, I was told when, as a bride, he made me wear black. Well, tonight, this sinner is wearing white.

With just one touch of green. I can't help but sneer at my reflection in the mirror as I pull my hair high, nestling the green silk hat on top of my dark waves. This thing that I've managed to keep and not yet wear, ever since Violet handed it to me years ago on another evening out, right here in Manhattan. The gift from Leah, the snake forever coiling around the silk brim in tight circles. My eyes stare into the serpent's emerald gaze, and I think: *What if Eve used the beast to escape?*

A rope of pearls around my neck, then I roll my sable gloves to my elbows and rearrange my face. I survey myself in the sweep of floor-to-ceiling mirrors. I've learned how to dress the part, haven't I?

I leave the bedroom to meet Hal, who is freshly shaved and dressed for the evening in a black tuxedo with golden cuff links, boater hat in his hands. But even though he's groomed and stylishly turned out, it's with bloodshot eyes that he takes in the length of my figure. He doesn't say anything about my white attire, though I wouldn't have minded if he had.

He is already deep in the drink; I can smell it. There's an empty scotch glass on the table, still perspiring in the heat. Beside it, that small black bottle with the stopper top. Morphine, as well as the booze. Usually these twin facts would fill me with molten dread, but tonight, they'll work in my favor.

"One last drink before we go, Mr. Thorne?" I ask, my voice silky.

He helps himself, I decline, and then he pats the pocket of his trousers. "Let me just . . ." I can tell he's feeling for that godawful revolver. Especially on a night like this one, out in Manhattan, *his* town, Hal will want it. Another fact that would ordinarily chill the blood in my veins. But tonight, it's exactly what I was hoping for. Exactly what I planned for. My tone low and conspiratorial, I whisper, "It's in the bedroom, on the dresser." A helpful wink. "Right where you left it."

"Oh, thank you." And to my relief, Hal doesn't look surprised at my assistance—only relieved that I know where he can find his gun.

WE DRIVE SOUTH in an open-topped motorcar, down along the Hudson in the direction of Bowling Green, where the crowds of humanity will be teeming in the streets, hoping for fresh breezes as the sun begins to dip.

"The chorus girl is back in her playground," I say, throwing Hal a nostalgic look as the city streets slip past.

I see the spasm of his cheek, the clenching and unclenching of his jaw. And then, with timing so perfect that I could not have orchestrated it had I tried, the hulk of the tower looms over us as we speed past Twenty-sixth Street. "Oh, look!" I point up at it, my features spreading into a broad beam. "So many memories."

A prick. And then another. I need to allow the slow boil to build. It appears to be working as he asks, without looking at me, "Memories . . . of?"

I sigh. "Oh, just of my jolly years here."

He nods once, a tight jerk of his chin, and then he glances out over the street. "Well, booful, tonight you make your triumphal return to New York City as Mrs. Thorne. Seated in the *audience*. Respectable. Saved. Beside me."

In response to my repeated requests, he's booked us two tickets aboard the *Virginia* for a pleasure cruise that offers dinner and drinks along with a variety show for entertainment. I always saw it as a step down in a girl's career, to move from a Broadway stage to a dinner cruise ship that tours the harbor. But this evening, it is precisely what I need.

The auto rolls to a slow halt before the pier, and Hal looks out at the scene. "I won't be sorry to sail from this Sodom," he says as the chauffeur opens the door.

As it always used to do, our arrival sparks a flurry of excitement from the small crowd milling about. New York's favorite starlet and her playboy millionaire, returned for a night on the town. I smile at them all as my husband steers me toward the walkway.

But I take my time, drawing in deep breaths, knowing what it is that awaits me once I board that cruise. It's like stepping from the wings out onto center stage. Just before we reach the gangway, I pause, feeling my stomach dip. Can I really go through with this? I close my eyes, my mind spinning back to only a few hours earlier, hoping to draw some much-needed fortitude from the memory. My solitary outing to the park, my discreet rendezvous with Penny. How I pulled my friend into a hug, whispering into her ear so that only she could hear, just in case Hal was having me followed. "You made it! Oh, thank you, Pen."

"Didn't I tell you I'm your lucky Penny? I'll always show up."

"Will he be there tonight?" I asked.

"Oh, he'll be there. I've fixed it all."

"Thank you," I said, my voice low and thick with the threat of grateful tears. "I've always been able to count on you."

"Who said you can't count your pennies?"

She'd given me a heartening wink, and then I'd said, "I wish you could be there with me."

"Ev, it's down to you now. You know it'll only work if I stay behind."

I leaned toward her for one final, bracing hug. "You know I'll never say good luck," she whispered into my ear.

"Naw," I agreed with a smile. "No showgirl worth her salt would dare. Besides, it's never been about luck, has it?"

"It hasn't," she said, brow creasing. "So you go out there and you stun them. No one can put on a better show, Ev."

And now here I stand, amid the din of the crowds and the rolling water and the waiting cruise, my husband turning to throw me an irritated look, wondering why I'm tarrying. "Showtime," I whisper to myself, pulling my shoulders back. And then, pretending that I don't see Hal Thorne's outstretched hand, I stride out over the water.

Chapter Fifty

Aboard the cruise, I finally take Hal's hand, and I pull him toward the far side of the deck. I waste no time in ordering him a double whiskey from a passing waiter. Then I say, "Let's watch as the lights flicker on behind Lady Liberty," and I fix my attention on him until I feel the ship pushing off from the shore. The low bellow of the whistle is answered by a cacophony of seagulls that scatter before us. The floor rumbles beneath our feet, and it feels as though I don't fully exhale until I am certain that we are well and truly on our way, trapped aboard this thing, with only water all around.

I lean on the railing. "It's grand, isn't it?" I ask, making my best effort to keep my tone breezy. Crisscrossed strings of light flicker over our heads, mirroring the lights of the city all around us. Slipping ever farther away, Manhattan shimmers like a mirage in the sultry summer heat. The soft notes of the orchestra waft over the crowd, and then a gong sounds.

"Time for supper," my husband says.

"And time for the show," I reply.

I take my husband's arm, and he weaves us through the crowd toward the grouping of dinner tables covered in white linen and fresh flowers. When Hal pauses, mid-step, and his grip locks around mine like a vise, I feel my entire body go rigid. I follow his stare. I know precisely what he's seen. *Who* he has seen.

Stanley Pierce is taking his seat at a table, front and center. Stanny is always front and center, best seat in the house. Heart in my throat, I throw a quick look toward my husband and see that his face has paled to a sickly white.

Nearby, the orchestra is still offering its jaunty notes, the lively crowd thrums all around us, but Hal stands silent and still as a stone. "Let's take a seat," I say, giving his arm a gentle tug. "Where's our table?"

"The Beast," Hal says, unmoving. His voice is low, more like a snarl than speech, but I've heard what he said.

"Oh?" I follow the jerk of his chin, pretend that I'm only now seeing Stan for the first time. I make a clucking sound. "So it is. Best seat in the house, like always."

Now Hal turns to me with a horrified look, and I can see that his eyes are ablaze. "But . . . doesn't seeing him . . . ? Aren't you . . . ?"

"Not surprised," I say with an unaffected shrug. "It's his town, after all."

"*Precisely* why I did not want to come back here," Hal growls, not even helping me into my seat. Meanwhile, I'm doing all I can to avoid meeting Stan's eyes. It might spoil everything if he feels I'm giving him an opening. Not now, not yet.

Hal has bought the entire table for the two of us, so there we sit, at a table set for ten, a silent pair. A steady stream of well-wishers approach Stan, just a few tables away, but no one approaches us. We must make an odd tableau, Hal stewing in a wordless fury so palpable that I can practically feel the heat seeping off his skin. And me beside him, his young showgirl turned bride, clad all in white.

I do my best to appear happy, perhaps even a bit giddy. The servers bring Hal another drink, and then they bring our food, and even though my stomach feels as though it's been yanked into knots, I eat as though my appetite is as lively as ever opposite Hal, who declares he has none, asking only for drink after drink.

As we dine, the showgirls file out and strut past the tables to admiring applause, all legs and feathers and sequins, before taking their places in two columns on the small raised stage before us. I watch them with apparent interest, and in truth I am impressed at how they manage to sing and move through their steps as the ship sways beneath us.

The mood on board grows ever more festive. All around us, revelers are enjoying their food and drink beneath the thatch of twinkling lights. The air has cooled a bit now that the night has darkened and the breeze has picked up. We have made our way out into the middle of the water, with the Hudson flowing to meet the opening of the Upper Bay, and Lady Liberty rises up just before us. The ship hugs the coastline around the harbor, the nearby shores dark and empty. My husband orders yet another drink as the girls take a bow and trot off for a quick break, having completed their first set.

It's showtime.

My heart hammering, I push back my chair and throw a sheepish smile toward Hal. "I'm feeling awful sentimental."

He looks at me askance, and I can see his distracted confusion. He's been deep in his own brooding—and his cups. But now he speaks to me for the first time since we've taken our seats. "What?"

I stand, keeping my body far enough away that he can't snatch my arm. "I think I'll put on a little show for my admirers."

"A *show*?" I can see it—the horror that grips his features. Hal is more shocked than if I'd just suggested we strip bare and jump in the harbor.

But I force myself to carry on, shrugging. "I guess I've still got the bug, after all."

"Evelyn Thorne, you will not play the dancing harlot as though—"

"How about if I play Evelyn Talbot for a little?"

Rage twists his face. And then, through pinched lips, he spits, "Sit down this instant."

I do the exact opposite, sliding another step away from the table. "Come on, now. You can take me from Broadway, but you can't ever take Broadway out of me."

"Sit down. I'm warning you."

"You fell in love with me up on that stage. You and everyone else, right?" And then I slip away before he can grab me and undoubtedly leave me bruised yet again. I know it's the confirmation of his worst fears: I'll eventually slip out of his grasp. No matter what he does to follow me or pray for me or lock me up or even hurt me, he will never in fact be able to hold on to me.

I saunter up toward the stage, fully in my role now, beaming at the revelers as I pass. I must win them over, and quickly. To my immense relief, many gasp in delight as I step up onto the empty stage. The orchestra pauses, and hundreds of eyes are turned on me, confused and expectant.

I raise my arms wide, flashing my most beguiling smile out over the eager crowd. "Good evening, all." I sweep the audience with my gaze. "Some of you may recognize me. I am—"

"Evelyn Talbot!" someone shouts before I can say my name.

"The Gibson Girl!" The crowd erupts in applause.

"The peach is back from Pittsburgh!"

"Ripe for only one night," I parry, offering them all a playful wink as I bring my hand over my mouth and flash a coy smirk. Laughter, more applause. They are eating this up. I've got them; they are game. I raise my arms high. "Let's keep that champagne flowing, shall we?" I place a hand on my hip and give a coquettish shimmy. "You *do* remember me, don't you?"

Patrons hoist their glasses, cheering me on. "I was hoping I might be able to do a little number for you. Would that be all right?" More applause, cries of hearty approval. I'm doing my best not to look toward Hal, who I know is seething, or Stan, who I'm sure is watching all of this, highly amused. Instead, I turn my gaze toward the orchestra musicians and ask, "Who remembers *Grande Dame Champagne*?" The musicians nod. It was one of my most popular shows. "Let's hear 'Can't Keep Me Down.'"

And as they begin the first brisk notes, I close my eyes and allow the familiar song to wrap itself around me. I tune out the delight of the crowd, the bright lights, and the movement from all of the tables, and slip back into the role that I played so popularly for so many nights. I remember the words—of course I remember the words—and the steps come to my feet with the familiarity of muscle memory.

As we build toward the crescendo of the song, I begin to

bounce lower and lower until I bend my knees deeply and then pop up, raising my arms and my feather bolero overhead. Just as I used to do from out of the massive papier-mâché champagne bottle each night. I kick my legs high, finishing off with a playful sashay of my hips as I strut across the stage. This is a scene that Hal came to watch often, though he later confessed to me how horrified he was at the fact that others saw me behaving in such a way. I know he's incensed now, but still I do not look toward him. The audience remembers it, as well. They are hooting and hollering.

A few tables away, Stan is joining in the din. As I did the famous move, looking like I'd just been shot from out of a champagne bottle, I heard Stan guffaw, saying aloud to anyone who would listen, "There's never been another one like her."

The audience is rapt, and I'm feeding off their energy. The dinner service carries on, with the handsome servers in their dark tuxedoes and starched aprons moving about, refilling glasses and clearing plates, while everyone else seems fixed in their seats, eyes on me. My husband more than anyone.

As the song finishes and they erupt with fresh applause, I raise my hands toward them, appearing to all as though I'm basking in their adoration when, in reality, I'm summoning from them the strength I know I'm about to need.

My breath is ragged, and my heart is pumping; it's been a while since I moved like this—but I can keep this up. I *must* keep this up. After a moment, I summon a breezy tone and tell them all, "It feels good to be back with you! Thank you, thank you." I blow a kiss over the crowd. "Can I do one more?"

Everyone in the audience hollers their approval, except for Hal. I know what he's thinking, in his misery: in spite of everything he's done, everything his mother has done, to rout the sins of Evelyn Talbot of Broadway, replacing her with the pure and obedient Evelyn Thorne of Pittsburgh, this wicked genie has slipped from her bottle. Defying him, deceiving him, humiliating him. He is betrayed.

I ignore his glower and banter with the rest of the crowd: "Now I'd like to slow it down, just for a moment."

They clap approvingly, and I carry on. "I'd like to offer this one up as a gift. To the one man who was always there for me. The man to whom I owe everything. I'd like to sing one of my favorite songs. And one of his, too, if I remember correctly. I'd like to sing 'To You, I'll be True.' "

The crowd is cheering again. Again I raise my hands, sweeping my gaze out over the audience before I land my eyes on the center of the crowd, looking at him for the first time. "Won't you please come up and join me on this stage, Mr. Stanley Pierce?"

Gasps from the entertained crowd. I see the surprise, and then delight, bloom across Stan's bloated face. Just a few tables over, Hal's face changes yet again, as well. It's a look I've never seen before, in spite of the fact that I've seen my husband frighteningly angry more times than I can count—Hal's expression now appears as though a living snake is writhing across his features, desperate to strike.

The audience offers up riotous applause for Stan as he lumbers toward me, all too willing to participate in this impromptu circus. I am fully embodying my role now; I await him on the stage, as if utterly delighted to see him. He seems to feel precisely that same way.

"Well, hello there, Mr. Pierce," I croon in my sultry stage voice as he huffs his way up onto the raised platform, coming to a halt right before me, his features upturned in a giddy and flushed smirk. "It's good to see you, sir. It's been too long, hasn't it?"

"Too long, Miss Talbot," he agrees, his voice thick and self-satisfied. Up close, I see how he has aged. It's been two years since I last saw him, but it looks more like a decade. His brow is rutted with new wrinkles; his thinning hair is almost entirely leached of its copper color. He is heavier and his steps are a bit labored. But he's thrilled to join me, that much is evident. When he speaks, the audience is hollering so loudly that I suspect only I can hear him as he asks, "It was you, then? The secret admirer?"

I quirk an eyebrow, and he goes on, "I got the invitation with the ticket to dine on this boat tonight, but never in a million years would I have suspected . . ."

"It's good to see you again," I say, hopping down and grabbing a nearby chair, which I slide onto the stage as I climb back up to stand right beside him. "Take a seat."

"Anything you say, Kitten."

I swallow back the bile that rises in my throat, keeping the showgirl smile plastered across my face. Then I give the orchestra a nod, and they take up the slow, crooning tune. I close my eyes, and I begin to sway. As the music surrounds me, I allow myself to be picked up by the song. By the words, by the tune. I start the steps. This song, being slower, calls for a sultrier, more fluid set of movements, and so here I am, dancing onstage for all these men. But as I sharpen my focus and look down at Stan, I make it clear that, most of all, I'm dancing for him. And he's drinking it up.

So is the audience. When I shimmy out of my feather wrap, tossing it toward the front table, the audience goes wild. All except my husband, whom I catch out of the corner of my eye, looking wild with rage.

It's you. It's you.
It's always been you.
To you alone,
I will be true.

The words come slow and smooth, like warm honey, and so do my dance steps. When I writhe my hips right at his eye level, Stan chortles, nodding appreciatively. I can't look at him; I cannot allow myself to wonder whether he's remembering those nights we spent together. I'm sure he is. But what matters more is that *Hal* is thinking of all those nights that Stanny and I spent together.

I pour myself even deeper into the music—into the role.

It's you. It's you.
It's always been you.
The other fellow,
he'll only be blue.

And then I do something that no one is expecting. I bring my hands to the buttons down the front of my dress and then slowly, languidly, begin to undo them, one by one. This was never part of the routine. Scandalized gasps, a few spurts of bawdy applause. The audience is titillated—they bought their tickets for a boat ride and a variety show of middling performers, and here they have Evelyn Talbot onstage, coming out of retirement and shedding her clothes for Stanley Pierce! The newspapers will go wild. And yet I'm only getting started.

I unclasp the final button and writhe out of my white silk dress, allowing the material to fall like water from my shoulders, catching for just a moment on my hips before I give them a quick shake, and the silk lands in a puddle on the floor. I stand onstage in only the skin-colored slip.

Stan is not even attempting to hide his lewd gape, but I do not allow myself to become distracted. Not by him, not by the enraptured audience, not by Hal fidgeting in his seat. I continue to sing; I continue to dance.

I am Salome, dancing the king to my bidding.

I am Cleopatra, charming the snake.

I am Helen, launching the ships full of jealous, lustful men.

I am Eve, offering the apple that shall be his undoing.

I dance them into desire, the bonds of their own doing.

I dance myself to freedom.

And just like that, as if I have been holding a string and I've now given it the final tug, my husband rises from his seat.

"*It's you. It's you. It's always been you.*" I keep dancing, but I can see it all out of the corner of my eye. Hal slowly walking toward us, his steps plodding, a predator with his quarry in sight.

"*That other fellow can never be you.*" I keep crooning, swaying my body in front of Stan, who remains seated, thrilled by the unexpected turn this night has taken. One beat more and now Hal is right before us, at the foot of the stage, close enough for me to lean over and touch him. But I do not even acknowledge his presence. The song is almost over. *Keep going*, I think. I keep dancing.

And then I see Hal reach to his hip. *Keep dancing.* An instant later I hear his voice, hoarse and rasping. He raises his arm as he shouts: "You ruined my wife! I know what you did! She's mine! She'll never be yours!"

And then Hal points his revolver at Stan. Startled gasps rise from a few in the crowd, only those close enough to see what is happening. This is the moment. I stop dancing. I step in front of Stan, putting my body between my husband and his target. As I lean forward to wrest the weapon from Hal's raised hand, gunfire rips through the languid musical notes, three times. Three shots. All aimed for Stanley Pierce, seated in a chair right behind me. Not one of them hitting its intended mark.

The orchestra halts, the instruments falling silent, as the crowd sputters with confused exclamations and then horrified shrieks.

I look down, first at my husband just below the stage and then at my midsection. A red blossom seeps across my thin slip, and I brush it with my fingers before I hold up my bloodstained hand.

More shrieks as understanding takes hold of some in the audience. This is not part of the performance. Hal Thorne, intending to shoot Stanley Pierce, has hit his beautiful wife instead.

I gasp. It's not pain I feel; it's triumph. Several audience members look around in bewilderment, some asking if this is an act. Surely this cannot be happening. They all seem paralyzed in their shock and confusion.

I clutch my waist as I stumble across and off the stage, away from Stan and Hal, and I don't stop until I've reached the far railing of the ship. In one hand I'm still holding my husband's gun. The other hand I raise, showing the smear of scarlet across my palm and fingers.

"*You* did this." I make eye contact with Hal first, then Stan. I hold their stricken, stunned gazes. Then I turn from them, tipping forward over the railing as Lady Liberty reaches skyward before me, her island perch rising up dark and close. I fall. And I don't stop falling until, gun in hand, I've tumbled into the water.

As I slip into the cool and quiet embrace of the waves, I am certain that everyone on the cruise saw my final scene: Hal shot to kill. And he's killed me.

Chapter Fifty-One

I knew the role; I played the part. I've always given them what they want. On many occasions—far too many, in fact—this has been what has kept me alive. Even when it wasn't the truth. Especially when it wasn't the truth. Even when it felt like a part of me had to die to do so.

Now all of me has died. And I'm finally free.

This isn't some fairy tale, and there's no magical wand or benevolent prince coming to save me. I realized there would be no happy ending—unless I decided to write it.

I want more than mere survival.

I want to *live*. At long last, I'm going to make that happen.

Learn to swim. And then you'll survive.

Walk fast before the snakes know you're there.

All the ways I've been told to live. All the ways I've learned to survive.

The water rolls over me, around me, through me, washing me clean. I release the gun, letting it plunge into the black water, and swim with all I have. I move under the water, hidden by the pitch-dark night. The ship grows smaller as all on board rush about. I had them all hooting and hollering my name; now they are hollering my name for a very different reason. Others are trying to restrain the madman on the deck as the engine pulls them too far away to see my receding figure, wrapped in night-black water, slipping away.

Find your light.

Now I move, quickly and quietly, before the light can find me. I swim toward the shadowed shore, the opaque outline of Lady Liberty's massive copper body rising up from her island perch. My lungs burn, and so does every muscle in my body, but I know I have to hang on. *Learn to swim. And then you'll survive.* I pull myself forward through the water until I hear the blessed sound, faint, but coming closer. Eventually the familiar voice mingles with the splashes of oars slapping the waves. "That you, Ev?" Just where she said she'd be. Meeting me just where I hoped I'd be, if the show went off as planned.

"Penny!" I gasp out, bobbing in the water, my breath ragged but strong. "Right on time."

"That's the thing about your lucky Penny," she says. "I keep showing up."

Chapter Fifty-Two

"Another ship," I say, throwing a sideways glance toward Penny, whose windswept hair is whipping cheerful circles around her face.

She leans on the railing, looks out over the rolling expanse of steel blue, and says, "I like the view from this one."

I turn to take in the scene: Lady Liberty, who first sailed in this direction in the name of freedom, now slips from sight behind us as Penny and I glide the other way, gazing out upon the open Atlantic and, beyond that, a freedom unlike anything either one of us has ever known. "Yes," I say, agreeing with my friend. "I do, as well."

On the steamer to Marseilles, we keep to ourselves. Penny transforms my famous dark mane of hair into a chin-length bob of burnished auburn. "Lady Liberty brought her copper this way, and you're leaving in some new copper," she quips, as I take in my changed appearance in the stateroom mirror.

We remain mostly in our rooms and on our own private deck, booked in Penny's name. If I do have to step out, I wear broad-brimmed hats, netted veils over my face, loose and dowdy clothing that conceals my famed figure. Anyone who saw me would think I was a wispy old widow, deep in mourning and disinterested in talk. It'll be the last costume I have to wear, and it's only for a few days.

I welcome the rest, especially after the past few months. Heck, the past few years. Our roomy and luxurious accommodations weren't a problem to acquire, since we've got more than enough money. Hal, as he always liked to tell me, had enough in his monthly allowance to support an entire family for a decade. He never even noticed the bills slipping away in recent months. And besides, he won't be needing the money anytime soon—he's just shot to kill in front of a hundred people. He's locked up and no one is much concerned with guarding Hal Thorne's cash for him. If it wasn't me, it would have been someone else who got to it.

"Saving up was smart, but the true stroke of genius was the gun," Penny says in a quiet voice. We are back belowdecks in our private stateroom. She chuckles, apparently pleased with herself for nabbing the prop firearm, at my request, from backstage in her theater, just before meeting up with me in Central Park. "But how did you switch his pistol out for the prop?" she asks.

I nod, feeling more at ease with each ocean league we put between ourselves and Hal, but I well remember how nerve-racking those last few days were, planning and preparing for every detail leading up to the ruse. "Hal was on so much morphine in our last days together—disoriented, forgetful. He'd slip off into spells where he'd sleep like a rock. That's when I switched out the guns. I tossed his real one into the lake in Central Park, shortly before I met up with you. The key was bringing the prop gun into the water with me when I went overboard, so that no one was the wiser."

Penny lets out a slow whistle. "You sure did play it well."

I throw her a wry smirk. "I *was* a rather famous actress for a time. Before all this."

"How could I ever forget?"

I sigh. "It's what got me into all this trouble to begin with."

Penny gives me a heartfelt nudge. "But then you got yourself out."

I fall into a moment of reflective silence until Penny says, "Some kind of swell final show you put on, Ev. Prop blood and everything. I don't think a single person aboard that cruise had a moment's doubt."

I meet Penny's gaze, saying, "I couldn't have done it without you. Not only the gun, the rescue in the rowboat. Getting Stan there, so Hal could go mad with rage. And for once, in public. So that not only I had to be party to it."

Penny nods thoughtfully; it was she who arranged the invitation to get Stanny on the same dinner cruise that night, sending a note from a "secret admirer" along with a ticket. Stan, with his shameless ego and the enticing thought of meeting yet another admiring and pliable young lady, hadn't hesitated for a beat.

There was only one more matter to settle once I knew that both men would be stuck together on the same boat, with Hal enraged and armed: all three of us had to play our parts. If I could make Hal jealous enough, he just might make good on the promise he'd been making for years, to kill the man who had "ruined" me.

Before I'd done my best imitation of Salome, I'd put one final note in the mail. A letter to Mr. Comstock, longtime enemy to Stan, erstwhile ally to Hal. Outlining in lurid detail what Stanley Pierce had done to me back when I was a sixteen-year-old girl first learning my steps on Broadway. *"Please, Mr. Comstock, my husband is a man so preoccupied with a woman's virtue that I fear he may take action on his own to avenge my debasement. I fear that my husband and Mr. Pierce, should they ever meet, may come to blows in a confrontation that could prove harmful to one or both of them."*

Salome herself could not have fixed it better, I dare say. Comstock has my written accusation against Stanley Pierce, one that now seems to shine with preternatural prescience from my watery grave. Let's call it my last will and testament—at last *I'm* writing the story. Comstock will be delighted and inspired to take action against Stan, and I have no doubt he'll print my entire letter in the papers. He'll ensure they both get what they deserve. Hal is already in the Tombs prison awaiting trial for murder. Stan will be called in for questioning—at the very least he'll face a scandal and public outrage; Comstock will see to that. Stanny and Hal can both answer for their crimes.

◆

My plan works. Comstock and his Society for the Prevention of Vice do go public with charges against Stanley Pierce of indecency and abuse, just as a judge and jury in Midtown Manhattan prepare to try Hal Thorne for murder. As we steam across the Atlantic, Penny and I read the news bulletins in the privacy of our stateroom. My murder has caused nothing short of a sensation. It's "the crime of the century!"

A Playboy Millionaire shooting to kill his rival and instead killing his beautiful Broadway bride.

As the ink pours out, what was dark for so long comes to the light. An employee of Mr. Pierce, who works in his tower, is quoted: "*We always knew that someone would come for Mr. Pierce eventually. We just figured it would be a father, not a husband.*"

Mr. Thomas Edison declares he will produce a nickelodeon moving picture about our sordid love triangle and its murderous end. He vows to speed production, predicting it'll bump aside *The Story of Jesus* as the nation's most popular picture.

My body is still the source of scandal and conversation; there are all sorts of theories on what happened to it. Other than its sinking into the harbor, some posit that Hal had his men recover my corpse from the water. Others claim that Stanny's men had my body whisked away. Or that I simply disappeared, that I was an angel of death, pulled up to heaven or down to hell. They are calling me "The Girl Houdini," my famous figure having vanished off the shores of New York City, never to be found. It's gotten so sensational that President Teddy Roosevelt has asked the papers to stop printing on the matter of my murder.

But they can't stop. Column after column speculates on how it all got so violent. Asking how I endured for as long as I did. Rumors, long bubbling under the surface, come gushing up. Speculation that Hal was a predatory fixture in the Tenderloin District for years before he moved me to Pittsburgh. So many girls, and even some young men, come forward with horrible accounts—canes, whips, welts. I don't doubt a single one.

Hal is being tried for the electric chair. Mother Thorne—I can see it in the headlines—is attempting to walk a tightrope between her son's act of murder and the question of his madness. "*My son is not mad,*" she insists. "*He was driven to a temporary madness by his love for that girl, by his virtuous desire to avenge the wrongs done to her by that beastly man. All my son ever endeavored to do was restore honor to his poor, fallen wife.*" I wonder how those words tasted coming out of her pinch-lipped mouth. Mother Thorne, who always lamented to anyone who would listen that I would be her son's undoing.

I'll leave all that to the jury. Hal's madness is no longer my torment, though I very much hope that the memory of me will be his. Perhaps now poor dead Mary Thorne won't be the only Thorne lady to haunt the family.

And I hope that Stan is in a tomb of his own, as well. I made sure to hold each of their eyes. To say, clearly, for all to hear, "You *did this*" to both of them. They each played their own starring role in the tragedy of my young life. As much as they hate each other, they were collaborators in their cruelty. And now I've charged them both, those two men who almost destroyed my body and my soul.

Almost. But they did not succeed. Because here I am, staring out at the waters that will bring me to freedom. I've survived the harrowing swells that threatened to pull me down, I've fought my way back to the surface, and now I'll choose a different shore.

For now, France. With the pretty little fund we have stashed for ourselves, Penny and I plan to set ourselves up somewhere beautiful and warm. Some place colorful—the shimmering aqua of the Mediterranean, the gold of the southern sunshine. I've still got that piece of paper from Philadelphia with an address scrawled on it. I already have a pair of friends who followed their dreams to France. "*Saint-Paul-de-Vence, Provence, France.*" I smile, giddy at the thought of how shocked—and delighted—Rachel and Leah will be when we materialize outside their door. I might just have to don a green snake as I knock. "*Don't believe that it was all Eve's fault.*" My guess? Eve just needed out of that garden.

Eve, yes. America's Eve. That's me, escaping a garden of delight that turned to hell. Surviving the fall and then learning how to climb back up, no longer interested in looking back as the men wage their wars in my wake.

Turns out a girl can write herself a happy ending and a new beginning, after all. It's not about luck or the kiss of a prince. And if there is magic involved, well, it comes from within the gal herself.

As I stand at the ship's railing on the final evening of the crossing, I know the next time the sun rises, France will be visible before me. I tip my head upward to catch the last few spears of the setting sun. I breathe deep of the clean, salty air. I listen to the distant caw of a bird that flies free overhead. And I savor the golden warmth as it shines on my skin, my hair, my face, my entire body. I know how to find my light.

Author's Note

THE STORY OF EVELYN NESBIT HAS FASCINATED AND HAUNTED me for years. I first saw images of Gibson girls hanging in my mother's bedroom when I was a girl. I was endlessly intrigued by the scenes of these elegant, busy women—this combination of cool and slightly intimidating sophistication mixed with the mundane activities of daily life. Nobody I knew dressed like that to, say, wash their hands. Plus, those piles of hair!

Fast-forward a few years, and my mother made an offhand comment one day: "Oh, the real Gibson girl, Evelyn Nesbit, her life was so tragic." Wait, there was a real woman behind these images? A true-life Gibson girl? And her life was full of drama? Tell me more!

I've learned as an author of historical fiction that inspiration can strike at any time. It's funny how a passing comment like this can lead to three years of research and a leading lady who takes up residence in my imagination. When I can't stop thinking about a particular historical figure or historical nugget, that's when I realize that I have met my next book.

But in the case of this novel, I found that my way into the story came, curiously, by finding the ending. And that was a different experience from how it's been with my other books, so let's start there.

While reading about the life of the historical figure Evelyn Nesbit, I came to realize that she had a *lot* of nicknames—a fact that you also know if you've completed *It Girl*. One nickname in particular leapt off the page for me: the Girl Houdini.

This moniker was given to Evelyn by a New York reporter because of the fact that—immediately after her husband pulled out his pistol to shoot and kill her former lover in front of the who's who of high society—Evelyn disappeared. As the crowd roiled across the chaotic Manhattan murder scene on a hot summer night, Evelyn, arguably the most recognizable person in America, vanished. For days, no one could find her, as the city's law enforcement, reporters, photographers, family members, and seemingly everyone else hunted for her. Where had the Girl Houdini slipped away to?

Evelyn was in hiding. Taking refuge, in the words of biographer Paula Uruburu, "in the tiny cramped apartment of her only real friend," a fellow chorus girl from her days on the stage. Hidden away with her one trusted ally, Evelyn wanted nothing more, as she later confessed, than to "bury herself forever."

But alas, Evelyn emerged. Seeing no other choice, the star with perhaps the world's most famous face reentered the maelstrom, much to the delight of the ravenous media, soon making miserably public appearances at the Tombs prison, at the police precinct, and in every newspaper in New York and beyond—and perhaps most painfully of all, throughout the "Trial of the Century" that followed, in which Evelyn was coerced into testifying on behalf of her murderous husband, lest she risk financial abandonment and social retribution by the powerful family into which she had married.

I could not stop wrestling with all of this as I read the details of Evelyn's life: her desire to escape, even to die, rather than to reenter the world and the mess that the men in her life had made. How close she came to making that happen. And yet how overpowering the forces were that ultimately drove her to decide she had no other choice but to testify on her husband's behalf, even as she was being labeled "The Cause of It All" and "the lethal beauty" by the papers and the crowds.

As I considered Evelyn's story as a subject for a novel, I realized that what I really wanted to do was imagine a divergent version—an arc for my leading lady that was inspired by Evelyn's life and yet one that explored this lifelong desire of hers to escape to freedom. For years, as the story swirled and the characters took shape in my mind with ever more clarity, I kept returning to the question: What if I give Evelyn the opportunity to reclaim her own agency, even to rewrite her own ending?

Evelyn spends significant time in these pages engaging with the tropes of Helen of Troy, Cleopatra, Salome, Eve—some of the other "lethal beauties" whose names and tragic stories we all know. In so many of these epic tales it feels like an unpleasantly recurring arc: the beguiling beauty drives the men to do bad things. The woman is essentially a tool or even an antagonist in service of the plot of the men and their kingdoms.

I thought, *What if I pull Evelyn from that relegated role and allow her to lead this story? What about* her *voice?* Not as she was told she had to speak on the stand by her murderous husband and manipulative mother-in-law, but as a reimagined narrator who ultimately breaks free and finds her own way? That felt exciting, compelling, and worthy of pursuit. And thus began the process of writing *It Girl*.

This is a work of fiction. While many readers undoubtedly recognize aspects of the historical figure of Evelyn Nesbit in this book's leading lady, I made the strategic decision on this, my eleventh published book, to change my heroine's name to Evelyn Talbot and, in doing so, take the creative space and artistic liberties that such a decision affords. Readers who are familiar with my work know that I've previously written biographical historical fiction that remains closely welded to the facts of my subjects' lives because, as I always say, history is juicier than fiction. I couldn't make this stuff up, so I'd be a fool *not* to stick closely to the history. And I've chosen my heroines because I found their histories to be so compelling and worthy of telling. And yet I see my job as first to listen for the story that is calling to me, and then to sit down and write the story that comes to me. This is how Evelyn's story came through to me. Thank you for allowing me the freedom to pursue her through fiction.

The raw material of Evelyn's history is murky at times. Even she, in her autobiographical commentary and writings later in life, admits to being a changeable or confounding narrator because of how complicated her feelings were on her own past. In dealing with the matters herein of murder, sexual assault, serious mental illness, and more, I did not wish to plant a flag into this material and lay down a version of this history for the reader in such a way that people might perceive it as my telling of fact. I needed the creative freedom and flexibility to explore the story and its characters and events—all of the dark and the light—with the license that fiction allows. Thus, I decided to alter the names of all my main characters and, as previously mentioned, reimagine Evelyn's trajectory.

That said, many of the details of Evelyn's life have been relayed in this book in a way that is essentially consistent with how Evelyn herself relayed them. This pertains to her early days first in Tarentum coal country and then Pittsburgh. True to the history was the sudden and tragic death of her beloved father, with whom Evelyn was incredibly close and from whom she derived her dream of attending college—if they didn't first run away with the circus together. Also pulled from the history are the details of her mother's emotional collapse and the need for Evelyn to begin working in Wanamaker's at age thirteen to help support her family, particularly her younger brother. She nurtured a lifelong desire to return to school but was soon noticed by a Philadelphia artist and recruited to work as an artists' model, with that early modeling work paying her a dollar a day and launching her swift rise to fame. While Evelyn did work during these early days with the likes of Louis Comfort Tiffany and Violet Oakley, I created the fictional characters of Leah and Rachel. I wanted Evelyn to have early friends and well-intentioned allies as she launched into stardom at such a young age. They presented a vision of another kind of free life as a woman, and I knew they would be a support to her, even after she moved on from Philadelphia.

Soon after she began her successful work as an artists' model, Evelyn relocated with her mother to New York City as they tucked her brother away at school in the Pennsylvania countryside. In Manhattan, Evelyn's star shone ever brighter as she worked with the likes of James Carroll Beckwith, Frederick S. Church, and, yes, Charles Dana Gibson, who called her "The Eternal Question" in what would become perhaps his most iconic work. The details of Evelyn's ascent to the stage are also based on the facts, including the scene when the Broadway agent tells her he's not in the business of employing babies before reluctantly hiring her with the tacit agreement that they would not discuss her age—a common refrain in her life. Shortly thereafter, as Evelyn became a smash sensation described with much of the laudatory language included in this book, she was noticed and admired by the predatory "Pharaoh of Fifth Avenue" and architect to the millionaires. The fictional character of Stanley Pierce is, as I suspect many have guessed, inspired by the figure of Stanford White.

Here is where things got even darker, both in my book and in the historical accounts. Evelyn averred all her life that "Stanny" groomed her, provided for her, then raped her at the age of sixteen. In her memoir Evelyn writes, "He dominated me by his kindness and by his authority. He abused the sacred trust that had been put into his hands" while her mother went away and left her in Stan's care. What followed was a sexual liaison between the pair that the shockingly young and tragically unempowered Evelyn mistook for love—until she discovered that Stan had many other young lovers, some of whose names he kept listed in a small leather book.

Around that time, Evelyn began a romantic relationship with a young cartoonist and aspiring actor by the name of John Barrymore. Much like the fictional character of Art Darrow in this novel, the true figure of Barrymore first admired Evelyn on the stage, courted her, declared his love and intention to marry her, then ceased his pursuit, leaving his "Evie" in the tightened grip of her mother and Stan. Evelyn blamed them for the machinations that led to the separation from her young lover, and rumors persisted that John Barrymore loved Evelyn for the rest of his life.

Shortly after that, Evelyn was pursued, relentlessly, by a Pittsburgh millionaire, the fictionalized version of whom I've named Hal Thorne. This character is inspired by the chilling figure of Harry Thaw, who indeed lived as lavishly as a royal and is believed to have inspired the popularization of the term *playboy*. The details of his outlandish courtship of Evelyn, his hidden depravity, his mental illness, and his deep hatred for Stan all did come from the history.

Evelyn, her mother, and Harry traveled together through England and France on a whirlwind trip much like the one in this book. Details such as the shopping sprees, the fight between Harry and Evelyn's mother, the awkward meeting with his aristocratic sister, and Harry's obsession with Joan of Arc's virginity all come from the history as well. There is evidence in the historical record that Evelyn had heard rumblings of her suitor's sins, but he presented a meticulously calculated version of himself as the faithful and generous supplicant while wooing his "booful." After many persistent proposals and seemingly earnest promises of love and support, Evelyn accepted the millionaire's offer of marriage after her mother abandoned her abroad, much like in this book.

Evelyn's life as a newlywed in Pittsburgh with the miserable Mother Thaw was much as I write it here with the character of Mother Thorne. Based in fact are the gloomy descriptions of the family mansion and the crippling loneliness Evelyn felt as a new wife, as well as the disapproval she fielded from her censorious, cold, and hypocritically pious mother-in-law. The family matriarch did all that she could to strip Evelyn of her agency, to ridicule what she saw as the pollution and failings of Evelyn's character, and to erase the accounts of the young woman's past as a performer and model. Even her disgust at seeing Evelyn's image on the Haudenshield's Christmas gift comes from the history. And yet her cruelty toward Evelyn paled in comparison to the emotional and physical abuse that Evelyn detailed receiving at the hands of her "Jekyll and Hyde" husband, who was jealous, violent, possessive, erratic, and increasingly obsessed with Evelyn's past with Stan.

Poor Evelyn, I thought. Yet again, a man had offered her a happily ever after, and once more, most disastrously of all, that happiness turned into a living nightmare. And this is when I started laying the groundwork for my character to begin finding ways to reclaim her power—and to write an ending of her own.

The reality is that in New York City on a sweltering summer night, Evelyn Nesbit's husband shot and killed her former lover on the rooftop of Madison Square Garden. Everyone there saw it, and Harry Thaw was taken to Murderer's Row to await trial and the expected execution by the electric chair. The powerful family into which Evelyn had married then placed much of their hope on her—expecting her to pull off the performance of a lifetime on the stand. They coerced Evelyn into testifying that her husband had been driven to a temporary madness by his love for his beautiful wife and his desire to avenge the wrongs of the predator who had abused her in her youth. This was to save her husband from the fate of the electric chair. It worked. And the true-life figure of Harry Thaw would go on to torment Evelyn, and himself, and many others, throughout the remainder of his life.

I decided that Evelyn Talbot, like Evelyn Nesbit, wanted something different. Instead of being told her role, what if she could instead be the choreographer of the stunning scandal? The Girl Houdini who *does* in fact escape with a loyal friend, leaving the men with their own mess and meeting more true friends in a place where at last she can be free. The great star would need to give the performance of her career—as though her life depended on it. Because, well, it did.

This was a time of tectonic shifts in society. Everything was changing, from how people saw the world (electricity! moving pictures!) to how they communicated in the world (the telephone! the camera!) to how they moved through the world (the motorcar! the subway! the airplane!) and so much more.

So, too, was this a time of shifts in how people saw women. This was the era that brought up a new crop of charismatic and independent young women—the first celebrities—who soared to the top tiers of society not because they were the debutantes and brides of the blue-blooded Four Hundred but because of how they performed and worked and, yes, aroused the collective interest.

In an age when everything felt fast and fresh and bright, these women danced on the new Broadway stages and dazzled in front of the new camera lenses. They showcased beauty and talent; they sparked intrigue and desire—and Evelyn shone the brightest of all, with a star power so brilliant that it proved to be both a blessing and a curse.

I was so captivated by this moment in time, this liminal era of transition from the corseted fainting spells of the Victorian era to the fast-paced dance steps of the roaring twenties, and the leading lady who came from nothing—and overcame everything—to take center stage.

Evelyn was so much more than a mere vessel through which both men and women might see their fantasies—both good and grisly—play out. Rather than the goddess or demoness, she was a mortal who felt, loved, thought, and dreamed deeply. A woman who lost so much but also fought for every single thing she had. She was a survivor, an artist, an adventurer, an icon. And if this tale can be likened to the fast-paced dances in which each of our showgirl's steps leads to the next dramatic turn, I am happy that Evelyn has had her chance to choreograph. I hope you enjoyed the show.

I AM SO unbelievably grateful to the historians, scholars, and biographers who shed light on Evelyn Nesbit's complicated, compelling, and fascinating life, particularly Paula Uruburu and Simon Baatz. Their brilliant biographical works examine and illuminate the moments both epic and intimate of Evelyn's story.

Thank you, Margaret Copeland Hunter, wonderful artist and friend, for answering my questions and sharing the most nuanced and thoughtful perspectives on live theater and the work of an actor. Your insights on everything from how it feels to sit backstage before a show to how it feels to harness the emotions of the people seated before you helped me to craft Evelyn's character as she reckons with her own star power and both the light and dark sides of being a beautiful young performer.

Most enlightening of all were the words of Evelyn Nesbit herself, given in two memoirs she penned and the interviews and testimonies she gave over the course of her life. While the newspaper clippings, letter excerpts, and notes to Anthony Comstock that I wove into this book are fictionalized, they are inspired by accounts and quotes from the era and its individuals. My earnest hope is to have offered a narrative in which the spirit of the times, this story, and the voice of its leading lady all shine through.

For those who wish to read further on the figure of Evelyn Nesbit and her times, I highly recommend:

Tragic Beauty: The Lost 1914 Memoirs of Evelyn Nesbit, by Evelyn Nesbit, edited by Deborah Dorian Paul
Prodigal Days: The Untold Story, by Evelyn Nesbit, edited by Deborah Dorian Paul
American Eve: Evelyn Nesbit, Stanford White, the Birth of the "It" Girl, and the Crime of the Century, by Paula Uruburu
The Girl on the Velvet Swing: Sex, Murder, and Madness at the Dawn of the Twentieth Century, by Simon Baatz
The Gibson Girl and Her America: The Best Drawings of Charles Dana Gibson, by Charles Dana Gibson
Broadway: A History of New York City in Thirteen Miles, by Fran Leadon
Historic Photos of Broadway: New York Theater, 1850–1970, by Leonard Jacobs
The Gilded Age in New York, 1870–1910, by Esther Crain

If you or someone you know is in need of assistance, you can call the National Domestic Violence Hotline at 1-800-799-SAFE (7233). Other resources may also be available in your area, including RAINN (1-800-656-HOPE) and Women's Law.

Acknowledgments

THIS SECTION GETS HARDER TO WRITE WITH EACH BOOK, AND that is a beautiful fact that I will never take for granted.

So many people have helped to make this book and my career possible. I would like to begin by thanking my readers. Your enthusiasm, warmth, and willingness to share my work make each new book possible. Thank you for joining me on the page, in person, online—and everywhere else we can connect. Here's to many more chapters together!

To the libraries and librarians: thank you for all that you do for so many communities, readers, and writers around the world.

I am so grateful to all the booksellers who spend each day supporting our stories and connecting books with the readers who will give the stories their meaning. You shape and sustain our communities.

Books change lives and indeed move the world. I'm humbled and honored to play a small part in our collective storytelling. Now, more than ever, we must share our stories.

My heartfelt thanks to the book club groups, reviewers, influencers, book community leaders, and podcast hosts who share our work and do so much to support readers and writers. I am especially grateful to Katie Couric and Shannon Gibson and the team at Katie Couric Media, Jenna Bush Hager, Lee Woodruff, Hoda Kotb, Kathie Lee Gifford, Sarah Ferguson Duchess of York, Christine Gardner, Mary Calvi, Zibby Owens, Carol Fitzgerald, Andrea Peskind Katz, Suzanne Weinstein Leopold, Lauren Blank Margolin, Leighellen Landskov, Robin Kall Homonoff, Jennifer Tropea O'Regan, Pamela Klinger-Horn, Bobbi Dumas, Elaine Ubiña, Jude Connally, Laurette Kittle, Sharlene Martin Moore, Tonni Callan, Jamie Rosenblit, Dallas Strawn, Aidan Donnelley Rowley, Jen at Electric Bookaloo, the Friends & Fiction Book Club, the Skimm, George Whipple, Chloe Melas, and so many others. A special shout-out to Annissa Joy Armstrong and the reading family at Beyond the Pages: Annissa, I hope you enjoyed your time dancing with Evelyn and the girls. My love to all the organizers of festivals and events and online forums where we connect with readers. This is the part where I cringe because I just know I am forgetting too many important names, and for that I am deeply sorry. Please know I am so grateful and I love each chance that we have to connect.

The writing community is made up of a warm and inspiring group of people, and I am humbled to consider so many of you my friends and creative confidants. Deborah Goodrich Royce, you were supportive of this book from the very start, when we first discussed whether Evelyn was more of a Marilyn Monroe or a Kim Kardashian. I'm so thankful for your hospitality as you welcomed me to your homes in both the Catskills and Connecticut so that I could see your original Evelyn art and soak up the rich scenery and mythology of these historic individuals. The day we spent together at the Onteora Club with Iliana Moore, studying the art and architecture of this era, was a highlight of the research process. Early conversations with Fiona Davis, Marie Benedict, Dawn Tripp, Lauren Willig, and Nicola Harrison on the topic of Evelyn and the early Broadway showgirls inspired me and gave me wind in my sails.

I am reluctant to name names because I know I will inevitably and inadvertently forget too many, but I wish to say how much I appreciate and admire so many of my fellow authors: Lynda Cohen Loigman, Annabel Monaghan, Lisa Barr, Kristin Harmel, Stephanie Dray, Susie Orman Schnall, Sarah McCoy, Rochelle Weinstein, Joy Callaway, Alyson Richman, Erika Robuck, Ariel Lawhon, Greer Macallister, Heather Webb, Samantha Greene

Woodruff, Pam Jenoff, Tatiana de Rosnay, Leslie Carroll, Laura Kaye, Kate Quinn, Brooke Lea Foster, Jacqueline Friedland, Michelle Moran, Abby Maslin, Martha Hall Kelly, Kristina McMorris, Jo Piazza, Natalie Jenner, Jane Healey, Kristy Cambron, Brenda Janowitz, Renee Rosen, Jenna Blum, Camille Di Maio, Elyssa Friedland, Yvette Corporon, Amy Poeppel, Emily Giffin, and Kerri Maher. You all make this solitary writing life full and rich.

This is the first time I've worked with an expert authenticity reader during the editing phase of the writing process. To my partner in this: I am so grateful for your wisdom, support, and insights. We come to the page and this material within the context of the twenty-first century, and this professionally trained educator and counselor helped me to process and present the events of this story in a way that—I truly hope—feels authentic and sensitive.

The captain of Team Evelyn has been my literary agent and friend, Lacy Lynch, who acts as my partner from the first idea through to the day of publication and far beyond. You shine bright, my friend, and I wouldn't want to do any of this without you. To the incredible "A Team" at House of Story, Dabney Rice and Alexandria Kominsky, I am so grateful to work with you. You make it look like magic, and you do it with grace and joy, but I know in reality it's all about the hard work, tenacity, and devotion to your writers. I'm lucky to be one.

Kara Cesare, I could use all the words, and yet there are no words for how grateful and overjoyed I am to be publishing another book with you. I thank my lucky stars every day that you are my editor and my friend. Your wisdom, thoughtfulness, and care make every step of the writing process better; my books and I are so fortunate to have you. My deepest thanks to the entire team at Ballantine, especially the brilliant Gabby Colangelo. It is such a pleasure to work with you. My special and heartfelt gratitude to Kim Hovey, Loren Noveck and the assiduous production team, Katie Herman, Megan Whalen, Taylor Noel, Chelsea Woodward, Kara Welsh, Jennifer Hershey, Susan Corcoran, Jennifer Garza, Paolo Pepe, Belina Huey and the art department, Pamela Alders, Sandra Sjursen, Elizabeth Rendfleisch, Michelle Jasmine, Jesse Shuman, and Sanyu Dillon.

A warm thanks to Emily Easton and Jill Santopolo, with whom I love writing and working, particularly in the wonderful world of children's books. I am so excited for all that we are doing together!

I'm forever amazed by and thankful to Lauren Auslander and the incredible publicity team at LUNA Entertainment. I write the books, but you give them their spotlight.

To Allen Fischer at Artists First: it's been a joyful and interesting adventure ever since the *Traitor's Wife* party over ten years ago. I'm grateful for your expertise and look forward to all that's to come in this next decade.

My thanks also to Haley Reynolds, Rebecca Silensky, Jan Miller, Shannon Marven, and the team at Dupree Miller for years of partnership and support.

I'm blessed to be a member of two big families, the one I joined at birth and the one into which I married. I love you and I am grateful for you all: my siblings Owen, Teddy, and Emily; sisters- and brothers-in-law; beloved nieces and nephews; cousins; aunts; and uncles. Louisa and Nelson, my parents-in-love—and Lulu is nothing like Mother Thorne. Mom and Dad, who gave me both roots and wings, in addition to so many book suggestions.

Like Evelyn, I cherish my friends so deeply. But unlike Evelyn, I am blessed to have more than simply "one real friend"—I love you all. You are my people, my chosen family who span every stage. My fellow chorus girls in this colorful dance of life.

And last but most of all, my love and gratitude to my husband, Dave, and our three daughters. Here's to the beautiful and real story that we are writing together each day. As you find your light, precious girls, always know that you are ours.

About the Author

ALLISON PATAKI is the *New York Times* bestselling author of *The Traitor's Wife, The Accidental Empress, Sisi, Where the Light Falls* (with Owen Pataki), *The Queen's Fortune, The Magnificent Lives of Marjorie Post, Finding Margaret Fuller,* and *It Girl,* as well as the memoir *Beauty in the Broken Places* and two children's books (with Marya Myers), *Nelly Takes New York* and *Poppy Takes Paris.* Her novels have been translated into more than twenty languages. A former news writer and producer, Pataki has written for *The New York Times,* ABC News, *HuffPost, USA Today,* Fox News, and other outlets. She has appeared on *Today, Good Morning America, Fox & Friends, Good Day New York, Good Day Chicago,* and MSNBC's *Morning Joe.* Pataki graduated cum laude from Yale University, is a member of the Historical Novel Society and a certified yoga instructor, and lives in New York with her husband and family.

allisonpataki.com
Facebook.com/AllisonPatakiPage
X: @AllisonPataki
Instagram: @allisonpataki